He's really here.

He's back on Ymir, back in the Cut, and for now he has no way of rectifying that, so he gestures the windows to clear.

The city has grown while he was away, the way a tumor grows. Gray concrete housing blocks are interspersed with the newer, cheaper version: spiraling coral grown from a remixed polyp geneprint, striped in lurid reds and greens and yellows. The traffic is thicker, a miasma of lumbering autohaulers, skeletal stripped-down bikes, floating drones, harried pedestrians. The atmosphere is still half-vapor, drenching the streets in filthy fog. Holos slash through the haze here and there, to signal a sex house or dopamine bar.

All of it seething under an artificial sky, a holo meant to help people forget they're living in a shallow wound in Ymir's crust. Instead of a sunrise he sees an aching white blank. Jagged black cracks flicker across it. Stray lines of code scroll through and disappear.

Still glitching. He was gone for ten years his time, twenty here, and the sky is still fucking glitching.

Praise for
Annex

"An exciting twist on a hostile-alien-takeover drama....Exhilarating." —*Washington Post*

"Rich Larson has an amazing knack for capturing the lonesomeness of growing up and how much random cruelty and steadfast companionship there is in childhood. Not to mention just how alien and scary families can be."
—Charlie Jane Anders, author of
All the Birds in the Sky

"*Annex*'s combination of a likable and diverse cast of characters with breakneck, engaging action—all against the background of an evocative and sinister world—make it an accomplished and impressive debut." —*Booklist*

"An energetic, nonstop adventure." —*Chicago Tribune*

"*Annex* is a ferocious sci-fi fairy tale—a warm, thrilling adventure about what happens after the end of the world. Both epic and intimate in equal measure, this one's a joy and a blast, from beginning to end."
—Cherie Priest, author of *Boneshaker* and
I Am Princess X

"Wunderkind Rich Larson's *Annex* gives us nonstop action set pieces as breathtakingly clever as they are relentless and a vivid, compelling cast. Sequels now, please!"
—Mike Allen, author of *Unseaming*

"Rich Larson presents a uniquely compelling apocalypse—equal parts frightening and touching."

—Alex White, author of *A Big Ship*
at the Edge of the Universe

"A thrilling and imaginative entry into the alien invasion genre with two fierce and desperate young protagonists you won't be able to stop rooting for."

—Fonda Lee, Nebula Award–nominated
author of *Jade City*

"Larson's breakneck pace end[s] up making [*Annex*] exhilarating, and well worth waiting for the next volume."

—*Locus*

"Deftly plotted and packing a few interesting twists, *Annex* delivers."

—*Kirkus*

By Rich Larson

Annex
Ymir

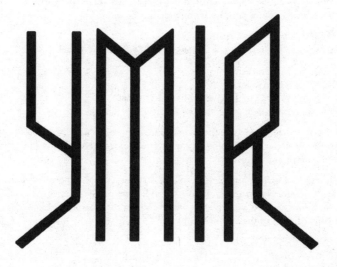

RICH LARSON

orbitbooks.net

Copyright © 2022 by Rich Larson
Excerpt from *The Body Scout* copyright © 2021 by Lincoln Michel

Cover design by Lauren Panepinto
Cover illustration by Arcangel
Cover copyright © 2022 by Hachette Book Group, Inc.
Author photograph by Micaela Cockburn

Orbit
Hachette Book Group
1290 Avenue of the Americas
New York, NY 10104
orbitbooks.net

First Edition: July 2022

Orbit is an imprint of Hachette Book Group.
The Orbit name and logo are trademarks of Little, Brown Book Group Limited.

The publisher is not responsible for websites (or their content) that are not owned by the publisher.

The Hachette Speakers Bureau provides a wide range of authors for speaking events. To find out more, go to www.hachettespeakersbureau.com or call (866) 376-6591.

Library of Congress Cataloging-in-Publication Data
Names: Larson, Rich, 1992– author.
Title: Ymir / Rich Larson.
Description: First edition. | New York, NY : Orbit, 2022.
Identifiers: LCCN 2021060514 | ISBN 9780316416580 (trade paperback) |
    ISBN 9780316416573 (ebook) | ISBN 9780316416566 (library ebook)
Subjects: LCGFT: Science fiction. | Novels.
Classification: LCC PR9199.4.L375 Y58 2022 | DDC 813/.6—dc23/eng/20220118
LC record available at https://lccn.loc.gov/2021060514

ISBNs: 9780316416580 (trade paperback), 9780316416573 (ebook)

Printed in the United States of America

LSC-C

Printing 1, 2022

For Megan & Peter
Kalena
Wesley
& Miles

CHAPTER 00

An enormous rust-brown bowlship, pitted and scarred from its journey, descends through Ymir's dark howling sky. Drones stream upward from the ice field to meet it, swarming like insects, tasting its hull with electromagnetic mouths and asking after its cargo. The bowlship reports nickel alloy, raw hydrogen, an inconsequential amount of human freight.

When it sinks into the frost-coated docking cradle, the heat of its stabilizers turns ice to vapor. A thunderhead of steam slams out in all directions. The bowlship groans and shudders and finally comes to rest. It opens itself to the tunnels below, where automated laborers and exoskelled dockhands await to begin unloading.

Past the alloy stores, past the hydrogen tanks, in the darkest gut of the ship: the torpor pool. Bodies churn in a slow current around the reactor, tangling and untangling, a drifting mass of frosty flesh. They are skeletal, emaciated from the long haul, and their skins are coated a slick milky white by the stasis fluid. They are clinically dead, but not legally corpses.

At the far end of the pool, a door folds open. Two dockhands step through in a gush of steam. One is carrying a long hooked pole on her shoulder. A tiny drone is clinging to the end.

"Rerouted the whole ship for one fucking body," she says. "Must be a company man."

"We giving him a private thaw, then?"

"Sending him straight north. They'll thaw him on the way."

The drone darts ahead of them, fairylike on gossamer rotors. Its scarlet laser plays over the drifting bodies. The dockhands wait while a spiny walkway assembles itself, sprouting from the reddish-brown wall to extend across the torpor pool. They trudge forward, footsteps echoing in the cathedralic space.

The drone slides under the surface of the pool with a muted gurgle. The dockhands follow its red light, and the one with the pole slings it off her shoulder. She eases it into the stasis fluid, poking between bodies until the magnetic hook finds a particular harness.

Together, the dockhands dredge their catch up out of the pool. The walkway grows a socket to hold the base of the pole. It slides inside with a rasp and click, and the man is hoisted into the air like a puppet, dripping fluid. The dockhands peer at him.

He's small, pallid-skinned and dark-haired. He has no lower jaw: between the blue curve of his upper lip and the rippled flesh of his throat there is nothing but medical membrane.

"Ugly fucker," the first dockhand says. She points to a geometric spiral on his neck, the biotech tattoo the drone scanned to identify him. "Company man, though. I was right."

"Looks a bit like you." The other dockhand blinks. "Sending him north, you said? Maybe he a cold-blood, then. A cold-blood company man."

"No such thing."

But when they load the body into a drifting sarcophagus for transport, she sees shins and feet cratered with scars. Her black eyes widen, then narrow, and then she spits. It trickles down the side of the man's frozen face.

"What's that about, then?"

She stares down at the body. "No such thing as a cold-blood company man," she says. "Only traitors."

"So *I* was right." He smirks. "Them cold-blood geneprints are real distinct. Sealie, yeah?"

"Half, maybe. Half-blood." She hinges the sarcophagus shut. "Company's mad to send him north. He'll be leaving in a spraybag."

They guide the body across the dark walkway, over the torpor pool, following the dancing drone.

CHAPTER 01

Yorick wakes up dead, which is never comfortable. His chest is a clamp, lungs frozen, no heartbeat. His limbs are phantom. The hindbrain panic swallows him whole. He knows nothing except that he is alone and terrified and in the dark; every sensory-starved nerve in his body is screaming it, and then—

A jolt of electricity digs its teeth in, and his heart stutters back into motion. He owns his chest muscles again, so he sucks down a breath, ballooning all the crumpled alveoli in his lungs. The first one always feels like sucking back broken glass. A rehearsed thought comes to him: *Nothing is wrong. You're coming out of torpor. Nothing is wrong. You're coming out of torpor.*

He gasps. Bucks. Waits for the firestorm in his nervous system to subside, for the world to stop lurching from side to side. He works on proprioception, finding his body in space. His arms and legs are spread-eagled, punctured in a dozen places by tubes that are pumping him full of newly brewed blood. A diagnostic droid is scuttling up and down his torso.

His prosthetic mandible is missing. Cold dry air rasps in his wound.

"Welcome back from the River Styx, Yorick."

Yorick's eyes are crusted over. He works his lids until he manages to free one from the gound. First he sees only a dark gray haze. Next he sees an orange blur, flickering through his field of vision too quickly to track. He knows from experience that this is the orange suit of a thaw technician.

"It's been a long time since we spoke last," the voice says. "Nearly two decades here. Half that for you, I believe, with all the time spent in torpor. I can see you've done good work in that span. Eight successful hunts. Do they ever permit you to keep trophies from them?"

Yorick knows the voice. His gut coils tight.

"I still think you did your very best work right here with me, of course," the voice continues. "Back in those early days of Subjugation."

The tattoo on his neck prickles. He knows the voice, but it was one he never thought he would hear again, and if he's hearing it again it means—

"I'm afraid this thaw's not taking place on Munin. You were rerouted in transit to solve a more pressing problem here on Ymir."

No.

No, no, fucking *no*.

"That seems to have spiked your adrenals, Yorick. Thrilled to be home, I expect."

Memories crash in. Phosphorescent flares lighting up the ice field, the skull-pulping sound of smart mines going off. An anonymous body shredded to pieces, steaming, another barely intact, wriggling through the snow and slicking blood behind. And the owner of the voice is there, too, one bony hand on his shoulder, saying *civilization costs*.

"I'm an administrator here now," Gausta says, voice sintered with faint surprise, as if she's still marveling at the fact. "Living just to the east of your old haunts, overseeing security for all of Ymir's northern-hemisphere extraction and refinery sites. Which brings us to why *you're* here."

Yorick wants to rage, to beg, to say that he will go anywhere, absolutely anywhere. Just not Ymir, the slushball of piss on the edge of the colony maps, the birthplace he swore to never set foot on again. But he can't speak without his mandible. He only manages an animal groan that startles the thaw technician.

"Eight days ago a xenotech incident suspended all labor in the Polar Seven Mine," Gausta continues. "There were grendels here after all, and we finally dug far enough to wake one up."

Yorick isn't afraid of the grendel. He's killed the grendel a dozen times on a dozen worlds; it's the job the company trained him for. He's afraid of everything else.

"It butchered a few miners and then disappeared, as a grendel is wont to do," Gausta says. "But the attack has reinvigorated anti-company sentiment here in the north. There are rumors of a strike. Fainter rumors of insurrection. We tread on thin ice."

Yorick finally pries his other eye open. The orange blob of the technician sharpens. Above it, he sees the hazy outline of a holo projected on a low plaster ceiling. He can't make out Dam Gausta's features, but he recognizes the predatory angles of her body. He remembers her in a chamsuit, her long limbs dissolving into the ashy snow behind her, her hooded head turning dark as the starless sky. Before that, in a bright yellow coat.

"The algorithm balked when I chose you for this job, Yorick," Gausta says. "You were only the third-nearest option, and the differential in transit cost was significant."

Yorick forces the memories down and works on focusing his eyes. Gausta's face comes clear, the wolfish gaze and jutting bones and swirled vitiligo skin. She's aged less than he has in twice the years, as perfect and awful as ever, the gengineered telomeres of a company higher-up at work. Her eyes are unchanged, the same silvery pits.

"But machine minds are so limited when it comes to sociohistorical context." Gausta gives her scalpel smile. "You understand this place, Yorick. Every day the mine remains shut and the grendel roams free, not only does the company bleed profit, but the locals' discontent festers. Stability degrades."

But it will never be stable up here; Yorick wants to scream it at her. The first colonists to come to Ymir were exiles and radicals. The generations born after were shaped by the cold and the dark into paranoid tribalists. He left because he didn't want to die, and now the company has returned him with a tattoo on his neck, a target on his back.

Gausta reads his ruined face, or more likely his jolting heartbeat. "It's been twenty years here," she says. "And you've undergone quite a spectacular rendering of flesh. Nobody will recognize you, Yorick. So long as you do your work quickly, and tread lightly on the ice."

CHAPTER 02

Gausta leaves, but her avatar lingers to give Yorick logistics: He will have one day to recover from torpor before he conducts his initial investigation of the site, accompanied by the Polar Seven's interim overseer. His pseudonym will be Oxo Bellica, to avoid Yorick Metu's lingering notoriety. His hunting equipment was not transferred, but will be reprinted pending ansible clearance. His clothing and mandible are nearly finished. He is three hours out from Reconciliation.

That last part jags him, but explains why the world has not stopped lurching from side to side. They loaded him straight from his bowlship onto the only passenger skid that heads north. Nobody in the north would ever call it Reconciliation, of course. It's the Cut to them, was the Cut before the company ever arrived.

Unless things have changed in the past twenty years—Yorick considers that faint possibility as the thaw technician retracts the tubes, freeing him from his plastic web. They're gentle with the flap of scar tissue and reconstructed flesh where his jaw should be.

"I can give you one more wake-up shot," they say, muffled by their mask. "Nod if you want it."

Yorick has been working mostly on clenching and unclenching his toes, wriggling his fingers, but he manages to bob his head up and down. Microneedles prick his neck, and a half second later he feels a chemical cloudburst, stimulants flooding his whole body. It rubs his nerves raw and makes him momentarily want to vomit.

The bed folds, easing him upright, and the diagnostic droid crawls off him.

"You ready to try walking?" the technician asks.

Yorick nods.

The technician nods at a chugging printer at the end of the compartment. "We'll go to that printer. Get you your clothes and your prosthesis."

Yorick grunts. He draws a deep breath, rubs the knotted muscles in his thighs. He holds the thaw technician's shoulder as he takes his first shaky step, timing it to the sway of the skid. He takes a second. A third. On the fourth his knees buckle, his head rushes, and he nearly takes the technician to the floor with him.

"Today's not going to be pleasant for you," they mutter. "Thawing you this fast, yanking you straight off the freighter without calibrating your chemicals."

Yorick shrugs his bony shoulders, gives the technician his own hideous version of a smile. He was not expecting a pleasant day anyway.

They stand him in front of the printer nozzle, just long enough for a patchy gray undersuit of spiderwool, then help him into his high-collared coat. The color is wrong, black instead of canary yellow, but it fits the same on every world. The boots are heated this time. He puts them on while he watches the printer work. It disgorges his rucksack next, a fabric shell that scuttles along on four stubby pneumatic limbs.

"Your prosthesis should be inside," the technician says. "Do you want my help with it?"

Yorick shakes his head, because attaching the mandible is something he does himself, alone.

"Okay." The technician scratches under their mask. "I'm getting off at Sants. I recommend you stay in here and rest. You're going to be sleepsick for a while. Fatigue, nausea, some body dissociation. Probably hit the peak in four or five hours." Their eyes flick to the tattoo on Yorick's neck, then away. "But you can do whatever you like. Your vitals cleared threshold."

A door dilates at the back of the compartment, and Yorick catches a brief glimpse of rocking corridor as the technician departs. He smells a whiff of dust and machine oil. Then he is alone with himself. He needs to rectify that quickly, so he rubs his thumb and pinkie together to beckon the rucksack.

It ambles over to him, sliding slightly with the motion of the skid, and peels open to display the exact same things as always. This is a comfort to him. Whatever world he wakes up on, the small orderly one inside the rucksack is unchanged. Basic black tablet. Coiled neurocable. Disinfectant brush. Microneedle injector. Rolls of gelflesh.

His mandible is in a slab of clear putty, still warm from the printer. He worms his hand past it, to the bottom of the rucksack, and finds the drug canisters. Immunosuppressors for his wound, phedrine for his mood—neutered company stuff, of course, not street-grade. But right now, even company phedrine will do.

He loads his injector with trembly fingers. When the microneedles punch through his capillaries it feels almost like sunshine. It's the closest he will get to it on Ymir.

CHAPTER 03

Yorick watches through the window as the skid churns along, throwing up a shroud of shattered ice in their wake. The sky is a black hole, all traces of starshine concealed by dense cloud. The only illumination comes from the skid's running lights, a sickly green glow, the bioluminescence of some eyeless creature gliding along the primordial seafloor.

They've already passed the cities, passed the graveyard of one-way ships that brought Ymir's first settlers and are still being digested for salvage a century later. They've passed the petrified forests and the airfarms that replaced them. This far north, the entire world is a single sheet of wind-scoured ice.

Yorick spots a herd of frostskimmers in the distance, leaping and gliding, attracted by the light of the skid. He observes them for a moment, then lets his phedrine high pull him farther along the swaying corridor. He hardly even minds that he is on Ymir, that he is heading north, that he is going to die there. His whole body is full of warm helium. He has the mandible tucked up under one armpit. His vague goal is finding the lavatory pod, where he will attach it.

The skid was noisy earlier, echoing with drunken shouts and laughter, a crowd of miners and a few fat-hunters swilling foamy bacterial beer in the corridor. Yorick kept his coat zipped to hide his lower face as he passed them by, but nobody glanced, too preoccupied by a wager: a tall bulky offworlder with an eye implant had bet they could contort themselves to fit in a standard-size sleepstack, claimed they were *all cartilage, nephew, skeletal mod.*

Now the corridor is dark, lumes dimmed by consensus, and half the skid's passengers have shelved themselves into the miniature mausoleum to rest, not to win wagers. Yorick suspects they are trying to sync for the same work rotation. He keeps his footfalls soft, trying to outquiet the rucksack padding silently behind him.

There's another window before the lavatory pod, and through it Yorick sees the one interruption to Ymir's cold horizon. It grows in the distance, a warped mound erupting from the ice, sheathed in nanocarbon scaffolding and coated in buzzing drones. As always, it's difficult to judge the size of it. Even veiled in human tech, the original architecture of the ansible has a disorientating effect. Workers take a certain depressant drug to mitigate it.

A memory flashes through Yorick's head, neural sheet lightning: trekking out to the ansible when he was fourteen, maybe fifteen, clambering over the blockade, seeing who could creep closest before the nausea and the brain-bend were too much to handle. He remembers the alien structure as an enormous face, carved from black rock, sutured with eerie blue lights.

It's the ansible that drew the first colonists here, the ansible that marks Ymir as one of the Oldies' abandoned worlds. The company took it over during Subjugation, and Yorick doubts anyone clambers over the blockade anymore. Not if they want to keep their skulls intact.

He feels unease trickle, icy, through his phedrine high. Partly for the memories, which he knows will only get worse the longer he's here. Partly because passing the ansible means they are barely an hour from the Cut. He knows this journey, this skid north, from what he thought was his very last day on Ymir. That day ended very badly.

Someone is puking in the lavatory pod. Muted sounds, throat and splash. Yorick's shrunken stomach gives a sympathetic ripple. He goes the other way, finds a vacant sleepstack. He peels down his coat just long enough for it to scan his company tattoo, then climbs inside.

CHAPTER -7

*T*he concrete cube of the apartment. Yorick and Thello are small, crouched on the floor, playing with rubbery yellow dolls they got from the toy printer. One is an exoskelled soldier holding a tiny howler. The other is a monster, a mass of spines and tendrils.

Their mother looms over them. "Where'd this come from, then?"

Her anger is a pressure drop; Yorick feels his chest tightening, his ears ringing. She doesn't mean the toys. She means the tablet dangling from her hand, the basic black square that the company men were giving away last week near the junk recyclers. She holds it casually, asks the question calmly, but Yorick can hear the needles underneath.

"Didn't steal it," Thello says. "Swear truth. It was for free."

"What did they tell you it's for?" their mother asks. The needles are sharpening. Yorick knows, instinctively, that it would have been better if Thello had stolen it.

"You can go on the net with it," Thello says, face flickering confusion. "Play. Learn things."

"Learn things from the company," their mother says, snarling the last word. "The Cut existed before they showed up. You learn that?"

Thello shakes his head, gledges pleadingly at Yorick. Yorick ignores him. Thello deserves this, for hiding it under the gelbed instead of in the spot behind the cooker.

"It was just smaller, that's all. Simpler." Their mother runs her frayed nail across the tablet's surface. "Just a chasm in the ice, deep enough to wait out the blizzards. Then we find the first vein of zinc, and suddenly the company wants to make friends."

"Nothing like that," Thello mumbles. "Learned about the Oldies, about the grendels—"

"So they come with buildbots, with bubblefabs, with air," their mother interrupts. "With gene scanners, credit, implants, and contracts. With smiles here." She drags a corner of her mouth upward with one finger. "And knives behind their backs."

Yorick has heard these words, or similar ones, a hundred times. He knows to nod and keep his mouth shut.

"They're not our friends." She holds out the tablet to Thello. "Smash it."

Thello, stupid little Thello, flushing and defiant, shakes his head. Yorick wants to hiss in his ear: you can get another one, it doesn't matter, just smash it.

"Or I will," their mother says, raising the tablet high.

Thello's eyes dart left. He shakes his head again, and this time he mutters something, too. "Our da, though. Our da was a company man. Everyone says."

Her free hand snaps out; there's the loud flesh-smack and then the red stamp on Thello's cheek. Yorick can phantom-feel the sting on his own. Their mother is trembling. Yorick's heart is pounding so fast. Everything can go wrong in an instant.

"I took it," Yorick lies. "I wanted to play the netgames. I hid it under the bed."

She doesn't seem to hear him, but when he reaches cautiously for the tablet she lets it go. Yorick sets it screen-first on the floor, then stomps hard, eliciting a bone-deep crack. Thello flinches. There are tears winding down his face, but when Yorick insists with *his eyes, his brother comes over. Thello stomps down on the tab-let, first hesitant, then with a growing ferocity.*

The smartglass crunches and squeals, a small symphony that blends with his sobs. Yorick monitors their mother's face until she turns stiffly away.

CHAPTER 04

Sleep doesn't come. His eyelids scrape. His bones ache. Every cell in his body is exhausted. But as the skid churns closer and closer to its destination, more and more memories come for him, chewing through the walls of the sleepstack. The last of the endorphins from his phedrine shot have crawled away on all fours. He feels unwell.

When he gets the wake-up chime, when he pulls himself out of the sleepstack, he feels like a ghost of a ghost. No time to attach the mandible. He'll do it at the hotel, with better hygiene. He taps the spot between his shoulder blades, and once his rucksack has climbed aboard he joins the crowd shuffling off the skid. Some are knuckling their eyes. Some reach for vapor pipes.

The stillness is eerie now that the skid has finally stopped. There's a hollow in Yorick's skull, the absence of a humming engine, as he heads down the ramp. The bay is lit by yellow pylons that jaundice the faces of the disembarking passengers. They're at the bottom of a massive downtube; when he cranes his head he can see the top sealing shut, a shrinking black pinhole.

His skin pebbles as he passes the magnetic clamp that holds the skid in place. Enormous mechanical puppets with dripping proboscises whir to life around the chassis, checking, refueling, scraping away the accumulated ice. A melting lump smacks the back of his neck and trickles down the nape of his coat, soaking into the spiderwool.

He barely twitches. His nervous system is running on fumes, feet dragging on his way to the security queue. The main skid terminal is dreamy familiar: coppery skeletal architecture, oxygen recyclers belching vapor, vaulted ceiling cloaked with schedule holos. The time display ticks forward, but for Yorick it feels like time is running in reverse.

There's no facelock up here, only a haggard man with a scanner wand and tablet. He's pure sealie, the dominant geneprint in the north: jagged cheekbones, pale skin, big black eyes to filter the gloom. Yorick used to wonder why the other children could see so much better than him in the dark. He didn't catch up to them until he joined the company and had his eyes peeled, standard mod for nocturnal operations—which was all of them on Ymir.

Yorick reaches the front of the queue. The man opens his mouth, to tell him to pull his coat down, then shuts it again as a notification flits across his screen. He gives Yorick a familiar twice-over, trying to judge him an offworlder or a cold-blood.

For once, Yorick is glad to be small for his geneprint, to have eyes with too much iris. The man judges wrong, and nods him through without a word. Yorick shuffles on. There was a wide scatter of accents and babeltalk aboard the skid, but now he hears the northern lilt emerging from conversations all around him.

Most of the conversations are about the grendel in the Polar Seven. Whenever a grendel makes itself known, so too do the fabulists. A person in a holomask is explaining how they saw a live one on Thoth, big as a frostswimmer, void-black hide and gnashing blue teeth that glowed in the dark. Yorick is too sleepsick to be amused.

He steps outside and sees a flash of busy street, twisty bio-organic structures rising from mist, a wrong-seeming sky. He inhales.

Mistake. The husk-dry air in the skid was filtered. So was the air in the terminal. The Cut's air is a soup of old grease, dirty fuel, human urination, and Yorick's first breath smashes nausea through his abdomen.

He thought his stomach would be safely empty after a few months in torpor, but when it heaves he starts spewing up rancid white stasis fluid. Without his mandible, half cascades down the front of his coat and half slides, searing, back down his throat. He kneels on the cement stoop as he retches again, so gravity can help.

When he stands up he sees a car waiting for him. It's an elegant gray gargoyle of a thing, conspicuous, drawing far more eyes than the man puking beside it. Yorick doesn't care. The Cut will know there's a company man here sooner than later, and he would collapse trying to walk. He stumps forward, dripping.

The car drifts backward, its side-door scanner blinking. Yorick can't curse without his mandible. He opens the collar of his slimed coat and turns his head, so his company tattoo can override whatever behavioral loop normally keeps the car from picking up vomit-covered passengers. This time it hunkers down and a side door folds open. He shrugs off his rucksack, tosses it inside, and follows.

Filtered air again. He sinks onto a leathery pew, stretching out lengthwise, and sucks it down in gulps. His head is swimming. His body feels like it's about to peel apart. This must be the peak the thaw technician predicted, come an hour early to remind him that humans are not lungfish; they are not adapted to being medically dead for months at a time.

The door folds shut and the car starts to move. He pinches the windows opaque with a trembly gesture, cocooning himself in the dark. His forehead is slick with sweat. He can feel the vomit congealing on his neck. He tries to focus on breathing. He listens to the muffled street sounds: shouting vendors, looping ads, warning klaxons. Cut sounds.

Finally he swings upright and opens the chiller. The rows of cold bottles are all glass, not edibles. He uncaps one, then rips a feathery fistful of spiderwool off his sleeve, wets it, and wads it up. He starts sponging the vomit from his face and neck, scraping off his coat.

The opaqued windows display the company pictogram, the one that looked so beautiful to him as a child, a sleek wasp silhouetted against a decahedral hive. It makes him feel a phantom buzzing in his thumb. He's really here. He's back on Ymir, back in the Cut, and for now he has no way of rectifying that, so he gestures the windows to clear.

The city has grown while he was away, the way a tumor grows. Gray concrete housing blocks are interspersed with the newer, cheaper version: spiraling coral grown from a remixed polyp geneprint, striped in lurid reds and greens and yellows. The traffic is thicker, a miasma of lumbering autohaulers, skeletal stripped-down bikes, floating drones, harried pedestrians. The atmosphere is still half-vapor, drenching the streets in filthy fog. Holos slash through the haze here and there, to signal a sex house or dopamine bar.

All of it seething under an artificial sky, a holo meant to

help people forget they're living in a shallow wound in Ymir's crust. Instead of a sunrise he sees an aching white blank. Jagged black cracks flicker across it. Stray lines of code scroll through and disappear.

Still glitching. He was gone for ten years his time, twenty here, and the sky is still fucking glitching.

CHAPTER 05

When the car pitches to a halt it dumps the last of the bottled water onto Yorick's lap, soaking him. The spiderwool clings cold to his crotch, but he can't hiss without his mandible. He picks up his coat, motions for his rucksack, and braces himself for the stink as the side door peels open. He's barely on the curb before the car gives an electronic bleat and whisks back into traffic.

Yorick stares up at the hotel the company has chosen for him. It dwarfs the buildings on either side, a sprawling mass of polyp grown over the skeleton of some converted foundry, burnt orange and pink inlaid with dull gray metal. The rows of black smartglass windows look like empty eye sockets. A sodium-arc sign vacillates between colonist characters and geometric company script:

SOUTHERN URBANITE MEMORY.

A yelp from behind him. Yorick turns and sees his rucksack wrestling with a child, squirming all four of its stubby limbs despite the makeshift jammer pushed up against its shell. He yanks it free and the girl stumbles backward, squeaking an obscenity.

She's small, even coated in a dozen ragged layers of recycled spiderwool. Broad face, thick bones, tousled orange hair echoing an ancient ice age. She's from Ymir's other colonist geneprint: a red. Her pale blue eyes are terrified.

Yorick remembers he's not wearing his coat. There's no collar to hide the missing jaw, the gaping scarlet hole dribbling spit and the last dregs of regurgitated stasis fluid. He takes advantage of her horror to reach down and pluck the jammer from a limp hand.

She blinks back on. "No, no, don't," she whines. "I didn't know it was your crawler, swear truth, I thought it was lost, I need that jammer, it's Masha's." She picks at the dirt and snot crusted around her mouth, staring at his wound in a way he still hates. "I have to bring it back or she'll beat me blue."

Yorick nods, and hurls the jammer over his shoulder into the thick of the traffic. The girl tries to dive after it; he snares her in place. They both get to see the autohauler slam past and crunch the jammer into black paste. He feels a shudder of shock go through her whole body. Then she starts to scream at him.

She chases him all the way up the steps, only stopping when the security guard slouches off their chair carrying a stunstick. She says *fuck you forever and ever*, then slinks away. Yorick displays the tattoo on his neck for scanning, then steps inside the hotel.

The lobby is dimly lit and vaguely embryonic. It's warm, at least, glowing orange heatlamps baking away the damp exterior chill. The deco is a blend of rusty metal parts and porous bone-colored coral. He can hear a low electric drumbeat and snatches of slurred conversation drifting up through a recessed doorway.

The phantom taste of alcohol makes his stomach buckle again.

"Good evening," comes a synthesized voice. "Are you Mister Bellica, reservation code 2840PK, scheduled for an indefinite stay beginning today?"

A droid pads out from the shadows. It's quadrupedal, about the size of a cat, a skeletal chassis with a holoprojector for a head and a single manipulator flexing up off its spine. Not the typical humanoid host.

Yorick doesn't like how *indefinite stay* sounds, not at all, but he nods. His joints feel loose and watery. He needs to get inside the room and onto the bed.

"If you are Mister Bellica, reservation code 2840PK, scheduled for an indefinite stay beginning today, would you please give verbal confirmation?"

Yorick wants to kick the droid into the nearest wall. Instead he squats down and points to the side of his neck.

"Apologies, I'm afraid I didn't hear you," the droid says. "If you are Mister Bellica, reservation code 2840PK, scheduled for an indefinite stay beginning today, would you please give verbal confirmation?"

Yorick considers tearing open the package and attaching his mandible in the lobby, no regard for sanitation. Instead he takes a rattling breath and tries to shape his tongueless grunt into an affirmative. The droid ignores him until his fifth attempt, at which point it skitters into a pre-programmed dance.

"Thank you for confirming," it burbles. "Welcome to Southern Urbanite Memory, Mister Bellica. We are pleased to offer you a double-luxury suite on the seventh floor of our hotel."

Its holoprojector blossoms to life, sketching a blocky map

of the lobby. Yorick watches a miniature cartoon of himself walk toward the lift. Past the lift. Around a dusty corner to the stairwell.

"I'm afraid the lifts are currently undergoing maintenance, but I would be happy to accompany you up the stairs."

CHAPTER 06

By the third floor, Yorick is crawling. His rucksack is still following him; he can hear the soft whine of its servos as it negotiates the steps. The host droid came, too. It matches his pace, slinking along beside him, chattering about the features and services of the hotel.

Yorick is in purgatory. His entire body is a dull ache. His limbs quiver underneath him. He can feel sweat trickling down his forehead, down the furrow of his shoulder blades. He has his coat pinned awkwardly under one arm, and the lingering stink of the vomit is getting worse.

His saliva glands are working again, which means he's leaving a glistening trail of drool on the concrete. He imagines a cleaner bot finding it and following it up the stairwell to join the caravan. But Southern Urbanite Memory doesn't seem like a place with cleaner bots to spare. The concrete steps are caked with grime. Before long, so are his hands and knees.

On the fourth floor, he has to navigate past a congealed brown puddle that triggers his gag reflex all over again. The abdominal spasms are knifelike.

On the fifth floor, he has to rest for a little while, temple to forearm, staring at a smiley face someone has gouged into the plaster wall. His rucksack bumps into him from behind.

On the sixth floor, he hallucinates. The host droid tells him the reason the lifts are down is because he tossed a small urchin's thieving tool into traffic, and that the Ledger of Universal Suffering is always balanced at Southern Urbanite Memory.

On the seventh floor, he nearly overshoots his destination, moving on sheer muscle memory, but the host droid steers him through the door. The long stretch of dehydrated mosscarpet looks as vast and merciless as an ice field. He braces himself against the wall and staggers upright, just in case there's someone else staying on the seventh floor. Crawling is for private functions. He keeps one hand on the wall as he stumps along, following the gamboling droid.

"Room 702," it announces. "Please provide a gene sample for secure future entries."

Yorick has already run his thumb through the drool on his chest. He pushes it against the door; the imprint of his thumb flashes red on the black smartglass. It swings open.

"Enjoy your stay at Suffering Urbanite Memory," he hears the droid say, and it pads off down the hall.

Yorick locks onto the bed, a massive white slab of mattress suspended by a magnetic yoke. He drops his bundled coat, crosses the room in three disjointed steps, and falls onto it. He kicks off his boots, scrunches his toes, waiting for the tremors to stop. For his heavy breathing to subside. The sheets are crisp and clean-smelling. The mattress is impossibly soft.

But once he has the strength, he hauls himself off the bed and toward the bathroom. His rucksack follows, clambering up onto the sinktop while he shucks the spiderwool off, exposing his torpor-pallid skin to the fluorescent light. The smartglass becomes a mirror. He sees skin shrink-wrapped to bone from the long haul, a rib cage like a clenched fist. The wound is unchanged, still gaping at him.

He claws the last linty strands of spiderwool away and washes his hands as thoroughly as he can stand. Then it's time to open the rucksack. He retrieves the brush first, dips it in a foamy blue disinfectant, and starts cleaning out the wound. The last flecks of dried stasis fluid dissolve. He maneuvers through rippled scar tissue, scrubbing away bits of trapped dirt and sebum.

He rinses once, twice, three times. Puts the injector to his carotid and takes the drugs that keep his immune system hobbled. Uses a roll of gelflesh to seal up his throat. Finally he slides the mandible out of its putty sheath and fits it into place.

It's not warm from the printer anymore, but it heats up when it mollybonds to the gelflesh and to the surgically implanted strips in his skull. Nerve endings meet their artificial conduits and he suddenly has bottom teeth, a lower palate, a chin. His tongue is back, a flexing worm-thing that always feels enormous for the first few minutes.

He works his jaw open and shut, observing the bare mandible in the mirror. It's an angular thing, black nanocarbon swatched with raw-pink polymers. The teeth are paradoxical ivory, small and perfect, displayed by the clear membrane of the lower lip. Something out of an anatomy diagram, or else a bad dream.

He kneads more of the gelflesh overtop, softening the sharp edges, concealing the hinges so only a hairline glasgow grin is visible. It mottles and pales to match his skin. It's not perfect, but it draws fewer eyes than a gaping hole. He pulls faces at himself, testing the range of his new mouthparts. He runs his artificial tongue along his upper palate. The lower.

The mandible makes an almost imperceptible hum, synthesizer ready to compensate for his damaged vocal folds. He exhales. Inhales. These will be the first words he has spoken on Ymir in twenty years.

"I have so much love to give," he says. The voice is reedy, feathered by an electronic razor blade.

His dark hollow eyes say otherwise.

CHAPTER 07

Yorick takes another half dose of phedrine, because he deserves it today, then steps into the shower. One blast of hot water, a slathering of soap, one blast of cold water. The shock of it makes his skin tingle. He thumbs the airdry and a warm gale sucks the moisture away.

Back in the bedroom, he takes stock of his lodgings. Aside from the bed, there's a kitchen corner with a foldaway table and stools. A wide closet with another slab of smartglass on it. A cooker, a washer. A cube of petrified wood serving as a nightstand, a slowly undulating sculpture doubling as a bio-lamp, and a truly stupid sort of chair that seems designed to seat two people facing opposite ways.

He drags the nightstand cube up against the same wall as the closet, leaving a precise gap between them, as is his custom. He remembers his reeking coat pooled on the floor. He opens the closet, pulls out a sealed canister. The geophage is curled inside like a pill bug. Kept frozen until someone needs an unpleasant job done—the parallels are not lost on Yorick. He pops the canister open and pours the stimulant in.

The geophage wriggles.

"We all have to earn our keep," he says, and carries it gently over to his coat.

The geophage slides out of the canister and lands with a plop, uncurls, sets to work deep-cleaning. Hopefully it has the metabolism to do his boots afterward. Yorick clenches his fist in the air to turn the lights off, then tumbles naked onto the bed. He's been asleep for months and all he wants to do is sleep more. The only problem is the dreaming. Inside the torpor pool he never dreams; outside it he can't stop.

"I hate this place so fucking much," he says, and shuts his eyes.

CHAPTER ~(#&−

The desert. Pale, irradiated sand stretching in all directions. Rippling dunes carved by arid winds. The sky overhead is an endless sea of stars, phosphorous constellations illuminating the void. A violet butterfly flits along beneath the starlight, coming to rest every so often on the bone-white sand. Two children are following it, the older tugging the younger by the hand.

The butterfly reaches its destination: a spar of black metal, half swallowed, jutting from the crest of the dune. It folds its wings and vanishes. The children come to the spar. They walk in a solemn circle around it. The younger takes a needle from his jacket and starts pricking the flesh of his hand until blood is welling and dribbling onto the ground. The older inspects his work, nods, and presses his punctured palm against the spar.

A tremor ripples the sand. Something massive, buried and forgotten, is clawing its way back to the world. It rises from the dune, shedding rivulets of slithering sand. The same black metal as the spar composes its geometric body. Ancient and sapient, a machine mind millennia older than anything made by men. It has no eyes.

The children are gone, replaced by a young woman whose entire body is covered in moving tattoos. She approaches the machine.

CHAPTER 08

Yorick's stomach is gnawing itself to pieces and it wakes him up. The dream stays crystallized for a moment, sensical, even meaningful, then crumbles away in the dark. His nausea is gone and now he's ravenous. He half climbs, half falls out of bed, which triggers the biolamp on, and goes to the kitchen to search for food. The cupboards are empty. The freezer has nothing but ice pellets.

"Hotel," he says.

No response.

"Southern Termite Memorial," he says.

"Good evening, Mister Bellica." The host droid's voice is too cheerful for the middle of the night. "How can I improve your lived experience?"

"Closest, quickest food."

"I'm pleased to inform you that our downstairs bar is always open and always serving a variety of local dishes. Would you like to place an order?"

The bar. Imagining the taste of alcohol doesn't make him feel sick anymore, and the chemical fates have decided he's fully awake, strung with a strange nervous energy. His eyes land on his coat, gleaming clean and fresh-smelling. His boots are immaculate. The bloated geophage has curled up and died off in the corner.

"I'll come down," he says. "Are the lifts fixed?"

"I'm afraid the lifts are currently undergoing maintenance."

"Right." He picks up the stiffening geophage and takes it to the trash disposal. "Into the long night," he mutters, tipping it into the hole. "Thank you for your sacrifice. Goodbye."

"Goodbye, Mister Bellica," the host droid warbles.

CHAPTER 09

The bar's deco is more of the same: polyp walls in deep reds and pale purples, derelict mining equipment oxidizing in the corners, sheaves of metal and cable hanging from the ceiling. One end of the place is dominated by a vaguely religious holo-mural, some angel or avatar wearing a gas mask.

He thought he would have it all to himself, but there are two drinkers sitting at the far end of the bar, both wearing the same kind of heavy thermal cloak, and a third stretched out behind a corner table, spindly legs crossed at the knee. A jungle of flexy pneumatic limbs is tending bar; Yorick heads for what looks like center mass. The gray countertop is playing a bright yellow ad.

He pulls up a stool, and a sensor swivels to greet him.

"What do you need?" The bar's voice is gravelly, brusque, a nice changeup from the host droid.

The pair at the end hear it and turn to look. Both of them are dark-skinned, androgynous, taller and bulkier than the typical Ymir geneprint. One has thick locs done up with a static clip in a slowly twisting, slowly writhing tower. The other has a shaved skull and an eye implant—fresh, judging by the vibrant bruising.

Yorick's sleepsick head is still fractured, but there's something familiar about them. They might have been on the skid.

"I'm waiting," the bar says.

Yorick doesn't meet the pair's gaze. "Food," he tells the bar. "Spicy as you can make it. Cook for standard enzymes."

"You want a drink?"

"Yeah. Give me a tank of..." He scans the parade of logos marching along behind the bar. "Whatever got brewed last."

The bar sets a metal cup down with one arm and fills it with another. "Looks like you did a long haul," it says. "You come off that bowlship yesterday? One docked in Shipfall?"

The gurgling nozzle moves away and Yorick takes the cup. The contents are white, foamy, slightly sour-smelling. "Yeah," he says, even though he's talking to an input-output algorithm that has no idea what it's saying. "Just thawed."

"First time on Ymir?"

He takes his first slug from the cup; it hits his empty stomach like mercury. "No."

"Couldn't stay away, huh. Missed the weather."

He takes another drink, this time holding it in his mouth, swilling it around. The mandible tongue has decent sensitivity. He can feel the frothy liquid sliding over it, and he can taste the tang of alcohol underneath the sour. He might even enjoy eating.

"What's your business?" the bar asks, setting down a steaming bowl.

"Hunting something," Yorick says.

"Fat-hunter, huh. So are them two." The arm bringing him a fork jabs it toward the end of the bar. "They're gearing up for the ice field soon."

Yorick doesn't want to explain the difference between

hunting frostswimmers and hunting grendels to an algorithm. He leans over the bowl and inhales. The smell of chili oil sets his stomach sloshing. He starts shoveling the spiced noodles into his mouth as fast as he can.

"Your gut shrinks on a long haul, doesn't it?" the bar remarks. "You're going to burst your stomach wall. The medics will be picking noodles out of your pericardium."

"Worse ways to die," he says thickly, mouth half full.

"Just do it ten meters from the hotel entrance, glutton. Or you ruin our fatality rating."

Yorick shakes his head. "Good algorithm."

"Huh?"

"I said you've got a really good algorithm." He tongues a flake of pepper out of his teeth. "Good conversational reads. They must have loosened a few machine mind restrictions while I was in torpor."

A pneumatic arm yanks his unfinished meal away with unexpected ferocity. "I'm not no fucking droid. I just use one to talk. Same as you with that jaw."

Yorick is still holding the fork. He finally reads the glowing yellow letters scrolling along the dull gray bartop: HUMAN OPERATOR, HUMAN OPERATOR, HUMAN OPERATOR. His eyes dart from arm to arm and find connective cable leading back to a recessed shelf in the wall. The black biotank is only big enough to hold part of a human.

There's a peal of laughter six stools down. The fat-hunter with the shaved head is grinning a blue-stained grin. "Called her a bar droid, didn't you? Nephew, we did the same thing first time we stayed up here. Get you a bigger fucking sign, Linka!"

"Read what's in front of your fucking face," the bartender says.

"She'll warm back up," the fat-hunter says, refilling their drink from a tall metal pitcher. "Sometimes the debodied stay touchy, you know?" They rap a meaty knuckle against the side of the pitcher. "Plenty in here. Have a drink with us, nephew. I heard you say you're hunting."

The other fat-hunter is less gregarious, still analyzing him through hooded lids, but they are also crushing a beautiful blue tablet onto the bartop, and Yorick hasn't had a hit of doxy in six months. Technically.

CHAPTER 10

The two of them are siblings: the one with the wriggling hair is Te and the one with no hair at all is Vesper. Both are nons, which is common enough on Ymir, something they say they appreciate. Once Yorick takes a snuff with them and settles onto his new stool, they burrow back into what feels like a cyclical argument about whether or not *fat-hunter* is a misnomer.

With alcohol and doxy swimming his system, Yorick can enjoy any conversation. His artificial tongue moves in a circuit around his tingling mouth. His head buzzes. He pours the drinks with rapturous precision, and when the pitcher runs dry he orders another from Linka, who is not a bar droid. Mostly he waits for Te to pull the doxy out again.

"Because it's not the blubber you're after," Vesper says. "It's the little beasties living in it. The little parasites. Here, nephew, have a stare." They pull a glossy canister out of their pocket, flick it transparent, and hold it up to Yorick's face. "This is what you're going to be risking your ass for out on the ice field."

He sees a chunk of yellowish-white fat. Then Vesper gives the canister a shake, and tiny flecks of light, miniature arcs of electricity, start moving under the surface.

"Biological superconductors," the fat-hunter says. "Just what's in this tube, worth about forty thousand."

"Treated, extracted, worth about forty thousand," Te corrects. "Don't wave that shit around." They yank the canister away and slide it into the pocket of their cloak. Yorick sees the edge of the bubble bag and tries to estimate how much doxy it might still hold. "We don't do the treating or extracting," Te continues. "We just get the fat. So we're fat-hunters, dumbshit."

"Between us, I'm glad we're on our last run," Vesper says, rubbing at their face. "With the Polar Seven shut down, with the southerly wind coming on, there's going to be a fucking swarm of amateurs out there trying to hunt. No hate on you, nephew. You hear about it, though? You hear about the grendel?"

Yorick wasn't intending to think about his job until the morning. "All labor suspended for the past eight days," he says. "Tensions are running high."

"This is what happens when you go too deep," Te says. "When you try take too much. I always said it. The grendels, they are here for a reason. Here to make sure we don't fuck up the colony worlds the way we fucked up our first one."

"Get comfortable, nephew," Vesper says. "Te has a thing."

"Fuck you, Vesp." Te slides their cup forward; Yorick refills it. "Humans are parasites, too, you know. That's swear truth." They pause. "Actually, detritivores. Since the Oldies are gone. We are detritivores feeding off the remains of an ancient spacefaring civilization that actually had its shit straight."

Vesper grips their own throat, an old Cut threat they must have picked up hunting. "Call me a detritivore one more time, Te."

"I don't even blame the grendels," Te says, ignoring their sibling. "They outlived their creators, right? Thought they were done dealing with little bags of meat."

Vesper bristles. "Grendel just killed a bunch of miners, you here on their world saying you don't blame the grendels—"

Te raises their voice. "Thought they were done, so they go dormant for a thousand years. Who wakes them up? Brand-new little bags of meat. Shit must be agitating."

"You acting like the Oldies just up and went extinct on their own," Vesper snaps. "It was the grendels, Te. You know it was the grendels who did it."

"Company talk," Te says. "Company line to suppress machine mind development, keep people all shit-scared of nonhuman intelligence. The grendels are still around because the Oldies built them tough, is all. Redundancy nodes and bioreactors and xenocarbon—"

"I hate you when you do this." Vesper is up off their stool. "Thinking opposite whatever I think just to piss me off. Linka, where's the toilet?"

A pneumatic arm points toward the back of the room. Vesper staggers away, heated, mumbling. Te's nostrils are flared. They pluck the bubble bag out of their cloak and start crushing more tablets onto the bar.

Yorick watches the growing mound of pale blue powder. He momentarily wants to explain that the neural nodes around a grendel's reactor are not redundancies, that they're actually linked machine minds acting in concert. But dissecting a grendel is tomorrow's work.

"Te," he says. "I don't blame the grendels, either."

"You agree with whoever's got the drugs," Te says, but hands him the straw.

CHAPTER 11

From there the night fragments. Vesper comes back to make peace. There are more clanking pitchers, more rounds of the sour drink. The world contracts into a blurry warm cocoon interspersed with bursts of sharp geometry. At some point Vesper disappears and reappears with a hunting tool, a sort of harpoon-syringe hybrid, not because they want to stab anyone but because they want to show it to Yorick and to Linka and to the spindly man at the corner table.

"Isn't it beautiful?" the fat-hunter asks, voice thick with emotion, laying it across Yorick's lap. "All shiny and sharp and phallic." They tap the circuitry inlaid in their bruised eye socket. "I got it linked to this little imp now, for targeting."

Yorick hefts it into the air and nearly drops it. Vesper curses at him; Linka tells them to get their gear out of the bar before she activates her security.

"Ex-con, Linka is," Te mumbles in his ear. The doxy has made them friendlier. "She was in one of them company prisons."

"Always have to stay for a southerly blizzard," Vesper says, oblivious. "Always worth it. The little ones spore, see, and that lures the big ones up. They like to taste it."

"Then we taste *them*," Te says, flashing their precisely striated eyebrows. "With the hook and the graft-knife."

Vesper takes the canister of blubber out of Te's cloak and balances it on their forehead, neck craned back. Yorick asks where they got the doxy, which is not neutered company stuff. Vesper points to the man in the corner. There's something spidery about him. He's wearing a black body glove and smoking from a vapor pipe. Dark sealie eyes, frozen half smile.

Te gives a shout of alarm. The canister wobbles, precarious, and—

11.2

"The locals up here, they got this bloodsport," Vesper says. "Real brutal shit, but real underground, too. They don't let just anyone come watch."

The three of them are in the bathroom; Yorick and Vesper are watching Te fix their twisted tower of hair in front of the mirror, deftly arranging the strands. Sometimes the mirror Te moves a little different from the meat Te, but that might just be the doxy messing with Yorick's sleepsick brain. Same for the feet marching back and forth beneath the toilet stalls.

"They wear these fucking shoes," mirror-Te says, with meat-Te's mouth moving a beat behind. Their teeth are stained blue from the doxy drip. "These *shoes*, Yorick."

Yorick can't remember introducing himself. Paranoia slices through his cocoon. He looks at mirror-Yorick, who must have told them his real name, because they are offworlders and heading for their final run on the ice anyway. Mirror-Yorick stares balefully back. He stretches out his arm, touches his doppelganger's fingertip.

"Fuck you forever and ever," he says.

Vesper and Te start to laugh. He tries to laugh, too, but mirror-Yorick's mouth just opens wider and wider and wider until it's a big black hole that's going to swallow the stars—

11.4

They're all at the corner table with the man in black, sitting in a shroud of smoke. Te hollows out their cheeks on the pull, then passes it to Vesper, who passes it straight to Yorick. He takes a short polite drag before he hands the vapor pipe back to its owner.

"This one, he's a artist," Vesper says. "You should have seen him play tonight. Little dopamine bar down the street, had the whole place packed and sealed."

The man's inchoate smile doesn't change. His mournful eyes are fixed on the pipe, which he is refilling with long graceful hands.

"Virtuoso," Te agrees. "Play us something. One of them colonist ballads. Ice and death and shit."

"Smoked too much," the man says. "Can't." His voice is soft and carries the north Cut lilt.

"For us." Vesper puts both palms together, supplicating. "For your favorite customers. We're keeping you afloat, nephew. Them miners aren't affording doxy, not with the shutdown."

The man shakes his head, adjusting something near his feet. For a moment his eyes meet Yorick's, and Yorick is certain he knows about the company tattoo hidden under his spiderwool, the same way he knows about ice and death and shit.

Te stands abruptly. "Vesp, where's the fat? Where's the—"

11.5

In the embryonic lobby: Yorick and Te are standing under a heatlamp while Vesper makes the host droid draw up a map of north Cut, the rough stuff past the refineries. Te has their canister of blubber cradled securely in the crook of one arm.

"By the way." The fat-hunter's voice is hushed. "What happened to your face, Yorick?"

"It's kind of a fucked-up story." Even with the mandible compensating, he's starting to slur his words. "You ever seen a wood thresher up close?"

Te shakes their head, making their locs writhe outward all at once like startled snakes. Yorick tells them the story by rote while Vesper argues with the host droid about the value of spontaneity over safety to a lived experience.

"We know a niece," they're telling the droid. "We meet her up, we won't have any trouble."

"I'm afraid it's against our policy to provide transportation to this sector of Reconciliation," the host droid says. "Southern Urbanite Memory prioritizes the safety of our guests."

"That is a nasty story," Te says, staring contemplatively up at the orange bars of the heatlamp. "Nasty, nasty."

"Yeah." Yorick is staring at Te's cloak. He pats his side, pocket-level. "You got any left?"

Te's eyes narrow. "What I say the last three times?"

He tries to remember. Vesper walks over, grim-faced, host

droid skulking behind. They pull Te aside and mumble into their sibling's ear. The paranoia hits again. His head throbs. The host droid asks him if he's enjoying his stay, and he says—

11.7

"History of this place is mad, nephew." Vesper is sitting with him on the hotel steps, under the sodium arc sign, face slashed in two halves by the pale pink light. "You hunt here long enough, you hear all about it. See, nobody wanted this snowball." They jab their finger into some invisible person's chest. "At *first*."

Yorick doesn't like history. The edible bottle they brought outside is empty now, so he is tearing spongy chunks off it, chewing the ale-soaked fiber. This is their final drink together. Te is off pissing, and then the fat-hunters have to do something, go somewhere. It's unclear.

"Had just a handful of colonists out here," Vesper says. "And all their kids were done exosomatic, modified. Cold-weather geneprints. Back then, starting out, they made surface colonies, not this cozy underground shit."

Yorick rips more pieces off the bottle, faster now, mashing them into his mouth and swallowing them in sticky lumps. The mandible can barely taste it, but taste isn't important. He needs the feeling of distension in his gullet, his belly.

"But whoever geoscanned the place, they fucked up, because they didn't scan all this zinc and silver in the crust." Vesper snatches the last rind of the bottle out from under Yorick's fingers and pops it into their mouth. Grimaces. "Nephew, this tastes like wood."

"At first," Yorick says.

"At fucking first," Vesper says again, and laughs. Their eye implant is a firefly hovering in the dark. "So, listen. The company finds that shit, because they always find that shit, and they come set up here on Ymir. This is forty years ago. Fifty, maybe. The colonists, the cold-bloods, they don't like it. But they been isolated out here. They don't know the company always *gets* what it *wants*."

The tattoo on Yorick's neck becomes a living thing, pulsing, pulsing—

11.8

"They're not coming back." A gravelly electronic voice. Linka, the bartender who is not a droid.

Yorick turns on his stool. "Who?"

"Your fat-hunter friends. They said so when they ordered you that." An arm nudges the bowl of oily noodles on the bar in front of him. "Remember?"

"Yeah, I remember."

"So what are you watching the door for?" she asks.

"Not sure." He rubs his face, feeling for the minute ridge where gelflesh meets real flesh. "Sorry I thought you were a droid. I'm sleepsick."

"You're dumbsick. You're also—"

11.9

Yorick is sitting cross-legged on the floor, facing the holo-mural, watching it swell and swell but never burst. It makes him feel vaguely religious. In his peripheral he can see that the man in black, the musician, is watching him. He climbs to his feet and the world slews to one side. It recalls the swaying skid compartment where he was so recently resuscitated.

His thaw technician would be disappointed by what he's done to his body chemistry since. So would Gausta—she would tell him he is sabotaging future iterations of himself, borrowing from tomorrow's happiness. But Gausta has her own vices. Bad ones, in the rumors. Yorick does not owe Gausta anything anymore.

He gets to the corner table, holds the edge of it for balance while he arranges his thoughts. "There's this song I heard, last time I was on Ymir. A dirge. It's about two children."

The musician is refilling his pipe again, every movement slow and drifting, like someone underwater. He blinks his dark eyes. "That's an old song."

"I would like to hear it."

The musician rolls his head to one side. "Not many people leave here come back."

"It's the weather," Yorick says. "Couldn't stay away."

"You always like that? Always echoing what other people said to you?"

"Yeah. Only way I can seem clever." He spies a gray bag sitting under the table with a distinctive shape tenting the fabric. He goes to yank it out; the musician stops his arm. Yorick grins his half-real grin. "I seen you switch the canisters. What did you put in yours? Kitchen grease?"

The musician gledges toward the bar, where Linka's arms are scrubbing the stools down. "I'm keeping it safe for them," he says. "If they took it north end, they'd lose it for sure."

"Play me the dirge, and by the end of it I'll have forgotten I saw," Yorick says.

"I don't know it."

"I know you know it. Everyone from this fucking place knows it." Yorick sways on his feet. "Play it, or I'll help Te and Vesper break your elbow bones."

"I don't think you'd do that," the musician says, with a semi-smile. "Don't think you're that sort."

"I contain multitudes," Yorick says. "And most of them are shitbags."

The musician gives him a long look. Then he reaches down and unzips the black body glove from his left leg, exposing a long bony limb that bulges in strange places. He rests his bare foot on the stool across from him. As Yorick watches, the pasty flesh of the man's thigh slides apart and his leg unfolds, insectoid, into a metal-stringed instrument.

He tunes, then sets his saw to the strings and starts to play. From the first note, Yorick's entire body remembers where it leads. His skin pebbles with it. The song ghosts through the empty bar, seeping into all the cracks. He lets go of the table and sinks to a crouch. The doxy is wearing off. The ache in his throat is like a chunk of hard plastic.

Yorick listens until the end, and when it's over he can't meet the musician's eyes. He goes to the bar and pays for his drinks, plus purge virus and a stimulant for morning, with his wet thumb. Linka doesn't say goodnight.

The trip up the stairwell is slow and fast at the same time, and then he's collapsing onto the hotel bed again. The smart-glass tells him he's due to meet the replacement overseer of the Polar Seven Mine in three hours.

"Southern Urbanite Misery," he says.

"Good morning, Mister Bellica. How can I improve your lived experience?"

"I need you to search a name for me on the local net."

"I'd be happy to do that. What is the name?"

Yorick stares at the ceiling.

"Apologies, I'm afraid I didn't catch that. What is the name?"

Silence.

"Apologies, I'm afraid I didn't catch that. What is the name?"

Silence.

"Apologies, I'm afraid—"

CHAPTER 12

Yorick doesn't sleep. He cleans his mandible in the mirror, then loads the purge virus into his injector, running a scan to make sure his antibodies are copacetic. As soon as it gives him the go-ahead, he plunges it into his neck. The virus will eat whatever alcohol his liver hasn't broken down. The doxy is already gone, leaving a trail of fried dopamine receptors in its wake.

He takes his immunosuppressants and showers again, luke-warm water this time. The night's events have already begun to slip away from him, swirling down the drain. The virus kicks in as he's climbing out of the stall. He heads to the toilet, squats, and starts shitting out gray sludge. He watches himself in the smartglass.

"I have so much love to give," he says.

Back to the shower for a remedial rinse, then to the spider-wool nozzle for a double-thick coating. He scrubs the blue stains from his real teeth—the artificial ones self-clean—then finds a dispenser disgorging some kind of scented clay and uses a pinch of it to slick back his hair. His reflection is still gaunt and sickly. Finally he takes the stimulant, tearing it open and squeezing it down his throat for slow absorption.

He's on the bed, skimming the official incident report from the Polar Seven Mine, when the host droid's voice blares through the room to tell him he has a visitor waiting downstairs. The overseer is early.

"Tell them I'm coming," he says. "Are the lifts fixed?"

"I'm afraid the lifts are currently undergoing maintenance."

Yorick puts on his coat and boots and heads for the stairwell; the hallway's desiccated mosscarpet crunches underfoot. He recognizes a few landmarks on his way down. The smiley face gouged into the wall on fifth floor. The coagulated brown puddle on fourth. By ground level, the stimulant has cleared the last of the night's smog from his head. Instead of bleary, he feels jumpy. Disjointed.

The smartglass windows have turned transparent to coax in the light, but there's not much of it. The lobby's only occupant is mostly in shadow. She's a giant, even by red standards: broad-shouldered, long-armed, young legs slabbed with muscle under spiderwool. When her pale blue eyes land on Yorick, they turn glacial.

Yorick recalls the brief. The giant is Fen, a mononym not uncommon among the surface clans. She arrived to the Polar Seven half a year ago as a transient laborer, but had her contract extended past the end of the blizzard season. She's young, very young. She must be competent, or she would not have been named interim overseer following the death of one Petra Zabka by grendel.

"Good morning," Yorick says.

The interim overseer ignores the greeting. "I'm to take you down the Maw," she says. "Follow."

"What about my equipment?" Yorick asks. "My hounds?"

The red nearly ignores that, too, but something folded in her massive hand starts to rumble. She grimaces down at it for a moment. "You can ask her," she says, then slips the company-issue holomask over her face, fastening a modified strap to accommodate her wide skull.

Gausta's features resolve from the pixelated blur. "Good morning, Oxo," she says, with a trace of amusement for the alias. "I hope you slept."

Yorick's not sure if it's her or her avatar, but he nods.

"There's been a licensing delay with the hounds," she says. "Increased security measures. I suppose one can never be too cautious, moving machine minds through the ansible." Her eyes flick left and right; the cam in the holomask's forehead swivels. "This must be what rebodying feels like."

Fen stiffens at that; Yorick can feel the red's distaste radiating outward.

"Hounds or no, you should familiarize yourself with the mine's environs in advance of your hunt," Gausta says. "Fen will escort you to the secondary skid terminal, and from there to the Polar Seven. I'll rejoin you underground."

Her face freezes and fades. Fen yanks the mask off and for a microsecond still bears the snarl that was hiding underneath. The flicker of malice floods Yorick's body with fight-or-flight, prickling his skin and bowels.

Fen's face smooths over. "Come on, company man," she says, and turns her broad back.

CHAPTER 13

The secondary skid terminal is only a few blocks away from Southern Urbanite Memory, which is likely how the company decided on his lodgings. Yorick can recognize it by the enormous uptube piercing the sky like a proboscis.

The hour is early, but the Cut is busy. Old men are dragging cooking vats out onto streetside conductor pads. Vendors are cleaning yesterday's skin and grime out of their gene scanners. A woman walks past carrying a spool of electric cable on her head like a halo. The sidewalk is already clogged with bikes and walking markets.

A block from the hotel, there's someone dancing naked. People part around them, unperturbed, and when Yorick gets closer he realizes it's just a mannequin advertising some sex house. All its jittering limbs are intact, but somebody has scrawled graffiti onto its muscly stomach. The wasp of the company pictogram, crudely anthropomorphized, humping a snowman.

Yorick follows Fen down the shopping alley that bisects the block. The red has her own gravity when she walks; the crowd seems to bend and split around her. Yorick is her irregular satellite. Halfway down the alley, Fen pauses at a particular vendor and buys a half-dozen steamed buns that quickly fog their plastic bag.

The smell triggers a memory: biting into wobbly dough, hot grease spurting down his hand, the savory vatmeat and browned onion. He would rather keep the taste memory intact than let his new tongue try to approximate it, but his stomach gurgles loudly enough for Fen to hear.

"Have you eaten?" the red asks.

"A while ago."

Fen doesn't offer, just knots the bag and continues down the alley. Up ahead on the corner, Yorick sees the little red girl, the one who tried to steal his shit. Today she's selling filter masks, flimsy pus-color things printed from bioplastic. Her face doesn't have any bruises, but they might be on her body instead, hidden under the linty spiderwool.

Her eyes flare with recognition as they approach: delight for Fen, confusion for the man trailing after her. Yorick's paranoia jabs him again, tells him this show is for his benefit, a way of reminding him that cold-bloods take care of their own and he is not their own.

But there's no show. Fen drops the bag into the girl's lap without breaking stride. Yorick briefly considers buying a filter mask, to demonstrate that he is not a soulless company man, but it wouldn't fit over his mandible. The little red girl scowls at him on the way past.

Outside the blue-tiled skid terminal, a handful of miners are playing dice on an overturned crate. Four sealies, two reds. All of them look up at Fen's approach; the dice keep clattering but it becomes performative, an attempt to mask the sudden stretched-wire tension. Yorick remembers Gausta's voice: *rumors of a strike.*

"What's news?" asks a man with cobalt-blue tats capping his cheekbones. "You here to put the company face on and tell us to go back down the Maw?"

Fen's nostrils flare. "Company sent us a grendel killer," she says. "I'm taking them under."

"That's a grendel killer?" A woman narrows her bloodshot eyes and waves a vapor pipe in Yorick's direction. "Don't look like a grendel killer."

"There's no specific geneprint for it," Yorick says.

She squints at his mandible. "Grendel fuck up your face, then?"

"Yes," he says. "On Baldr."

Fen doesn't let him tell the story. "Be gone when we get back, Wickam," she says, addressing the sealie with the facial tats. "You lot strutting about here helps nothing."

The miner called Wickam folds his arms across his concave chest, plants his feet. "Easy for you to play both sides, Fen," he says. "Things get messy, you can always fuck off back to your surface clan. Some of us, we got stakes."

He points to a scar on his arm: an indenturement implant, paying off damages from Subjugation days. Yorick thought that would all be over by now.

"What happened to *fuck the company*?" Wickam asks. One of the others giggles low in her throat, anticipating Wickam's next words. "Or are you letting the company fuck you now?"

The dice stop clattering. The scene ices over. Then Fen moves, and she does it fast, suddenly looming over the man like a thunderhead. Yorick can see Wickam's bony knee start to quiver. But the sealie's brave from the vapor pipe, and he meets Fen's cold eyes.

"You want a jig, you tell me now," the giant says. "If not,

you keep your mendacious fucking mouth shut about what you don't understand. And you go home."

A vapor pipe can only do so much. Anger is radiating off Fen's body, and Yorick can imagine those blue-veined hands crushing a throat with ease. Wickam can probably imagine worse. The miner blinks his oil-black eyes. Then he crumbles, and slides out of the way without a word. The others keep their heads down as Fen strides to the terminal doors.

"Mendacious," Wickam mutters. "Fuck's that mean, then?"

Yorick follows Fen in. The secondary skid terminal is cramped compared to the main, space for just a half-dozen transports arrayed around the uptube he saw from the street. Fen uses her thumb to unlock the smallest skid from its clamp. Lightweight, roughly oblong fuselage, anchor spikes equipped to tether it to the ice in a blizzard.

She doesn't ask for help, so Yorick watches her haul the skid to the uptube all on her own, muscles furling and unfurling under her spiderwool. It thunks into the uptube shaft and bobs there, suspended.

"Looks like tensions are running a bit high," Yorick says, trying to gauge how much of the red's anger, if any, is performative. "How far is the mine?"

Fen blanks him, expressionless, and climbs into the skid. Yorick has a premonition: Fen knows. The overseer spotted some bit of evidence, maybe saw through his spiderwool somehow, saw the scars on his shins. She knows that Yorick is the worst sort of company man, the kind who betrayed his own blood during Subjugation.

As he follows Fen into the skid, Yorick reminds himself that he's only been thawed for a day, and that paranoia is a symptom of sleepsickness. That extended torpor often causes heightened anxiety, minor audio hallucinations. His nervous system was frozen for months, starved for input, and now it's readjusting to the land of the living.

He straps himself down. An electronic voice recites safety protocol while they drift to the dead center of the uptube. Fen grips the handles above her orange head. Yorick wraps both arms around himself, and a second later the uptube sends them hurtling toward a hole in the sky.

CHAPTER 14

The skid stays low, hugging the ice, and the rush of wind becomes familiar white noise. The glow of the Cut's blister roof has already receded in the distance. The uptube spat them out thirty klicks from the Polar Seven Mine, and Fen is quickly making up the difference, controlling the skid's throttle herself.

Yorick stares out the side window. They are back under Ymir's real sky, the howling black void, and as they soar across a frozen lake the skid's running lights throw their wobbly reflection back at them. The ansible lurks in the distance, pulsing electric blue. His hounds are bogged down somewhere inside its quantum anatomy, cycling through the procedural diagnostics that ensure they haven't gotten too clever.

Without his hounds, without his nerve suit, this meatspace visit to the mine is very nearly pointless. Gausta must know that, so Gausta must want him there for some other reason. Yorick ponders it as the Polar Seven approaches, entrance demarcated by glowing yellow pylons, and wishes he'd brought something to drink.

Fen starts to slow as soon as they pass the first marker. By the time the mouth of the downtube appears, they're moving at the perfect speed to drop right in. Yorick braces himself, but the down is gentler than the up, and aside from a slight bubbling in his stomach his body barely notices it. The skid settles at the bottom of the tube and its running lights shut off.

For a moment there's perfect darkness. He feels Fen moving in the black, undoing her harness. Sudden fear jabs through him. Fen and Gausta have conspired. He knows it in his gut. They've brought him here to kill him and hide the corpse deep, deep.

Yorick focuses on his breathing. The biolamps around the edge of the downtube swell to life at last, leaking blurry orange light through the skid fuselage.

"I have so much love to give," he says—aloud, by accident.

Fen's voice is acidic. "What?"

Yorick undoes his harness. "Nothing."

The skid clamps itself to the rim of the downtube and Fen exits first. Subtracting her weight makes the vehicle surge a half meter higher; Yorick has to jump down. His boots echo when they hit the dirt.

The main shaft is an enormous hub hollowed out around the downtube, lit by clusters of biolamps awoken by their arrival. Smaller shafts branch out in all directions, following veins of zinc through Ymir's crust, winding deeper into the dark. He sees the glinting metal vertebrae of hauling tracks, but nothing moves on them.

"You worked underground before?" Fen asks.

"A few times," Yorick says. "Grendels like to burrow deep."

"Same as the company." Fen jerks her head toward a polyresin structure on the other side of the downtube; judging by the web of electric cables, it houses one of the mine's main generators. "Glue bath's this way."

Yorick follows her around the edge of the downtube. The bio-lamp lighting is dim, slightly hellish, limning everything in furnace orange. They are deep enough in the earth that the frigid air of the ice field is a distant memory. Sweat is already soaking into Yorick's spiderwool, and he knows they're not done descending.

Fen ducks through the polyresin door; a moment later the echoing shaft is filled with a low hum, power restored to the necessary hauling tracks. Yorick hears a sloshing noise and follows it around the corner of the generator hut. The glue bath is a small circular pool, maybe two meters across, fed by a chugging black fabricator. A waxy yellowish skin on the surface begins to churn, dissolving into itself. Fen shows up to scoop the last of it away with a long-handled skimmer.

The bath's contents are glossy and clear now, swirled by sluggish ripples—organic membrane, grown from a tweaked tardigrade geneprint. Ship technicians use the same stuff for vacuum work. Yorick assumes it's cheaper for the company to repurpose a bowlship's fabricator than to print individual heatsuits for its miners.

Fen strips down, peeling off her spiderwool. The miner's legs are laced with telltale scars—one fresh scab on her shin stands out, reddish black on anemic white. Yorick sheds his coat and boots, removes the spiderwool from his arms and torso, but keeps his lower body covered. He doesn't want his legs naked in front of the red.

"Eyes shut, don't breathe in," Fen says, then lowers herself into the bath. Her shoulders scrape the sides. The membrane closes over her head for one second, two seconds, then she tightens her grip on the rungs and levers herself out. She doesn't drip. The membrane warps the light, sending rainbows across her face when she turns her head.

"Now you," she says. "Two seconds is enough."

Yorick stands on the lip of the bath. It makes him think of torpor, except by the time he gets dumped into the torpor pool he's already clinically dead. For this he has to climb in on his own. The membrane wriggles at him. He eases himself down, shuts his eyes, sucks in a deep breath, and goes under.

The membrane is cool and dry against his skin, alive, undulating slow and steady. His tailbone grazes the bottom of the bath, and he settles there. No sounds from above. No light behind his eyelids. It's tranquil. It feels almost like not existing. He imagines expelling his air and inhaling the membrane instead, letting it flood his lungs and baptize him inside out.

Massive hands, Fen's hands, hook him under the armpits and drag him out of the bath. Yorick opens his eyes—the membrane allows them a small air pocket—and sees the red is giving him a strange look. He was under longer than he realized.

"Two seconds is enough," Fen repeats.

"Sorry."

Fen dons the holomask again, pulling it taut over her glistening head. Gausta's signal has to bounce far and deep from her house on the ice. Her face jitters, freezes, but her voice comes clear.

"Hello again, Oxo. I hope you and Fen are getting acquainted." Her wolfish smile stutters wider and wider. "Let's go have a look at the kill site."

CHAPTER 15

Track Five is unfinished, only a few kilometers long. They rattle down its magnetic spine in an empty ore-scoop, moving through an increasingly narrow tunnel, then continue on foot from its terminus. The air is hotter down here; the membrane stays cool against Yorick's bare skin but starts to snag on his spiderwool.

"No visual record of the attack," he says, recalling the brief. "Why?"

He hears Fen shape a breath, but Gausta interrupts. "We have Fen's deceased predecessor to thank for that," she says. "He lobbied quite strongly for decreased worker surveillance. Farcical at the time, and now deeply inconvenient."

"No cams in the tunnels?" Yorick presses, charting the muscle tension between Fen's swooping shoulder blades.

"As I understand it, they are triggered only by seismic shift or gas leak," Gausta says. "The grendel was not classified as either. We've modified the parameters since, but the grendel has yet to make an appearance on the feed."

They pass through a gauntlet of stalled extractors, jagged silhouettes looming from each side of the tunnel. The ground grows uneven. Every few steps, Yorick trips, catches himself.

Fen somehow knows without looking where the divots are. As the slope of the tunnel increases, the heat ratchets upward. Sweat trickles down his spiderwooled legs, puddling in the membrane under his feet.

His calves are aching when they finally see the end of the tunnel. A single enormous digger sits there, drill plunged forward into the rock face. The ceiling is low enough now that Fen has to stoop, but she does it with practiced ease, still holding the biolamp steady.

In the orange illumination, Yorick sees the machine has been smashed, leaving a deep gouge of crumpled metal and torn wiring. Dried blood is crusted onto it in a splash pattern.

"Here...we...are." Gausta's micvoice chops and echoes. "Show him."

Fen taps the holomask, widens the projection. Gausta vanishes, and the tunnel fills with corpses. Yorick is standing ankle-deep in one of them. For an instant there's a phantom stench in his nostrils, the death smell, and his stomach gives a dangerous lurch. But it's only a holo, and the eviscerated miner has no scent.

He takes a long look. The body is nearly split in two, cloven from shoulder to groin, shards of rib cage jutting at odd angles. Their torn-open membrane puckers and curls around the wound. Their limbs have been shorn away. Their face is strangely relaxed.

"I was impressed upon by the brutality," comes Gausta's wavery voice. "I had never seen...aftermath...one would..."

"Cayetano," Fen says dully.

Yorick recalls the name from the incident report: indentured worker, six years in the Polar Seven Mine, three in the Polar Four before that. The ferocity of the damage is consistent with the ferocity of a grendel woken from hibernation. They tend to disassemble their victims.

He moves around the holo-skinned tunnel, over digital dirt coating actual dirt, to inspect each body in turn. Fen names them all, even though they are all just rearranged meat. It reminds him of a colonist ballad, one of the gruesome ones. The fourth corpse is draped across the digger. She's a red, shorter than Fen, head hanging at an ugly angle. The grendel presumably picked her up and smashed her onto the machine, snapping her spine.

"It's rather reminiscent of Subjugation days," Gausta says. "Smart mines had a similar way of strewing pieces all about."

Yorick doesn't want to think about Subjugation days. "Where's the fifth body? The old overseer?"

Fen answers. "Zabka wasn't found."

"He's listed as a casualty, not a lost miner."

"Membrane degrades after eight hours," Fen says. "Zabka's been missing eight days."

"The drones have found no sign of him." Gausta's voice has solidified. "But the auxiliary tunnels are extensive. Fen suspects he fled, and later asphyxiated in some hidden crevice."

Yorick is not particularly curious. He's exhausted, and angry. He could have loaded this holo at the hotel and inspected it there. Either Gausta dragged him to the mine because she wanted to bait Fen with the sight of fellow miners shredded to pieces, or Gausta dragged him to the mine because she knows he spent last night drinking and snuffing doxy. She always was a sadist.

But Yorick is not a recruit anymore. He claps his hands together. "Yeah," he says. "Yeah, well. Without hounds and a nerve suit I'm as useless as either of you. I think now we head back to Reconciliation and get a drink. My buy."

Fen grunts, a surprised sound, but waits for Gausta to speak.

"If you really feel you've gleaned all you can from this, Oxo," she says. "I'll advise you when your equipment is ready. In the meantime, do try to sleep a bit."

Fen switches off the holomask and the bodies disappear. She yanks the company tech off her face. Yorick is not expecting gratitude, but maybe some flicker of relief that Gausta's game has been cut short. Instead, Fen's nostrils are flared with disgust, and her pale blue eyes feel more like a blizzard than ever. It's the kind of hate that could collapse a star.

Yorick's sleepsick brain assures him, in a chemical whisper, that one of them will have to kill the other before he can leave Ymir. He is too dehydrated to piss himself.

CHAPTER 16

For today, Fen lets him live. The giant doesn't speak on their way back across the ice, and when they return to the skid terminal Yorick slinks off without attempting a goodbye. The terminal entrance is empty now, the crate shoved to one side and the miners long gone. He keeps his head down on the short walk to Southern Urbanite Memory. His unease comes in peaks and troughs.

As soon as he's back in the sanctuary of his hotel room, he tells the smartglass to call Dam Gausta. He is drenched in sweat from scaling the stairs, and his heart is pounding at his ribs. His hands shake. He tears off his boots and hurls one at the wall while the call loads. When Gausta's marbled face appears on the smartglass, he hurls the other.

"Hello, Oxo," she says, unperturbed. "You look unwell."

"There is no one for whom it is well," Yorick says, by rote, then snarls. "What do you expect? Bringing me to Ymir, sending me to the bottom of a mine with an untagged grendel and a giant clanner who wants to snap my neck. Without any of my shit. Without even a fucking graft-knife. Do you want me dead?"

"Of course I don't want you dead," Gausta says. "The company values you very highly."

"What was that all about, then?" Yorick breathes. "Was that for Fen? She's hiding something, yeah?"

Gausta only blinks. "We can discuss this later, Yorick. Get some sleep."

Yorick eyes the smartglass. He unclenches his fists. "You're not really there, are you?"

"Very perceptive," Gausta's avatar says. "I'm attending to other concerns. If there's anything else you'd like to add, please be brief."

Yorick considers all sorts of brief additions, none of them polite. "Nothing else," he says. "No."

He blanks the smartglass, then climbs onto the bed. He draws his knees to his chest and wraps his arms tight around them, curled in on himself like a fetus.

Outside, he keeps the chin of his mandible higher than the chin of whoever's across from him. He slouches and spreads. He takes his space like a gas giant, making his body as big as he can. All of those habits were gouged into him here on Ymir when he was still a child. Inside, when nobody can see him, he always makes himself small.

Exhaustion catches him up and shuts him down. Too many hours wandering through the mine with his nerves knife-edged. Too many hours doing whatever he was doing last night. Too many hours in the land of the living. He falls asleep like falling off a cliff.

CHAPTER **#>`

*T*hey are building a human skull in orbit, an enormous orb of nanotube and alloy slowly gaining the crude dimensions of forehead, cheekbone, jaw. Yorick watches it grow in the sky, with the knowledge that he has watched it for years. He sits at the top of a wind-pummeled hill. Gnarled bushes curl back against the gale; red-and-gray lichen swatches the boulders. Someone is sitting beside him, but he doesn't turn to see who.

"Let's play the grendel game," says a child's voice.

Yorick feels the warm weight of a needlegun in his hand. When he looks down he finds the weapon is made of flesh and teeth. Its skin is joined to his skin and he can't ungrip it.

"Not like that," the boy says, because now Yorick has the needlegun pressed up against his small forehead. Yorick explains that he doesn't know any other way to play the grendel game, and he pulls the trigger.

Up in the sky, they are giving the skull a face. Buildbots crawl across the surface, sheathing the alloy with swathes of pale plastic, installing pitch-black chunks of carbon in the eye sockets. It's not Yorick's face, but it's close. He starts to clap.

CHAPTER 17

He wakes up with strains of an old dirge growing through him like vines, tethering him in memories. The time display on the smartglass shows late evening. His head is muddled but one thought comes clear: he needs to get off this world. Every second he spends here erodes him, and the past is forcing its way through the cracks.

He pushes away the dream, the face in the sky, the needle-gun, and tries to focus on current problems. Gausta is yanking him around. The grendel's whereabouts are unknown. His equipment hasn't been printed. A giant red wants to murder him for some reason. Another red, much smaller, wants to murder him for taking her jammer.

He rubs his eyes and unfurls himself. He takes his immunos, then a double dose of phedrine, liquid sunshine to help insulate him from his paranoia.

A few drinks will help even more. Yorick puts on his boots and heads for the stairs, not bothering to ask if the lift has been fixed in the six hours he's been asleep. The ascent and descent has become its own comfortable kind of hell. He knows he is helping to balance the Ledger of Universal Suffering.

He's winded by the time he's on the ground floor. He walks

across the lobby with his hands on his head, wheezing. Entering the hotel bar kicks off cell division in his cerebellum. Scant memories of the prior night start to multiply. He recognizes the tangle of pneumatic arms behind the bar, stools that screech when dragged, a holomural that he no longer loves. For a moment he superimposes a pair of fat-hunters at the end of the bar, one with revolving hair.

But apart from him and a black-clad man at a corner table, the place is empty. Yorick picks a stool. Yellow script is scrolling across the bartop: HUMAN OPERATOR, HUMAN OPERATOR, HUMAN OPERATOR. He feels an echo of shame, distant through his phedrine high, but can't quite remember why.

"What do you want?" asks an electronic voice.

"Something to drink." He looks over the logos, picks a stylized black hole. "That one. Half tank."

"Eating?"

"Anything spicy," he says. "I got standard enzymes. Cook for standard."

"Yeah, I know," the voice says. "Dumbsick."

Yorick feels a prickle of familiarity. "We met last night."

"Yeah. Obviously." An arm picks a metal cup from the hanging rack, flips it, and fills it with what looks like bacterial beer. "When do you go fat-hunting?"

"I told you I was a fat-hunter?"

"You did. Te didn't believe it, though. Said you didn't know shit about the industry."

Te. He remembers Te crushing doxy onto the bartop, adjusting their hair in the bathroom. He takes a drink; the bacterial beer is bitter and somewhat watery. His eyes slide around the bar and come to rest on the man in the corner. He has a flash of the man's leg unfolding, bone replaced with fluted black carbon.

"Did I talk to that man?" he asks.

"What man?"

"The person in the corner."

A sensor behind the bar gives an exaggerated swivel. "Nobody there."

The phedrine keeps him steady, but Yorick is suddenly worried that the black-clad man and his wide sealie eyes are a hallucination. He finishes the watery beer in a few gulps. It's awful, but he orders a full pitcher and another cup. The pneumatic arms dance and weave behind the bar. Linka. Her name is Linka, and she's not a droid. She's just debodied.

"How long have you been running this place?" Yorick asks.

"Two years."

"Before that?"

"Before that I was incarcerated. Company prison. Very fun. Drink your fucking drink."

Yorick drinks his fucking drink. A few minutes later she sets a steaming plate onto the bartop, stringy peppers and hashed vatmeat. He thanks her and carries everything over to the corner table, slopping beer on one hand and scorching his fingertips on the other. His hallucination looks up.

"I won't have more doxy for another couple days," he says.

"I don't do that shit anymore," Yorick says. He offloads his plate, sets the pitcher in the middle of the table, and juggles the two cups down beside it. The musician watches him. Yorick remembers that now, that he's a musician. He remembers the beautifully haunted voice and a stridulating instrument built surgically into the man's lanky leg.

"She grows those peppers," the musician says, nodding at his plate. "She has a hydroponic garden in the back. I helped her plant."

"You sure you exist?" Yorick asks.

The musician shakes his head.

"The bartender said she can't see you," Yorick clarifies.

The musician's dark eyes flick toward the bar. His half smile is pained. "When we're having an argument, she pretends I'm not here."

"Very fun." Yorick pours a beer and slides it over. "I'm Oxo. I'm not really a fat-hunter."

The musician slides the beer back with two long pale fingers. "No. You're a company man. Probably you're here for the grendel."

"Probably." He lifts the cup. "You don't drink with company men?"

"I don't drink." The musician taps the side of his neck. "You're smart to cover that tattoo. People have a long memory up here. Longer than the rest of Ymir. They remember Subjugation. They remember killers with tattoos on their necks."

"I wasn't here for that," Yorick lies, so easily.

The musician's eyes narrow. "But you know the dirge for dead children."

Yorick drinks, wipes a trickle off his mandible. "I heard it before, yeah."

The musician's eyes are obsidian shards now, sharp enough to pierce Yorick's phedrine insulation. "You could pass for old blood here," he says slowly. "Old blood. Cold-blood. You could be part sealie. Maybe that's why the company picked you."

Yorick doesn't answer. He starts to eat, peeling the peppers apart with his hands until orange grease stains his fingertips. When he chews, the mandible makes a faint clicking. He didn't notice it last night, but now it's only a matter of time before the sound drives him out of his mind. He points to the musician's leg.

"You get that biomod here in the Cut?" he asks.

The musician strokes his own kneecap. "There's a woman in the recycling district. She custom prints, does bio-installations. Nobody better on the whole world."

"Maybe you could put me in touch," Yorick says. "I might want to get a new prosthesis."

"Give me the blueprint, I can run it to her for a fee," the musician says. "Just not tonight."

Yorick looks around at the empty bar. He waves an encompassing arm. "Is it always like this? Just you and Linka?"

The musician gives a delicate shrug. "The bar and hotel are company-sponsored. People don't like that lately." He pulls up the time display on the table's surface. "And today, the miners are busy." He gives him a pointed look. "It's the ninth day."

Yorick keeps his expression blank. "Of what?"

"The wake." The musician's smile grows, stretching across his pale face like a wound. "The Cut will be a little strange tonight. A little wild. I'll be in high demand."

"So it's a party?" Yorick asks.

"Yes," the musician says. "A death party."

Yorick knows that now is the time to stay put. To stay safe. He can drink himself into a stupor in the furnished oblivion of his hotel room, order the host droid to bring an endless parade of bottles up the endless staircase. He can gorge himself until his shrunken stomach is screaming, then throw it all up in the toilet. Those are a few of his many pastimes.

"What's your name?" he asks.

The musician blinks. "Nocti. We've been introduced before, Oxo."

"You think I can pass for colonist geneprint, right?" Yorick says. "Old blood, cold-blood?"

"I think so. Yes."

He should stay in the hotel room until Gausta contacts him to tell him what's really going on. He has every reason to hide. Ymir is not his world anymore, if it ever really was, and he is not wanted here. The tattoo on his neck, the things he did twenty years ago, make him the enemy.

But he knows better than to be alone with his memories. The alcohol is already blending into his double dose of phedrine, bright and warm, and if the musician is out of doxy, it means the doxy is elsewhere.

The Cut will be a little wild tonight, and Yorick never could turn down a death party.

CHAPTER 18

Nocti is reluctant, even after Yorick offers him the rest of his phedrine—company-grade is still good enough to be cut with something more potent and resold. Yorick understands his reticence. Bringing a company man to a miners' wake is a stupid thing to do.

"Keep that tattoo covered *well*," Nocti says, watching the bar. "And cover up your face, too, if you can. Some people already been speaking about you." His eyes aren't on Linka's pneumatic arms; instead they drift farther back, to the black biotank set into the wall. The northern lilt in his voice is growing more pronounced. "Get you a mask on the way, maybe."

Yorick nods, still coaxing the last dregs of bacteria beer out of the pitcher and directly to his mouth. He carries the empties back to Linka while Nocti packs up the phedrine vials in his bag.

"They don't like warm-bloods at this sort of thing," the bartender says, taking the dishes out of his arms. "Don't like off-worlders. The performance isn't for you."

For an instant Yorick wants to tell her he was born on ice, that he's as much a cold-blood as anyone else on Ymir. But it's true in all the worst ways, and the fewer people who know it the better. He is Oxo Bellica for a reason.

"I'll be careful," he says.

"I don't care about you." A pneumatic arm jabs in Nocti's direction. "I don't want you to get in the shit and drag *him* down into it with you."

"Do you love each other?" The question comes out of him unexpectedly, and Linka doesn't answer it. He waits for a beat. "If I get in the shit, I don't know him," he says. "I'll pretend he's invisible."

Nocti is already motioning for him at the exit, so he licks his thumb and pushes it against the bar's gene scanner. Linka doesn't say goodnight, but one of her sensors turns to watch them leave. They go through the lobby, where the host droid scampers forward to ask Yorick how it can improve his lived experience, and continue out the glass doors.

The Cut's temperature drops in the evening, to maintain the illusion of a day/night cycle. Yorick's breath tumbles out into the cold air as a frosty cloud. He looks down the street, sees a cacophony of neon in the vapor murk. Some of the polyp structures have their own bioluminescence, glowing ghostly blue. The artificial sky is dark and seething with static.

Distant music, a harsh electric drum, drifts on the air. He hears shouting. Singing. He suspects he'll recognize the songs when they get close enough.

"The Cut always looks better at night," Nocti says. "It becomes a different animal." He pulls his coat shut and it molly-bonds, giving off tiny tendrils of steam as they start down the steps. He has a rolling limp. Yorick wonders if it came before the instrument or after it.

"You grew up here?" he asks, knowing the answer.

Nocti nods. "Snow-eater. I grew here, I shrank here, I loved here, I died here."

"You look really healthy for a corpse," Yorick says, and it makes him recall the bodies in the tunnel with a buzzed detachment. "Did you ever work in the mines?"

"No. Linka did. Before." Nocti pauses and turns. His pallid face is twisted. "She's not voluntary," he says. "She's not one of those Baldr technomonks. I don't want anyone to go around thinking that."

"She told me. Prison."

Nocti gives an eyeless smile. "Prison," he says. "But I'm going to get the money for a transplant. I'm saving, saving. Get her out of that biotank and into whatever body she wants, and then everything will be how it was. Or close enough."

He starts walking again, and Yorick falls in beside him. They plunge down one of the Cut's winding side streets, an artifact of early colony construction, pre-grid. He smells something acrid. The electric drum is getting stronger, and now there's a metallic rattling, too. People are wailing. People are laughing. People are making guttural animal sounds.

The street twists one last time, and they find themselves in a crush. Mourners and revelers are the same thing here, and they're packed shoulder-to-shoulder, shouting, singing. Some of them are wearing masks—not filter masks, but funeral masks, the blank white kind with slitted eyeholes that Yorick remembers so well. Almost everyone is holding a drink or a vapor pipe or both. He looks around for sources and sees a huge dirty vat set up down the way, probably holding rotgut brewed from the dregs of dregs of dregs.

Nocti pushes a funeral mask into his chest. "Wear this," the musician shouts in his ear. "The wake is farther up."

Yorick doesn't bother explaining that he'll have to take the mask right off again in order to drink. He puts it on, feeling the plastic rasp against his mandible. He remembers the first time he wore a funeral mask, back when he was small, and how the anonymity made his blood rush. That feeling of disappearing was the first thing to ever intoxicate him.

He picks a discarded cup off the ground. It was mistaken for an edible—the brim is chewed. He holds it as a prop as he follows Nocti up the street, away from the vat. When a drunken woman spills her drink, he slips the cup into the parabola and catches a few milliliters. He lifts his mask to sample the vatbrew. His artificial tongue burns and puckers.

Up ahead, the performers are in their frenzy. The scene is lit with reddish biolamps, maybe taken from the same mine that claimed tonight's dead. Ragged cloaks of synthetic fur, holomasks of empty eye sockets and snapping jaws, hoods crowned with skeletal branches: the grotesques. They stomp and howl, clanking their chains in time to the drum.

The shades dance around them, mostly women, some men, some nons, all their graceful bodies netted in pulsing white lights. It is ethereal and hideous and beautiful, and it makes him a child again.

Nocti is shouting in his ear; Yorick retreats back into the crowd with him so he can hear. "I'll show you the ghosts," the musician says. "After that, you should go back. I can lead you to the mainstreet."

Yorick nods, follows Nocti down a narrow alley decorated with moving graffiti. At the end of it, the dead miners, each one cobbled from a hundred old holorecords. They are standing in a circle of printed lanterns, dried dark flowers, food offerings. They look around, cross their arms, fidget, and blink. They don't speak.

Other tragedies have been commemorated on the alley wall.

Yorick's eyes are drawn to one piece of graffiti in particular: the company numeral for seventy-eight, the number some cold-bloods now skip when they count. Below it, the colonist character for *sleep-at-home* or *cradle*. People have a long memory up here. Yorick knows he should have expected it, but the sight still splits his stomach in two.

He is about to turn and leave when one of the ghosts moves its head just so.

Yorick freezes to the spot. His sleepsick brain is thrown into overdrive. He is hallucinating. He tears off his mask, ignoring Nocti's hissed protest, and walks closer, pushing through the gaggle of mourners. The ghosts have their names etched into the air with them. He sees Cayetano whole and unmarred, Nam Ocet with her spine in one piece.

The last ghost is Petra Zabka. He only knows the name from the incident report and asset records, but he knows the face from all his best and worst memories. He knows it from the decade of bad dreams he's had since leaving Ymir. The face in the sky, the boy with the needlegun pressed to his forehead.

His younger brother is older than him now, shaped and bent by long years in the mines. His name, his real name, the one Yorick couldn't bear to search for, would sound wrong coming from the mandible.

But Yorick finds he has to say it anyway. He lays it into the cold air like the first stone of a cairn: "Thello."

The world is carouseling. Blurry. Something is squeezing his chest, constricting his lungs like rubber. He squats to the ground and takes as deep a breath as he can. Then he's up, stumbling back through the crowd. Past a startled Nocti. Past the performance, the grotesques, still howling, shuffling. Mourners and revelers are joining in now, linking arms to dance with the shades, tipping back a grotesque's holomask to pour the vatbrew down her throat.

Yorick pushes upstream, against the crowd coming to dance for the dead. Two revelers with their middle legs bound together hobble into his path, cursing each other; Yorick skives around them and snatches one of their bottles on the way. Half spills out, foaming to the ground. He drains the rest. The vatbrew burns all the way down and claws his belly.

Nocti reappears out of the crush, mouth billowing smoke, but Yorick shoves him away, keeps moving. He hooks down a familiar alleyway and the music dulls. The air feels colder, wrapped damp around his bones. The night feels darker. He's heading deep into the north end now, where the hotel would never send its guests. The way home is so familiar.

CHAPTER -6

*H*e and his brother are skulking out of the north end, electrified by the darkness, jittery from midnight adrenaline. They're heading to the fountain. It's a new thing, a company thing, a sleek black plinth full of bubbling clean water. A drone guards it during the day, to keep people from pissing or spitting in it.

Ever since it was installed in the square, Thello has watched it. Yorick has noticed. Now they peer around the corner of an apartment block and find the fountain undefended. There are pale blue lights at the bottom of it, turning the bubbling water into something unworldly. They creep to the base of the plinth, shuck off their clothes, climb up and over.

The cold water bites at first, making Yorick's skin pebble. He sees the same goose bumps on Thello's darker skin, but his younger brother is unbothered, wearing a wide grin. He splashes his hand into the water and tracks the shimmering arc.

"I didn't think we'd actually do it," he says, wonder in his voice.

"I said we would."

Yorick stretches out against the side of the fountain, extending his arms how he sees the older children do, making himself big. Thello mimics him from the opposite end. Up over their heads, the artificial sky is functioning for once, showing a sea of bright white stars and a pair of crater-pocked moons—the view from Ymir's surface if the cloud veil were ever to dissipate. Their mother hates it. Yorick is ambivalent. Thello is fascinated by it, which is why Yorick chose tonight.

"I'm going up there someday," his brother says, pointing with a dripping finger. "On a big bowlship."

Yorick tilts his head back. "No, you're not," he says, mostly on reflex. "Bowlships only bring people. When they leave they're all full up with zinc. And dirt."

"I'll hide in the zinc and dirt, then," Thello says.

Yorick considers arguing, or plunging his brother's head underwater, but he shuts his eyes instead. He's content here. Feeling the tug of the filtration system on his skin, the small warfare of it. Smelling chlorine and night. Listening to his brother cup and pour, cup and pour, entranced by their transgression.

"I'll go to some other world," Thello says a while later. "And you'll come, too. And nobody will ever call us half-blood again."

Yorick jerks upright. "Who?" he demands. "Little Braun again?"

Thello's not-quite-sealie eyes skitter sideways.

"Did you hit them?" Yorick demands.

Thello sullenly shakes his head, and for a moment Yorick feels so hot with anger that the bubbling water could be boiling. He wants to grab his brother and shake him, make him understand what Yorick has always known in his cells: they need to be tougher and louder and bigger and colder than everyone around them, or they'll never be cold-bloods.

But tonight is for Thello and his artificial stars, so Yorick locks his tongue. His brother shifts and fidgets in the water across from him. There is a seething dark silence between them now, like the silence before their mother explodes. Yorick stares at the sky until his anger leaks away.

"If we're going offworld, we have to practice for the torpor," he finally says. "Hold your breath. We'll go under on three."

Thello blinks, then peels a hesitant grin. "Okay."

"One," Yorick says, watching his brother's eyes squeeze shut. "Two."

They drop down under the surface, and Yorick imagines it: an icy pool of stasis fluid, company bodies on their way to do company business. Then he grabs his brother by the ankle, making his hand a grendel claw. Thello wriggles free and comes up spluttering, but laughing, and they chase each other in circles through the clean water.

Overhead, the false sky starts to flicker.

CHAPTER 19

Yorick lopes past a hundred small scenes: a woman slouched on the curb, bent intently over her own foot with a pair of pliers; two people fucking in an alleyway, forming one shuddering shape; children flipping a lost cleaning bot over to watch its legs wriggle in the air. A hundred miniature universes of hurt and happiness, but mostly hurt, here in the Cut.

He gets deep enough a meatman starts following him. "Hello, offworlder. Hello, hello." The voice is a diseased croon. "You look so lonely. Boy, girl, non? What's your preference?"

"My preference is nothing," Yorick says, trying to push the northern lilt through his mandible.

"Real meat, we have. No holos, no mannequins." The meatman grins with metallic teeth. "What we have, you don't get in your company hotel, offworlder."

"Not a fucking offworlder."

"Yes, offworlder. Fucking. You are beginning to understand."

Yorick keeps his mouth shut, keeps his eyes peeled for the jumpers that often accompany a talker, until the meatman shrugs, spits, and drifts back toward the wake sounds. Alone again. His feet carry him on automatic, another left, another right, and he rounds the last corner.

He stops when he hits the warning holo. Flickering red, chest-high. It circles the darkened block like static fire. Looming above it, his old home: a crooked stack of concrete cubes. Company architecture, a hive built for human insects. It used to seem big as the world.

Yorick squints at the holo. Not a biocontamination notice, just a demolition order. They'll be clearing out the concrete and putting polyp in. He looks down and sees he is still clutching the funeral mask in his torpor-pale hand. He puts it back on, less to mourn, more to hide. He is an intruder, after all. He should not be here.

He steps through the warning holo. For a moment, the red light bisects him, splits him into two Yoricks: One who left, one who stayed. One who hates, one who loves. Then he's inside the demolition zone, facing the entrance to the place where he grew up. He refuses to look down at the concrete stoop, afraid to find stains.

He keeps his eyes on the door instead. He remembers how it grew frost in the night, back when the Cut's temperature regulators were still being worked on. He remembers how he and Thello used to race to it, and the day Thello was finally faster.

The door is dead. He has to give it a charge from his tablet before the electronic lock flares to life. Then his tattoo overrides it, the physical mechanism churns and clunks, and he pushes his way inside. No squatters, no sign of any. The entryway is dark and deserted.

The lifts are dead, too, but Yorick is accustomed. Southern Urbanite Memory trained him for this. He stumps up the stairs, following the pale square of light from his tablet. It goes fast, then slow, dreamlike. Once a shriveled biolamp, crusty and weeping, responds to his footsteps with a faint pulse of orange light.

He is young again, creeping back into the apartment after a night at the pits. He can almost hear Thello crawling up the steps behind him. They have to be quiet. Their mother is passed out in her orthochair. If she wakes up, she might wake up angry.

Yorick finds his way to the right floor and the right door without any conscious effort. The route is still hardwired into his body. He holds his tablet light up to the gene scanner, almost expecting to see a familiar smeary handprint on the pad. This door is as dead as the exterior one, so he hooks his tablet in.

When the gene scanner hums on, he doesn't even think to use the tattoo. He pushes his hand against the pad. It turns pebbly, licking his skin like papillae spines. He imagines it tasting twenty years of blood and stasis fluid on his skin. Judging, weighing.

The door unchokes.

Yorick steps inside, and it feels like he is at the bottom of the sea. Not from the dark, but from the pressure. Gravity is doubling itself, crushing down on him. He can barely lift his feet. He should not be here. He is an intruder.

The apartment has grown smaller. When he sweeps the tablet light around it he expects each wall to last longer than it does. He expects the ceiling to be higher, a cracked concrete sky. The space feels like a trap, like jaws, everything tilting inward. For a wild moment he expects Thello to step out of the dark with a needlegun.

Yorick finds the gap. It's shrunk, like everything else. Just a sliver of space between the wall and the rust-coated cooker. It wasn't just for when Yorick and Thello played the grendel game. Sometimes their mother was the grendel, and Yorick would let Thello stay in the gap, stay in the safespot, while Yorick took the beating. It could only fit one of them at a time.

He puts his shoulder into the cooker. It slides and screeches, digging a furrow in the floor. When there's just enough room, Yorick folds himself into the widened gap left behind, wedges himself tight. He waits to feel safe. Instead he keeps picturing Thello hiding there, only now Yorick is gone. Yorick left him behind.

He hears an ugly electronic warble and realizes he's sobbing. The mandible never knows what to do with the noise. It sounds like a droid trying to imitate pain. He hates that.

"Hello? You in here?"

There's a figure framed in the doorway. Yorick tenses, watching for a certain twitch of the head, a certain bounce in the feet. He knows it's impossible, but maybe it isn't. Thello exists in a Schrödinger box. He's young and old, dead and alive, decomposing inside the Polar Seven and hiding here where they both began.

Nocti steps inside. Yorick feels an implosion in his gut, relief mixed with disappointment mixed with phedrine and alcohol and hash.

"Fuck did you take, Oxo?" the musician asks, folding his lanky arms across his chest. "This place is set to come down. Probably full of cutworms." He blinks his oil-black eyes. "Come on. We'll get you back to the hotel."

Yorick can't move. He stares at the empty corner where the orthochair ought to have been. He remembers sitting in it with Thello, waiting together for their mother to come home from the mine, watching procedurally generated goretoons on the apartment's cracked smartglass.

Every so often Thello would sniff the headrest of the chair, because it smelled like her, and Yorick would tell him how fucking stupid that was, but when Thello wasn't looking he would sniff, too. They were always dreading her and pining for her at the same time.

Sometimes she crept home from the bar instead of the mine. She was softer when she drank. It blurred her anger out. He remembers the night she stood over his bed, mumbling apologies, half nonsense, already too late.

Always too late, and time can't run in reverse.

"Nocti, I'd like you to go the fuck away," Yorick says. "Unless you found doxy."

The musician hesitates. Then he sits down across from him, raising a puff of chemical-smelling dust from the floor. His bony black-clad foot touches the toe of Yorick's boot. The point of contact is so small, but somehow it moves through his whole body, activates nerves he didn't know were starving.

"I'm not an offworlder," Yorick says, hoarse and hollow.

"No," Nocti agrees. He rakes a circle in the dark with one skinny finger. "This where you stayed, then? Growing?"

"Yeah."

Nocti looks around, peering through the gloom. "Old woman name of Basta lived in this block, I think. Used to give me puffs off her pipe if I brought her scrap."

Yorick chokes on a laugh. "Yeah. Yeah, we used to bring her shit. She wasn't so old then." He tips his skull back against the wall. "She gave us bacteria samples once. To try brewing our own beer. We hid it in..." He points out the doorway. "This bucket, in the back of the maintenance room. Fed it and skimmed it for a whole week before we drank it."

"Disgusting," Nocti says.

"Yeah. Made us sick."

Half true. It made Thello sick, enough so that their mother noticed the smell, but after the beating Yorick snuck back to the maintenance room and finished the bucket, crouched in the dark, scooping the dirty liquid to his mouth with his cupped hands. It made him feel safe for a little while.

"Dangerous for you to be back here," Nocti finally says. "People will realize."

Yorick gledges over. "You're not going to tell them?"

"No. If you're here to kill the grendel, your past's not my business."

They sit in silence for a while, a softer silence than Yorick anticipated, but he can't let it last long. "Petra Zabka," he says, forcing the wrong name out of his mouth. "The overseer. You know him at all?"

Nocti shakes his head. "People say he was good. They say he took care of his miners." He shrugs his sharp shoulders. "But they'd never say otherwise on the ninth night. You want to speak to someone who knew him, knew him well, you speak to Fen."

Yorick remembers the snarl on the giant's face. "Fen," he echoes.

"Big red clanner," Nocti says. "Her and Zabka, they were close. Close like kin."

Yorick blinks hard behind the funeral mask. "That doesn't mean anything," he says, with ice filling his belly. "Not a fucking thing."

The musician's forehead creases.

"Where is she tonight?" Yorick asks. "I want to speak."

"You want to die," Nocti says, and he sounds sad about it.

CHAPTER 20

Nocti's not coming, but that's for the best, because Yorick knows in his bones that he is going to get in the shit. He joins a trickle of revelers heading for the old foundry, enough of them to render him anonymous, one of a half-dozen mourning masks bobbing in the dark. There's an electric current in the air, different from the one at the death party. Deeper, more dangerous.

The first time he went to the pit he was nine years old; Thello was six and followed him, even after Yorick stamped down hard on his small bony foot. They were always enemies until other enemies made themselves known. That night was the same. Thello came limping and sniffling after him, and Yorick only circled back when he heard the drunken mutter of a red walking past: *ugly little half-blood, company grub, wailing, wailing.*

Thello had their mother's sealie eyes, wider and blacker than Yorick's, but their offworld father's skin, melanin made for sun. It stood out in the street. Other children would pinch or rub it. Usually Yorick chased them off; sometimes he would only watch. Sometimes he was tired.

But that name, *half-blood*, always had danger behind it. So that night Yorick circled back for his brother, and they entered the foundry hand in hand.

Tonight he goes with Thello's ghost. The man running the door is a red, nearly as big as Fen but with a more developed fashion sense. Large swathes of his skin have been replaced with clear bioplastic, displaying the flayed muscle underneath. His cheeks are pierced with dermals.

"Take the masks off," he says. "No masks inside, you know that. Take them off."

Yorick uncovers his face just before he gets to the door. There is a fragile glass moment where he nearly slips through, where his eyes are dark enough, skin pale enough, swaggering walk north-end enough. It shatters when the doorman catches sight of him.

"Who the fuck are you?" he asks.

Yorick pulls a name from recent memory, feels for the most natural lie. "Vesper," he says. "I worked with Cayetano in the Polar Four. Came for the wake."

"This isn't the wake."

"Yeah. Nocti told me I ought to come here after."

The doorman frowns. "I don't know you. I never knew Cayetano much."

Yorick nods to his plastic-capped flay. "You get that done in the recycling district? Heard she's the best. Might get a new jaw while I'm here."

The man unbristles, just slightly. "Chlora? She's good. Beskidu and Woad, though, they're the best."

"Not what Nocti said."

"Everybody's got one masterpiece in them. Nocti is hers." He tilts his head. "Get in, you're holding the line."

Yorick is inside before the last word passes the man's lips;

he can't let him reconsider. The smell of dust and old metal greets him as he enters the foundry. It hasn't changed much. The vast dark space is still a labyrinth of derelict machinery. The smelting pit, illuminated from above with surgical bright floodlights, is still the only part that matters. He follows the anticipatory rumbling.

Metal bleachers soldered from old parts are racked around the edge of the pit. Spectators are climbing to empty seats, making the whole structure sway. He sees a few tufts of orange hair in the crowd, but none of them are Fen.

Yorick elbows his way to the edge and checks the pit. The sloped sides have permanently imbibed bloodstains. The metal bottom is hidden by a layer of fresh silicate, hard-packed for ease of movement, bright white for visual contrast and to mimic the snow. Two fighters are already limbering up. The first is a sealie, lithe and balletic as he leaps and stretches. The second is a red with animated tattoos moving along her broad shoulders. Not Fen.

Not Fen, but Yorick is transfixed watching her buckle her shoes. The rasp and click echoes up out of the pit, amplified by speakers, and the sound triggers a cascade of memories in his pounding skull. He remembers him and his brother worming to the front of the crowd to watch through gapped legs, remembers someone stepping on his fingers and breaking the littlest one.

A followcam is circling over the fighters' heads like a buzzard. That's new, and so are the screens suspended by metal cables from the ceiling, each one showing a different angle on the pit, the crowd. For the briefest moment, one of them backgrounds a giant in a furred cloak. Yorick blinks, spins, trying to figure out the cam placements.

There. Fen is on the far side of the pit, heading for the back of the stands. Yorick leaves the railing and pushes through a compacting crowd. Down below, the jig is starting. The fighters are moving to a relentless beat, flexing their arms and legs, tiptoeing forward, back, forward again.

Fen knew he was no ordinary company man, right from the start. She recognized him, recognized his telltale half-sealie genes, because Thello had told her about him. And now Yorick wants to know what else Thello told her, wants it badly, desperately. He is halfway around the pit when someone takes his knees out from under him.

He slams into the floor and all the wind leaves his lungs in a single grunt; for an instant he is back on the medibed, inhabiting a dead man's body. He gasps for air. The mandible makes it into an electronic rattle.

A sealie face looms into view, cheekbones tattooed with stylized cogs. "Hey, company man."

Yorick keeps gasping.

"Seen you at the wake," the miner says. "You liked that? Seeing how we send off our dead real proper? Last time the company thugs were here, it was a strike-break." He's drinking from a bottle; some of it drips onto Yorick's forehead. "They killed fourteen snow-eaters. Picture that wake."

Yorick doesn't want to picture that wake, or any wake.

"And then you decided to come get some culture," the miner says. "Come see a show. Right? You almost look like you belong. Thought you could snake in."

Yorick's breath is finally back. He tries to sit up; a heavy boot stomps him down again. The sealie's friends are here, too. He swallows. "I came to see Fen."

It was the wrong thing to say. The miner's eyes narrow to

slits. "Fen invited you?" he demands. "Fen invited the fucking company man?"

"Just heard she was fighting tonight," Yorick says, shifting tracks. "I like fights."

"She was last night. Maybe her last jig ever, now she's a fucking overseer." The miner takes another swig from his bottle. He grins across at someone Yorick can't see. "But you. You like fights, company man?"

Yorick's heart thuds hard. "As a spectator," he says. "I'm here for the grendel."

The miner ignores him. "Tell Koto I'm taking their slot," he says. "And then get this fuckwit some shoes. Some culture."

CHAPTER 21

Yorick wraps his feet slowly, methodically, and fortunately nobody is paying him much attention. The miner with the facial tats, whose name he recalls now is Wickam, is arguing with the sealie woman who owns the pit. Twenty years ago it didn't have an owner, but it didn't have stands or screens or followcams, either.

"You bring him here just to jig him?" she demands, hands on her head, exasperated. "You're drunk, he's drunk, you say he's from offworld, it won't be a fight."

They're in a polyresin bubble behind the stands, a barebones prep room with a medibed and drug shelf and gelflesh incubator. The roar of the crowd is dulled.

"He'll have a bit of fight in him." The miner's eyes are shiny. "At least a bit. He's the company man they sent for the grendel." He reaches for Yorick's neck; Yorick slaps his hand away the first time but misses the second. The spiderwool peels back. "See?"

The owner's eyes flicker. "You kill a company man, you bring the shit down on everybody," she says, but she's no longer looking at him. It's a bad sign.

"No kill," Wickam says. "Blunted shoes." He takes her

hands off her head and laces them into his own, tenderly. "I'm your fucking brother, and I need this. Blunted shoes."

She looks at him wearily. "Blunted shoes," she echoes. "Just make it quick."

"I'm here for the grendel," Yorick says, but nobody's listening. He starts flexing his calves and ankles.

CHAPTER 22

They get a shot of phetamine before the fight. Yorick knows he's risking serious infection by using the same battered injector as Wickam and a hundred other filthy miners, but when they hand him the dose he doesn't hesitate. The bite of the needle is delicious in its own way, and then the phetamine flash-floods his nervous system, sets it crackling.

If phedrine is sunshine, phetamine is moonlight. No warmth, just a cold blistering rush, stronger than doxy, that sharpens the world into glass and makes his senses sing. He normally avoids phetamine, but at this exact moment he can't remember why. His whole body is humming.

"I'm not going to make a joke of this," Wickam says. "The jig shouldn't be a joke. It's a beautiful thing. A kind of dancing, a kind of dying." His eyes are solemn. The phetamine renders his face in flawless geometry; Yorick almost wants to touch it. "Find the dignity."

"Yeah," Yorick says. He looks around for chalk, to grit his grip, but doesn't see any.

"Don't curl up or beg."

"I have so much love to give," Yorick says woodenly.

Wickam seems to understand. He nods. They sit back and

listen as his sister announces the new slot. Her amplified voice echoes. *Offworld man comes to our wake, comes to our pit, thinks he owns it, thinks he owns us, thinks he wants to fucking* jig.

"Alright." She ducks back into the room. "They're hot. Get in the pit."

"I owe you," Wickam tells her, and she agrees with a twitch of her nostrils.

Yorick lets his opponent lead the way. As soon as they step out of the prep room, the noise goes up a decibel. The crowd has swollen while they were inside, and the owner's improvised speech was a good one. The people in the stands are baying for blood. He looks around at the blur of angry faces, and for a moment they are all one single organism, multilimbed and ravenous.

The crowd sounds get muted as he follows Wickam down the ladder. The pit is its own world. A little girl is tamping fresh silicate onto the floor, covering over the dark spots. She looks up with keen black eyes. She probably wants to be a fighter when she's older, the same way Yorick and Thello and other scared children did.

He watches Wickam strap on his shoes. They look well-made, rubbery custom mold with a burnished metal toe guard. The backheel spike is replaced by a dull knob, as promised, and the mount where the main sickle should be attached is empty. Sparring shoes, but they whistle and shriek through the air with each practice swing. Sparring shoes are still enough to crack bones.

His own shoes are too big by half. He starts tearing the spiderwool off his arms, stuffing it into the interstices, hoping to pack it tight enough to keep his feet from sliding. Wickam watches him do it. Yorick lurches upright and takes a few test-ing steps. The silicate crunches slightly underfoot, well packed. The traction's decent.

Yorick watches how Wickam warms up and carefully copies the motions, loosening out his arms, swinging his legs. When Wickam bends and stretches, Yorick bends and stretches. When Wickam leaps, Yorick leaps, if more clumsily. His whole body is singing with the phetamine and with its own auto-brewed adrenaline. Through the rushing in his ears, he almost doesn't hear the music start.

Rattling drums. Shrieking strings. For a moment he pictures Nocti sawing furiously, playing the song on his vivisected leg. A synthesized chant fills the background, voices crackly with distortion. Wickam is moving to the music. Creeping forward, rushing back, following the beat. Yorick stands flat-footed, how an offworld company man would.

But every part of him is spring-loaded. He knows the pit better than anyone fighting on the ninth night—all the good jigs are on the eighth—and his body knows exactly what to do.

He'll just have to ignore it.

Yorick flails forward and the miner's first strike sends him reeling; a toe guard finds his floating rib and seems to deto-nate there. He staggers to one side of the pit, clutching him-self. Overhead, the crowd howls. He dives in again, swinging one foot in an ugly arc. Wickam knocks it aside, metal jarring metal, and comes around with his backheel.

The knob connects with Yorick's thigh. Nerves flare. Mus-cles seize. He drops to one knee, screaming. All he has to do is get the shit beat out of him, and he'll be allowed to limp back to Southern Urbanite Memory as a Chastised Warm-Blood Company Man. He's only half acting. The jig is not something you forget, but it's also not something you can leave for ten years and come back to easy.

He gets upright, taking the space Wickam gives him. He flexes his fingers, readies his arms, because any offworld fighter will have given up on the shoes by now and try to grapple instead. The miner dances at him. Yorick grabs for his swinging leg, misses. The next blow hits his stomach and folds him in two.

Purple blots bloom in his peripherals. The crowd makes a savage and joyful noise, because Ymir hates him. Ymir has always hated him. When the miner comes at him again it feels, in the air, like Thello's little feint-and-go. He answers it the same way he always did, and the muscle memory takes his opponent's legs out from under him.

Wickam lands harder than he ought to. Too surprised, maybe, to break the fall properly. His face is transmuting shock to suspicion, but in the rush of adrenaline Yorick suddenly doesn't care. If Nocti knows, if Fen knows, then the whole Cut might as well know.

He scuffs the floor with his toe, sending up a tiny spray of silicate. It's the oldest taunt on the world, and it brings Wickam surging to his feet.

Yorick swarms him: high knees, kicks mixed with jabs, elbows, all the patterns he burned into his nerves in another life. He is not here for the grendel. He is here for the pit. His knee finds a gap and snaps Wickam's head back. His backheel hits and tears Wickam's lip open, sending a spurt of blood skyward. He has so much hate to give.

A riposte slips through. The impact nearly takes his shoulder out of its socket, and the pain wipes his head clear. Wickam the miner is eyeing him, bobbing on his toes, blood dripping down his chin. Yorick sees the same disgust he saw on Fen's face in the mine. The star-collapsing hate.

"Mendacious means lying," Wickam says. "Some people, they floated the idea. They said you looked like one of us. Not full sealie, but some kind of mix. Some kind of half-blood."

Up above him, the crowd has stopped roaring. It's a buzzing now, insectile, ominous. They're busy realizing the company man in the pit is the very worst kind of company man. The people at the railing start to clamor.

Wickam wipes at the blood, smearing it sideways across his face. "Me, I said the company wouldn't be stupid enough to send a traitor back here. But they did, didn't they?"

Half-blood. The word filters down from the bleachers. He hasn't heard it in so long. He remembers whispering it to himself at night, over and over, until it finally turned into meaningless syllables. *Half-blood. Company grub.*

Wickam grins a leaky red grin. "I'm going to do you like the old days." He goes to the side of the pit and slams his hand against it. "Real shoes!" he shouts. "Real shoes!"

Yorick's mouth is bone-dry. His limbs are trembly. The phetamine crash is coming soon. He knows the only way he will survive this is if someone stops it. If he loses, he's dead. If he wins, he's dead. Voices are raised against each other in the crowd, debating his identity, debating repercussions. *Killing a company man will bring more company men*, they say. *Probably even maiming one*, they say.

It doesn't matter. Someone is already lowering new shoes into the pit. Wickam inspects them, tosses them over, reaches for his own blades coming down in a black box. Yorick pulls his numb feet out of the sparring shoes. One of his toenails is battered blue.

Even though he is about to die on the world he swore he'd never come back to, he has to admire the craft of the new shoes. They have adjustable ribbing, to make sure they fit right, and the sleek toe guard ends in its own little spike to supplement the main sickle. The blade curves up from the top of the shoe like a beckoning finger, razor-sharp, agleam with oil.

He drags his thumbnail lightly, lightly, along the inner edge. It leaves a furrow; any more pressure would cleave through. The flat of the blade is warm. Someone sharpened these shoes only minutes ago. Someone wants him to win.

Yorick looks across the pit at his opponent. Wickam's main sickles are barbed, made to hook and drag. They glint in the floodlights as he stalks closer. The music is off. The crowd is still divided; there's a scrap at the railing, people shoving and shouting. He can tell from the look on Wickam's face that the miner doesn't care about any of that. This is not a normal jig, where second bloodshed forces a stop, where the loser can signal surrender.

He gets his shoes buckled on the instant before Wickam flies at him. The barbed sickles slice the air and make it hum. He hurls himself backward, dodging one kick, blocking another. Metal gnashes metal, tangles. Wickam pushes down on him. Yorick can feel the man's elastic strength, the muscle hewed by years in the mine. It's folding his leg back on itself.

He twists free just before his knee joint gives out. The sickle shrieks, spitting yellow sparks. He staggers to his feet and runs for space. There's not much of it. Wickam follows, chasing him around the wall of the pit. Yorick hears him dragging the tip of his toe guard along the base—scrape, scrape, the second-oldest taunt.

The followcam dips and swerves and nearly hits Yorick in

the head. He's at the ladder now. He grips the highest rung he can reach, jerks himself into the air just as Wickam catches up to him. A barbed sickle clangs against the spot where his legs were a moment earlier. He tries to climb higher, but his shoes scrabble and slip.

Wickam curses; his sickle is trapped, hooked under a rung. Yorick misses it by micrometers when he falls, slamming into Wickam's shin instead. He hears a pop and Wickam howls as they crash to the sand in a tangle. Yorick rolls away coated in blood. He thinks it might be his; he can feel an oozing hot pulse on his calf.

They clamber to their feet. The followcam is revolving over their heads. Wickam circles right, hobbled, favoring his left leg. Yorick mirrors him, dripping a red track through the silicate. The noise of the crowd pitches up at the sight.

Wickam feints, retreats. Yorick barely registers either. The phetamine clarity is leaking away. His limbs shake. His stomach is churning on the coppery smell of his own blood.

Their jig ends with no tactic. No pattern. No art. They both have tired legs and sweat-stung eyes, so Wickam trips on one of Yorick's discarded sparring shoes, and as he stumbles forward Yorick kicks three times. The first carves a furrow across the miner's chest. The second misses. The third is nearly caught, caged for a crystalline moment between Wickam's hands, but the blood makes things slippery.

Yorick forces his foot through, and his sickle gashes Wickam's throat open. It sprays a wild pressurized arc, splattering the followcam. One of the hanging screens turns red. Yorick and the miner look at each other as Wickam sinks, silently, to a crouch. Slitting the carotid is not like slitting wrists. He knows Wickam will only be conscious for another ten, twelve seconds.

He needs to say something reassuring. Tell him they'll patch it with gelflesh, brew him a transfusion. Tell him his sister probably loves him, loves him a lot, or she wouldn't have given him the slot to jig a company man. Tell him they're all on the same skid departing into the dark.

The bleachers are silent. The followcam scrubs its lens, and Wickam reappears on the screen between streaks of scarlet.

Yorick doesn't say anything. He unbuckles his shoes, pulling them off his bloody feet. The pit smells like a butchery. He goes to the ladder and starts to climb, focusing all his attention on one rung at a time, clinging with crash-weak fingers.

It takes an eternity to get to the top. He staggers for the exit. He feels people moving behind him in a pack, feels the collective gaze like a needle between his shoulder blades. They let him step outside, into the cold Cut air, before the beating starts.

CHAPTER 23

One of them has a hand wrench, and the first swing obliterates his mandible, pulping the bioplastic, powdering the circuitry. The shock wave rattles through his skull and he goes blind watching explosions behind his eyes. His legs give out of their own accord, like a puppet getting its strings cut, and he's dimly glad. It means he doesn't have to feel guilty about going to ground.

The blows rain down on him, and he curls up. He can't beg without his mandible. The only sound he can make is a shapeless groan. They stomp and kick but none of them are wearing jig shoes, so dying is going to take a little longer. Someone is yanking at what's left of his prosthesis, trying to rip it free from his face.

Yorick realizes this is why he came to the pit. This is the damage he wanted. He is balancing the Ledger of Universal Suffering. When the pit owner raises her wrench, tightens her grip, preparing to shatter his skull, he's almost grateful to her.

The swing is interrupted. A massive hand rips the wrench away and suddenly Fen is looming overhead, holding the heavy tool like a twig. She's still wearing the furred cloak, and for a moment in Yorick's pain-scorched brain she really is a grotesque from the underworld, a towering demonic apparition.

"Fuck are you doing, Fen?" the pit owner snaps.

"Got instructions," the red says. "Go back in. All of you. I'm dealing with him."

"Wickam was right," the pit owner snarls. "Company owns you now, don't they? At least Zabka didn't lick their fucking boots."

Fen drives the wrench into her diaphragm. She drops. The nearest miner lurches forward; Fen hooks their leg and gives them a knee to the face on their way down. Yorick's eyes are still warping light. It makes the violence blurry and oddly soft. He can't tell how many people are standing in the alley, but he hears feet shuffling backward.

"Wickam was a waste," the red says. "I'm glad he's dead. Now go back in."

The pit owner is still winded. She's just starting to sputter as the other miners drag her back into the foundry. That leaves Yorick alone, and incapacitated, with the red he was so certain wanted to murder him. He tries to move. His head is pounding, and breathing feels like a saw edge. He suspects a fractured rib, dislocated shoulder, bruised flesh all over the place.

Shards from his broken mandible are embedded in one cheek. The cut in his calf has its own little heartbeat.

"Can you walk at all?" the red asks.

Yorick gives an incremental headshake; it sends spikes through his neck.

"I'm going to carry you to the mainstreet, then order a car," Fen says. "Show it your tattoo and it should take you to the company clinic." She crouches down, slides a brusque hand under Yorick's torso, the other under the bend of his knees. "Thello's call, company man. Not mine."

She lifts, and the motion floods enough pain through Yorick's nerves to send him to the void.

CHAPTER -5

*T*he autohauler lot. Someone has hacked one of the older vehi-
cles' halogens, providing a burning white spotlight. Yorick is fifteen, growing fast, all gangly limbs. Too old to have Thello always
following after him. He came alone, and now he finds his way
quickly to the stolen vatbrew, drowning his usual self with it so he'll
be able to speak more easily to Tuq and Mara and the rest of them.

He's still swigging from the plastic carton when someone he
doesn't know drifts up, someone who already has mine-muscle on
their arms and scruff on their face. "This him?" the red asks. "This
Yor?"

Tuq has a gleam in her oil-black eyes. "Yeah," she says. "This is
Yorick."

The red wraps one hand around his own throat. "Tuq says you
been speaking too much shit," he says. "Says you want to jig."

Yorick stares at Tuq, whose friendship he earned the hard way,
with sparring and blood, who now has lied him into this for no
reason, no reason at all. Tuq only smiles. Her doxy-stained teeth
shine poisonous blue in the dark.

"So I'm going to shut you up," the red says. "You got shoes?"

Yorick always has his shoes, and there's a part of him that
always wants to jig, and he can tell from the sway and slur that his

opponent is heavy drunk. So he doesn't try to duck away. They shove him into the halogen glare and someone starts the music. The red has a greedy bleary look on his face. He grips his throat again.

Yorick slips into the jig rhythm, then ignores it, darting through the lull and driving his metal-toed foot into a meaty thigh. The red has reach, but he's so much slower than Thello. Yorick dips in and out, picking his spots, a slow demolition. The red has bad lungs; he's gasping before Yorick even starts to sweat. Tuq and Mara and the rest are whooping, jeering, saying fuck him up, Yor, get to the blood, fuck him up good.

The red taps ground before he bleeds. He slumps off into the dark while everyone else crushes into the halogen light, crowding around Yorick to slap his head and thump his chest. The victory is a crackly electric rush he feels in his whole body.

Then the company drone comes swooping in, blaring at them about property violations, and everyone scatters. Yorick sprints after Tuq and Mara, to the swathe of fence that sags low enough to climb. The drone zeroes in on them, wailing, wailing. Mara imitates the noise, gives a wild laugh, and Yorick laughs, too, invincible.

Mara's already on the other side when Tuq and Yorick crest the fence. The drone has them in its laser light, trying to scan their faces. It doesn't matter. They're nearly away.

Yorick tries to slide over the top of the fence, and something claws him back. He looks down, sees one of his jig shoes caught in the wire links. He yanks. Yanks again.

"Tuq!" he shouts. "Tuq, pull me up!"

Tuq crouches there at the top, hood pulled up to hide her face. "Better if they catch someone," she says, with a brutal shrug. "Better if it's you."

Yorick stares, uncomprehending.

"*See you when you're out of the tank,*" Tuq says. She winks, like it's a private joke between them, and drops down to the other side of the fence.

By the time Yorick extricates himself, the drone has scanned his face and two security guards are waiting at the bottom with stun-sticks. He climbs down slow and numb. They prick his thumb for gene confirmation, then cuff his hands. He waits for the beating to begin. A company man in a bright yellow coat shows up instead.

Yorick recognizes her vitiligo face. She used to hang around the recyclers, handing out food packs or tablets. As a child Yorick thought she was strangely beautiful. She looked more like him and Thello than anyone else they knew. Mara always called her hideous.

Sometimes she sat and watched him and Thello spar, back when they were just learning the jig, until one day someone called her a babyfucker and told her to get off the world. She left with a cold smile and he never saw her again.

Until now.

"Hello, Yorick," she says. "Tired of it?"

He blinks.

"You can try, try, try all you like," she says. "I grew up in a place like this. Everyone the same but me." She shakes her head. "They're never going to love you."

Yorick feels his ears go red. He doesn't know how she knows, how she burrowed so deep into his private thoughts and opened the black box.

"You always do well on the tests," she says. "Very well."

Maybe that's how she knows: from the twice-a-year tests they have to take to live in company housing. Gut biome, brain activity, blood, and reflexes. Nonsense questions asked by an algorithm. Screens that flash images, usually of hideous violence.

"You can get off this world," she says. "You deserve better." She taps a finger to her throat, and Yorick sees the tattoo, a subcutaneous swirl of circuitry. "You and Thello both."

His brother's name jars him.

She notices. "He tested well, too," she says. "Particularly in xenotech sensitivity. Children born near the ansible usually do." Her eyes turn warm and worried. "But he's lacking in a vital area."

Yorick already knows which. Thello can't crush a wingless wasp under his thumb. He can't keep sparring once he draws blood or sees too much pain.

"Not enough aggression," the company man agrees. "No willingness to exert force. That's why life here will be difficult for him."

"I don't like hurting people, either," Yorick says, which is half a lie.

She gives her cold smile again, as if she can see the electric way he felt tonight in the autohauler lot when the red collapsed in a heap. "We wouldn't take you offworld to hurt people," she says. "The company's not threatened by people."

Yorick is too old and too young to recognize the lie.

"There's a game you and Thello used to play," she says. "Do you remember it?"

CHAPTER 24

Yorick wakes up in the company clinic, on the last medibed in a short row of them. He recognizes the electronic symphony of blips and chirrups from the many machines keeping watch over his body, and when he opens his eyes he sees familiar sights: pale green walls, gelflesh incubator, a squid-like teledoc sliding along its groove in the ceiling.

The company clinic is the same on every world, and Yorick knows it well. He feels comfortable, even though his last swathe of memories is all blood and fear. It's probably the opioids.

Gausta's voice mars the high. "Nostalgia, was it?"

The question is rhetorical, and Yorick could not answer it anyway; his mandible is gone. He raises a clumsy hand and finds his face is studded with regrowth tags. His old wound, his familiar wound, is protected by membrane.

Yorick returns reluctantly to his body. His left leg is elevated, calf already gelfleshed shut with a lone regrowth tag sticking out of it. His torso is encased by a purring plastic shell, subsonics knitting his fractured ribs back together at speed. He's naked otherwise, and the tug of a catheter tube along his thigh makes him wonder how long he has been here.

"An overwhelming wave of nostalgia," Gausta continues, "that carried you from the comfortable amenities of your hotel all the way to the fighting pit, where you exsanguinated a miner and were then beaten half to death by his angry relatives."

The teledoc has turned off his drip. He can feel a chill creeping in under the high. It sends him back to the pit with Wickam, watching the miner sink to his haunches, drench the white silicate with bright red blood. He went to the wake last night. He went to the apartment. He went to the foundry. Things went wrong.

Then he remembers the ghost of Thello-called-Zabka. He remembers Fen's words as he was lifted into the dark: *Thello's call.* It releases a rush of chemicals that sets the monitors chirping.

Gausta's face flickers onto the teledoc's bulbous white body, looming over him. "You've been here two days, and the entirety of the Cut is already baying for your head," she says, voice hard but a faint glimmer of delight in her eyes. "I told you to tread *lightly.*"

Yorick barely hears, because Thello is not dead. Thello escaped the grendel at the end of Track Five, or was never there at all but saw the opportunity to kill a false identity, maybe to assume another. Yorick can think of only two reasons for Thello to move under Petra Zabka: either because the name Thello Metu is yoked to that of Yorick Metu, Ymir's greatest traitor, or because he wanted to hide from the company algorithm.

Thello is alive, and he arranged for Yorick to be here. For him to have good shoes in the pit, for Fen to protect him from the mobbing miners. All Yorick's churning thoughts crystallize into a single spar of fragile ice: maybe his brother has forgiven him, the way he sometimes has in dreams. They're not always playing the grendel game. Sometimes they're walking in the snow, or sitting in a dopamine bar, and talking about nothing at all.

"But perhaps I should take a portion of the blame," Gausta says. "My avatar wasn't very forthcoming in your last conversation. Perhaps your foray to the pit was an ill-advised attempt to investigate the Polar Seven's temporary overseer for yourself."

Yorick stares into the center of Gausta's holographic face, waiting for her to divulge, to confess. She must know Zabka is Thello. She must know he's still alive, and that the grendel attack was a smoke screen for something else, something Yorick can't guess at. This is why she brought him to Ymir. To hunt his brother.

"I believe you are right to be suspicious of Fen," Gausta continues. "The surface clans are disappearing, but those who remain often harbor insurrectionist sympathies. I promoted her to keep a closer watch on her activities, and I sent you to the mine with her to glean your unbiased opinion. Do you judge her to be a destabilizing influence? Is she using the grendel attack to foment unrest?"

She doesn't know. The realization relieves him and angers him at the same time. Gausta doesn't know. Thello was hired by algorithm under a borrowed identity, and even now that he's one of the first five xenocasualties on Ymir, she doesn't recognize him. She only knows that Fen is a clanner, and clanners can't be trusted.

"I understand that she intervened in last night's little melee," Gausta says. "But that might have been a calculated measure. She is not so brutish as she looks."

Yorick stares at the wall.

"There is a tablet on the tray beside you." Gausta's voice turns impatient. "The teledoc tells me you are fully lucid."

Yorick takes it off the tray and pushes his thumb to the gene scanner. It boots up to a blank white screen, fresh snow. His hand hovers over it. Gausta's silver eyes are burning, almost febrile. The grendel was always tertiary for her. She wants blood.

Fen has no influence. He writes it in geometric company script, learned on the black tablet she gave him so many years ago. *Miners don't trust her.*

Gausta's face slackens, disappointed, then she nods. "We isolated her too effectively, perhaps, by making her overseer," she murmurs. "And during last night's misadventure in the Cut? Did you hear any whispers worthy of our attention?"

Yorick hears Fen's words in his ear again. His heart starts to pound. It's better that he doesn't have his mandible for this conversation; his ruined face will give nothing away. He scrawls a single jagged shape on the screen, one of the colonist characters that eventually bled over into company script.

Nothing.

"Well, you were quite fucking intoxicated." Gausta's voice is airy again. "I've allotted you one more day to recover, after which you'll return to the mine and do your job. The hounds have been uploaded and your equipment has been printed." She gives a conspirator's smile. "I signed off on the autopsy, by the way. As he was still under contract." Her hand appears in the holo; she drags one gnarled finger across her throat. "Beautifully done, Yorick. He must have gushed like a fountain."

She disappears, leaving him with the memory of Wickam's startled black eyes, his bubbling, his burbling.

Yorick uses the tablet to request more pain-eater. He pushes the icon over and over until the drug wraps warm around him and forgives him his sins. The dreams are strange things. Hybrid things.

CHAPTER :#%>>

*T*he concrete cube of the apartment is crawling with wasps. His brother is sitting on the floor, in the gap between the cooker and the wall. Sometimes he is a child playing with a needlegun; sometimes he is old, a fidgeting patchwork of holos. Yorick needs to persuade him of something. He starts catching the wasps, scooping them into a metal cup, to make him understand.

"What do you need?" Linka the bartender asks. The black biotank is sitting in the corner of the apartment, in the corner where their mother's broken-down orthochair normally sits. Yorick realizes the wasps are her body now, and putting them in the cup is the same as tapping her on the shoulder, getting her attention.

"He can't drink," Thello says, a boy's voice. "It'll go out the hole."

He made a mistake. They're in the hotel bar, not the apartment. Thello is sitting at the corner table, old and weathered. Yorick carries the wasps over to him. It's been too long since they spoke, so he tells his brother about the bartender, how she is not a droid or a technomonk.

Thello is only half listening, to punish him. He keeps his dark eyes on the holomural, and when Yorick follows his gaze he sees a grendel, xenocarbon body unfolding from the ice field. Snow is drifting into the bar, dancing wind-whipped patterns across the floor.

"Skulls and hips are too big for cremation," his brother says. "You have to grind them up."

Yorick puts his hand into the cup of wasps, because it's a game Thello might like. The stingers puncture him over and over and—

CHAPTER 25

He wakes up with his hand tingling, pinned beneath him. The pain-eater cocoon has peeled away, leaving dull aches through most of his body. The room is dark. Now that Gausta is gone, the holoprojector has rendered it as a frozen cavern, classic psycho-aid for pain management. The algorithm never figured out that snow was a stress trigger for him.

The holographic icicles hanging over his bed look sharp enough to puncture organs and he has another flash of Wickam, sinking to his knees.

He reaches for the company tablet. A time display in the corner swells when it notices him looking: 0438. His sleep cycle is slowly realigning. He presses his thumb to the gene scanner and connects to the local net. As Gausta promised, his hounds have been transferred from the ansible to a black box, a hidden pen where they slaver and pace.

A grendel's body is only one avenue of attack. The other is its mind, and for that the company fights fire with fire, with semisentient programs designed to overload their quarry. Using them to slice anonymously through Ymir's net is a misallocation of company resources, but Yorick has no intention of logging the action.

He searches for Thello Metu, the way he wanted to that first night. The data comes in a cascade: public cam footage, locality records, payment records, every time and place the company algorithm tasted his genes.

Yorick's chest folds in on itself as he watches his brother age, each year carrying him toward the gnarled miner in the holo. Thello's chubby cheeks hollow out and grow bristle. His scrawny limbs grow muscle. His eyes grow tired. The webs of social molecule shift around him; Yorick sees faces he recognizes, more and more faces he doesn't. He wonders at friends, lovers—Thello often had those, needed them in a way Yorick never understood. Once he sees a child.

His brother slides through one decade, the start of another, then disappears. Yorick blinks, retraces. Thello's last entry into the local net was six years ago, aged twenty-seven. He spent his last dregs of credit on surface supplies, thermal gear. He was last seen by a surveillance drone, crisp footage of him striding through the skid terminal.

Yorick watches it on loop for a minute, trying to imagine his brother abandoning the Cut for the ice. Their mother took them to the surface only once. It was to visit their grandmother, who still lived in one of the crumbling surface colonies. Back then the first uptube was still a skeletal frame swarming with buildbots, so they took a conveyor to the surface, slow and creaky.

He remembers the creeping cold, worse the higher they rose. Their mother had wrapped them in so much spiderwool they could barely bend their arms, but by the time they reached the surface terminal, Thello was blue-lipped, Yorick numb-toed. From there they trekked south to the colony, a collection of bubblefabs and ice-houses, most of them in disrepair.

Only a few old men were outside, and Yorick recalls their mournful black stares, the same stare their grandmother gave when she finally saw them. She had stopped speaking by then. She rubbed her hands together over and over, like a goretoon glitching, and forgot to turn the heating pipe on. Their mother sent them outside to throw snow at each other, and when she joined them a while later she was red-faced and trembling.

Yorick searches for Petra Zabka next. He finds a wide scatter of individuals tied to the name, most of them clanners registering for work contracts in the mines. He sifts through pale faces, searching for his younger brother turned old. A pattern establishes itself: Thello has been transient for years, wandering from one mine to another, always volunteering for deep work, dangerous work.

For a moment Yorick hears a musician's soft voice in the dark: *You want to die.*

But Thello is not like him, and he wasn't wandering. Yorick traces the geometry of his brother's brief contracts, the later ones usually twinned to those of a giant named Fen. Their ill-fated stay in the Polar Seven is double the duration of any other. Maybe they just got tired of the cold. Yorick suspects otherwise.

Fen knows what's going on, and the deep mine is as good a place as any for private conversation. Heart thumping, Yorick finds the overseer's company tag and taps out a simple message in company script, nothing to raise the suspicion of an avatar or algorithm: *I need a spotter in the mine tomorrow. Meet me in the skid terminal at 1500.*

He wasn't anticipating a swift reply, but it arrives instantaneously: *Send a work contract for standard emergency pay.*

Yorick does. Then he plunges deep into the company system and uses the hounds to scrub the worker profiles and surveillance footage where Thello appears as Petra Zabka, replacing his brother's face with a sallow conglomerate of a dozen different clanners. The trespass makes his stomach clench. Gausta would not forgive him this.

But Gausta has kept him in the dark and used him like bait ever since he arrived to Ymir. She doesn't deserve his trust anymore, and Yorick can't risk her interfering with the chance, the fragile chance, that when he finds Thello they'll embrace, and all the bad years will peel away like dead skin, and they'll be brothers again.

CHAPTER 26

Southern Urbanite Memory has seen changes in his absence. When he gets out of the car he notices passersby giving the hotel steps a wider berth than necessary. The hotel's one security guard has fissioned into two, both of them brandishing chitinous black guns along with their stunsticks. The hotel's switched-off sign has a ragged hole burned through it.

The little red girl is selling her filter masks on the other side of the street. When she spots him she makes a gesture with two specific fingers, Cut shorthand for *fuck your dead*.

He returns it, then climbs up the steps. The guards at the top scan his neck without looking him in the eye. They don't ask to see inside the bag the clinic loaded with phedrine for him. He walks into the lobby, which is as empty as ever—at this point he suspects he might be the only guest. The host droid comes trotting up.

"Welcome back, Mister Bellica. I have some news I think you'll be happy to hear."

"Lifts?" he asks, using a fresh copy of the mandible Wickam's sister smashed to bits. The medroid helped him attach it before he left, maneuvering around the few regrowth tags still sticking out of his cheek.

"I'm afraid the lifts are currently undergoing maintenance."

"What's the news, then?"

"It's news I think you'll be happy to hear. Several packages arrived for you while you were away."

"Yeah." He pauses. "What happened to the sign outside?"

The host droid does its jittering dance. "We are glad to have you staying with us again, Mister Bellica," it chirps. "I would be happy to accompany you up the stairs to your room, which is a double-luxury suite on our seventh floor."

"What happened to the sign outside?" Yorick repeats. He eyes the recessed doorway in the red coral wall, the one that leads to the bar.

"I'm afraid it was accidentally damaged by an improvised explosive," the host droid says. "Our security detail has since been doubled in order to prevent further accidents. Southern Urbanite Memory prioritizes the safety of our guests."

He heads past the droid and down the short twist of stairs. The bar is dark when he enters, lights dusked low. The rusty mining equipment casts jagged shadows in the corners. The table where Nocti usually sits is empty. Behind the bartop, Linka's pneumatic arms are a strange sculpture, frozen mid-motion.

Yorick feels trepidation moving ice up and down his spine. "Linka?" he calls. "You there?"

The arms don't so much as twitch. He walks to the bar, eyes on the black biotank installed behind it. The stool screeches against the floor when he takes a seat. The sign is still scrolling along the bartop: HUMAN OPERATOR, HUMAN OPERATOR, HUMAN OPERATOR.

"I'm always fucking here."

Her electronic voice undoes one of the knots in his chest. "Where's Nocti?" he asks.

"Yeah, it's probably better if I don't tell you that," Linka says. "He has to stay low for a few days. Think you know why."

Yorick suspects, but he shakes his head. "He didn't come to the foundry. He wasn't there when I got in the shit."

"You used his name to get inside, and someone saw him with you at the wake." Linka's voice is fainter than usual. "You let us think you were just some offworlder. If he knew you were a blood traitor, he never would have taken you."

"Yeah." Yorick looks at the holomural, the halo, the gas mask. "It felt good to have a friend for a little while." He doesn't know if her sensors are watching, but he twists a knuckle against his temple. "Dumbsick."

"Don't." One of Linka's manipulators snaps shut, echoing in the empty bar. "You *knew* it would fuck him over if someone found out, and you did it anyway, and now he's fucked over. You got your little paid stay in meat repair. He got his place gutted, his whole stash stolen. If he'd been there, they were going to play his leg."

Yorick's imagination flashes Nocti babbling, begging, as the miners tear open his body glove and dig their thumbs under his kneecap. He sees the instrument unfold, blossoming out of Nocti's flesh, sees the pit owner raise her wrench, drag it along the strings—

The anger has to go somewhere, but Fen is a hard target, and Yorick is a company man.

"Still eating their own," he says, biting out the words. "Fucking Ymir."

Linka's arms jerk.

"Fucking Ymir?" she echoes. "Those dimskulls after Nocti, if they were here right now I would drown each and every one of them in the brew barrel. But in a month they'll be in here yocking and drinking, and Nocti will be right here laughing along with them."

"That makes it even worse," Yorick says, and thinks of long-gone Tuq abandoning him in the autohauler lot with a wink and a smile.

"You want to know who eats who?" There's a choppy staticky sound, and he knows the synthesizer is trying to approximate either laughing or the other one. "Did Nocti smoke enough to tell you how I ended up in a company prison?"

"A strike."

"The Polar Three strike, yeah." Linka's voice grows louder. "Eight years back. We striked, and I got arrested when the company came to break it. Other people got killed. They put me in a box, and when the box got full they put me in a smaller box, and when that got full they carved me up."

"No pain," Yorick grates, heart thudding hard. "It's a temporary measure, and there's no *pain*—"

"I got to watch. The teledoc sawed me off at the second vertebra, and I got to watch my body get fed to the bioprinter. Raw mass for food or for organs or whatever the fuck the company needed more than I needed to have my own fucking body."

Yorick has a splintered memory of the teledoc saw, buzzing over him like a wasp, cutting away his mangled jaw. He tries to imagine it cutting away everything below.

"And now that I'm released, the company sponsors me. They pay for the biotank. Pay for the fluids. I exist because the company lets me exist."

"I can help get you a transplant." Yorick swallows. "Get you rebodied. I can do that."

"Right. And then everything will be fucking beautiful again." The choppy sound comes again. "Nocti's already writing the song in his head. The ballad. But nothing's the same after the company touches it. If I rebody I won't even be the same person." Linka's synthesized words tumble over each other in a rush. "Different nerve mass. New gut flora. Some stranger's muscle memory. I'd rather be half of me than turn into somebody else, and Nocti can't fucking understand that, and neither can you, company man, so you can keep your transplant and you can *fuck* off."

The arms behind the bar spasm, lashing in all directions. He jumps back. His stomach is sick and hot. His pulse is pounding in his ears.

"I didn't put you in the box," he says. "I didn't make you strike, or make Nocti come to the wake with me. You picked your own fuckups. We all picked our own."

She doesn't reply. Her arms go still again, branches of a petrified tree.

CHAPTER 27

None of the nozzles work without Linka's say, so he leaves the bar, brushing past the host droid in the lobby one more time on his way to the stairwell. The bartender and the musician are not important, not compared to Thello. His brother is alive and close by—the thought is still dizzying. Hiding somewhere in the Cut, or out on the ice. Waiting for a reunion.

Yorick makes his tally in the Ledger of Universal Suffering: up seven flights, down the crunchy mosscarpet hall, all the way to room 702. The clinic did its work well. He can move with only a slight ache in his repaired ribs, the smallest twinge in his calf. It feels like the last of the sleepsickness is gone. It feels like he's young, healthy, cells on their way up instead of down. More likely the clinic pumped him with slow-release endorphins as a goodbye gift.

Other gifts are waiting inside the room. The first crate is chest-high, dull red, heavy enough to indent the floor. He wonders who brought it up the stairwell and hopes, vaguely, that they did it with a hover. The other two crates are smaller, black, printed with the company pictogram on each face. He goes to the red one first.

It tastes his genes, folds open, and reveals the nerve suit:

a living mass of intercalated conduits and sensor cilia, bone-colored, molded to his exact proportions. He misses it when he goes too long between jobs. He dreads it, too.

Yorick strips off his clothes—the clinic printed him trousers and a hooded shirt, not flimsy spiderwool—and folds them. The closet smartglass shows the cuts on his face are already fading white scars. The bruises mapped across his whole body have receded to a few dark spots, mostly around his reknit ribs.

The cut on his calf has disappeared entirely. It won't join the old marks, the permanent marks, from jigs he fought before he had access to regrowth tags and stemtech. Maybe that means he'll forget Wickam entirely. That would be good. Maybe there are other people he's already forgotten.

Yorick takes the nerve suit out of the crate. Xenotech sensitivity is a condition found in disparate populations across all colonized worlds, always in the second generation. Babies born near Ymir's ansible, or under Tyr's crumbling skyways, or in the cloud lattice of Hod—anywhere human detritivores feed off the Oldies' infrastructure—develop a novel sensory pathway.

The company's nerve suit sharpens it to a razor. He steps into it now, letting it close around him. Internal calipers pierce his skin in a dozen places, chining him with minuscule filaments. He turns the suit on and the world turns inside out.

All his other senses recede. He plunges into a seething darkness that somehow plugs his ears and olfactories, too. He feels a wasp in his skull, a sickly sweet static lurking somewhere behind his eyeballs. Every hair on his body strains upright, or maybe strains toward the source, the black hole tugging him into its gravity well.

Even from inside this hotel room in the middle of the Cut, so far from the ice, the ansible is overpowering. He'll have to adjust the suit's filters when he gets to the mine, or the grendel's whispers will be lost in bad noise. For now, he lingers just long enough to load the hounds, transferring them from their firewall pen, then switches the suit off and puts his clothes back on overtop.

He goes to the weapon crates next, unpacking all the vicious tools the company has created or modified for grendel hunting: a carbine loaded with radioactive rounds, a sleek white howler they always give him even though sonic weapons only ever work once, a rack of tiny flicker bombs. Below those, for intimate range, they've printed him a needlegun.

He slips the spiny shape from the cradle, turns it over in his hands. The familiar weight makes him shiver. The grip licks his thumb and recognizes him. It's not a standard arm for grendel hunting, but it used to be his preferred weapon. Gausta must have specified its inclusion.

Same goes for the graft-knife, a fleshy prehensile whip tipped by a butcher blade. It's the sort of tool fat-hunters use for flensing, once they get to the delicate parts, or often for brawling. Fine for flesh, but it would never make it through grendel hide, and if he gets close enough to try it he's already dead. Gausta always did have a tenebrous sense of humor.

Yorick thinks of his impending conversation with Fen, the two of them alone in the dark of the mine, and attaches it anyway.

CHAPTER 28

The Polar Seven's temporary overseer is waiting outside the skid terminal when he arrives, her plus two unexpected companions. The company combat drones hover over her sinewy shoulders, planar, vaguely corvid. They bristle with autocannon. Judging by the restrained fury in Fen's stance, they've been shadowing her all day.

When one of them grows Gausta's face, Yorick feels no modicum of surprise. "Hello, Oxo," she says. "It seems you've made an excellent recovery."

"Seems so," Yorick says. "Yeah."

"We're fortunate that Fen here was on hand to intervene," Gausta says. "Though I'm afraid she's received a flurry of death threats since. Providing her some additional protection was the least I could do." She gives a beatific smile. "And perhaps they'll be useful in flushing out the grendel."

Yorick eyes the drones, digests the lie. "I don't want them in the tunnels," he says. "The grendel starts mimicking their feeds, I'll be chasing shadows all over."

He waits for Gausta, or more likely her avatar, to verify the fact that Yorick has always hunted without drone support, that feed interference is a known hazard. He made the information a little easier to find last night.

"That's a pity," she finally says. "I'd hoped to watch you work. See the bloom of those seeds I helped plant so long ago. You always had such a talent for finding and brutalizing."

"I'd like to find and brutalize this grendel and then get the fuck off Ymir," Yorick says, keeping his face blank. "You ready, Fen?"

The giant nods, stiff; Gausta recedes with a permissive smile. The drones don't follow them inside the skid terminal. They drift higher instead, circling the uptube like buzzards.

Fen has already prepped the skid. Yorick straps down his weapons and gets to his chair just before the uptube pipes them up through the sky and the sudden acceleration makes his gut into a trapdoor. There's a pressure change as the skid pierces the blister roof; one of his ears pops. Then the skid is moving horizontally again, plowing across the ice field toward the Polar Seven. Fen peers into the dark, hands welded to the throttle.

Yorick's questions are already clawing up his throat. He swallows them back down, like swallowing bile, because Gausta abandoned the drones too easily. Her avatar is probably lurking in the skid's circuitry, listening for suspicious language, or maybe she put a cutworm-sized surveillance droid somewhere on Fen's body.

He's surprised when the red speaks first.

"How many grendels have you killed, company man?" She asks it with her gaze still fixed to the smartglass window, to the endless snowscape turned sickly green by the skid's running lights.

"Eleven," Yorick says, recalling all of them.

"Eleven of eleven."

Yorick shakes his head. "Three I never found. Sometimes they just disappear."

Fen's brow furrows, but she says nothing else. They pass the first pylon, and its yellow glow filters through the skid's fuselage. The Polar Seven entrance appears up ahead. He knows why miners call it the Maw, but this time he really sees it. The broken ice ringed around the downtube becomes jagged teeth. The hole itself becomes a gullet.

Yorick hears Linka's voice in his ear: *You want to know who eats who?* He thinks of his mother and brother, bent and battered by their years in the mines.

The skid descends.

CHAPTER 29

Yorick skips the glue bath this time—he doesn't want the membrane touching his nerve suit—but he spreads a coolant paste on his face and hands while Fen finds herself a pair of goggles and the stored pheromone that turns off the biolamps. They retrace the steps they took three days ago, down Track Five, and diffuse the chemical as they go.

The nerve suit does its best work in darkness. As the luminous orange scales fade to black, the tunnel becomes chthonic. He feels like a shade, drifting through the mine with his feet barely touching the ground. Fen could be a grotesque. He keeps remembering another colonist ballad he wanted Nocti to play for him, the one about the dead man who tries to escape the underworld.

He knows he's not here for the grendel. The deeper they go in the mine, the tighter the knots in Yorick's organs. His sleep-sick paranoia is crawling back. Maybe the moment he keeps turning over in his mind, Fen saying *Thello's call, company man*, was only a pain hallucination, bruised neurons. Maybe she only said it to lure him here.

Fen's face, gleaming under membrane, gives nothing away as they approach the kill site. Yorick can still remember the placement of the holos, the four dead miners. He remembers how Gausta's micvoice wavered and chopped. If she has a droid on Fen, they must be testing its transmission range by now. Yorick's heart begins to hammer.

The hammering intensifies when Fen wordlessly leaves the track, veering down an ancillary tunnel. Yorick checks the metal plate welded to the rock. The number is 517, and underneath it a yellow hazard holo warns about gas leaks. He feels for the coil of the graft-knife against his forearm, then follows the giant inside.

The tunnel is cramped: half a meter of clearance on either side, less overhead. With Fen in front of him, he has no hope of seeing where it leads. They move along a gradual curve, heading north, away from the bulk of the mine's excavations. It feels vaguely familiar. Dreamlike.

He switches on the nerve suit, because the grendel won't respect their desire for private conversation if it comes across them in the dark. The ansible flares in his head like a star going nova. He tamps it down, pares it away. He listens for the grendel, splitting his attention in two: half for an ancient war-machine springing from the blackness, half for Fen whirling with a weapon drawn.

Fen stops walking. Yorick tenses, dials down the nerve suit. He readies himself as the red wriggles sideways into a crevice, aided by the slippery membrane. But Fen doesn't emerge with a pirate-printed blockgun or illegal hunting rifle. Instead, her hand dwarfs a jammer, not so different from the one Yorick recalls tossing into traffic a few days ago.

It whines to life, buzzing between them in the dark. None of the tension seeps out of Fen's hunched shoulders. "If it was to me," she says, "I'd have killed you down here the first day. Whether Dam Gausta was watching or not."

Yorick goes cold. He considers hitting first, letting the graft-knife fly. He can carve through the membrane into Fen's bulging jugular before she strangles him.

"Thello keeps telling me monsters can be useful," Fen says, with a storm building in her voice. "We'll see. We'll see about it. And the instant you're not useful, company man, you're dead."

Yorick's mouth is dry. His mandible clicks when he speaks. "So where is he? The Cut? The ice?"

"He's here," Fen says. "He never left."

Yorick recalls what Fen told him about membranes dissolving after eight hours, about dehydration and heat exhaustion. There's no way Thello has survived down here nearly two weeks. There's no way Fen could have brought supplies to the shut-down mine without attracting Gausta's notice. The impossibility jags.

His nerve suit starts to whisper.

Yorick unslings his carbine. The ansible is still looming, a singularity leagues away, but the nerve suit has fished out something else, distinct and moving. He amps the sensitivity and feels the grendel's approach, feels its body displacing air.

"The grendel's in the tunnel," Yorick says. "Sixty meters behind you, closing quick."

Fen eyes the nerve suit. She doesn't run, just drops to a squat, leaning her head back against the tunnel wall. Waiting. "Put that down," she says. "You're locked anyway."

Yorick checks the carbine, then the needlegun, then the howler. The gene-coded triggers on all his weapons have been rusted over with malicious code. The hounds should have been awake by now, sniffing out the grendel's familiar electric signature, but he can't reach them. He looks at the makeshift mechanism clutched in Fen's hand.

Not a jammer, or at least not only a jammer. Gausta's words dart through his mind: *not so brutish as she looks.*

The nerve suit's whisper becomes a soft scream. If he is going to die to a grendel, of course it will be here, in Ymir's belly. Not scaling a beautiful limestone cliff on Baldr, or adrift in the shifting metallic cloudscape of Hod. It will be here, in the sweating black. Just like any indentured miner.

"Put it down," Fen repeats, placid now beneath her goggles. Resigned to be torn apart, or maybe it's something else.

Yorick peers through the sights of his locked carbine, but readies himself to use the graft-knife. He'll have to lop Fen off at the wrist, smash the not-jammer against rock so his carbine can recognize his sweat-slick hands, so the hounds can hurtle across the gap at their prey.

Then Thello comes strolling out of the dark.

Patchwork surface gear, dark goggles, but Yorick will always recognize his way of moving. He is skinnier than he was in the holo; his unzipped thermal vest shows a concave chest and jutting ribs. His face is bloated, overgrown with bristly beard. His eyes are made into black holes by the goggles.

And strolling behind him, mimicking his motions, a hulking shadow composed of rust-red flesh and gleaming black xenocarbon.

Yorick hears an echo of Fen's voice in his head: *Monsters can be useful.* Thello comes to a halt, staring. The grendel does the same, slipping from its bipedal contortionist act into a shifting mass of insectile limbs and razor-tipped tendrils.

Yorick's subconscious has spun this scene for him a hundred different ways in a hundred different dreams, but never like this. Thello peels off his goggles with a sweat-suction pop. His eyes are weary, bloodshot, cratered by deep wrinkles. But they're Thello's eyes, and they root Yorick to the spot.

A red filament slithers from the grendel's body into his brother's waiting hand. Yorick watches, uncomprehending, as Thello feeds it into the swollen corner of one glassy eye. A ripple goes across his sweat-studded face. His eyelid flutters.

"Yeah," he says, in a voice that has somehow barely changed at all. "This is him. The one they sent to catch you."

The filament retracts, and Thello's eyes refocus.

"I didn't know how it would feel," he says. "Seeing you like this. After so long." He gives a tight shrug, and says nothing else.

CHAPTER 30

They give him an antisensory hood, the kind technomonks use for meditation and other people use for sex games. Yorick doesn't like either of those things. Fen makes no move to force it over his head, though, and the grendel stays crouched behind Thello, sprouting and resorbing sensory stalks but otherwise calm in a way Yorick has never seen before.

"I can't stay out here long," Thello says, twitching how he twitched a lifetime ago, impatient for the toy printer to turn their dirty plastic scrap into fresh figurines. "We have to go somewhere else to talk."

Yorick still has his nerve suit, and he still has the graft-knife coiled warm against his forearm, so he pulls the antisensory hood on. His eyes fill with purple-gray static. He can't hear anything, not even his own breathing. He thinks of Linka the bartender drifting in her biotank. Somebody clasps his hand and leads him off into nowhere.

It all feels unreal: this reunion in the Maw, his younger brother turned old, the pale-eyed clanner and the docile grendel. Most of his mind is floating, shock-tossed. A small corner of it is plunged into ancient memory: a child's voice babbling in the dark, nonsense syllables drifting up to the concrete ceiling, on and on until he has to put his arm against Thello's mouth, so their mother won't do worse.

Talking to the grendel, Thello muttered the next morning.

You don't talk to grendels, Yorick said. *You hunt them. That's the game.*

There have been several attempts to communicate with grendels and no recorded successes. The machines self-immolate if captured, and in the field their only reaction to drones, droids, or humans is extreme hostility. But somehow Thello has found an exploit, a buried vulnerability in the grendel's machine mind that no hound has ever scented.

Thello always was good at finding hidden things.

CHAPTER -4

Yorick wanders through a polyp-walled barracks, holding a basic black tablet aloft, trying to find the best pocket of connectivity. The company's new net is still crawling its way across the world, and the Cut is far away. Finally Thello flickers onto the screen.

"Hey, company man," he says. Lately Yorick can't tell what his brother means by calling him that. Thello's face isn't as transparent as it used to be. "When are you coming back?"

Training and mods happen in the south, in the capital, where the company has already wrapped itself into every function of colony government. Shipfall is different in many ways. For Yorick's whole life he's met echoes of the same person over and over, either a dark-haired sealie with spindly limbs or a red with thick muscle and fiery orange hair.

In Shipfall there are hundreds of different geneprints, brought to Ymir on company business, and nobody knows the word half-blood. He has been in the capital eight months, eight months of microsurgeries and running sims with the other recruits. The tattoo will be coming soon.

"Soon," he says. "How is she?"

Thello glances over his shoulder. "Old," he says. "Old all at once." He hesitates. "She took her clothes off yesterday. She stood around looking at something that wasn't there. Kept saying she was going up to the ice fields."

Part of Yorick thinks: good. Their mother deserves her confusion, her weakness, after all the bruises and handprints she put on them, all the poisonous words she poured in their ears. Part of Yorick wants to weep. All of Yorick knows that once their mother is gone, there will be nothing tying him and Thello to Ymir anymore.

"It'll be different when you come back," Thello says. "Things are changing. Things are bad."

"With her?"

"No." Thello's eyes wander left. "With everything. They're trying to break the strike. More bowlships keep coming in, offworld workers from the mines on Baldr. The contracts keep mutating. People are fucking angry. Something's going to happen."

"It doesn't matter," Yorick says, even as his chest constricts. "We won't be here when it happens. We'll be gone."

Thello looks right at him now, but almost like he's a stranger.

"You remember that night in the fountain?" Yorick says, trying to find a crack in his blank face.

"Yeah," Thello says. "The fountain. Someone dumped a skimmer carcass in it last week. Turned the water all pink and bloody." A pained smile twists his mouth. "People are saying it should be a company man next time. Mostly they're joking."

The silence again, seething. Yorick is relieved when the connection cuts out. He hesitates, hesitates, then finally speaks another call onto the screen. The company man in her bright yellow coat appears, or maybe just her avatar does. Yorick can never tell.

"What's happening in the Cut?" he asks her.

"A vestigial but inevitable reflex," Gausta says. "Rebellion. It's always part of the process."

Yorick's stomach churns. "What will you do?"

"We're evaluating our options," she says. "We want to avoid an extended conflict. We have no wish to waste company resources and northerners' lives." She gives him a penetrating look. "It's the same old calculus. Kill a few, save noncount."

Yorick knows she was listening to the call with Thello, but it hardly matters. All he can think about is a crowd of drunken miners catching sight of Thello's half-blood face in the shadows of some bar, thinking he's an offworlder, dragging him outside. They put their jig shoes on and stomp and slice until he's a heap of mangled meat.

"You understand what it's like here," Gausta says. "You understand there's no other way." Her fingers run along the shape of her tattoo. "But you can help make it quick. Almost painless. Compared to grendels, it'll be easy."

Yorick knows it won't be.

CHAPTER 31

They walk the underworld for what feels like an eternity. Every so often an anonymous hand pushes softly on Yorick's head; he ducks to fit under a dipped ceiling or support beam. Even rendered deaf and blind, he can tell they're moving north, in a tunnel too cramped and jagged to have been hewn by automated diggers. The air is stifling.

Before the antisensory hood went on, Yorick caught a whiff of Thello's sweat. He holds the familiar scent in his mind, and it acts like an accelerant, making the memories come faster, cleaner. He is being carried along invisible rails. Internal, external.

There's no point in struggling.

CHAPTER -3

*T*he training sims are cut short, and Dam Gausta sends him back north with a handful of other recruits. But not to the Cut: to the ice instead, to the company camps ringed around the ansible like black fungi. The soldiers there are offworlders, unaccustomed to the cold and dark, but they do their work calmly and with a strange tenderness.

It extends to Yorick and the other recruits, too, once they take their first pheromone bath. The company soldiers don't seem to resent being taught to navigate the snowscape by foreigners half their age. There is no suspicion, no reflexive hostility. No anger.

Not even when the northerners strike first, as Gausta predicted they would. A group of disenfranchised miners and territorial clanners blow a hole in an orbiting bowlship using a munition assembled from company components. The satellite view circulates through camp: a hundred corpses leaking out into space in a frozen nebula of stasis fluid.

Yorick and the other recruits can meet each other's eyes more easily after that, knowing they are saving Ymir from its own barbarism. They start taking the same wardrugs that bond the company soldiers together and sometimes make them laugh uncontrollably, an atavistic pack behavior. They start the slow and bloody process of Subjugation.

In the Cut, the insurrection is dissected by algorithm, all the bonds of social molecule between sympathizer and radical laid bare in a matter of days. Minor offenders are sent to the mines with indenturement implants. Major offenders, or those projected to be, are imprisoned. But the actual malefactors, the ones who blew the bowlship, are already out on the ice.

Those are Yorick's work. Hunting for rebels with springy red hair, like the woman who used to watch him and Thello when their mother was long away, or rebels with dark sealie eyes, like the sad old men in his grandmother's village. The clanners' brutality makes it easier. When they catch one of the other northerner recruits on a patrol, they open her veins with a hundred cuts and bleed her out into the snow.

The only lull in the violence is brought by blizzards. Storm season blinds the company's sensors and grounds their flyers. It forces the insurrectionists deep into their makeshift burrows. The Cut is no longer an option, but the extremist clanners never needed it. They use repurposed hibernation equipment, crude torpor pools, to hide from Ymir's anger. They have for generations.

Yorick tells Thello lies. He says he is in Shipfall still, hunting simulated grendels. He says the violence will end soon, as if he knows. When Dam Gausta visits the camp for a personnel inspection, yellow coat swapped for a chamsuit, she pulls him aside and offers to generate him an avatar to make the lying easier.

A week later, she appears in his goggles. "Hello, Yorick," she says. "I hope you're well."

"There is no one for whom it is well," Yorick says, because that is their shared joke, sliced from some ancient ballad. He doesn't think the other recruits know this joke or take these calls in the night, but maybe they do. Maybe they all have small bargains of their own.

"Thello's still safe," Gausta says. "I have a drone watching when he leaves the apartment, but it's rare these days."

Yorick knows why, thinks of their mother's slow descent, feels a gut-churning guilt. He reaches on instinct for the injector beside his bed.

"You've been doing hard things up there, Yorick," Gausta says. "Hard, necessary things. I've been watching." She looks at him, and for a moment her silver eyes are soft and sad. "The algorithm has found a way to end the surface conflict. You are the only one who can do this job, Yorick. I wouldn't ask you to do it otherwise."

CHAPTER 32

Yorick's nerve suit is whispering again. Not from the grendel he feels loping along behind him, and not from the ansible, still a distant event horizon. The whisper grows as the passage shrinks. Eventually disembodied hands stop him, pluck at his knees, and he realizes he's meant to crawl. He feels a stream of cool air up ahead, paradoxical. It turns his spouting sweat into gelid slime.

He crawls, eyes and ears straining pointlessly inside the hood. The tunnel has inclined a half-dozen times, small shifts upward, but nowhere near enough to spit them out at the surface. This pocket of cold, this building murmur of xenotech, is something else.

A hand grips his ankle; he stops moving. Another hand peels the antisensory hood away. His eyes see only spots, but a rush of sound thunders through his skull. His own labored breathing, his thudding heart, the scrape and scritch of his eyelids. The others are even louder: Thello's clothes rustle and shout against themselves; Fen's lungs are bellows.

The sound of the grendel, the click and squelch, sends one more dart of adrenaline down Yorick's spine. He's only ever this close to a functioning grendel when things have gone very wrong for him. Things might still go very wrong for him.

"You'll want the nerve suit off," Thello says, in a deafening whisper. "For your own safety."

Light is beginning to trickle through Yorick's optic nerve. Recessed in the rock ahead, a small sheet of metal, the dimensions of a door. There's a locking pad where the handle would be. Thello's arm reaches past him, offers a palm, and the door groans open. Cold air rushes out like a ghost, accompanied by a familiar lambency.

Yorick manages to switch the nerve suit off before it flenses him. The unshielded xenotech beyond is bright and active; even without the nerve suit's amplification he feels a hit of nausea. He realizes they have followed the grendel home. He sucks in a breath of icy air and crawls through the door.

CHAPTER -2

Yorick leaves camp in the dead of the night cycle. An unmarked flyer carries him north, drops him on the ridge with a chamsuit and a black box. Gausta comes with him: a voice in his ear, a miniature face in his hood's combat display. Even with thermal coils wrapping his entire body, even with half-sealie genetics and the company's metabolic tweaks, the cold bites.

The wind does worse, slicing to his skeleton, shattering ice against his chamsuit. He moves low, following the digital directions in his goggles. The trail pulses arterial red in the dark. He climbs. He crawls. The blizzard batters and shrieks at him. Once it nearly plucks him off his feet and hurls him into the void.

By the time he finds the maintenance shaft, he barely knows who he is, why he is there. All he wants is to go inside and be warm. He rubs his chest with stiffening hands while the company tool, a binary beast they call a hound, does its work. The shaft shutters open.

"Way down we go," Gausta says, silver eyes flashing.

Yorick descends, clumsily at first, then more easily as his circulation returns. The howling wind cuts away. Its absence leaves a cavernous hollow in his skull. At the bottom, he switches on his chamsuit and the chromatophores turn him into a sooty ripple. He moves through the maze of Laska's Cradle exactly how he did in the sims, heading deeper and deeper.

The first deviation is minor: In the sims he smelled nothing. Now he smells his own fearful sweat, pungent, sour. Gausta assures him the chamsuit contains it.

The second deviation is major: In the sims his path led him to the munitions cache, to the clanner-hacked smart mines and homegrown biobombs. In the sims Yorick's black box rendered them unusable, turned them to sludge. Their destruction tipped a panoply of small scales. The war withered. The algorithm rejoiced.

He has been led to the hibernation pod instead. It's a crude imitation of bowlship torpor, more of a pit than a pool, but it churns the same cargo: naked bodies with frosted flesh, tangling and untangling. It's hypnotic. He verifies the map in his goggles, trying to pinpoint some error in the reconnaissance.

"No mistakes, Yorick," Gausta says, soft. "This is just where you're needed."

Yorick stares at the black box.

"There are seventy-eight people in there," she continues. "I won't call them insurrectionists, or clanners, or otherwise dehumanize them. Of those seventy-eight people, three planned the initial bowlship assault. Two more directed the raids on the mines. Some are gifted in tactics, others only in charisma or brutality. All are dedicated, ready to prolong this war for a generation."

Yorick subvocalizes his question. "The algorithm?"

"A catastrophic failure in this hibernation pod will break the spine of the surface resistance," Gausta says. "Subjugation will advance unimpeded. The algorithm predicts 4800 ± 100 casualties averted. Most of them northerners."

Yorick goes to the lip of the torpor pool and crouches there. Tendrils of vapor rise from the surface of the stasis fluid. Clanners drift just below it, eyes gummed shut. He can feel the cold coming off them. Bile rushes up his throat; he swallows it, mutes his groan.

"They're already dead, Yorick," Gausta says. "Now, in the hibernation pod. A few years from now, in the war. I'm only asking you to excise the slice of time between those two points, and in doing so save thousands of other lives. There will be no pain."

Most of the clanners are reds—broad-faced, foreheads plastered with flames—but Yorick sees a sealie who looks almost like his mother. He waits for her eyes to spring open, dark and accusing. She would hate him for this. She would beat him for this. In a way, this moment is the culmination of all her sins. Not his.

"After this, offworld," Yorick whispers. "No more people. Only grendels."

"Two berths on the next bowlship," Gausta says. "It's arranged. It has been for weeks."

In his head, Yorick understands the numbers: he is trading 78 lives for 4800 ± 100 lives. In his gut, Yorick understands that he is trading this torpor pool for another one, the one that will carry him and his brother away from Ymir forever.

"Thello will never know," Yorick says, without meaning to.

"No," Gausta agrees. "He wouldn't like this very much."

A timer in Yorick's peripheral starts to pulse. The patrols, the ones he thought were guarding a weapons cache, will be coming back soon. He straightens up, nearly falls. His legs are weak and watery, but when he goes to the black box and opens it, his hands stay smooth. There's a small canister of biophage inside. He carries it to the edge.

The frozen clanners and insurrectionists won't feel any pain. In a way, he envies them. He remembers the bowlship blown open in orbit. He remembers Canna, the recruit who was exsanguinated on the ice. He drops the canister into the pool. The stasis fluid swallows it whole.

Yorick is kneeling, packing up the black box, when the torpor pool begins to bubble. The bodies slowly become a pinkish soup of denatured proteins. He watches them dissolve for as long as he can, because somebody has to watch, then slips away. He thinks of the company fountain, of the frostskimmer carcass dumped inside.

He chants the words in his head: Thello will never know. Thello will never know.

CHAPTER 33

The passage unfurls into something otherworldly. Everything is moving without moving, swelling in perpetuum. A high-vaulted ceiling erupts, ribbed with beams that bend and jut like broken limbs. The floor becomes an intricate web, slate-gray cut through with recursive channels. Yorick's eyes slip and slide off the inhuman architecture, and a new tide of vertigo sets him afloat.

"We have dampers," Thello says. "Here."

Yorick hears the click of an injector being loaded, then it's pushed into his hand. He stabs himself. Breathes. As the vertigo dulls, he forces his eyes to follow the curve of the chamber. He still half expects to see drifting shades, shambling grotesques. He accepts it. This kind of site sets off the same synapses as deep-sea dives and old religion, magneto-cranial stimulation and falling dreams.

"It's beautiful, isn't it. And terrifying." Thello is crouched beside him, swigging from a water sac. "I guess you've probably seen better. Maybe on Tyr."

He passes the sac to Fen, who attaches a sort of metal straw and jabs it through her membrane to drink. A red-and-black flash in Yorick's peripheral makes him remember the grendel.

It scuttles past him—quadrupedal, vaguely reptilian—and heads deeper into the den's rippled gray architecture. Yorick tracks it with his aching eyes.

The light comes from wet green veins in the floor and ceiling, illuminating the grendel as it ambles down a row of strange shapes, maybe sculptures, that loom and recede. They remind Yorick of bones grinding in sockets, stubborn children slowly shaking their heads. Staring at them too long prickles the back of his neck.

One shape doesn't belong: a solitary digger, twin to the stalled machine at the end of Track Five. The man-made angles of its chassis are comforting. Its geometry makes sense in all the brain-stem ways the chamber doesn't. At the far end of the cave, he sees more human traces. A cluster of bubble-fabs. A tool-strewn workbench. Drooping biolamps. A small generator.

His brain takes in these small details, rotates them, observes them from all angles, and even before he sees the moving silhouettes inside the bubblefabs, he knows it's too much equipment for a two-person operation. He remembers Gausta's fears of conspiracy.

This is where the grendel woke up, but it didn't tunnel out on its own. Thello-as-Zabka must have scrubbed the mine's maps, kept all the digging unlogged, as he and Fen and whoever else slowly worked their way here. They freed the grendel on purpose.

Yorick's throat is mummified dry, but the mandible compensates. "What is this, Thello?" His voice is hoarse. "What are you doing?"

Thello twitches slightly, and Yorick realizes it's the first time his brother has heard him speak using the mandible, heard the soft buzz of it. He takes the water sac back from Fen, guzzles a last mouthful, and passes it to Yorick.

"It's the grendel game," he says. When he pulls his goggles down, his eyes are bright. Feverish. "You been having odd dreams, Yorick? Since you thawed?"

Yorick feels like he's having one now.

CHAPTER 34

They talk in one of the bubblefabs, so its curved walls can provide a breaker against the cave's disorientating tide. Thello goes in first, then the grendel, then Yorick, with Fen looming behind him like a thundercloud. The entrance mollybonds shut with a wet sound, sealing the four of them into a dark room that smells of gasoline and yeast.

Thello swings up onto a battered orthochair and Yorick sees a ghostly glimpse of their mother, laid out exhausted after her shift. The grendel moves to the corner of the bubblefab. It's bipedal again, crouching. The hump where its head would be is orbited by jagged fragments, a rotating crown.

Fen detaches Yorick's useless weapons—the carbine off his back, the howler, the needlegun from his hip—but misses the graft-knife, sheathed flat and fleshlike against Yorick's forearm. She takes up position behind him, blocking his egress, and Yorick can feel the future violence radiating off her: *The instant you're not useful, company man, you're dead.*

But that's a backdrop. Yorick's preoccupation is with Thello and the grendel, the grendel and Thello, two elements that have somehow become entwined. He keeps picturing the red filament—a tool, not a weapon—sliding into his brother's eye socket, burrowing all the way to his gray matter. He's never seen that before. Not on any world.

Thello observes him from his sagging throne. His dark eyes snag on the mandible, but only for a moment. "You don't look that old. They must keep you in torpor a lot. Keep you in transit." He pauses. "How long has it been for you?"

"Ten years," Yorick says.

"More, here," Thello says.

"Yeah."

It feels unreal and ordinary at the same time, speaking to Thello. Yorick wants to throw his arms around him and embrace him. He wants to wrap his hands around his throat and hurt him. He knows Fen will stop him before he does either. Fen, or maybe the grendel seething slowly in the corner.

When Yorick turns his head to watch it, it mirrors the motion. "How long has it been behaving like this?" he asks.

Thello blinks. "Since we were children, I think. They've been trapped down here for a long time."

Yorick feels an old flare of children's anger, for his brother deliberately misunderstanding. "How long have you been controlling it?" he clarifies. "When did you find the exploit?"

"I'm not controlling them." Thello looks repulsed by the idea. "We have an understanding. A deal."

The world tilts. His first thought is that Thello's damper drugs are bad grade, cut with cheap benzo, and two weeks of hiding in this nightmare architecture has loosed him from reality. A grendel's machine mind is complex enough for cognition—some theories put them equal to vatgrown dogs, others leaping far past humans—but the processes occur in a lockbox, and their response to all stimuli is insensate aggression.

The company algorithm has never managed to build a base language, not in a billion simulated iterations. You can't talk to grendels.

"What interface?" Yorick asks faintly.

"All in here. All wetware." Thello puts a crooked finger against his skull. "Right to the lobe is best, but they can broadcast, too. They use memories. Dreams." He blinks. "They've been trying to talk to you for a while now."

Yorick thinks of his vivid midnights, his half visions. He stares at the silent grendel. "This is valuable," he says. "This is more valuable than all the fucking mines combined."

Fen gives a contemptuous snort, but Fen is not the one who can speak to the grendel, and Yorick sees it now, why he's been brought here. Thello wants him as his intermediary when he negotiates with the company.

"What do you want?" Yorick asks.

He is already anticipating a likely list of demands: amnesty for company prisoners, clone-grown bodies for Linka and the hundreds like her who lost the chop lotto, erasure of indenturement contracts, blinders on the algorithm. The company will batter it down to size, but they'll acquiesce. Not everyone is Gausta, nostalgic for bloodshed, and access to this grendel's machine mind is potentially worth more than all of Ymir.

Thello doesn't say any of those things. He looks over at the grendel, then back to Yorick. "The ansible," he says simply. "We want the ansible."

Yorick gets a nonsensical image, company droids loading the massive xenostructure into a delivery crate, then realizes what Thello means: he wants to plug the grendel into Ymir's node. Thello wants the one thing the company will never allow. They barely let hounds through the ansible; there's no fucking chance they let a sapient warmachine tap in.

"When Fen locked your weapons, that was grendel code," Thello says. "With the ansible, they can do that all across Ymir. They can disable every arsenal, erase every gene record, dissolve every implant, even drop the satellites out of orbit if we ask them to." His eyes glisten and burn. "We're going to undo Subjugation."

Yorick stares. Twenty years later, and somehow Thello is still a child, not understanding. The company has hollowed Ymir out and poured itself into every crack. This world can't survive untethered from company credit, company infrastructure. The swollen cities won't empty themselves back onto the ice to hunt and migrate and play at being clanners.

Time can't run in reverse.

"Not just here, either," Thello finishes. "On every world. We're going to unmake the company, Yorick."

"You've been down here too long." Yorick taps his head. "Or maybe that thing drilled holes in your cerebellum."

Thello shrugs. "It doesn't matter what you think of it," he says. "It's been a long fucking time since I cared what you think. Probably longer than you realize. But you're here, and you can help us."

Yorick doubts it; Thello's plan is a delusion, a dangerous one. But he hardly cares. A question has been assembling itself in the corner of his mind, a question that somehow means more than collapsing the company or putting out the sun.

"Did you know it would be me?" he asks. "When you heard the company was bringing a grendel killer, did you know it would be me?"

Thello's face softens for a moment, and he looks almost like Yorick remembers him. Then he speaks. "No, Yorick. When Fen found out who was on the bowlship, that was the first time I thought about you in years. Years and years."

The words hit his gut like cement. For a moment Yorick wants to peel back all the gelflesh, show Thello the memory he cleans and maintains every day of his fucking life. He wants to scream his pathetic buzzing scream.

"But it makes sense," Thello says, meeting Fen's eyes over Yorick's shoulder. "Since Dam Gausta is head of operations now, and you were always her favorite tool for dirty work."

"I forgave you," Yorick says, choppy, distorted.

Thello's eyes dull to exoskeleton. "Yeah, Yorick. You probably did. You have so much love to give."

The venom in his voice makes Yorick flinch.

"You'd do it again," Thello says. "I'd do what I did again. We haven't changed any." He nods his head at the grendel. "But this, this is a change. This is a chance."

"What do you want from me?" Yorick asks, meaning it in every way possible.

Thello's voice is flat and vicious. "I want you to do what you do best," he says. "Save your own skin. Slide across to the winning side. Tell a few lies and slit a few throats."

Yorick feels something buckle and split in his chest. He feels cold rushing into the gap. Thello has not forgiven him. Thello never will.

"I did it all for you," Yorick says, biting the words. "Especially what I did in Laska's Cradle." He feels Fen the clanner tense behind him, rising for the bait, and Yorick is a collapsing star now, so he finishes the job. "I whispered your name when I dropped the biophage in."

A big hand smashes into the back of Yorick's skull, sends him reeling, and this is the damage Yorick wanted, Yorick *needed*, so he rolls and sends the graft-knife whistling through the air in a savage parabola. It slashes Fen's membrane-coated knee, comes away bloody.

Fen doesn't make a sound, just lunges for the knife's prehensile stalk, teeth bared. She's impossibly quick for her size, but the graft-knife has had hours to bond, and Yorick can move it like he moves his own nimble fingers. It dances under her, plucks at her back.

This time she grunts. He jabs again and again, searching for a femoral artery. Blood is welling into her membrane, a cloud of dark red ink. Then she gets hold of the stalk and snaps its cartilage spine with a single torsion.

Yorick's new limb goes numb; nerve feedback deadens his arm, too, and he doesn't have time to detach the graft-knife with his other because Fen is on top of him now, a knee in his ribs that could crack them apart with one more pound of pressure. The blood he drew is swirling across her pale skin, still trapped by the membrane.

"I learned about you when I was imp," she says. "When I was small. Yorick the Butcher. Yorick-Who-Cooked-the-Cradle. We made a little rag doll of you and tore it all to pieces."

She jerks the graft-knife free from his forearm, trailing its wet neurocable. Her knee leaves. His lungs uncollapse. The jig lasted a moment, only a moment, but Thello watched it from his orthochair without so much as a flicker. Thello, who used to get sick at the sight of blood. The grendel hasn't moved a micrometer, maybe too busy composing its fucked-up dreams.

"Anything deep, Fen?" Thello asks.

Fen touches a finger to her scored back. "No. Nicks."

Yorick hauls himself slowly into a sitting position. He can already feel the bruise blooming on his sternum. "I'm not useful to you," he chokes, still shaking angry, craving hurt. "I can't get you the fucking ansible. Don't have clearance. Gausta's the one who brought the hounds through."

"We don't need clearance," Thello says, trading a glance with Fen. "But we need you to keep Dam Gausta looking in the wrong places."

"She already knows something's wrong," Yorick says dully. "Especially now me and Fen dropped off her signal map."

"So convince her. I know you can be convincing." Thello pulls something from under the orthochair, a smooth gray pellet suspended in insulatory gel. "Everything you did back then, you did for yourself," he says, digging the device free. "You'll do this for yourself, too. Fen and the grendel, they've been recoding some old company tech. You remember gutjacks?"

Yorick watches the pellet unfold on Thello's lined palm, prickly origami.

"Early days, before they had the indenturement implants worked out, they used these to keep miners from deserting," Thello says. "You were never in the mines. You might not be familiar."

Yorick is familiar. They fed them to prisoners in transit, too.

"It attaches to the stomach wall," his brother says. "If it doesn't get the right chiral molecule every three days, it wakes up, and the detonation rips you apart from the inside out. If we send it a particular signal, it wakes up, and the detonation rips you apart from the inside out."

Love is so close to hate. Yorick feels an old fury in every cell of his body, the kind he used to feel in the pit, the kind he used to feel when their mother was the grendel. He looks at it again, lurking in the corner. An open strip of vermeil flesh in its hide is extruding something, tiny lumps poking and bursting through. Off-white, conical.

Teeth.

"In three days, all this will be finished," Thello says. "You'll get the chiral molecule. The gutjack will turn into harmless proteins. You'll be free to go back to drinking and drugging yourself to death." He raises the gutjack. "Until then, you do what we tell you."

Yorick knows he is never getting the chiral molecule, not if Fen coded the gutjack, not if Thello still hates him the way he hated him when the needlegun went off. He is the ghost here, not Thello. He is the flickering holo at a wake. As far as his brother is concerned, he died the day he left Ymir.

But he is outnumbered and unarmed, and in a way he is getting what he deserves, so when Thello's fingers wrench his mouth open he doesn't lunge or bite. When Thello drops the pellet onto his tongue he doesn't spit it out. It tastes like ash and numbs his throat on the way down, becomes a faint worming pressure in his belly.

Fen stays long enough to run a scanner over it, making sure it roots properly, then she goes to the other tent to muck out her membrane and patch her cuts. Thello doesn't even look at him. He watches the grendel instead, still seething in its corner.

"You trust it?" Yorick asks.

"I know them better than I know you, Yorick."

"Those four miners it shredded. You know them well?"

"I knew them. Yeah."

"But you sacrificed them. You traded them."

Thello's face contorts. "No," he says. "It was a reflex." He stares at the silent grendel, but Yorick thinks he is picturing the sundered bodies. "They still have—subroutines. Things they can't always override."

"Oh," Yorick says. "Just like our ma, then." Thello flushes at last, a telltale darkening of his cheeks, and Yorick feels a muted pleasure. He points to the fissures in the grendel's black xenocarbon where raw-looking tendons peek through. "Those red fibers are human," he says. "The grendel took bits of your miners and played with them. Spliced them into its hide."

He is seeding doubts, planting pupae that can hatch in the night. He's finding nerves.

"Recycled them," Thello says woodenly. "The company does it to the living."

He peels open the bubblefab and Yorick follows him into the cave, leaving the grendel to its machine thoughts. The dampers have had time to take effect. He can observe the architecture with only a faint unease. Either the xenotech has its own sort of cooling system or there's a shaft somewhere, a chimney leading all the way up to Ymir's icy surface.

"We'll take you to the main shaft to make the call," Thello says. "You'll tell Dam Gausta the grendel ambushed you, cut up Fen. You chased it down an auxiliary tunnel and got lost. You need more time here in the Maw." He unfolds the antisensory hood and hands it over, locking eyes. "If you stray, if you try to warn her, we blow the gutjack early."

The thing pulses in Yorick's stomach.

"Get her attention off Fen, if you can. There's more work to do in the Cut." Thello pauses, his not-quite-sealie eyes narrowing. "You went to the old apartment the other night. Why did you do that?"

"I thought you were dead," Yorick says. "I wish I was right."

He pulls the hood over his head. The dark static is comforting.

CHAPTER -1

*T*he Cut is silent when Yorick steps out of the terminal, leaving the last row of heatlamps behind. Cold air slices at the bends of his knees. It's like walking into an unloaded simstage: the streets are indistinct, cloaked in vapor, and nobody's in them. A pulsing red curfew notice scrolls through the blank gray sky. Harsh company script, no attempt at colonist characters.

This will be his last day under the suffocating artificial sky, breathing foul soup for air. Tomorrow the bowlship launches. He walks the familiar route to the apartment block in spiderwool instead of combat gear, a scarf wrapped carefully around his tattooed neck, needlegun hidden in his coat. He passes a cleaner bot scrubbing graffiti, the anti-company tag smeared half away. He doesn't look closely, in case it's the one that mourns Laska's Cradle.

He turns the corner and sees his brother waiting on the apartment's cement stoop. Yorick's heart turns to helium. Thello is safe, whole, healthy-looking. Nervous, maybe, for the company drone drifting nearby to make sure the curfew is respected. It swoops over at Yorick's approach; he pulls his scarf down on automatic and lets it scan his neck.

"Hey," he says, while the laser light traces his tattoo.

Thello watches with worried eyes, and doesn't reply until the drone has retreated. "Where were you, Yorick?"

Yorick doesn't flinch. "I'm sorry," he says. "I'm sorry you had to take her to the recycler yourself."

Thello blinks. "You didn't miss anything," he says. "There was no dirge. No wake. Company won't allow them yet." His voice fissures. "Where were you, I said."

"They had to keep us in Shipfall until things died down here," Yorick says, keeping his pulse slow. "I told you. But it's over now. Nearly over. The algorithm is drafting an armistice."

Thello gives a raw, cracked laugh. He rubs furiously at his eyes, and Yorick sees they're red from a vapor pipe or from crying. He looks up. "Where were you really?"

Yorick's helium heart plunges. He doesn't answer.

"I know you been out on the ice. Someone saw you." Thello wraps his arms around his bony knees. "You didn't see them. You were busy."

Yorick imagines a hundred things he might have been doing while a spy or sympathizer watched from hiding: repairing sensors, setting smart mines, loading prisoners. Bad things, but not unforgivable things. Not out on the ice.

"She recognized you from how you were cleaning the blood off your boots," Thello says shakily. "You do it the same way you clean your jig shoes. She showed me the clip off her goggles."

Fresh sweat is trickling down Yorick's rib cage, soaking into the spiderwool. His stomach churns, but he tells himself this is for the best, this flaying, this exposure, because it hides the darker deed. Now he needs to explain to Thello, about how Subjugation is a natural process, like entropy or erosion, and in the end Ymir will be better off, and even if it's not, it won't matter because tomorrow they'll be climbing out of the gravity well, sailing into the stars—

But his throat is screwed shut.

"Maybe they forced you. I thought that. I hoped that." Thello puts his finger to his head. "The wardrugs, or neurocables, or... I don't know. But it wasn't like that, was it?" Another raw laugh, closer to a sob. "You just saw who was winning."

"We don't owe anyone here anything," Yorick says hoarsely. "I did it so we could leave. So nobody will ever call you a half-blood again." He falters, blind and desperate. "You remember that night in the fountain?"

Thello's face is disbelieving, disgusted. "I don't care what a few dimskulls call me," he says. "Not everyone is like that. And even if they were, every single one of them, they wouldn't deserve the company." His mouth twists. "But this is some sort of revenge for you. Revenge on our own home. Our own people."

Yorick stares. Their mother has infected Thello, used her death-bed to slip through his defenses. Maybe she told him she always loved them, told him all her anger was the fault of the company man, told him they belonged to Ymir no matter who told them otherwise. Or maybe it was someone like Tuq, who could act like a friend until the knife went in.

He remembers all the times he protected Thello from their mother, from the other children, from his own weakness. He did his work too well. Now his brother thinks if he keeps pretending, keeps playing at being a cold-blood here under the artificial sky, they'll love him someday.

"It's over now," Yorick says, forcing the words through a bone-dry mouth. "No more people have to die. The armistice is coming."

Thello has tears tracking down his cheeks.

"Come on," Yorick says. "Everything's over. She's over. Ymir's over."

Thello isn't moving. Yorick will have to do it by force, drag Thello onto the bowlship, hold him while the technicians prep him and plunge him into the torpor pool. One long frozen sleep, and they'll wake up far from Ymir. He has years to make things right, to bring his brother around to understanding, once they get away from this poisonous fucking place.

Thello reads the shift in his body language, and as Yorick steps forward his brother levers upright, knees bent, hands loose. The company drone spins, interest piqued. But this is not going to be a jig. There's no time for it, and Yorick doesn't want to hurt him. Instead he slides the needlegun from his deepest coat pocket.

"Yeah," Thello says, flushed red, trembling angry. "You better. You better fucking shoot me, Yorick. I know it was you who boiled Laska's Cradle."

The world inverts.

"What did you say?" Yorick asks, in a hollowed-out voice that can't possibly be his.

"I called you that night." Thello smiles a horrible smile. "To tell you our ma was dead. You cried for her. You said you would miss her. So I knew it was the avatar again."

Yorick's heart pounds. "That doesn't mean anything."

"Tell me where you were, then." Thello's eyes are cold, cold. "Now."

Yorick knows it's too late. Knows he should leave. But he's rooted to the spot by all the months of exhausting microsurgeries and sims, all the weeks hunting on the ice, all the hibernating bodies swirling deep in Laska's Cradle. All for nothing. His hand moves without him, drifting upward, tugging the needlegun with it. His whole body is burning, trembling.

"They'll never love you," Yorick tells his brother.

The company drone snaps its cam shut.

Thello's eyes winch wide. Then he dives for the needlegun, teeth bared, face contorted. They slam into the concrete; the flickering sky pinwheels overhead and—

CHAPTER 35

He blew half my fucking head off."

Yorick has been turning the memory over and over, slicing his fingers on it. After so many years locked away, it's still pristine, razor-sharp. It feels more real than what happened in the cave, his younger brother turned old, the grendel squatting silently behind him, the mad plan to loose it into the ansible. But he knows that was real, too, because of the gutjack pulsing in his stomach.

"Most of the time, I tell people a grendel did it," he says, staring through the skid window at impenetrable rock. "Sometimes, other stories. Ordnance accident on Hod. Trying to kiss a wood thresher on Tyr. I do that one when I'm drinking."

Fen led him through the mine for another small eternity, until his muscles ached from the constant microadjustments, the uncertainty of moving into a void. Now the hood is off and they are back in the skid, sitting at the bottom of the downtube.

"But it happened here on Ymir," Yorick continues, running a finger along the hairline hinge of his mandible. "He ever tell you about it?"

Fen isn't talkative, maybe resentful of the gelfleshed gouges in her leg and back—more proof that what happened in the cave wasn't some torpor-induced hallucination. She keeps her attention on the skid interface, adjusting the signal.

"They scraped it all off the stoop," he says. "Teeth and bone splinters and a chunk of my tongue. None of it was viable, of course. When I woke up in the clinic, when I saw myself in the smartglass for the first time, I thought I was having a nightmare. Thought *I* was a nightmare."

Fen's eyes finally flicker over. "Was there pain?"

Yorick shakes his head. "They shut half my nerves down and drugged me to shit," he says. "The pain was later, when they put the conduits in for the mandible. It was a lot of pain, if that comforts you. Or arouses you. I was never sure how different those are."

Fen seems to consider it for a moment, then returns her gaze to her work.

"Him mauling my face, that was the first time he ever got his hands dirty," Yorick says. "Has he done it since? Or is that what you're for? He's hiding in the mine while you go back to the Cut and take the shrapnel. From the other miners, from Gausta. You know she's going to throw you in an interrogation pod as soon as she gets the chance."

"I'm not scared of the pod," Fen says flatly. "I done it before."

"You'll do it again," Yorick says. "For Thello, and his dreams. *His* fucking dreams."

"Our dreams. Ymir free and the company dust." Fen's face is full of scorn. "You think this is some dirge about you and Thello, some fated thing. It's not."

"What is it, then?" Yorick asks.

Her nostrils flare. "It's about Ymir and every world like it. So if I have to go back to the interrogation pod, so be it. If I have to work with the monster who killed Nam and Cayetano and Brills and Mala, and the monster who cooked the Cradle, I'll do that, too."

Yorick feels a savage delight and an ache in his chest at the same time. "Greater good," he says. "The tired old calculus. The company told me the same thing when they sent me to Laska's Cradle. We're all running the same numbers." He stares into Fen's glacial blue eyes. "But the company is a big beast. You're going to have to sacrifice a lot more than seventy-eight people to bring it down. By the time it's over, you and Thello, you'll make me look like a fucking monk."

Fen shakes her head. "Not if the grendel can do what Thello says."

"Fuck Thello," Yorick says, tipping his own head back against the window. "The company was going to arrest him for it, you know? Debody him, probably. I got him clemency instead. I had to beg, but I did it. I looked out for little brother one last time."

Fen ignores him.

"I heard you two are like kin," Yorick says. "You better hope his aim is still shit."

Fen puffs air and her massive shoulders twitch, maybe an aborted laugh. When she turns around, there's no levity. "I'm starting the call," she says, holding out his dead carbine, the one they'll use as a prop. "Are you ready?"

Yorick nods. He puts one hand to his abdomen. The pulse of the gutjack is more in his head than his pylorus, but it's there, waiting, lurking. In a way, it's his friend. The chiral molecule is never coming, and he's nowhere near the company clinic that would be able to dissolve the gutjack without setting it off. That gives him only three days to live.

It focuses things. He is drifting into a black hole, and before the end he's going to pull everything he can in with him: Fen and her venom, the grendel that's been fucking with his dreams, all of Ymir if he can manage it. But Thello especially. Thello who blew his face apart, who rejected all his love and even his forgiveness.

Thello, who still thinks he can play games with monsters.

CHAPTER 36

Yorick tells lies while Fen oversees from off-screen, miming violence with her eyes. Either Gausta or the algorithm must detect something beyond hunter's adrenaline in his elevated heart rate, in the traitorous dilation of his pupils, because she asks him, pointedly, if he is well.

"There is no one for whom it is well," Yorick says, taking out his carbine. "Especially those who nearly got eviscerated by a grendel an hour ago."

Gausta's face swells onto the skid's smartglass window. "I've had no signal from you or from Fen for the past three," she says. "Explain."

"This grendel has a new trick," Yorick says. "It can talk."

Her brow rises slightly. "Is this humor, Oxo?"

"No." He tugs a gossamer cable from the skid interface, pries open the port in the carbine's grip, and links them. "There might be traces, still. It blocked our signal anywhere below the main shaft. Locked my weapons when we got close. Locked the hounds. I've never seen a grendel do that."

Gausta's eyes narrow as she takes in the scan. Yorick observes it on the smartglass, rotating the spiky black aberrations in the needlegun's gene memory. Compared to the grendel's other behaviors, compared to it wriggling its tendrils into Thello's skull, this is nothing. But it should be enough to give Gausta pause.

"Clever of it," she says. "How close did you get?"

Fen shifts in his peripheral.

"Close enough your overseer took a few wounds," he says. "Mostly incidental. The grendel was coming for me, licked her on the way past."

"Yet here you are alive."

"Got the howler on manual just in time. I didn't do much damage, but the grendel spooked and ran. Fen got us back to the main shaft."

Gausta says nothing, but he can see her weighing the story. "And where is she now?"

"Patching up," Yorick says. "There's an aid station here."

"And the grendel?"

"Gone deep again. Nerve suit's getting nothing." Yorick lets some real anger show, lets it tighten the parts of his face that can still tighten. "I'm switching everything over to manual. Taking the genelocks off. Then I'm going after it again."

"A strange one, this grendel." Gausta's silver eyes are unreadable. "I suppose it follows. Most of Ymir's natives are a bit mad."

For a moment he's tempted to tell her just how mad. But then Fen will blow the gutjack, and Yorick will never get the chance to take his brother's delusions apart and grind them to dust in front of him. He needs to make his three days count.

"I'm staying here until I find it," Yorick says. "Might take the night cycle. Might take another day. I'll call when it's dead."

"You don't wish to rest and re-equip in a less subterranean environ?" Gausta asks.

"I've got what I need," Yorick says. "But I'm sending Fen back to Reconciliation. She's a hazard here. Breathes too loud."

Gausta runs her tongue along her blocky white teeth. "If this grendel is so unusual, and is able to interfere with company signals, perhaps you could do with more experienced reinforcement."

"I can find it," Yorick says, bristling. "Give me a day and a bit of fucking faith."

Gausta's eyes narrow. He wonders if he's played it wrong.

"I've never doubted your capacities, Yorick," she says. "Update me in six hours."

Fen nods in his peripheral. Acceptable terms.

"Best send your overseer to the clinic when she arrives," Yorick adds. "Grendel wounds are unpredictable. Xenocarbon does odd things to flesh."

Gausta gives an uninterested nod and ends the call. Yorick watches the realization move across Fen's broad-boned face, watches it transmute to rage. She opens her mouth to speak. He interrupts her, just in case the gutjack has a verbal trigger.

"She would have noticed," he says. "Gausta's the one who equipped me the blade. She knows the difference between grendel serrations and graft-knife." He gives the giant a bland smile. "This is a chance to seal cracks in our story. Head off her doubts."

They are alone here in the dark skid, and Yorick is anticipating more violence, almost praying for it. He's lost his way to Thello's triggers, but Fen's are obvious, poison-bright. She observes him for a moment. She must observe people in the pit the same way, a predatory mix of anger and calculation. But this time the violence comes soft.

"No wonder he always hated you," she says.

Yorick keeps his face hard. "Thello will say the same thing. The wounds need to be consistent with the story. He probably knew it already. Probably hoped I would tell you and save him the ugly conversation." He mimes a grendel's clenching claw. "Good thing you're so willing, Fen. To make sacrifices."

The slap rattles Yorick's skull, ripples the gelflesh that conceals his mandible. He blinks away the oil spills and sees Fen staring down at him, expressionless, seeing past him somehow. He knows she is picturing it: even if the grendel keeps its reflexes in check, even if Thello stays tethered to the beast by tendril, it won't be like a teledoc doing it. It won't be clean.

Yorick only feels guilty until he remembers Canna, the nineteen-year-old recruit who clanners like Fen cut open and bled out on the ice. Compared to that, this is nothing.

"Ymir thanks you," he says, and his mandible buzzes against the distorted gelflesh, so he peels the gelflesh away, exposing the pitch-black polymer underneath. His reflection in the dead smartglass makes him look like a grotesque, an avenging tormentor from some colonist ballad. Yorick the Butcher. Yorick-Who-Cooked-the-Cradle.

There might be more names to come.

CHAPTER 37

They don't let him watch, but he never wanted to. The sounds are bad enough. He can hear through the glistening wet wall of the bubblefab as the grendel retraces Fen's wounds with one of its flickering serrations, dragging open the small incisions that were only just beginning to knit shut under gelflesh. Meat sounds only; Fen makes no noise. Her big lungs must be held tight.

Yorick sits and waits until another of Thello's clanners, anonymous behind scarf and surface goggles, comes to get him. In the next bubblefab over, the orthochair has reconfigured itself so Fen's weight is supported even as her back and left leg are exposed. It trembles slightly under her bulk. Thello sits beside her, jaw clenched.

"You're right," he says, looking up. "The company would have noticed." His eyes catch for a moment on Yorick's exposed mandible. "Verify the wounds."

Yorick verifies the grendel first. It's back to its customary corner, maybe watching, maybe oblivious to everything outside its own machinery. If there is fresh blood on one of its limbs, it doesn't show in the dim light. Not everyone has acclimatized to Thello's new friend; Yorick can smell sour fear on the clanner behind him. Maybe they played some version of the grendel game when they were young, chased some snarling sibling through the snow.

Yorick goes to the orthochair. Fen's blue eyes track him as he comes closer, but their fury is dimmed—Thello must have given her pain-eaters. He wonders, briefly, if he might be able to filch some. He's already missing his phedrine; the damper drugs dance all around that neurochemical itch without actually scratching it.

He gets as close as he dares. He peers at the reopened gash on Fen's leg, then the ones scoring her back and shoulders. Still shallow, but the edges are jagged now, and the grendel left tiny flakes of xenocarbon behind.

"They'll pass, yeah."

"Good," Thello says. "Your turn now."

He jerks his head, and the grendel crawls forward, somehow pushing its top half through its bottom to form a single oversized pseudopod. For a moment, Yorick thinks that Thello, soft-stomached Thello, wants to balance the Ledger of Universal Suffering by having the grendel slice him up. But it's not a serrated limb that emerges from the machine's boiling mass.

"They're curious about you," Thello says heavily. "They want to talk."

Yorick stares at the rust-red filament snaking toward him. "Get that thing away from me."

"They won't damage anything." Thello's attention is split between the grendel and Fen, who is moving sluggishly in the orthochair. "They just sponge your patterns. Ask you—questions."

"Your own private interrogator," Yorick says, and it puts an image in his head, a motley communion of miners and clanners tipping back their heads for the grendel's tendril.

"Doesn't work that way," Thello says. "It might not work at all. You never had the dreams when we were children."

An even darker thought wings across Yorick's mind: Maybe Thello is not to blame. Maybe his brother is only a puppet, and the grendel is manipulating him to its own ends. But fine-tuning a human brain is on another magnitude of difficulty from manipulating company code, and it wasn't the grendel that pulled the needlegun trigger twenty years ago.

The machine creeps closer. The clanner behind him seizes his shoulders, holding him in place. Yorick feels a kick of panic, less for the possibility of it going wrong, of the grendel lobotomizing him, and more for the possibility of it going right. He doesn't want anybody joining him in his head, dissecting his thoughts, observing his secrets. Half the time he can barely stand to be in there by himself.

He twists away from the bobbing filament, and the grendel stops short. It waits. Part of its body rotates toward his brother, who is sealing Fen's remodeled wounds with gelflesh again.

"Go ahead," Thello says, distracted, impatient.

Yorick keeps his head craned to the side. The grendel squats there, its hide slowly roiling. Then the filament retracts, and it ambles back to the corner of the bubblefab. He feels his tremor of relief mirrored in the clanner behind him.

Thello's eyes flick briefly between him and the grendel. He shrugs his bony shoulders. "Alright," he says. "Take him back to his tent."

Yorick's captor wheels him around, shuffling him toward the bubblefab entrance. The grendel makes no protest. Thello doesn't even watch him leave. His brother's only concern is Fen, coming stiffly now off the orthochair. She finally breathes, a long slow grimace. Thello reaches an unnecessary hand to steady her. The tenderness on his face makes Yorick hurt.

He looks away, and somehow locks stares with the grendel, eyeless but alert. It raises one spiny limb, maybe a goodbye wave. Then the clanner is pushing him out the suppurating door, back into the cave. The architecture swells behind his eyes.

"I need more neuroleptics," he says. "More dampers. I got high sensitivity."

"You got habits," the clanner says, a non-sounding voice, thick northerner accent. "Seen the sucker mark on your neck. Ugly as the tattoo."

Yorick's fingers trace the place where he usually jabs himself. "That's for anti-immunos," he says. "I need those, too, or this mandible's going to fall off and I'll have to eat through my ass."

The clanner snorts. When they open the neighboring bubble-fab, the one where he's being kept, they hover. "People been say you're the Butcher, but I don't believe such. He would be old by now. And he'd be bigger, too, I think."

"There's no specific geneprint for it," Yorick says. "Can you get me my drugs?"

The clanner nudges him inside and seals the door.

CHAPTER 38

Yorick has to find other ways to entertain himself. He tries to count, from blurred voices and shadows, how many heads Thello has recruited to the cause. Most of them seem to be clanners, probably Fen's kin. There must be more malefactors in the Cut, who secured the damper drugs and smuggled them into the mine.

Gausta was right: insurrection has been stirring. This is not a bitter miner building a biobomb, or a clanner shooting down a glitchy company drone that wandered too far across the ice. This has gravity. The wonder is that it's gone this long undetected. Even if the cold-bloods have kept their mouths shut and their ranks tight, the company algorithm should have sniffed out an operation of this size by pattern-matching alone.

But maybe the algorithm needs the insurrection to fester, to gain some critical cancerous mass, before it debrides it entirely. Subjugation is a long and complex process. Or maybe it's the grendel's work. Maybe it's been whispering to the company algorithm the same way it whispered to Thello, sending it electric dreams.

Yorick walks from the center of the bubblefab to the wall and back, three strides each way. He drinks from the half-empty water sac. He does a few of the breathing exercises a puffy white medroid in the company clinic once taught him.

Trying to escape is useless; Thello will be only too happy to blow the gutjack and fill the gaps in his plan some other way. Trying to remove the gutjack is useless, too. He remembers a determined prisoner who drank three cups of smuggled vatbrew and slit herself open, yanked it out. He remembers it took six or seven geophages to clean out her cell. Gutjacks are designed to stay put. They trigger the instant they leave their warm acid bath.

Yorick sits down, wishing he had something to drink or smoke or snort. That makes him think of Linka in her empty bar and Nocti lying low somewhere in the Cut. Maybe he's strumming his leg and composing a sad ballad about it.

"There's another old dirge I wanted you to play," Yorick says to the absent Nocti. "You might know it. You might not. It's about a rich man who dies. I don't remember how. Probably he's caught in a blizzard and the cold stalks him in endless circles and finally reaches into his chest with its icy jaws and eats his dark warm heart. That's how people always die in these things."

Yorick can hear the dirge in his mother's tired voice. He can picture her in the orthochair, staring up at the ceiling, eyes half shut, reciting the story while he and Thello sit listening at her feet. One of those counterfeit glimmers, one of those gossamer bubbles of happiness that burst the next time they were too loud or hungry or looked too much like the company man.

"So his shade goes to the underworld," Yorick continues. "I think the underworld must look something like this. There's a couple grotesques who show up to torment him, pull his toenails out and all that—I guess shades still have toenails. But he's a rich man, so he buys them off. Hires them, actually. He promises them fuel and blubber and his own jig shoes. Says they can wear one each. In exchange, they have to help him escape."

Yorick lies down on the slick floor of the bubblefab, lacing his hands behind his head. This part of the dirge needs a slow ascent. He imagines Nocti sawing away, the music blossoming bittersweet in the dark, sadness stitched with a whispered hope.

"He wants to go back to his family," Yorick says. "He misses them. But shades can't leave the underworld, because they don't have bodies. So the grotesques have to build him a body. They don't know much about that, but they do their best. I always liked this part when I was a little imp. Them building it.

"They go to the forest and break branches, because they think the petrified trees are bones, the same as we have in our skeletons. They go to the craters and scrape lichen off the rocks, because they think it's hair. They kill a frostskimmer out on the ice, so they can use its sails as skin. And to make the eyes and mouth, they take a shard out of the blackest part of the sky."

Their mother always pointed up when she said that part, and they tipped their heads back, and instead of cracked concrete ceiling, Yorick remembers seeing Ymir's starless sky. He tries that now, looking up into the ceiling of the bubblefab. He sees nothing in particular.

"They take all that shit back to the underworld and piece it together," he murmurs. "Branch bones, animal skin, lichen hair. The rich man's shade, he's not happy with it, but it's better than nothing. He climbs inside and makes the body come to life." He pauses. "There is a guard at the mouth of the underworld. I should have said that before. There's a guard with a big snuffling nose instead of a face, two nostrils where the eyes should be."

The gutjack pulses in his stomach. Yorick slides one hand from behind his head and lays it across his abdomen instead. He flutters his fingers against the nerve suit's dead skin.

"The rich man walks right past the guard, who can only smell deadwood, dry lichen, skimmer carcass. He walks right out of the underworld. The grotesques are so proud of their work that they follow him, dancing all the way. He goes straight to his big ice-house, to see his family."

Yorick imagines the man in his makeshift body shambling across Ymir's surface, slip-sliding over the ice, desperate for his reunion. It interplays with another image: a prisoner fleeing camp on foot, on Yorick's watch. He remembers waiting with a mixture of dread and anticipation for the gutjack to go off, for the prisoner to crash to the snow, shredded inside out.

"But the rich man's children don't recognize his empty sky eyes," Yorick says. "And when he opens his mouth the only sound that comes out is howling wind. They think he's a monster."

Yorick strokes his own face, feeling the hinge where flesh meets mandible. The gutjack seems to wriggle in his stomach, as if it knows the gambit that has occurred to him, the idea that makes his heartbeat upshift. His palms sweat.

"His oldest daughter, she grabs his rifle and chases him out," Yorick says. "He has to run. But when he runs he knocks over a tank of fuel, and when she shoots at him she sets it alight. The fireball burns her up on the spot. Leaves just her skeleton, charred, black. The flames spread and the ice-house starts to melt. The walls collapse in. His other children are trapped under the snow. He tries to dig them out, but his dead-wood hands are too brittle. They snap. They splinter."

The prisoner who fled across the ice never collapsed. Their gutjack never went off. Yorick had to shoot them in the back instead, splintering their spine with a tracking round from his carbine. He was reprimanded for it—he'd missed an order, tagged by a glitch in his goggles as low priority.

"His children suffocate, one by one, and their shades slide up out of the snow, one by one. All of them are weeping. They float away over the ice, to the tunnel all shades are drawn to, the one that leads to the underworld. He chases after them, but his deadwood feet are so slow. And when he gets to where the tunnel should be, it's gone. He has a body now, so he can't find it."

Yorick opens a tiny nacelle in the underside of his mandible. His fingers find the microtool he uses to tune his nerve conduits, to do minor repairs. To try to get rid of a clicking sound.

"The grotesques pull the blubber out of the rich man's storage huts," he says, no longer for Nocti. "They feast on it. They find the rest of his fuel, and they use it to start a bonfire on the ice. I think they burn his sleds. Anyway, he sees the fire and comes back. He tries to make another deal with the grotesques, but they're not listening. They got everything they want.

"So he throws himself on the flames, thinking if he dies a second time, his shade can go join his dead family. The lichen shrivels up. The skimmer hide twists and crackles. But his petrified bones don't burn. The heat can't touch his sky eyes, his howling mouth."

Yorick's mandible is company tech. So is the gutjack, even

if Fen and the grendel have corrupted it. They speak the same language. He inspects the contact points on the microtool, then slips it back into its groove. It might work, but it won't be enough on its own. He's going to need something sharp.

"The man can't die a second time," Yorick says. "The grotesques think that's funny. They dance circles around the bonfire, wearing one jig shoe each. Eventually, he gets up. He wanders off into a blizzard. That's how it ends. Our mother never told us what it meant. I never asked her."

A distorted silhouette appears on the other side of the bubblefab wall. For a moment Yorick is still a child, and he knows he's conjured the makeshift man from the story, made it angry with his shit recitation. He tenses, scrumbles upright. Then the shadow resolves, and he realizes it's someone carrying his squirming rucksack.

The bubblefab peels open to let Thello in. He has the rucksack in one hand and a pair of bioplastic cuffs in the other, the kind ringed with nematocysts that sting in response to sudden motion—more old company tech. He tosses them over. The little orange polyps ripple in their grooves.

"Put those on first," Thello says. "You remember how they work. Then we'll get you your immunos. You tell me what to load and I'll do the injecting."

Yorick tries to read his brother's lined face. Maybe Thello is cultivating a bit of goodwill for whatever happens next in his mad plan, whatever they still need a company man for. Maybe Thello just wants to see him wearing the same cuffs the company clamped people with during Subjugation. Yorick doesn't really care about the motivation if the end result is him getting a hit.

He picks the cuffs up, very slowly, and slips his hands inside. The gel cushioning is surprisingly comfortable. His brother sits down across from him, and Yorick sees that they didn't bother trying to hack the kit's genelock, just slit it open with a knife. Its squirming pneumatic limbs make him feel a small, nonsensical pang of guilt.

It passes when Thello pulls the frayed fabric wide, exposing its contents—picked over but intact.

"The yellow one," Yorick says, trying not to sound too eager.

Thello inspects the little vial, then shakes his head. "That's phed."

"Label's wrong," Yorick says. "The seal broke on my immuno canister, so I transferred it."

His brother tips the vial, watching the viscosity as the liquid slides end to end. "That's phed," he repeats. "Stop fucking around, or you get nothing."

Yorick wants to claw the disdain off Thello's face, but the cuffs read the signs and give a warning pulse. The cool gel can turn to acid barbs in an instant, and then it's a feedback loop of agonized writhing until the body exhausts itself. Not many people can hold still when the cuffs start to sting.

"Gray one," he says. "Blue sigil. The injector knows how much to load."

Thello sets to it. "You like phedrine now," he says, in the same question-not-question mode that always pissed Yorick off when they were younger.

"Sure."

"Used to always be doxy. You and Tuq always had blue teeth."

"Doxy kicks different every place you go," Yorick says, the older brother again for a strange moment, bestowing the bad knowledge their mother won't. "Phedrine's more dependable.

And I got a taste for it when I was in the clinic having my face reassembled."

Thello's eyes dart to the mandible again, and Yorick regrets the jab. He doesn't need his brother thinking about the mandible. He angles his head so Thello will be looking at his neck instead, at the company tattoo and the flaky red skin around his overused injection point.

His brother hesitates for a moment, then plugs him with the anti-immunos. The microneedles bite deep. Yorick's head rushes.

"She told it different, near the end," Thello says. "That ballad."

Yorick stares. He wonders how long his brother was crouched listening by the bubblefab wall, wonders if Thello saw, in blurry silhouette, the microtool come out of the mandible. "She was telling you ballads?"

"Telling herself them," Thello says. "How you just did. Especially the kind where someone wanders off into the dark to kill themselves." His face works. "When she told that one, she said 'company man.' Not 'rich man.' She made it so it was a company man trying to buy his way out the underworld."

"That's anachronistic of her," Yorick says, and resists the temptation to ask if she ever gave the company man a name, if it was ever his name. There is a reason he left for Shipfall in the dead of night.

Thello tucks the injector back into the kit, keeping his eyes there. "She was halfway to the underworld herself by then. I was hoping the grotesques pulled her finger- and toenails both." His mouth thins. "But even when we were imp, I never needed her to tell us what that one meant. Thought it was obvious."

"Sure."

"Dead things have to stay dead," Thello says stonily. "People who leave can't come back." He nods his head at the quivering door. "It's been five hours. Time to call Gausta again. Keep it short, keep it sharp, and I'll give you the phedrine after."

"Sure," Yorick repeats, and this time he is glad for the mandible's toneless buzz.

CHAPTER 39

When the hood comes off again, they're in the main shaft. It seems bigger, emptier, now that the skid is gone. Yorick blinks the static from his eyes, looks around. Thello was the one leading him this time, through a series of turns and forks Yorick is sure were subtly different from the ones he took with Fen. The grendel accompanied them.

"There's a holorig in here," Thello says, opening the door to the generator hut Yorick saw earlier. "Tell her you're still hunting. Try for another six hours. She should have other things on her mind by now."

Another six hours. It's not unfeasible. Yorick has hunted the grendel for days at a time before, tracking it across vast salt flats or creeping like a cutworm through fog-shrouded ruins. The Polar Seven's tunnels are deep and extensive, and he's already told her this grendel is abnormally clever. He takes a last glance at it—the machine is scuttling up the craggy wall of the shaft, animalistic again—then follows Thello into the polyresin hut.

His brother puts him in front of the holorig and tightens the projection cone. It's a battered thing, cracks running through the bioplastic, a long sliver sticking off it. Yorick traces it with his eyes. Thello traces him, up and down, evaluating.

"You peeling the gelflesh off your prosthesis, will that mean something to her?"

"I'll just tell her the heat was making it droop," Yorick says.

Thello considers it, then goes to the aid station on the wall. Its white shell is flecked with blood, likely Fen's. While his brother retrieves a roll of gelflesh, Yorick reaches forward and adjusts the cracked projection cone.

"Here," Thello says, back with the roll in hand.

Yorick takes it wordlessly, starts working the gelflesh over his mandible. The motions are practiced, automatic, but concealing the mandible while Thello watches makes him feel strangely furious. It's like they're pretending that last day on Ymir never happened, the way Yorick tried pretending for so many years. Like they're pretending Thello never grabbed the needlegun.

Once color seeps into the gelflesh, matching to Yorick's skin, they make the call. Gausta appears in full body this time, which makes him think it's her and not her avatar. She's sitting lotus-legged on some distant floor, unclothed, chin propped on her laced-together hands.

Yorick normally pictures Gausta in her bright yellow coat, the one that contrasted so sharply with the gray spiderwool and blue-black thermal gear favored in the Cut, or in her military chamsuit. The sight of her without either jars him for a moment. She dispenses with the pseudonym, too.

"Hello, Yorick. Have you found our elusive grendel?"

"Not yet," he says. "It has about a hundred fucking hidey-holes to pick from. I've been moving on foot to keep things quiet."

"You may have company soon," Gausta says. "This closure has gone on far longer than anticipated. I've suggested we remodel work contracts for the Polar Seven Mine, offer a hurtpay increase for xenocasualties, and send them back to work." She gives a tranquil smile. "The news has not been well received in Reconciliation."

"I'll find it," Yorick says.

"They're quite testy already," Gausta says, unhearing. "It seems you set something in motion with your bit of fun in the fighting pit." She blinks. "The family of the deceased, this Wickam Pajet, are clamoring for blood. As if the cold-bloods don't kill a dozen of each other in the jig every year."

Thello remains stock-still where he stands outside the projection cone, but Yorick sees a tendon move under his jaw.

"Yeah," Yorick says. "They always did like killing their own. Give me another six hours."

"There was an impromptu remembrance in the north end today," Gausta says, eyes gleaming. "Supposedly for Wickam Pajet, but with seventy-eight attendees—not the subtlest nod to Laska's Cradle. There are rumors that the company man in the pit was none other than Yorick the Butcher."

Yorick's heart stutters. He watches Thello in his peripheral, trying to read from his brother's body language if this was the work he needed done in the Cut, if Fen has been stoking this anger.

"I imagine they'll be burning you in effigy soon," Gausta says, still smiling her contented smile. "Six hours, you said?"

Yorick's stomach clenches. The gutjack throbs. "Six hours, yeah."

"Are you cowering down there, Yorick?"

Yorick blinks.

"Are you afraid your presence in the Cut will set the tinder alight, and you'll be caught in the flames?" Gausta's voice is airy, innocent. "Simply because someone tossed a half-grown biobomb at the facade of your hotel? Simply because the cold-bloods are being cold-bloods?"

Yorick remembers the ragged hole burned through Southern Urbanite Memory's signage. "I'm doing the work you brought me here for," he says, even though he knows in his bones that she brought him here for lighting tinder, that she always intended for his identity to be uncloaked.

"You don't need to worry about retribution from the locals," Gausta says. "I have measures already in place. But if you're wallowing down there in the mine, you won't be able to enjoy the show."

She ends the call. Thello disables the holorig. His face is etched with worry, but his jaw is set, determined. Yorick recalls the expression from the first time his brother sparred with one of the older children, one of Yorick's false friends who had twice his reach and muscle. Maybe Mara.

He remembers feeling a fierce electric pride every time his brother slipped a gap or hooked a leg. He remembers a boiling frustration every time his brother didn't hit hard enough, every time he hesitated. Thello took a beating that night.

But that was a different life, maybe a different Thello. His brother is old now, hardened by the mine and the ice, powered by twenty years' worth of gangrenous cold-blood anger. Yorick knows he is going to hit as hard as he can. Which will make it that much better when Yorick disassembles his plan and drops him right into Gausta's soft and hideous hands.

He runs his artificial tongue through half a mouth, thinking of the pain when the conduits went in, the loneliness of the clinic where Thello left him for dead.

"Can I get the phedrine now?" he asks.

"In the tent," his brother says. "And you should try to sleep off it. Tomorrow's going to be strenuous."

Yorick doesn't doubt it. He has to survive tonight first, though.

CHAPTER 40

They give him the phedrine, and food, too: a bowl of flash-cooked noodles and a long strip of cured meat. Skimmer, judging from the blue tinge. He remembers dreading wild meat as an imp; the cold-bloods gobbled it down but Yorick and Thello were always liable to vomit it back up. He knew it was some shameful weakness imbibed from their anonymous father. He didn't learn for years and years that their half-sealie enzymes were struggling through alien protein chains.

Yorick is hungry enough now to give it another attempt, but he doesn't. Instead he drops the meat into the small red waste bucket they gave him, then empties his bowl after it, stomach groaning regret as the spice-smelling noodles splash down to mix with his own dehydration-yellow piss.

Temptation removed, he sits down at the far end of the bubble-fab, where his silhouette is least distinct to his neighbors, and waits. The phedrine extends his patience. He can drift there and think of nothing at all as the noise from outside—muttering voices, humming machinery, preparation sounds—slowly subsides.

The cave's strange sourceless light dies off, too, leaving only the biolamps. Yorick wonders if the grendel's done that, if it's accessed some hidden xenotech lampswitch for the benefit of Thello and his clanners' sleep cycles. He arranges the inflatable pillow and thin blanket left in the corner of the bubblefab, ready to fake slumber if someone comes for the bowl.

Nobody does, and eventually the biolamps start to blink out. Yorick peels all the gelflesh off his mandible again, joins it to a lump he pocketed earlier when he was with Fen. He opens the nacelle and retrieves his microtool. He reaches into his boot and finds the shard of bioplastic he snapped off the holorig while Thello was turned away.

It's time. Yorick's modded eyes have adjusted as well as they can to the dark tent. Now he visualizes himself in a company clinic, but not as the patient. He is going to be the teledoc, smooth and unhurried, unable to doubt itself. Of course, the teledoc could go laparoscopic, or better, feed him a little origami nanosurgeon to slide down into his esophagus and manufacture the chiral molecule without setting off the gutjack.

Yorick will have to do things the old-fashioned way, with a large abdominal incision. He uses the back end of the microtool first, abrading the tip of the shard to a crude scalpel, sharp enough to pierce skin and hopefully muscle. He peels his nerve suit down past his hips and etches himself a target under his lower left rib.

He has the same company modifications as any other foot soldier. His body chemistry is shock-resistant, and wounds heal fast. He remembers a squadmate who dug shrapnel out of her hip and abdomen in the field, but she was following the motions of an animated surgeon in her goggles, and had numbing tabs besides.

Yorick has the dregs of his phedrine high and his own grasp of anatomy, gutjack placement. He can't even run a sim first.

An image creeps through the back of his mind: Ymir's most hated traitor bleeding out in this bubblefab, exsanguinated. He uses the thought of Thello's dispassionate face to trade dread for anger. Anger for focus.

He takes a deep breath, and starts to cut.

CHAPTER 41

It starts off so well.

His skin splits easily. He only needs a bit of pressure to get the shard through, to widen the incision. Watching his hands, his smooth-slow hands, he feels almost like he's watching an animated surgeon. Blood seeps out, a red flower blooming on his torpor-paled belly. He wipes it away with his forearm and peers through his abdominal wall.

What he sees is a nauseating tangle, slick and raw-pink. His heart speeds up. He needs the pylorus, the lowest twist of stomach, where a gutjack takes root, but he can't extract a single feature he recognizes from the quivering mess. He takes a guess, moves the shard, and suddenly the trickle of blood becomes a gush.

Panic slams through the last of his high. He felt nothing tear, felt only the slightest give, but somehow the blood is pouring now. He sees Wickam, sinking to his knees in the silicate pit. He sees Canna spread-eagled in the snow, pumping her life away through a hundred cuts.

There is no one for whom it is well.

He drops the shard and scrabbles for the gelflesh. He tries to find the source of the bleeding, tries to feel it out by pressure.

He tears off clumps and slaps them everywhere he can reach. Blood spurts through his fingers and he is not a teledoc and he is not the clanner who nearly escaped, he is Yorick the Butcher, Yorick-Who-Pricked-the-Artery, and it was dumbsick to think he could do this in a dark bubblefab—

The gushing stops.

Yorick barely dares to exhale, afraid of dislodging the gel-flesh and letting whatever vein he nicked burst back open. He chants another borrowed phrase in his head: *Nothing is wrong. You're coming out of torpor. Nothing is wrong. You're coming out of torpor.* He lets the air out of his lungs one molecule at a time. The gelflesh holds. He inhales, just as slowly. The gelflesh holds.

His trembling hand finds the shard. He wipes it off on his thigh. There will be infection, and foreign bodies, but it's hard to care about that right now. He studies the tangle again, sponging away the excess blood. He swims through half-remembered anatomy games on a company tablet, medroid projections in the clinic, every time he ever saw his body or another torn open.

He picks a new pylorus, and this time, when he wriggles through the gap the gutjack is waiting, clinging to his stomach lining with its tiny spines. It's a small piece of tech, a simple piece. It only has two real functions. Cold-bloods are much more familiar with one than the other.

Yorick reaches for the microtool.

The gutjack gives a curious pulse.

CHAPTER <<`#&

*Y*orick and Thello are dredging their mother out of a torpor pool. They stalk around the edge with their hooks at the ready. Electricity hums the air, but they are not inside a freighter or bowlship. They are not at Laska's Cradle, either, which is a relief to Yorick. He knows Thello has forgotten about that, and he doesn't want to remind him.

They are in the cave. The pool's pallid glow illuminates living stone, splitting spars, architecture that looms and retreats ad nauseam. They are in the cave, which means the grendel is somewhere nearby. Yorick crouches down at the edge of the torpor pool, searching for their mother's mine-bent body in a frozen sea of corpses-not-corpses. The current swirls them in a slow vortex.

"I found her insides," Thello says, lifting his hook with a smile. Yorick nods approval at the dripping tangle, the stumps and sacks and tubes. Thello starts rinsing the stasis fluid off them with a hose. Yorick returns his attention to the pool.

He spots his mother's bobbing back, knobby and scarred, but the current reverses, drags her the wrong way. He follows. Every time he closes, the current changes. Back and forth, back and forth, like a stuttering mechanical clock. Every time he tries to use the hook, she drifts just out of reach.

The stasis fluid is only hip-deep, so Yorick wades into the torpor pool, sloshing through human freight. Bodies drift and bump up against him, frost-furred. His own skin is steaming. Thello tells him to look for the one with the hole in her belly, and it's because all of the not-corpses have the same shifting face: sometimes their mother's face, sometimes the face of a little red girl.

"Come on," Thello says, in his old-young voice. "Before it gets too deep."

Yorick starts to tell him the stasis fluid is only hip-high, and the bottom of the torpor pool drops away. He kicks, flounders. The not-corpses bob, limbs churned by his waves. There is nothing below him. The stasis fluid reaches down forever, milky white, impenetrable. Hiding something below him.

Something old, and patient. Yorick feels it moving. Thello is at the edge of the torpor pool, and he says it's a leviathan: ancestor to the frostswimmers, ten times the size and long extinct. The company found only ossified remains when they sounded underneath the eastern ice.

The stasis fluid starts to ripple. Yorick sees a woman with a dark hole punched through her stomach, and he swims. The surface is choppy now, stirred to frenzy by the leviathan readying to breach. He clambers over bodies. He ducks under them. He grips his mother by both her gnarled hands and she opens one bright black eye to greet him.

The stasis fluid is bubbling. He chokes down mouthful after mouthful as he hauls his mother toward the edge of the pool. Thello is dancing there, sometimes old, sometimes young. His jig shoes are gleaming. Freshly sharpened. He is waiting for the leviathan, because that was the whole point. Yorick is chum. They agreed.

He finds a final thrashing passageway to the edge of the pool. His mother climbs out, calm, unperturbed. He realizes she never needed his help. She was part of the performance. He turns, and sees the creature erupt from the stasis fluid. Its hide is gleaming black with lava cracks of red flesh.

Not a leviathan. There was never a leviathan.

Only a grendel in the shape of one, stretching its body impossibly vast and membrane-thin, hollow on the inside. It rises, shedding stasis fluid in rivulets, weeping cold white streams. Smaller now. Smaller still as it wriggles over the edge. The size of a skinny child, but ready to jig. It's grown serrations all up and down its legs.

Their mother sits up to watch, spooling her intestines back inside her. Yorick can't hear her, but he sees her purple lips forming familiar words. She hands him the needlegun.

CHAPTER 42

Yorick wakes up wailing, but he locked and muted his mandible for just this reason. All that escapes is a muffled groan, even though it feels like he's splitting in two along the fault line of his crude surgical incision. He stuffed and sealed the cut with gelflesh, and knotted a strip of blanket tight around his middle, but some small shift in the night has dragged things apart.

Now his whole body is trembling. Supercooled sweat is sliming his back, stinging his eyes. He worms back to his original position on the floor of the bubblefab, trying to move as slowly as possible. Trying not to picture the unset gelflesh stretching like vatcheese. When he's curled fetal around the incision again, the agony dips to discomfort.

His head clears enough to realize he has company. A monstrous shadow looms from the opposite side of the bubblefab—not the makeshift man, and not Thello with his drugs. The grendel looks like some sleep-paralysis demon. A ripple goes through its hide and Yorick sucks in a sharp breath, accidentally triggers another cascade of pain.

It knows what he did. It sensed it somehow, or maybe just recognized the foul coppery smell of spilled blood. He waits for it to grow jagged serrations, come finish the job. He waits for it to signal Thello, bring him and a half-dozen sleep-eyed clanners running. Instead it extends the filament again, looping and carving through the air.

Yorick's pulse moves up his throat. Maybe the grendel wants to confirm its suspicions before it signals Thello. Maybe it knows nothing, understands nothing, is too far removed from the human lens to understand betrayal or captivity. Maybe it's just a machine with a glitching algorithm Thello paints over with his own intentions.

The filament snakes closer. Another, stranger possibility comes to Yorick: this is a Faustian deal. The grendel wants to slide inside his gray matter in exchange for its silence. He turns his mandible back on and speaks in a humming whisper.

"You're not going in my head. Fuck off."

The grendel ripples again and mimics a face: strands of fibrous muscle and shards of xenocarbon knit together into a rough imitation of human features. It brings fragments of dream back to the surface of Yorick's neural sea. He remembers Thello strapping on his jig shoes, their mother reassembling her innards, the grendel erupting from the bottom of an icy torpor pool.

The grendel has already been in his head. It was crouched here directing his dreams.

"Fuck off," Yorick says, pleading now.

The grendel opens its gash of a mouth, and the voice that comes out, filtered through flesh and alien alloy, sounds like a thousand buzzing wasps. It pointillates the skin on the back of Yorick's neck.

"They want to talk."

Thello's words, recycled. Yorick recognizes the intonation.

"Talk about what?" he asks, transported back to Linka's bar for a moment, mistaking her for a mindless droid—he can't make that mistake again.

"The ansible." Thello still, faint echoes of his northern lilt in the swarm. "It's beautiful, isn't it. And terrifying."

Yorick has never thought of the ansible as either. It's landscape, an immovable behemoth on Ymir's snowy horizon. He is trying to decide whether or not to reply when the grendel's voice shifts, like it's putting on some demented holopuppet show, and recycles words Yorick only vaguely remembers saying.

"This is valuable. This is more valuable than all the fucking mines combined." Its voice shifts, turning soft, clipped, an imitation of Gausta pulled from his blurry post-thaw memory. "Thrilled to be home, I expect."

Yorick stares, trying to piece together meaning. The filament moves in a slow circle, but it's clear the grendel won't bruteforce the interface. A normal grendel would have no qualms about that. A normal grendel would have torn him to pieces by now.

"Yorick the Butcher." Its voice mutates again, approximating Fen. "Yorick-Who-Cooked-the-Cradle."

Yorick's curiosity seeps away to make room for his anger. He remembers the grendel is only pretending at restraint. It already rifled through his hippocampus without permission, bled his memories and dreams together, watched them unfold. Maybe as far as the grendel is concerned, it's all a holopuppet show. Some flimsy organic drama. Some dim amusement.

He has nothing more to say to it.

Well. One thing.

"They're going to vivisect you in a company lab. Render you down to molecules."

The grendel is silent for a moment, then lurches forward. Yorick tenses; the muscle contraction sends a searing wave through his abdomen. But the grendel stops short, hovering overtop of him, pointing a tendril downward. Yorick looks at the red blot showing through his blanket.

"Verify the wounds," the grendel says.

It steps over him, opens a slit in the bubblefab using some stored trace of permitted gene. It melts away into the dark shifting cave.

CHAPTER 43

Morning comes and Yorick is alive. He's stiff from hip to rib but the pain has receded to a dull throb, only jagged if he twists. When he undoes the knotted blanket and peels it away from his midsection, he finds a rubbery pale swathe marbled with streaks of red from the excess blood. The gelflesh has bonded as well as he could have hoped.

He pulls his dead nerve suit back up his torso, slowly, gingerly, and seals it. Then he works on mobility, feeling out the safest way to step, to crouch, to bend. By the time Thello comes to get him, he can hide most of the tightness and swallow back most of the pain. His brother is wearing full thermal gear, goggles slung around his neck.

"Time to talk to Gausta," Thello says. "Hood."

Yorick takes the antisensory hood and shakes it out; the motion sends tiny barbs of pain across his abdomen. The long blind wander to the main shaft will not be easy. But Thello has a thousand things moving behind his exoskeleton eyes. Maybe his brother won't notice if he's clumsier than usual, if he hisses and grunts here and there.

"You did it again," Thello says, tapping his jaw. "Why?"

Yorick feels a dart of ice down his neck. He forgot to cover the mandible. Even if he'd remembered, all the gelflesh is used up holding his guts inside him. He meets his brother's gaze and dredges his hate to the surface, a twisted body from a torpor pool.

"You said something before," Yorick says, softly, to keep the words from stinging his abdomen. "The first time in the tunnel. You said you didn't know how it would feel, seeing me like this." He taps the mandible. "How does it?"

Thello shakes his head. "It doesn't feel like anything," he says.

"They probably treated you like a fucking hero, afterward. Shooting a company man in the face and getting away with it."

Thello stares at him, then puffs half a laugh. "Fuck you, Yorick. Fuck you. I got no sympathy left." His voice shakes angry. "Hood. And before we call Gausta, you cover the jaw."

Yorick takes that anger into the void with him. When he slips the hood over his head, to begin his final tour of the underworld, he sees violent images in the static.

CHAPTER 44

Gausta is slow to answer. Her avatar jitters on the holo-rig, clearly split between a dozen different tasks. Yorick exchanges pleasantries with it, tells it the grendel has slipped through his fingers again, tells it he is laying traps along Track Five and Track Six. Finally the vitiligo face contracts, a tension in the neck Yorick recognizes as masked excitement.

"You get all that?" he asks. "You look busy this morning."

"You have no idea," she says. "Do you recall my prediction? Of malcontents burning you in effigy?"

Yorick grimaces; it flexes the new gelflesh coating his mandible. "Yeah. I recall."

"They've skipped that step." Gausta nearly wriggles. "They're burning down the whole of Reconciliation. Using half-grown biobombs and a zinc splitter stolen from the very mine you wander through so fruitlessly."

Thello seems to swell in his peripheral, maybe proud of Fen's work.

"We were too quick to ease the yoke. I've said it a thousand times." Gausta's silver eyes are splinters. "Policy change is long overdue. We've made eighteen in situ arrests, double that for algorithmic arrests. But now the clanners are joining the festivities, battering away at the Polar Six extraction hub with antiquated attack drones. It's quite a sight."

Yorick thinks back to the machine sounds he heard through the bubblefab wall. Drones being armed and loaded, maybe running more of the grendel's code, something that let them stay off the company sensors until it was too late. His wound throbs, skin tugging on gelflesh.

"What do you want me to do?" he asks.

"I want you to leave the fucking grendel, obviously," Gausta says. "I've diverted surface drones and a hot-squad, but the latter's at least an hour away. You have your carbine. You remember how to kill clanners. Their drone operators are using shortwave. Get position on the rear of the Polar Six and find them."

"My contract was for grendel work," Yorick says, automatic.

"Your contract has been amended," Gausta says. "Which you'd know if you weren't so busy playing hide-and-find in a signal-sucking hole in the ground."

Yorick stares at her. "Getting agitated doesn't suit you so well."

A flicker passes through Gausta's eyes. "There is no one for whom it is well, is there, Yorick?"

Thello motions from outside the cone, impatient.

Yorick keeps his attention on Gausta. "I'm well," he says. "I'll do it. I just don't like having my contracts fucked with." He tips his head to one side. The spinal cartilage crackles, like an old man's back. "I'll be there as soon as I can."

"You'll be compensated," Gausta says. "The hot-squad will meet you there."

She ends the call. Thello is still for a moment, reviewing the conversation, dissecting it. Then he turns off the holorig and stands.

"Am I going to the Polar Six?" Yorick asks.

"No," his brother says. "Hood."

CHAPTER 45

When it comes off again, Ymir is howling. The voice matches the cold that has crept steadily through his bones for the past several minutes, as they rose higher and higher on some sort of platform, an improvised lift that swayed and lurched under Yorick's feet. Every time he tensed to regain his balance, he felt the incision tug.

Now the platform is still, but he finds he can't relax any part of himself. Not with Ymir's pitch-black sky shrieking through the porthole overhead, not with the adrenal current crackling through the narrow vertical shaft. Blurred bodies are moving all around him, clanners checking each other's surface gear, fitting their breathers. One of them dumps a bundle at his shins.

"Here's yours, Butcher. Keep that gutjack good and warm."

Yorick waits for his eyes to adjust to the light, reddish-orange, cast by biolamp. Then he gears up: one-piece thermal suit, clawed boots, mantle with a hood that's much thicker than the antisensory one but equipped with goggles and earports.

All of it is typical clanner patchwork, repaired a hundred times over, punctures sealed with silicate or impact gel.

Whoever patched the series of tears on this mantle's back stylized them into plunging meteors, etched tails behind them. He can admit there's an artistry to clanner gear. Same as jig shoes, same as the Cut's best biomods. Ugly-beautiful.

He hinges too deep putting the boots on, and something shifts, throwing a hot lance through his midsection. He hisses inward.

Above them, the porthole grinds all the way open. The wind's howl doubles, banshee-like, until Yorick seals his hood. The earports filter it to a background roar and amplify the more immediate sounds. Normally there's a talknet, too, but he hasn't been linked. He looks around through the goggles, lenses painting the shaft an eerie pale green.

He finally sees the grendel, clinging to the wall over their heads with several long spiny limbs. Its shape reminds him of the gutjack, just for an instant, before it reconfigures and scurries up through the porthole. The clanners are beginning to follow it, scaling a short metal ladder with the uncanny grace that only comes from half a lifetime in surface gear.

Yorick knows he will be clumsy, and the incision is already clawing at him. He searches for Thello, his specific way of moving, but can't extract him from the others.

Someone who isn't Thello prods Yorick in the small of his back. "You next," they say. "Careful of the first rung."

Yorick nods. It's a short climb, and the microspines in his boots and gloves know when to anchor, when to release, but by the time he gets to the top his entire body is slicked with sweat. His breath is a rattling gasp inside his hood. Something has torn; he is sure of it now. He pictures stomach acid seeping through the fissure, pooling in his pericardium, eating his organs.

Thello's fault. Thello's fault, and Thello will pay for it in the same transaction he pays for Yorick's jawbone turned to splinters. He kneels there in the snow for a second, then he tamps down all the fear, all the pain, and levers himself upright. He realizes this is the first time in twenty years that he's stepped foot on Ymir's wind-scoured face.

The dark extends in all directions. From the inside of a skid, cocooned in metal and electronics, the surface might as well be a holo sliding along the windows. Actually standing on it, boots holding to the hardpack while the wind whips and slices, the surface is real in all the worst ways.

There is a reason the clans were dwindling even before Subjugation. Even modded to handle the dark and the cold, humans crave their inverse. Even if the company never came to Ymir, mass migration to the Cut was inevitable.

The clanners are digging something out of the drift, hacking at the snow with heated shovels. He recognizes the tarped shape of a sled, the kind that runs on blubber well or gas badly, and it reminds him of his grandmother's crumbling surface town. They're intent on their work. He could start off across the ice and nobody would notice.

The grendel would notice. It's stalking around the edge of the biolamp's faint orange pool, extruding and retracting small cilia, tasting the wind, maybe gleaning something from the composition of the snow or the subtle tug of Ymir's electromagnetic fields. Yorick stares off into the gloom.

An electric-blue pulse interrupts it. He feels a jolt of surprise as he reorients himself; the shaft spat them up much closer to the ansible than he realized. Maybe part of his dread is the faint ripple of xenotech. It's been a while since the last round of dampers.

The grendel notices it, too. Its body splits and pivots, the whole upper half rotating to zero in on the distant ansible. The pulse comes again, a nocturnal flower blooming and withering, a giant's eye opening and closing. The grendel rears up on two spindly stilts. It shudders, contorts, cilia telescoping to tendrils that wave in the wind.

Yorick thinks of the ballad, the grotesques dancing around the bonfire.

"You're with me," a clanner says, and this time it's finally Thello's voice. Yorick memorizes the specifics of his brother's mantle as well as he can. It has a splash of white on the shoulder, a handprint. From the size of it, Fen's, who wanted to be here on the ice in spirit while she sets fires in the Cut.

Yorick doesn't speak—no need to speak, no need to risk tipping Thello off with a ragged breath—but he follows his brother to the sleds. There are three of them, machine beasts stripped down to their skeletons for speed and fitted with oversized engine cowls for silence. One is already crewed, a pair of armed clanners hanging behind their driver. The other two are still being fueled and deiced. The chemical spray forms a steaming fog.

When Thello gives him the nod, he climbs into the bucket. His brother clambers up behind him. The non who gave Yorick his surface gear, who didn't believe he was Yorick the Butcher, walks a circle around the machine. They make some final adjustment to the cowl, casually sweep a fringe of icicles off the sled's front. They crank the fuel port shut.

Another pulse from the ansible, and this time it illuminates a flock of security drones. They're streaming away from their usual hunting grounds, heading for the Polar Six instead. Thello's goggled face turns to track their exodus.

The non swings nimbly into the driver's spot. The grendel boards last, folding itself against the back of the vehicle. Two sleds are already hurtling off into Ymir's gullet; now their own vibrates to life. There is no insulation to soften its vicious rattling. Yorick grunts, doubles over, and just before they leap away across the ice, he realizes the trip is going to shake his gelfleshed wound apart.

He mutes his mandible.

CHAPTER 46

They're running dark. The handful of animals that evolved in this lightless icescape navigate mostly by sonar; skids and sleds are equipped to do the same. They fly across the hard-pack like a trio of shades, and Yorick tries to imagine himself bodiless, to project himself into the rushing nothing. His body is a bad place to be.

The vibration of the engine feels like white-hot tongs prying at his belly; every dip or swerve of the sled widens them. He has to lean forward, press himself into his forearm, to keep it at bay. If Thello sees, he will think he's hunching into the wind. Yorick clamps his artificial teeth to his old ones and waits for it to end.

The sled in front banks, throwing up snow spray. The wake whips over them, battering his face, polygonal flakes turned a pale radioactive green by his goggles. Their driver banks to follow. Yorick can't see their destination approaching. Can't feel it, either. The dull dread-and-nausea is masked by the sharper kind from his fraying wound.

But the exterior ring of the ansible must be close. If they hurtle past the invisible boundary line, they will only have a few moments to regret it before the autocannons go off, and his bloody work with the shard and microtool will have meant nothing. He gauges distance in his head, guesses at their speed. He feels a bubbling relief when the sled decelerates.

They come to a halt thirty meters from a pair of frostskimmers. Yorick remembers the herd he saw on his way north. These two are nearly ready to spore; aside from the bulbous embryo pouch both are spindly, emaciated. The membranous sails that carry them across the ice are rotting off. They're sniffing at something in the snow.

One lowers its blunt head, and its fading phosphorescence illuminates a spattered dark parabola. The third skimmer is half a skimmer: its rear limbs are intact, splayed crookedly on the hardpack, but everything beyond its jointed middle is a mass of shredded meat. Tendrils of steam are still rising from the carcass.

It marks the boundary line as well as any hazard holo. Its butcher is just beyond, a glossy black autocannon that looks vaguely organic, almost elegant. Yorick knows it's one of many. The autocannons sprout from the snow all around the ansible's exterior, a fairy ring of brutal deterrent. Thello must know that, too.

"Stay there," his brother says, and Yorick can detect an undertow of excitement in his voice, the faint echo of a child's anticipation. It reminds him of the night they crept to the company fountain, one of those small perfect moments that in the end meant nothing at all.

Diverting half the security drones is worthless if they can't creep across the boundary line, so Thello must have some plan, hopefully one that doesn't smash Yorick's own to splinters. His brother climbs off the sled, and the grendel follows him. Yorick stays, and concentrates on breathing. The inside of his thermal suit is slick and sodden. He pictures a trickle of blood mixing with his sweat.

Their driver cranes forward, inspecting the dead skimmer. The other two have spooked off. "Should have learned by now to not follow the blue light," the non says. "Dead right before it was bent to spore. Sad thing."

Yorick doesn't see how it makes any fucking difference. He will never spore, either. But the driver turns, like they want him to answer, and they catch him with his hand splayed to his abdomen. Their eyes are hidden by their goggles, but Yorick imagines a flicker of suspicion. He keeps his hand where it is. Acts as if it's a casual placement, not an attempt to hold his organs in.

"Thinking on the gutjack," the non says. "Good. Keep that bare in mind." They lean forward and thump Yorick in the belly. "Mortality moves on us all, doesn't it, Butcher?"

Yorick doesn't process the words. He's distracted by the supernova. The agony's so bad that for a moment he thinks the gutjack has detonated, somehow triggered by the driver's half-curled fist. The muted mandible muffles his howl, but his vision swims, goes black. He wills himself still. He forces himself to inhale.

He slips sideways out of the bucket and crashes to the snow. The driver's noise of surprise comes distant, through a foamy roar. Bodies move over him. Hands yank his mantle open, then his nerve suit. Ymir's breath is merciful for the first time he can remember. It numbs his wound. Nearly quenches it.

"He cut it right out himself. Fucking—"

"Nah, no. Still in. Still see it on the screen, on the scan."

He briefly hallucinates. The ice becomes a bartop, and the gloved hands inspecting his patchwork gut become Linka's telescoping arms. She sterilized them in her strongest vat, and now she is going to put him back together. She is a human operator. Human operator. Human operator.

"*Tried* to cut it right out himself, didn't fucking say anything, should—"

"Blow it now. Blow it here, and leave him with the skimmer."

Yorick sees Thello standing over him, recognizes him by the white handprint. He can picture the expression under his brother's hood. It's the same one their mother had when she stared down at Yorick during a beating. Dispassionate, disconnected from any false bonds.

"What did you do, Yorick?" Thello demands, dropping to a crouch. The question hangs in the cold air between them, brittle. "Tell me. Quickly. What did you do?"

Yorick's head is so fractured he tells his brother the truth. Luckily, his mandible is still muted. He undoes that with his tongue and tells a half-truth instead. "Nearly got it out," he rasps. "I fucked up. Had to stop. Teledocs, they make it look easy."

Thello gives an angry twitch, shaking off an unseen insect. "Couldn't just sit in the fucking bubblefab." He turns and somehow grabs a tablet from the air. "Gutjack's still active," he says. "Still responding."

Thello's eyes slide away. Yorick follows them to the grendel, a slow-shifting shape squatting by one of the sleds. Its full attention is on the ansible again. Its cilia are straining toward it, magnetized. There will be no rust-red filament to influence his brother's decision. Yorick doesn't know if that helps or hurts him.

"We'll need his tattoo," Thello says, voice flat. "He has to be alive for it. We give him a shot and keep going."

There are no murmurs. No dissent. Thello has earned these clanners somehow, even without Fen here to loom and snarl. Soft-stomached Thello. It makes Yorick strangely furious, adds another sort of fuel to his conflagration. The fury matches the agony.

Then the agony ends, ushered away by the jab of an injector, and he promises some drug-dazed god that he will never disparage company phedrine again. Someone adds a fresh layer of gelflesh to his exposed stomach, finishes it with a numbing spray that gets mostly sucked away by the wind. They start sealing his thermal suit back up.

He could probably do it himself, but he doesn't want to. He wants to lie in the phedrine puddle forever, staring up at Ymir's starless sky, insulated against everything that hurts. But the bliss is fleeting. By the time his mantle is back on, the pain has returned as a dulled but persistent throb. He uses it like a war drum, pretends it's urging him to his feet.

When he straightens up, he is face-to-face with Dam Gausta. And another of her. And another.

CHAPTER 47

Thello always was a clever imp. Gausta would be proud, or at least amused, to see what he's devised here: holomask feed from her stored conversations with Fen and Yorick, spliced and smoothed to create ten blinking, scowling incarnations. Autocannons are indiscriminate, but Gausta is paranoid. The clanners have found a blind spot where her face is concerned.

Thello checked each holomask himself and gave out a final hit of neuroleptics. Now they approach the boundary line at a crawl, sleds throttled down to ensure the autocannon has a clear view of their many luminous faces. Yorick wonders how many times they have tested the exploit, if any of the frostskimmers that wander across the boundary do it wearing holomasks.

The bisected carcass lolls slightly in their wake, animated by the engine-churned snow. Yorick sees a similar shudder go through their driver's back. But they pass the blood spatter without adding to it. The autocannon swivels. Stutters. Yorick imagines it trying to clear its carbon-shelled head.

Normally a simple machine like this would kick the anomaly up to the company algorithm, or at least shuttle it sideways to its fellow sentinels, to decide by aggregate how to treat a silver-eyed crowd of company higher-ups. But today, with the Cut in chaos and the Polar Six under attack, a glitching auto-cannon is low priority.

They slide past, and Yorick counts the meters. Tries to remember the range. When the driver's shoulder blades slump, a small implosion of relief, he assumes they've left it. There's still a scatter of security drones somewhere up above them, but the sleds are small targets running dark. Their cobbled-together chassis give off no signals.

Nothing but ice between them and the ansible now. Yorick knows the human crew there is minimal—even with high-grade damper drugs, the company has to rotate its troops through. If they have a grendel behind them, and Yorick in front of them to open doors with his tattoo, nine clanners with blockguns and hunting rifles might be enough.

Thello thinks so. Yorick can feel his brother's leg jumping and knocking against the side of the sled, the same tic he had before jigs. For a moment it syncopates with the throb in his belly. He thinks again of the prisoner sprinting, slip-sliding, their mad run through the camp perimeter. They probably felt the same way Thello feels now.

The holomasks come off. The sleds pick up speed again, three magnetic grains skittering across Ymir's surface, drawn inexorably to the ansible. Invisible rails. Everything is on invisible rails. They slalom the occasional drift, snow swept up into small dunes by invisible hands. Yorick's incision throbs.

For the miners or clanners who swallowed gutjacks during Subjugation, they were a brutal deterrent. For the company, they had an extra utility: sometimes gutjacks belonging to algorithm-selected prisoners would glitch, allowing escape so long as a twitch-fingered recruit didn't interrupt. Then the gutjacks' dormant geotags, frequencies relegated to a tiny sliver of the electromagnetic spectrum, would wake up and start whispering.

Yorick had to wake his manually. It was a long, bloody hour with the microtool.

Their driver's head turns. Yorick tracks, peering through the veil of snow. In the distance, off to the south, he sees the running lights of a company flyer. It's heading for the Polar Six Mine, carrying the squad Gausta requisitioned from the garrison in Sants or Shipfall, ready to help him hunt down a handful of drone operators.

His gutjack seems to shiver, whispering a language nobody has used for years, one nobody would listen for. Not unless Yorick told them to.

"There is no one for whom it is well," he says, knowing the wind will strip it away before it reaches Thello's ears.

They hurtle on toward the ansible. It's massive now, the size of some folktale frostswimmer or extinct leviathan erupting from the ice to breathe. Yorick ignores its brain-bending geometry, watches the sky. He wishes he could watch Thello, too.

A dozen black boluses plunge from nowhere and detonate the snow around them. Ionized air shivers through Yorick's mandible, licks his skin with static. It rips the heart out of the sled engine. The vehicle jolts, shudders. Yorick barely feels the motion tug at his gelflesh. He's wiping his goggles clear, already anticipating the next act, the follow-up to the emps.

Their driver twists at the frozen throttle, begging and then bargaining with it as they carve out a stop. The other sleds are dead, too, one stalled out on their right, the other somewhere behind them.

"Fuck," the non says. "Fuck, fuck. Thello?"

Thello doesn't have an answer. The company flyer banks hard, drawing a jagged circle in the umber. Then the security drones that have been coalescing overhead, running dark, drop down in a furious swarm. Yorick is the black hole that draws them in.

CHAPTER 48

The drones' first salvo fells most of the clanners; the driver is one of them. Yorick watches shock rounds batter their hunched back. Impact alone knocks them halfway off the sled, then the rounds flatten and activate, clinging like limpets, and convulsions send the non the rest of the way down into the snow. They're safer there.

They're not important. Yorick twists around, ignoring the sear of torsion, to find Thello. He needs his brother to know it was him. He needs to look him in the eye. But Thello is already off the sled, crouched at the engine cowl.

The grendel is with him. Its hide is almost bubbling, tongues of xenocarbon curling outward, coronal plasma from a seething sun. Agitated by the emp, or maybe by its assault on the ansible coming apart so quickly and completely.

Yorick feels a small savage pleasure in that, but the grendel is tertiary. He hauls himself off the sled and lands badly. Pain finds new pathways, somehow shooting from his abdomen to tear through his hip and thigh. Two clanners who dove clear of the first salvo are firing back, blockguns chattering, reverberating in Yorick's skull.

It feels like Subjugation days. He leans into the pain and

levers up to his knees. Thello is busy, back turned, prying at a panel on the engine cowl. The grendel shields him, enveloping him like a bizarre exoskel. Thello's goggles are pulled down, and there's a filament wriggling into the corner of his eye, between the frost-licked lashes. Yorick feels a crackle and roar in his chest.

The pair move in perfect sync; Thello frees the panel and the grendel drives its tendrils inside. A meatier tendril, more a tentacle, snaps from the back of its body to scythe down a drone that dips too close. The sled engine's fried circuitry hums and sparks.

Yorick knows they're trying to escape the firefight, but that's not why he hurls himself at them. In the moment, all he wants in the entire fucking universe is to sever that filament between them, send the grendel back to its black box and Thello back to his flesh one, stop them fucking *talking*, because you don't talk to grendels, you kill them—

They see him coming and the grendel flicks him away; right before the xenocarbon club smashes him off his feet Yorick is reminded of his mother's backhand, brutal and casual. He lies gasping in the snow. Ymir spins around him, nearly dumps him off.

Thello will trigger the gutjack now. Yorick wasn't able to disable the detonator. Didn't even dare to try. He will die staring up at a sky with no stars.

A sky full of company drones that for some reason, maybe the collapsing neurons in Yorick's brain, are beginning to cannibalize each other. He watches one turn on the murmuration, spitting shock rounds at its neighbors instead of the scrambling clanners below. Traitor. The other drones will never forgive its trespass.

Yorick shakes his head clear just as the sled roars back to life. Thello is in the driver's spot now; the grendel's still wrapped around him, shrugging off the shock rounds—there's a reason they give Yorick radioactive ammo and nanocarbon fléchettes. Gausta probably thinks she's doing him a favor using nonlethals, making sure he doesn't die in a hail of friendly fire.

She doesn't realize he's already dead. Already a flickering ghost at a wake. Thello doesn't need to blow the gutjack, doesn't care either way. The emptiness is worse than hate.

The sled lurches forward. Because he is already dead, Yorick rolls across the churned-up snow and throws a hand against the metal skirting. He grips hard. The glove's microspines activate. Thello twists the throttle, and they slam off across the ice.

CHAPTER 49

Yorick's shoulder wrenches from its socket, a soft wet pop hidden by the roar of the sled. Even filtered through the earports in his hood, the engine sound is skull-pulping—the grendel didn't get the muffler rig back online. He is deaf, and mostly blind from the snow spray battering his face. He scrabbles his feet for purchase, bouncing off the hardpack, off the side of the sled.

His arm stretches. Stretches. He has a brief flash of a fathunter wriggling their way into a tiny sleepstack, saying their skeleton is all cartilage, good and flexy. His nerves scream. He screams, too, a harsh electric cipher. Then the sled banks, swinging him against metal, and his dislocated shoulder clacks back into place.

He gets his other hand on. The shoulder pain downshifts to join the rest, so he climbs, driven half by reflex, half by hate, up the back of the sled. The microspines in his boots anchor him when he reaches the top. Thello is obscured, still hiding halfway inside the grendel's mutating body. Beyond them, the ansible, impossibly big, swallowing up Ymir's horizon. It puts helium in Yorick's forehead.

The company flyer comes from nowhere, strafing low. Emps

erupt in the snow ahead of them; Thello snaps the steering column left. They slew hard, tipping almost parallel to the ice before the sled's gyros bob them back upright. Yorick's goggles are scrubbing themselves clear, but not fast enough. All he sees is pale green rime.

He rips them off and catches a disjointed image: Thello's lanky arm emerging from the grendel's red-and-black rorschach, his hooded head turning. Yorick lunges at them, not caring if the grendel's serrated limbs slice him apart. All he wants is to end this game.

He leads with his lowered head, diving into the grendel. Something gives: flesh, not xenocarbon, something picked off the massacred bodies at the end of Track Five. He claws past it, reaching for Thello. They bank again, and Yorick sees the wind-sculpted drift just before the nose of the sled plows into it, sending up a wave of shattered crust.

Force snaps the microspines in Yorick's clinging boots. He's hurled upward; so is Thello, both of them still latched to the grendel. For an endless nanosecond they all hang suspended in the dark. Yorick has a giddy thought in his hindbrain. Time has stopped. It might even run in reverse.

Then: crash.

CHAPTER 50

Back in the torpor pool, cold stasis fluid all around him. Yorick's head is fragments, bits of brain orbiting his pounding skull, but he knows something has gone wrong. Torpor pools are designed for the clinically dead. Conscious means alive, means he is going to starve slowly to death as the bowlship crawls from one world to another.

He tries his limbs, praying the bowlship's sensors will notice irregular movement. They move through snow instead of stasis fluid, and reality snaps back into place. He picks up. Down. Readies himself, then starts digging with numb hands. Every motion sends him afterspikes of pain: shoulder, stomach, now neck from the impact.

He imagines it helping him, keeping his muscles hot as the snow tries to sap them cold. He digs. His lungs winch tighter and tighter. For a terrifying moment he wonders if he's inverted, burrowing deeper under the surface, dooming himself to suffocate.

Then he pierces the drift and sees Ymir's black sky. He pushes his head clear. Inhales thin air. He fumbles his goggles back into place. The sled is half buried, overturned, gyros finally losing to gravity. Sparks fizz from its dissected engine cowl. Beyond it, a drooping autocannon. Beyond that, the ansible, smaller again.

The wrecked sled's flicker illuminates a body. His heart crashes against his ribs. Another flicker, and he sees the body split apart, twins coming unjoined as the grendel disgorges Thello from a fleshy cocoon. Yorick was tossed clear on impact, into the soft belly of the snowdrift, but Thello and the grendel landed on hard ice.

Yorick thrashes the rest of the way free, shedding snow as he staggers forward. The grendel hunkers over Thello's prone form. The filament probes the air between them. Yorick reaches on instinct for his carbine, for his howler or needlegun—all gone. His toe catches a jagged spar of ice. He stumbles. The grendel pivots.

A nonsensical splinter of dream comes to Yorick: the grendel wants to jig.

Instead, it runs away. He watches it go, reaches again for his phantom carbine, but of course the grendel's not running from him. The company flyer is setting down. Yorick can feel the hot blast of its breath on his back, feel it hammering the air. Company signals are finally flaring through his tattoo again, ghostly vibrations in his mandible.

He confirms his identity and ignores the rest. Ignores the grendel loping away across the ice. He goes to his brother like it's one of his dreams, feet floating. He finds Thello broken: His left leg twists strangely beneath him. Blood pumps from one mangled hand. Maybe he split it grabbing for the skirt of the sled; maybe it got caught and chewed apart in the grendel's shifting body.

Sweat is freezing in halos around his dark eyes. His gaze is alert. Alive.

"It doesn't feel like anything," Yorick says. He has to howl it, to make sure Thello hears him over the shriek of the wind, the roar of the flyer.

His brother's intact hand twitches. Yorick watches it move sluggishly across the ice, up onto Thello's chest. It fumbles to a pocket on the front of his mantle, just below Fen's white hand-print, and strokes the enzyme zipper.

Yorick knows what's inside. A verbal trigger would be too prone to error. Thello has kept things simple. Corporeal. A small mechanism, fed off his own bioelectricity, that will trigger the gutjack at the touch of his thumb. Yorick thinks of seizing his brother's arm, twisting it, snapping it to match his demolished leg.

He crouches down and unwraps Thello's scarf instead. He finds the spiderwooled gap between hood and mantle, and puts his hands around a bobbing throat. The microspines cling. He thinks he can feel a tiny wriggling pulse below them.

"You or me, Thello," he says. "Do it."

The pocket peels open. Thello worms his fingers inside.

This is the right way to end the ballad. Thello pulls the trigger again and sends Yorick to the void. There will be nobody to beg the company for clemency. His brother will be debodied, fed to the recycler, and drift in biotank purgatory for as long as the company can keep him there. Maybe decades. Maybe centuries.

If there is an underworld, some hidden quantum kingdom their mother's stories unknowingly intuited, their shades will eventually meet there and start the cycle over again.

Thello's fever-bright eyes are glassed over now, dull from shock. He doesn't have company modifications. Yorick wills him on, how he did in the jigs, as his trembling hand emerges from the pocket. The trigger is small and cylindrical, coated in graphene. When it tumbles out of Thello's stiff fingers, when it clatters onto the ice, Yorick's heart stops.

He releases his brother. He crabs backward, scrambling through the snow. He stares at the tiny medicine capsule, the not-trigger, that Thello pried from his pocket.

"These past few hours have been quite eventful, haven't they, Yorick?" Gausta's voice in his ear, her hand soft on his aching shoulder. "I'm pleasantly surprised to see you alive."

Yorick can't reply. His mandible is intact, functional, but the flesh parts of him are not. He looks up, thinking for a moment that Gausta has come in person to comfort him. To assure him he did hard but necessary things.

The company soldier wearing Gausta's face checks his vitals, running a scan wand up and down his body. He imagines it finding nothing but slick black ice.

CHAPTER 51

They have a teledoc in the back of the flyer, and it confirms all of Yorick's fears, all of his failings. The fallen capsule has his chiral molecule jellied inside. The teledoc feeds it to him, prodding it into his slack mouth. The gutjack sees its perfect mirror and dissolves into harmless proteins. He feels it as a soft implosion.

"A grendel that talks." Gausta has no holo now; her voice comes disembodied. "A grendel that cooperates with an insurrectionist crew of miners and clanners in order to gain access to our ansible. This really is a fascinating deviation."

Yorick has told her what he knows, told it mechanically, reflexively, as if he was a recruit again and she was the company man in the yellow coat. She has told him a few things in return. The Cut is quiet again, locked down tight by swarms of redeployed security drones. Half the hot-squad is moving by skid to hunt down the clanners at the Polar Six Mine.

The other half is here. They followed the gutjack, the same digital whisper that attracted the ansible's remaining security drones, and cleaned up the aftermath of the ambush. Yorick is not the only one lying in the back of the flyer. The clanners from the sleds are arranged all around him, still studded with shock rounds. Their jerks and twitches are smaller now that their nerves are exhausted.

"We didn't see your clever monster from the flyer," Gausta says. "Our troops on the ground didn't see it, either. Though they were, admittedly, focused on your safe retrieval."

The teledoc shuttles to the next patient over, and Yorick pulls himself upright. "Doesn't matter," he says. "I saw it. If it can't get to the ansible, it's heading back to the cave. Back to the mine. It knows it can hide down there forever."

He has to think tactics. Think hunting. He can't think about the body at the edge of his peripheral, the limp hand being stapled shut by a whirring white tool, the blood being suctioned away by a puckered bioplastic mouth. Hands are so full of veins.

"The same place Zabka hid, I assume." Gausta's voice is thoughtful. "After his supposed demise."

Hearing Thello's false name again jolts. Yorick thinks for a moment that she must be doing it intentionally, mercifully, trying to distance him from the moment in the snow and the body beside him. But then he remembers his alterations to the company records, and remembers that here in the flyer, still wearing surface gear, Thello looks like any other clanner.

The teledoc is done with the hand. Now it goes to the leg, slicing the thermal suit away for access. The small blade snicks and sighs.

Yorick presses his eyes shut. "There's a shaft that goes vertical, all the way from the cave to the surface," he says. "You have the geotag trail from the gutjack. We can follow that back to the shaft." His closed eyes only make the sounds of the teledoc more vivid—shifting bone now, as it sets the wrecked leg. "Either we find the grendel on the way, or we find it down below."

"And the remaining conspirators?" Gausta's voice is almost joyful. "Did they all vacate their hiding hole? Or are there more of them waiting below, anticipating revolution?"

Yorick thinks back to the bubblefabs, to his blind head-counts. Maybe there's a rearguard, or maybe every able body left to do Thello's work, whether on the ice or in the Cut. He doesn't know, but it doesn't matter.

"More of them," he says. "More prisoners. More blood."

Gausta pretends not to hear the last bit. "Then we'll drop the other skid," she says. "The skid will go to the shaft, quickly and quietly. The flyer will watch the Polar Seven's main entrance—the Maw, as they call it. In case it regurgitates any fleeing insurrectionists."

"I'm going in the skid," Yorick says, because he needs to be anywhere but here.

Gausta is silent for a second. When she replies, the concern in her voice sounds almost real. "Your entire torso is a patchwork of badly bonded gelflesh, Yorick. Better you watch from the flyer while the teledoc works on you."

"The teledoc can have me after. You need me now, for the grendel."

"You said your nerve suit is rendered useless in the cave. You'll just be a soldier."

"Good." Yorick looks at the squad members moving around him, the way they cock their heads, the near-instantaneous ripple of body language. "I'm nostalgic," he says. "I miss the hyena."

He can picture Gausta's distant smile. "So do I," she says, then, switching code: "Because the teledoc advises against your participation in this raid, you will not be eligible for additional hurtpay if you sustain further injuries or exacerbate current damage. Do you accept that?"

"Yeah. Accepted."

"If you find the grendel, try to take it functioning," she says. "If it self-immolates, as I understand grendels are wont to do, so be it. My main concern is that no insurrectionists escape the long bed they've made for themselves."

"I understand."

"Alright, Yorick," Gausta says. "Go have your fun, then."

The teledoc slides back over, baring an injector. He's so grateful he almost sobs.

CHAPTER 52

Yorick knows, in theory, that he's falling apart. He knows he should be watching this raid from a distance, with a forest of stemtags stuck in his belly. But as the skid hurtles across Ymir's ice, halogens cranked to catch the grendel's silhouette, he feels goddish. His body is a bundle of razors and electrical wire. Everything around him is bright, humming, clean.

He's amped to the gills on hyena and pain-eaters. He can feel the former doing its work as he looks over the squad—*his* squad. Eight company soldiers in raid gear, swaying with the motion of the skid. With their hoods down and chamsuits active, sponging up the gray textures of the interior, they look like eight debodied heads.

But he doesn't want to think about debodying, about Linka in her biotank or prisoners under the teledoc. He only wants to think about his squad. They're young. Smooth faces, raw eyes. Most of them look like offworlders; two look part sealie, but they're from the south, where the company rooted early and deep, so they've never been called half-blood.

All eight of them are so beautiful, so good—the way they angle their shoulders, the way they hold their weapons—it makes Yorick's throat ache. Hyena does that. That's why it's the wardrug he loved and hated most back in Subjugation days.

It comes on like phetamine at first. Laser-scoured focus. Boosted reflexes. Mitochondrial explosions of speed and stamina. But in conjunction with company pheromones, the behavioral tweaks come out to play: upped affection for anyone giving off the right scent, and upped aggression for anyone who's not.

Yorick still remembers the first time he took hyena. He cried inside his tac hood, fogging the goggles, overwhelmed by the cell-deep knowledge that his squad loved him and he loved them. He couldn't move, let alone run surface drills. The soldier who injected him apologized. They said they must have miscalibrated, made the dose too high.

The comedown was a sick shivering thing, and Yorick avoided the drug for weeks afterward out of guilt. He felt like he'd somehow betrayed Thello by using it. He was haunted by the fragile happy memory of it, by a ghost of serotonin.

Now guilt and confusion are impossible fractals. He feels no anger, no anguish, not even prefight fear. The hyena washes all that away and replaces it with a diffuse happiness, anticipation bubbling up underneath. The world binaries: friends inside the skid, targets outside it.

"Bleak up here, isn't it?" The hot-squad's leader is beside him, smiling out the window. "So dark. Like the bottom of a sea."

She's not from here. Her eyes are heterochromatic. Her skin is deep brown. Her face is small but her hands are brawny and bony, combat implants bulging under the flesh. Every part of her is so perfect.

"There's a sea, too," he says. "Out east, under the ice."

She cocks her head. "Right. Right. I remember the school-sim."

Yorick feels his head cock the same way, and when she touches him, idly adjusting his shoulder cam, he feels a thousand tiny hands sprout from his skin and strain for hers. Out of all the drugs he used to approximate desire back when he was young, back when he felt ashamed to lack it, hyena came closest. It's the only thing that ever made him want to touch gently.

"That's the sea where they found the giants' bones," says another soldier, one of the part sealies. "The leviathans."

"I know a woman says those were the Oldies." This soldier has gleaming silver teeth. "When the grendels came for them, they genejacked themselves into big old fishes and hid down there in the dark. Tried to wait them out."

"We can ask," the part sealie says. "We can ask the grendel when we find it. This one talks."

"The algorithm will talk to it," Yorick corrects. He feels a rhythm in his skull, a buzz saw coming online, going off. "You and me are going to hunt it."

The reminder of his differentiation, that he's a stranger brought in by bowlship, not a fellow soldier from the garrison, reignites their curiosity for a moment. Eager eyes flick across him, lingering on his mandible. Yorick feels no shame. The pheromone comfort fills the whole skid, makes it safe as a womb.

"We're going to hunt a grendel," says the soldier with the silver teeth. "And have a few insurrectionists for afters."

They give a happy shudder, and Yorick feels it, too, the sly electric thrill of violence to come. The shudder catches, rippling through the entire squad. Then the giggling, the one side effect the company never managed to excise from their favorite wardrug. Yorick doesn't think they tried very hard.

When silence is essential, hot-squads mostly use pictograms and directionals anyway, no mics. When silence is not essential, there is something about being stalked through a battlefield by oil-black laughter, giddy and predatory, that makes enemies lose their nerve.

He squeezes his eyes shut and ignores the impulse. It's his own small tradition, this vestigial defiance. He always held out against the laugh for as long as he could—maybe trying to assert mastery over his chemistry. Now, when he closes his eyes, he sees mangled Thello in the snow. He sees the chiral molecule that his brother couldn't have meant for him, but did.

It doesn't matter. Hyena makes everything simple: get the grendel, get off Ymir. Gausta will have a bowlship waiting for him. A torpor pool, waiting for him. He'll sink under the stasis fluid and sleep with no dreams. Maybe she can even put him on the long orbit, a slow loop through company space, and by the time he thaws nobody will know about Yorick or Thello Metu.

The buzz saw comes again, choppy, vibrato. Yorick finally recognizes the sound: his own giggle, forced through the mandible's synthesizer. He's joined the laughing already. He was the one who first set it creeping through the skid.

That makes him laugh even harder.

CHAPTER 53

The geotag breadcrumbs lead them to a metal-plugged hole in the ice, northeast of the Maw. Yorick knows he emerged from it only a few hours ago—him and Thello, the grendel, nine clanners—but it feels like a different lifetime. A different Yorick.

Now he's the ninth man of a hot-squad, the ninth head of a beautiful and dangerous organism. The tac hood is so different from the hood he wore down below. Instead of black static, he sees everything: heat trails wafting through the air, quicksilver echoes, color-coded swathes of background radiation.

His chamsuited squadmates are visible again, betrayed by their scalding blood, their thudding organs. Their vulnerability makes him squirm. He needs to keep them safe, needs it like oxygen. The talknet tags each of them with vitals, objectives, directionals. He can see the ghosts of where they intend to be next, like motion blur run in reverse.

The giggling has stopped. They're focused now, studying the cave layout Yorick dredged from rough memory. Hyena doesn't play well with neuroleptics, so they're going down without damper drugs. Only one soldier has done ansible shifts, but all of them have simmed combat in xeno-architecture, and the company's sims have only gotten better in the past two decades.

They know what to do. When the skid shivers to a halt, Yorick knows, too. They spill out of the hatch, establish sight lines, converge on the entrance. He slips into his spot on the flank like slipping into a familiar coat, the one the company always prints for him. He barely feels the cold. Raid gear doesn't have thermal coils, but on hyena it doesn't matter.

Hot-squads run hot.

A simple pictogram shuttles from point to point in Yorick's hood, successive confirmation: bare ice, no sign of the grendel. Maybe they passed it on the way; it could have burrowed into the snow and they thundered past unseeing. Maybe it beat them back here and is waiting down below. He scans his empty stretch of ground one more time, then adds the final all clear.

The squad has consensus. Two sniff the metal plating for explosives or dead man's traps; a third readies the thermite lance. It hisses to life, a miniature sun gushing sparks into the void. The hyena makes Yorick feel like he can track the trajectory of each and every one.

The burn illuminates a few details he missed last time he was here. He sees a snow ridge shaped by hand, not wind. Telltale ripples of melt and refreeze. If this was the clanners' only way in and out of the cave, someone must have seen them out here. Seen them hauling supplies over the ice, sending them down.

But if it was reported, it was probably reported to Petra Zabka, Polar Seven overseer. Yorick shakes himself. His nearest squadmate mirrors it.

The lock melts; the lance goes dark; gloved hands reach into the steam and haul the metal plating away. The squad leader puts Yorick's ghostly future self beside her. He steps forward and peers into the shaft. It's smaller than it seemed in the dark, maybe a quarter the diameter of the mine's main entrance. Not wide enough to drop a skid.

He inspects the rickety lift, cannibalized from bits of hauling track, that he rode to the surface. There are gaps in its metal floor. He crouches to look through one, and way down below he sees the faint alien glow of the cave. He remembers another long climb, a lonely one with an unpleasant task waiting at the end.

The squad leader touches his elbow. He wonders if she knows about Laska's Cradle. Maybe it's part of the prep for surface work in the north. Or maybe the company has expunged it from their net entirely, the way Yorick tries to expunge it.

"Nothing triggered," the squad leader says. "Good and ghostly so far. We can drop a drone—a quiet one—to clarify your map."

The cave layout he shared in the skid reappears in his hood. The drone would do better, but Yorick is wary after seeing the grendel's newest trick, the way it made the ansible's sentinels turn on each other. Not worried—he can't be worried on hyena. But wary.

"If the grendel's down there, it might hack and jack it," he says. "This one talks."

She nods. "Alright. Better to go in blurry than hand over our own eyeballs." She stares at the mouth of the shaft; he pictures the beautiful blue-brown dyad behind her goggles. "No drones. All weapons on manual, how you said. Shielded talknet."

"Are we climbing?" Yorick asks, flexing his hands. These gloves aren't as warm as the last pair, but they have other advantages: a sheathed claw for combat, hydrostatic muscles and cilia for climbing. Better than microspines, but it's still a long way down. The incision he can no longer feel might split open from the repeated motions.

She regards him briefly, then shakes her head. "We'll use spiderlines. Good and fast and quiet." Her voice carries a zen sort of pleasure, like the plan is something pulled from a fond reverie. "Chamsuits are built to fool humans," she says. "Do they fool grendels?"

Yorick looks down at the small feedback cascade where her camouflaged hand imitates his arm, his camouflaged arm imitates her hand. "Sometimes," he says, feeling an incongruous grin on his face. "But this one's a quick learner. And usually, down in the dark, they adapt to see infrared."

"*We* see infrared." She sounds almost offended; Yorick understands why. Hyena doesn't like having its dichotomy—us or them, friends or targets—bridged by similarities. "I guess if we need to, we can drop flares and fuck all visibility equally." She rubs absently at his arm. "Work by echolocation instead."

Her orders scroll through Yorick's hood. The thermite lance flares again, this time to cut the bottom out of the lift. Two squadmates haul a portable fabricator to the lip of the shaft. It starts to spin, regurgitating silvery-gray strands that come out gleaming wet, wafting steam.

By the time the hole is ready, so are the spiderlines. Yorick watches the first soldier step up. He can tell from their movements that it's the one who shuddered, the one with silver teeth. The acid-yellow tag over their head calls them Piro.

Yorick helps them hook on, mollybonding the line to the back of their chamsuit. Another squadmate checks the tensile. Taps their shoulder twice. Piro crouches at the edge of the hole, then tumbles forward, diving into the dark. Yorick feels a warm flush of pride for their grace, their fearlessness. He hooks on next.

"Way down we go," Gausta says in his ear.

Yorick can't tell if it's her, or her avatar, or his own memory. He dives.

CHAPTER 54

The fall feels good. The spiderline spins out behind him at the perfect speed, a hair from freefall, and the skeletal harness in Yorick's raid gear is there to distribute gravity's crush. It turns the rushing dark to a buoyant cloud. He can see his squadmate below him, sense the one above him. The hyena makes it feel like they're sharing a dream.

Then the shaft opens up, and it goes nightmare. The dark peels away, replaced by the sourceless light, almost day, almost night, tingeing everything a poisonous pale green. There are jagged shapes hurtling out of the walls, or seething just beyond them. He can't tell if he's falling down or up. Maybe the spiderline is retracting, pulling him back to the surface.

He switches fully to infrared. The architecture around him turns uniform, everything the same cold shade of violet. It cuts his vertigo as he decelerates. The spiderline brings him to a smooth halt, his toes just scraping the floor. Piro has their carbine drawn, sighting angles; Yorick frees them from the line and takes their place.

The cave is a gelid sea of purple, bubblefabs rising off to the left like red-orange islands. He unracks his carbine, then covers his squadmate while they chase and replace their doppelganger, getting deeper position. The next squadmate has already touched down. He feels their gentle hands unhooking him from the spiderline.

In moments, eight of their nine are fanned out across the cave's shifting floor. The part sealie called Shammet is kneeling, hit harder by the brain-bend; Yorick feels a pang of mirror neuron worry. The squad leader pictograms a little company soldier ducking out of a firefight, flashing the okay: *if you can't ride it out, stay down.*

Yorick adds his assent to the digital wave, throat welling with empathy, then they stalk forward as eight. He scans his wedge of ground and ceiling for any sign of his quarry. Any flashes of waste heat. Grendels run hot, too. Nobody's ever managed to reverse-engineer the pulsing semiorganic reactors that power them.

Most Oldie tech is beyond detritivores. As they push forward into the cave, moving low and quiet, they enter the row of structures Yorick remembers from his brief captivity or else from a bad dream. He sees them as avian skeletons hatching from trapezoidal cysts, then biomechanical trees sprouting downward into the earth.

Maybe the grendel knows what they're for, if they're art or machine or natural extrusions of the unnatural biostone. Yorick doesn't talk to grendels, though. He hunts them. It's been a long time since he hunted in a pack, but the hyena in his bloodstream makes it feel like he never stopped.

The next pictogram is pincered arrows, revolving eyes, a snarl of tendrils. Yorick understands it in his central nervous system, his distributed gray matter, more than he does in his brain: *we clear the bubblefabs, but stay watchful for the grendel.*

He follows his grainy electric ghost along the left flank, gliding between two glowing orange squadmates. They close in on their assigned bubblefab. The red blobs differentiate to their individual heat sources. He sees a sputtering cooker, scalding mugs forgotten on top.

Three bodies—the count is confirmed over and over in his hood. Three clanners in argument, their booming muffled by the bubblefab walls. He can't split words from the northerner cadences, but he can tell they're agitated, maybe scared. Hyena is excited by that. He can feel the giggle building in his throat. He verifies his mandible is muted.

The other pincers of the squad arrive at the other bubblefabs. They report no occupants. Some iterations of the pictogram droop slightly, wistful. Scant targets. Yorick sympathizes, but he's also glad to be one of the shooters. His blood is humming. The bubblefab membrane isn't reinforced. A shock round should penetrate with minimal deviation.

He scopes, finding the center mass of a blister-red body.

A directional bursts in his hood. His head swings, yanked to the firework going off over Shammet's. Her vitals are flaring. She's not screaming, but she's gurgling, a weak wet sound that comes loud on the otherwise silent talknet. She is struggling against air.

He drops the infrared, and it inverts. Shammet's chamsuit is barely visible, a nauseating ripple of green and gray, but the grendel is clear. Its body is all spines. Half are coated in blood. One plunges into Shammet's blurry head, and Yorick almost feels the bone crunch.

Hyena bays and weeps.

But it knows she's dead, so when he snaps his carbine over from shock rounds to shredders he uses a wide spray. His nanotipped rounds join an entropic hail; every squadmate with an angle raised and fired simultaneously.

The grendel doesn't collapse. It vanishes, reappears two meters left, holding the remains of Shammet's corpse over itself like a shield. It drops her. Flickers again, a glitching holo, and is suddenly halfway to the wall of the cave. Flickers a third time, and disappears.

Yorick has no time to figure out this new trick, how it turned its miasmic body into a chamsuit. The squad leader pulses an urgent reminder in his hood, another directional, just before the bubblefab breaks open. The clanners spill out: two with blockguns, one hefting a fat-hunter's harpoon. He wheels and rescopes to his assigned target.

The pair with blockguns go down twitching, but Yorick's clanner does something else. The man's body from hip to rib cage turns to chunks and spatter. The cloud of blood and fabric and bone fragments seems to blossom outward, and in that adrenaline eternity Yorick has time to remember that all weapons are on manual, and he never snapped back to shock rounds.

Hyena shrugs.

Three targets are incapacitated; the fourth will take more work. He pivots back into place, resorbed by the pack, and they hunt. Confirmation loops through his hood: nothing on infrared, now nothing on standard optics, either. He flips filter to echolocation and sees a jumble of shapes, silver on black, none of them the grendel.

He remembers the jammer in the tunnel. The security drones that turned cannibal on the ice. He unmutes his mandible, but the squad leader is quicker.

"It's in our goggles," she says, using the talknet, no easy

pictogram for something that has never happened or even been simmed before. "The grendel's hacking and jacking our feed. Hoods off, implants off if you have them. Naked eyes only."

Yorick shuffles through the spectrum one more time, sees a brief glance of Shammet's sundered body slowly fading to bluish purple. Then he undoes his hood and peels it away from his sweat-slimed face. The cave feels like a living thing again, swelling and contracting. Shadows are not where they should be. The floor seems to be shrinking away from his feet.

Hyena whines, amped nerves overloaded, but it quiets when he sees his squad. They're a ragged row of floating faces, and they're as fiercely beautiful as ever. Stepping off a never-ending precipice is nothing if he does it for them. He forces his way forward.

They comb the cave, find the tunnel entrance still genelocked shut. They fire exploratory rounds on Yorick's call, first shock, then shredder, into the walls and ceiling. The architecture absorbs most of them scarlessly, seems almost to swallow them. None of the rounds drive the grendel out of hiding.

On Yorick's other hunts, on Wodin and Hod, his quarry was savage, single-minded, no smarter than a vatgrown dog. This one is so different. The grendel has been awake for a long time, trapped deep underground. It's patient. He has that memory again, of Thello babbling in the dark, and pushes it away.

The row of structures pulls him in. He angles toward them, drifting slightly out of sync, stretching the invisible tether between him and Piro and the soft-footed squadmate called Nim. They tweak their own trajectories to accommodate him. His chest chokes up with momentary gratitude.

The structures have mutated again, less Euclidean than ever. It brings his vertigo back and reminds him they can't stay down here much longer without damper drugs. Maybe the grendel knows that. Maybe it's waiting them out, waiting for the brain-bend to pulp their cerebellums.

Yorick moves down the row. His nerve suit is stashed in the skid. If he retrieves it and gets it tuned right, using it in tiny bursts, maybe he can stand the interference just long enough to get a glimpse of the—

It erupts from the structure, or was the structure. Yorick has no hood to send the directional for him, to warn the squad, and as he goes for the trigger the grendel's serrated limb drops through his carbine. The weapon cleaves apart in his hands. Another limb hooks his legs; he amps his mandible to scream but the cave floor slams the wind out of him. He only makes a humming wheeze.

The grendel swells above him like storm cloud. He sees the punctures across its body, places where shredders managed to burrow through xenocarbon. The elastic red cracks are all sealed up now. All except one, a gash opening over his head. A mouth.

For a vivid moment he knows the grendel is going to eat him. It will render him down, recycle his traitor's anatomy. Then the wasp voice swarms his ears:

"Don't, Yorick. Don't fucking do this."

Thello's voice in pantomime, pitched too high this time, nothing Yorick remembers hearing. It's making its own scripts now. He thrashes against its weight, trying to free his pinned arms. The grendel's red mouth turns inside out, fractures, reforms as a tendril. It looks wet in the cave light, a wriggling eel. Yorick kicks.

He smells ozone. A squall of shock rounds hammers the grendel from all angles, sparking and sizzling. The overspill bristles his skin as static, stands his body hair on end. But the squad won't fire shredders until he's clear; he knows it in his bones and it makes him want to weep. He focuses on freeing his left arm. The socket is still loose.

He waits for the tendril to sharpen into a spine, to drive through his neck. It doesn't. It goes even finer, becoming the rust-red filament he should have expected from the start. It traces his face, searching for an entry. The grendel wants an explanation.

Yorick jerks his head back, but a pincer clamps around his skull, holding him in place. The filament hisses into the corner of his eye how it did to Thello. He feels it wriggling, sliding past the tear duct. Brushes a nerve, makes him see sparks, and then—

Two children are walking through a desert. Snow, not sand. They are not hand in hand. The older is moving quick and determined, the younger is trailing behind, weeping. They crunch through the snow. They breathe small packets of steam into the icy air. A butterfly is leading the way. The butterfly is a dirty metal drone, buzzing and clacking.

They crest the wind-carved snow dune. On the other side: the ship, a towering freighter, cradled and ready to be launched. The older boy starts to run, skidding down the slope. The younger follows, keeping pace.

"Don't go," he says, in a strange buzzing sob. "Don't go, don't go, don't fucking do this, don't—"

Outside himself, Yorick feels the filament yank backward. It slithers along his orbital. His vision swims. The grendel is somewhere above him; he can feel it shuddering, contorting itself. His left arm feels nearly free. He wrenches it the rest of the way, blind and enraged. He unsheathes the combat claw in his glove and slashes in a wild arc.

The blade splinters on xenocarbon, no better than a graft-knife, but he manages to wrap his hand around one of the grendel's limbs. Hallucinatory afterimages are still stamped behind his eyes: the freighter rising up out of the snow, Thello's pleading face.

That never happened. That never happened, and Yorick is going to tear the grendel apart for piping one more bad dream into his head. He pulses his grip to activate the hydrostatics; silicate muscles swell and climbing cilia burrow into the grendel's slippery armor. He is hanging off the sled all over again, desperate, hideously angry.

Hyena emerges—confused, half drowned—from the neural flurry. It howls along. Shock rounds are still slamming into the grendel, latching where they can, ravenous lampreys. One of its serrated limbs scrapes up and down its own hide, cutting them away. The sound shivers through Yorick's mandible and screams in his real teeth.

The rounds are replaced faster than the grendel can shed them. All seven squadmates have sight lines now, and Yorick is the anchor keeping their target in one place. The grendel reshuffles its body, compacts itself. Then a popping sound, and suddenly he's pulling nothing. Momentum sprawls him again. His skull bounces off the floor.

When he comes up, glove welded to an abandoned spar of flesh and xenocarbon, he sees the grendel fleeing. Its body has streamlined to a single pseudopod, and it moves like some demented spring, end over end. Yorick feels a laugh crawling up his throat, but it doesn't emerge. He unlocks the glove and gets to his feet. Gathers himself. Staggers forward to join the pack.

The grendel has given up its meatshield, and the squadmates circle and backpedal to make sure it doesn't find another.

Shock rounds become shredders. Yorick can hear the giggling. They pen the grendel in and disassemble it with scalpel-tight bursts. Every limb it churns out becomes a stump. It scuttles one way, then the other, slowing.

As it collapses to the shifting floor of the cave, Yorick feels almost ashamed, which means the hyena is wearing off. The grendel is only a grendel in the end. But before the final gust of razor-rain, the one to finish off its half-exposed reactor, the squad leader raises her fist. The carbines go silent.

"Still functioning," she says, with a no-longer-cherubic smile. "Incapacitated. Good."

Four squadmates stay with the grendel, scopes up. Two go back to the bubblefabs to check on the prisoners, maybe turn down the shock rounds and give them a hydration pack. One goes to Shammet's corpse and starts spraying it down with membrane for transport.

Yorick does nothing. Hyena is dead. Maybe the grendel's filament poisoned it somehow when it hotwired his neurons. He crouches on the cave floor, head down, eyes shut. Pain starts filtering back in. His skull throbs countertempo with his shoulder. His patchwork belly is pressed against a running engine, slowly heating up.

Behind his eyes, he sees bodies. The clanner he shredded by accident. The miner whose throat he slit open in the jig. The prisoners twitching in the back of the flyer. The mangled grendel in the cave, mangled Thello in the snow.

Yorick opens his eyes and stares at the receding floor instead. He hunts for his sizzling hate. He hunts for his satisfaction, his triumph, his anticipation for the torpor pool. They all elude him, scurrying off into dark corners.

A minute later the squadmate called Piro joins him,

squatting down to put an arm around his back. They rub
gently at Yorick's exhausted flesh, careful of the shoulder, no
doubt minding the injury notifications in their reactivated
hood.

"Did it speak to you, then?" Piro asks. "With the little
worm?"

"Sort of," Yorick says.

Piro's head swivels toward the quivering grendel, then they
tap a finger against one goggled eye. "Nim, she thinks that's
why it wanted our hoods off. So it could get in our brains."
They pause. "What did it feel like?"

Yorick gets another sheet-lightning flash of the two children
stumbling down the icy dune. The grendel's imitation of Thello's voice, droning and sobbing. Piro's hand keeps moving up
and down, up and down, on his bent back. It doesn't belong
there anymore, or Yorick doesn't belong under it. Hyena is
decomposing in the dirt.

"Bad," Yorick says. "It feels bad."

Piro nods, like they expected as much. Their hand drifts
away.

CHAPTER 55

They put the grendel in a box—a dull gray faraday cube, no internal sensors for it to hack and jack—and shuttle it up to the surface. Gausta's other troops are waiting there, done with their warwork at the Polar Six. Yorick feels no trace of pheromone affection for them. He watches them load the grendel, then the two new twitching prisoners, then finally the two membrane bags.

Both are a red mess; both are handled with a casual precision. Hyena doesn't care for corpses. Yorick can only tell his dead clanner from Shammet by the heavy snow boots, somehow untouched by gore. He stares at them for a little while, the way he stared at the dissolving bodies in Laska's Cradle, then boards his own skid.

He goes back to the Cut and back to the clinic, back to his miniature world of medroids and drug dispensers. The journey is a blur. Gausta's avatar whispers to him about prisoner processing, riots quelled, necessary things. The teledoc welcomes him with phedrine and then resumes its work, reopening him to regrow the torn fascia it only patched over in the back of the flyer.

He sleeps through the hyena comedown, avoids the ugly morning, but he pays a different price. More dreams, bad ones. The neural aftermath of the grendel's filament plumbing cracks in his gray matter. All of them involve the needlegun.

When he wakes up to Dam Gausta's beautiful mottled face, he has a nonsensical bone-deep fear that he has only just been thawed, just been sent north, that everything was a holoplay he will have to perform all over again.

"It must have been a very strange reunion," Gausta says. "Between you and your brother."

Yorick feels no jolt of surprise. Thello's deception was never going to stay intact.

"Was it his clever grendel that scrubbed his real face from the company net?" she asks. "Or was it you, Yorick?"

Yorick works his mandible, unstiffens his silicone tongue. "Does it matter?"

"It's a personal curiosity," Gausta says. "You've been impressive here. Your dalliances are small in comparison to the destabilizing catastrophe you preempted." Her silver eyes are guileless, wide. "In the end, you did what was necessary. I'm pleased for you. Perhaps proud of you, though I can take no credit for innate capacities."

"When's the bowlship?" Yorick asks.

"Tomorrow morning," Gausta says. "A freighter, carrying zinc to Munin. You've earned your rest, obviously."

Yorick tries to feel the stasis fluid on his skin already, surrounding him, submerging him, but his other question bobs him to the surface. "The prisoners? The ones from the ansible?"

A hook tugs the edge of Gausta's perfect lips. "Interrogations are under way," she says. "I may do a few myself. They're being held at a temporary site while we scour the Cut—scour Reconciliation, rather—for the final few conspirators. My briefly tenured overseer chief among them. She's quite skilled at hiding for such an enormous individual."

"What about Thello?" Yorick asks. "His leg?"

Gausta blinks, a minute flicker of annoyance. "I was hoping you'd severed the last tendrils of that parasitic fraternal attachment," she says, "when you sliced open your own abdomen to sabotage the gutjack *he* placed there."

Yorick sees the gutjack bristling in Thello's palm. He sees the medicine capsule tumbling into the snow, chiral molecule coiled inside.

"He nearly finished the job, didn't he?" Gausta asks, stroking her jaw. "Yet you ask after his *leg*."

Splintered dreams churn with Yorick's memories now: the concrete stoop becomes the lip of a torpor pool, the needlegun becomes a grendel's serrated arm. He needs to get off Ymir. He needs to get off Ymir and never come back.

"I'm more interested by the red," Gausta says, eyes gleaming. "Fen. She looks the part of a fearsome revolutionary, doesn't she? Her youth and physicality will make the debodying all the more poignant. All the more potent."

The teledoc on the ceiling is hideous now, sinister. Yorick shuts his eyes and prepares his last question. "Are you well, Dam Gausta?"

A small pause. He can picture the small crease on her forehead. "There is no one for whom it is well," she says, completing the verbal loop, the one that assures them both they are speaking in privacy. "Do you have something more for me, Yorick?"

Yorick opens his eyes. "All those times you visited me when I was in orbit. When I was having my face put back together. Were any of those really you?"

Gausta stares back at him. "Of course, Yorick. The company values you very highly, and so do I."

Yorick considers it, considers two trembling quantum branches, truth or lie. He realizes some things can be true and not matter at all.

"Then don't bring me back here," he says. "Don't you ever fucking bring me back here."

Gausta slowly nods. "I understand your sentiment completely," she says. "It's such an ugly place." She pauses. "Your bowlship launches early tomorrow. I've assigned you protection for the intervening hours, as your weapons have already been recycled. Is there anything else I can do for you?"

Yorick realizes there is. "I want its arm," he says.

Gausta blinks.

"In the cave, during the raid, I tore its arm off," Yorick says, keeping his voice flat. "You asked if I ever keep trophies. I want the grendel's arm."

"How macabre," Gausta says, amused. "I'll see if it can be arranged."

She dissolves away. Yorick exhales. He reaches without looking, finds the same company tablet he always finds, and pulls it onto his lap. He sees his reflection for a moment, haggard, red-eyed. His request for more pain-eater blinks through, accepted.

He sits back and waits to feel good. The teledoc is still above him, a frozen insect. He searches its body for the surgical saw, the one they use to debody prisoners, but doesn't see it.

CHAPTER 56

Two drones are waiting for him when he finally emerges from the clinic, his pain-eater allotment exhausted, his body as whole as the company can make it. They dip to orbit him, stunners unsheathed and swiveling. Gausta's protection is obviously not meant to be discreet.

It's getting dark. The artificial sky is dusked down to a charcoal gray. The east end is still glitching. Yorick watches errant code drizzle through a gash in the firmament. He stares up at the drones, tapping one fingernail rhythmically against his freshly printed injector. The clinic sent him off with phedrine, but he's craving something else.

"When's curfew?" he asks.

The drones stare back, their carmine cams unblinking. One of them does a little loop in the air. They're not equipped to talk, not even to blare company announcements.

He starts to walk, and his new friends fall in behind him. His vague destination is Southern Urbanite Memory. The umber streets are empty. Swatches of bioluminescence start appearing on the way, sleepy eyes blinking open. He thinks of the pulsing ansible, which in turn makes him think of the grendel, and of Thello, and the mudslide will begin if he doesn't stop it now.

When he spots an autobrewer, he scans his neck and buys a glass jug of bacteria beer, the enormous kind that has to be drunk fast before the carbonation dies. Or drunk with other people, but Yorick has never liked that as much.

"Last night on Ymir," he says, raising it in the drones' direction.

They say nothing back.

Yorick names them Te and Vesper, after a pair of half-remembered fat-hunters from the last time he got shitfaced on Ymir. Then he starts that particular process all over again.

CHAPTER 57

The Cut becomes a different animal. The air turns cool, and thick as blood. Vapor-shrouded streets bare their neon skeletons. Yorick remembers when this place nearly belonged to him, and feels nearly happy for a moment. He refills the jug from another storefront nozzle. It's paler this time, bitter. He gulps deep to savor the crackle and bloat in his gut.

Most shops are shuttered. He sees traces of the riot in fire-scarred walls, detritus scattered across the paving. Cleaner bots scuttle here and there, digesting chunks of plaster and shards of glass. He watches one choke down a sliver of broken window. The tinkle-crunch of the denaturing smartglass is oddly melodic.

One of the scrap shops is open, illuminated by an argon-splash sign. The drones follow him there. At the dilating door, he pauses.

"Wait here," he tells drone-Te, or maybe drone-Vesper. "Need to grab something."

He flows down the steps into a sea of jumbled components and circuitry, parts diverted from the recyclers. He starts combing the mess for what he needs. The beer buzz makes his motions feel more intentional and more important, more fated maybe. The pieces come to him, the way they always came to Thello.

He carries the scattered anatomy to an old woman with a shaved head. Her left arm is withered, encased in exoskel that was self-assembled, and she doesn't look at him while she scans his tattoo. She wraps the components and spraybags them. Yorick drinks the last of the bitter beer and swills it around his mouth. The jug emptied too quickly.

He takes the bag in one hand and holds the glass jug in the other. He thinks he will feed it to the cleaner outside, to hear its shivering music, but when he steps out of the scrap shop the cleaners have all scurried away. The artificial sky is black.

Yorick heads for the hotel again. The drones bob along behind him like bad thoughts. Cowardice demands another drink, so he watches for another autobrewer. The walk is shorter than he remembers, though, and he finds the red girl on the next corner. She's squatting stubbornly behind her rack of filter masks. The street is dead empty of customers.

Her blue eyes flit past him to the drones, and her scrawny body tenses. Yorick holds up the jug, corrects, holds up the bag. Components clack together inside it.

"For the jammer," he says. He dredges a name out of the hazy sleepsick memory. "For Masha's jammer."

The girl stares at him.

"That supshop down the street," he says, setting down the bag. "You can go in, eat whatever you want, get some to take away. I'll pay it."

Her stare shifts to his neck, where he is no longer bothering to hide the tattoo. Her lips twist. For a moment she looks just like Fen. "What do you got instead of blood?" she asks. "What's the other half?"

Yorick sloshes the jug of bacteria beer. "You want a coat?" he asks. "Boots? I'll pay the printer."

"Half-blood," the girl says, serrated, gleeful. "Half-blood, half-blood, half-blood."

"What's that mean?" He crouches down. "What the fuck does that mean?"

The girl recoils, eyeing his mandible. She clenches her jaw shut.

"I used to hunt scrap," he says. "Fed it to the company recyclers. They fed us back. Got more food from them than I did from my mother." He pushes the cold glass of the jug against his forehead. "You get food from your mother?"

Her glacial blue eyes barely flicker at the word.

Yorick knows he is ranting at a child, but the words keep spilling out. "People up here, they don't care about their own. They care about deciding who's not. It's an ugly place. It's so fucking ugly."

"You're fucking ugly," the girl says, pumping bravado into her small voice.

He stands up and nudges the bag of parts toward her with his toe. "Just take it."

"You're fucking ugly," the girl repeats.

Yorick wants, momentarily, to unhook his mandible and show her the ragged hole. But then he remembers she's already seen it. She saw it the first day he staggered up the hotel steps. "I'll open the tab for you in the supshop," he says. "It'll close tomorrow when I go offworld." He hesitates, grimacing. He asks. "You know anyone with blue teeth?"

The girl looks at the drones again. Shrugs.

"Alright," Yorick says. "Bye."

"Bye," she echoes.

CHAPTER 58

There's a walking market ambling slow circles around Southern Urbanite Memory; Yorick catches it up and buys a small cold bottle of seed liquor. The beer was working too slowly, making him bloated and tender when what he needs is the hollowing out. He dulls the olfactories in his mandible and takes his first swallow.

It burns, but the burn softens everything else, starts to melt the wax. After his second swig he turns his olfactories back up, stops cheating. The taste is disgusting. He stands there drinking, sometimes sloshing it into the gutter, until the drones circling overhead seem less like pests, more like pets, sleek and friendly and clever.

The Cut becomes blurrily beautiful. Its neon and biolamps, its filthy alleys, its wood-faced inhabitants. When the walking market's selection screen goes dark and he sees his own reflection, he's beautiful, too. The shadows hide the trench of his glasgow grin, the hinge where mandible meets flesh, and they hide his half-blood eyes. He can imagine Nocti's there instead, or his mother's. He gets another bottle for the hotel room.

He sways over to the supshop, drawn to the smell of hot yellow grease. He doesn't know how to open a tab only for small dirty children with orange hair, so he opens it for anyone who walks in, slivers off his anonymous block of company credit. He weaves in and out of the food stalls without speaking, and buys everything he wanted to buy as a child.

Smoked and spiced crickets, doughy pockets full of vatcheese and red sauce, greasy rinds, tubes of bright blue jelly. He finds steamed buns that smell almost as good as the ones Fen bought. He leaves the skimmer meat where it is.

There are company foods, too, things that are the same on every world, how phedrine is the same. He buys a packet of the sugared shells that a company man in a yellow coat used to sometimes hand out. He meanders back to the red girl's corner to waft her the smells, remind her of the tab, but she's gone. Spooked by the drones, or more likely by him.

But his body is filling slowly with helium, so it's hard to feel bad about that. He floats up the hotel steps, leaves drone-Te and drone-Vesper to make friends with the sullen security guards outside. He floats past the dark doorway to Linka's bar. He floats above all the shit in his head.

When the host droid skitters over to greet him, he doesn't even ask about the lifts.

CHAPTER 59

Up the stairwell, the penultimate seven-flight stagger. Past the puddle, past the smeared smiley face, into the corridor. The dead mosscarpet is beautiful. Every step crackles and crunches. He skips his way to room 702 and fumbles a hand free; the door licks his thumb.

It feels like sanctuary when he steps inside and the lock buzz-clunks behind him. He is safe from the cold-blood stares in the street, from the red girl's small contemptuous voice, from the drones that might grow Gausta's face at any second. He's alone and ready to celebrate his final night on Ymir.

"Stubborn Urbanite Memory," he says. "Play me some music."

He trips on something, nearly drops his grease-spotted cone of rinds. A long black box is lying on the floor. Gausta has managed his goodbye gift. He leans down and taps it with his finger, leaving a pock of red sauce. The box turns transparent, revealing the grendel's flash-frozen arm, its lavascape rimed with frost. He sees the imprint of his raid glove. The cilia burrowed deep.

Yorick stares at the detached limb. It's macabre, and wasteful, too—xenocarbon can be repurposed, even if it can't be reverse-engineered. But the grendel wanted him to have it. He is almost sure of that now, after a dozen jagged dreams. Maybe it's meant to be a reminder of his many sins.

He waits to feel bad, but he can't. He's past tender. He's hollow now, in the best possible way.

"What sort of music would you like to listen to, Mister Bellica?" the hotel asks.

"Compose something." Yorick touches his face and feels a half-mandible grin. "Please."

He shoves the box into the smartglass closet.

CHAPTER 60

The hotel has been learning from Nocti. Yorick hears the ghost of those same strings, can almost see the musician and his peeled-open leg. He imagines the hotel collating sounds from Linka's bar, sieving out melodies, reassembling the patterns that made heads turn and conversations taper. It adds a clacking drum, electronic pulses, whispering voices.

Wake music. It sounds like wake music. Yorick snakes his head to it as he goes to the kitchen corner, spills his bags on the fold-down counter. He eats standing up. Even with his olfactories cranked, the tastes are shades of what he remembers. Indistinct. He was hungrier as a child, and he had a fully flesh mouth, and maybe that makes a difference.

But he's a different kind of hungry now, so he keeps eating. Tastes matter less than the textures, the temperatures. Those matter less than the consuming. He needs to fill his mouth, his gullet, his stomach until it aches. He wolfs down the steamed buns and packs the splintery crickets after them. Sauce spills down the front of his coat.

He shrugs it off, lays it carefully on the floor, and the room is hot now so he strips the rest of his clothes off, too. He folds them and drapes them on the nonsensical chair. He inspects his belly in the smartglass mirror. The incision has dwindled to a pale pink scar. He feels the weight of his full stomach behind it, a painless pressure.

The teledoc told him not to eat. He remembers that now. His regrown tissue is still delicate, and he has torpor in the morning.

"Humans are detritivores," he tells the mirror, and shoves the last bun into his mouth.

CHAPTER 61

His boots disappear for a while; he circles the whole room searching before he feels them still on his feet. The hotel's music has evolved, looping through itself. Maybe the temperature flux is part of the performance. He's cold again, shivering, so he throws the sauce-stained coat back over his naked body. The geophage he must have freed from its canister splats to the floor.

He scoops it up, apologizes, cradles it in one arm while he stumbles over to the heating vent. The warm air ripples away his gooseflesh. The geophage squirms, searching for mess. Yorick pats it absently as he stares at the gap between the closet and the cubic nightstand. He pictures Thello crouched there, small and teary-eyed.

He pictures an older Thello diving across the concrete stoop, coming up with the needlegun, taking aim. He can't remember which hand his brother used to pull the trigger. The memory keeps splintering, reassembling.

There's a cold weight in his coat pocket. He reaches inside and finds the second bottle from the walking market, still chilled. The prescience astounds him, the prescience of the less-fragmented Yorick who bought it for him, knowing he would need it in this precise slice of time.

It uncaps with a comforting click—

61.1

He is drinking with the geophage, or at least near the geophage. The little vatgrown creature sucks the stains out of his coat while he sits and watches and swills stinging mouthfuls from the bottle. He finished the food before he thought to offer it any. His fingertips are shiny with grease. He is glutted, distended.

"He blew half my fucking head off," he tells the geophage.

Yorick mimes the act, raising his hand with two fingers forming the blunt mouth of the needlegun. His arm shakes. He sees himself in the smartglass closet again. He remembers the grendel's limb is boxed up inside it.

"There was a therapy algorithm in the clinic," he tells the geophage. "They told me to pick a phrase. A verbal anchor. Something to focus on while they put the conduits in."

His overfull stomach heaves. It's time to hollow out again, before—

61.3

The world slants on his way to the toilet. He falls. The room hurtles around his head and chyme sloshes in his stomach. Some comes burning up his throat. He swallows hard and lurches back to his feet, unbothered. He is safe here. Insulated. He is a child hiding in the maintenance room, drinking from the bucket.

Yorick kneels on a smooth cold floor. He crawls his hand deep, past his artificial tongue, past the gelflesh that keeps his wound sealed tight. He hits the familiar flap and his gag reflex finally kicks. Slurry gushes out hot, half digested. Wave after wave of it: erupting from his mouth, leaking out his nostrils, aching his ribs and making the incision burn.

He empties out, and for a beautiful moment time runs in reverse. The geophage has followed him to lap up the floor spatter. He watches it work for a while, then sways upright, pedaling the air. He goes to the sinktop to clean his mandible.

He won't remember tonight, this last night on Ymir, and tomorrow he'll climb from the wreckage and leave forever. He ducks his head under the cold gush of water. Emerges dripping.

"Practicing for torpor," he tells the geophage.

He thinks of two children stumbling down a snowy hill, Thello's buzzing voice: *take me with you, take me with you, take me—*

61.5

Yorick is stretched out on the floor, back arched, trying to make his spine crack. He can feel air bubbles lurking in carti-lage. The geophage has curled up and died. The hotel's music has gone on too long and begun to cannibalize itself. Its syn-thesized instruments stutter, disjointed, arrhythmic. The whis-pering voices sound like people he knows.

"Southern Troglodyte Mezzanine," he says.

"Good evening, Mister Bellica," comes the host droid's voice. "How can I improve your lived experience?"

"Need a car," he says, sitting upright. "Up north end. To find some doxy."

"I'm afraid it's against our policy to provide transportation to this sector of Reconciliation," the hotel says. "Southern Urbanite Memory prioritizes the safety of our guests."

"It's fine, because—" Yorick shuts his eyes, losing the sentence. "It's fine. It's company business." He swallows back an aftersurge of bile. "You know anyone with doxy?"

"I'm sorry, I'm afraid I didn't catch that."

He pries the boots off his feet and carries them to the smartglass closet. He stares at his reflection again. The boot dangling from his fingers becomes a needlegun. Somewhere a company drone snaps its camera shut.

Don't, Yorick. Don't fucking do this.

Yorick's heart strums his ribs. The stoop, the drone, the needlegun. The stoop, the drone, the needlegun. He thought that was going to be his last day on Ymir. It nearly was. He drops the boots and slides the closet open, braced to see the grendel in full, somehow regrown from its severed limb.

All he sees is Gausta's black box.

61.8

"Sunburned Urbanite Mammary."

Yorick has wedged himself into the gap between the closet and the nightstand, shoulder blades flush to the wall. He is not sure how long he's been here. Oily tears keep sliding down his face.

"Yes, Mister Bellica?"

He rubs his head. "Turn off the music, please. And send a droid up with a purge virus. I need to be my—I need to have my faculty. Faculties. More than one."

"I would be happy to do that for you, Mister Bellica."

The music ends. The silence pounds.

CHAPTER 62

Southern Urbanite Memory brings him his discreet black phial of purge virus on a mirror-bright tray. The host droid watches while he takes three tries to load the injector. He finally puts it to his neck. Microneedles punch through skin with a metallic whisper.

"We noticed that you are ending your stay with us shortly," the host droid says. "Southern Urbanite Memory will be very sorry to see you go! Would you be interested in offering feedback on our services?"

Yorick's head rushes off his shoulders. He sways. "Everything was good."

"Earlier during your visit, you noted a *bad smell* in one of our double-luxury suites, room 702. Was that bad smell addressed to your satisfaction?"

Yorick sniffs the air. "Yeah. Think so."

The host droid dances, delighted. The purge virus kicks and Yorick feels a sick shiver go through his whole body. He barely makes it to the shower before the first wave of byproduct from his deep-cleaned liver and bloodstream lavas out.

"Would you recommend Southern Urbanite Memory to

other company employees?" the host droid asks, stopped politely outside the bathroom.

Yorick's gut is a pressure cooker. He clutches a corroded handgrip on the shower wall, ignoring the chirp of the droid until it wanders out, shutting the door behind it. He lets the purge virus work for a while, rinses himself periodically.

But he knows he can't be fully sober for this, either. He'll lose his nerve. He staggers out of the shower and goes to Gausta's gift.

CHAPTER 63

Grendels have distributed processing, a dozen odd nodes that are in constant flux around the reactor—not unlike the nervous systems of the cleverer cephalopods, the ones the company breeds on some colony worlds for marine work. Humans have an echo of the same in their limbic system, in reflex and instinct.

Yorick feels instinctive now, as he opens the box and pulls out the grendel's severed limb. The xenocarbon stings his palms. He lays it on the puffy white bed, then hunts his tablet, finds it facedown on the counter. There is a fresh crack in the screen, a Cut in the ice. He forgets dropping it. It's functional, though, and boots with no issue.

He teases a gossamer thread from the tablet, searches dumbly for a corresponding port on the grendel's armor. Lets it slither back, and runs a touchless scan instead. He finds the small node midway up the limb. Something is still moving inside, a slow churn of code fed by the last dreg of energy from an absent reactor.

He needs an intermediary, but when he taps into the local net his hounds are gone. He combs the whole Cut for them, not understanding, squinting at the blurry screen. It takes him a full minute to remember that the grendel has been caught. His contract has been completed. The hounds have self-deleted.

They were fully useless down in the tunnel, but he needs them now that there is no rust-red filament to accept or ignore. He needs an interface to access this small near-dormant fragment of machine mind. The hotel net might be enough, but without his hounds he has no way of cutting inside. Southern Urbanite Memory is only so accommodating.

There is one other person who might be able to do it. She fucking hates him.

CHAPTER 64

Yorick only remembers his boots halfway down, so he enters Linka's bar barefoot, wrapped messily in spiderwool, the grendel's limb tucked under his armpit. His empty belly is refilling with dread. He dreads speaking to Linka, and he dreads the things he will do to make sure she helps him.

But prying open the node, accessing the buried sliver of the grendel's mind, is more important than anything else now. It drives him across the darkened bar. His bare feet slap, leaving wet crescents behind. He accidentally stepped in the fourth-floor puddle.

Linka's frozen arms are where he left them. He sets the grendel's on the bartop and pulls out a screeching stool. He can feel his pulse under his tattoo.

"I need your help, Linka," he says. "I know you're here. You're always fucking here."

No answer, no motion.

"I'm sorry for what I said last time. About paying for your transplant. About everyone making their own fuckups. It was stupid."

Nothing.

"Only two days since that, right?" He climbs carefully onto the stool, stares at the vats. The purge virus has barely finished with him, and he wants a drink. "Mad days, though. Two mad days in the Cut. You and Nocti been alright?"

He leans forward across the bar, willing her to respond, ears strained for her synthesized snarl.

"I need your help," he repeats. "There's something I need to see. Something I can't get out of my own head. I need you to use your neural construct to hook me and this node into the hotel net. Deep as you can." He pauses at the intersect of two fragile quantum paths. "I know you can do it, Linka. I know you're the reason the lifts don't work."

She bites at last, her electronic voice approximating disdain. "Right. I hate company men so much I hacked the lifts to make them walk."

"That's not why." Yorick puts his hand on the grendel's limb. "Help me do this, Linka, and you never have to see me again. You and Nocti will forget about me fast." He takes a slow breath. "If you don't help me, or if you try to fuck this up for me, the drones and guards outside come crack the lift open."

"So?" Linka snaps, buzzing.

"So no more lying low for Nocti," Yorick says. "Except for in a company prison. I don't want that, so fucking help me."

Linka doesn't speak for a long moment. Yorick imagines the dancing synapses in her skull, the face contorting in the dark of the biotank. She knows him well enough to know he'll do it. She knows he's a black hole.

"Okay, Yorick," she says, because she even knows his real name now. "Okay."

He wanted her to rage at him, curse at him. Her fear makes him feel so sick.

CHAPTER 65

He lies on the bartop with the grendel's cold limb resting on his chest. Linka's arms whir around him, over him, trailing electrode cables. She tethers his scalp to her biotank, tethers her biotank to the grendel's sluggish node. They become a trinity.

"The hotel's going to notice this," Linka says flatly. "What I did, my blind spot, I did that slow. Took six fucking months. I made sure I didn't wake up any subsystems, made sure I covered my tracks." One arm above his head helps another switch manipulators, go from a gripping claw to a microtool. "This isn't like that. This is a deep hack all at once. It'll trigger countermeasures."

Yorick adjusts the spiderwool clinging to his groin. "I'll be quick."

"You'll have to be." Linka's arms pause. Shiver. "Okay. Ready. I'm plugging you in."

A firework detonates behind Yorick's eyes and his whole body spasms. His back arches. Finally cracks. Then his body is gone, and he's seeing through Linka's eyes, through her many arms. Hyperreal textures in panorama: the foam topping the vats becomes a cumulus cloudscape, the bartop is an endless gray plane. His foot rises off it like a sheer cliff.

For a nanosecond he sees through her other cams, too, sees not just the bar and lobby but slices from all over the hotel and even outside it, all the cams she's managed to pirate or rig up on her own. He catches a glimpse of a familiar figure clad in a black body glove.

Then it falls away, and he's drifting in an electric sea. Southern Urbanite Memory churns all around him, its behavioral loops and processing patterns, its guest data and infrastructure. He sees an echo of simplistic machine pleasure from positive customer feedback, Oxo Bellica, room 702. He sees the wandering host droids as fingers tapping out a listless rhythm.

Something else is in here with him, another intruder. Yorick turns his un-head. The fragment of the grendel is now a swirl of foreign code, shifting, mutating. Not so unlike its corporeal self. It stretches its digital tendrils, maybe by reflex, sampling a swathe of the hotel's data. Its movements are sluggish, clumsy.

The tendrils retreat as Yorick approaches. "It's me," he says, knowing he might be talking to nobody, knowing this fragment might be nowhere near sentient. "I need you to show me something." He tries to crouch on un-legs, make himself smaller, slower. He doesn't want to trigger any shadows of the reflex that killed four miners. "You've been in Thello's head."

The fragment ripples. Yorick hopes it's recognition.

"I need you to show me the day I lost my jaw," he says, and far away he feels his heartbeat accelerate. "Not my memory. His. Show me the stoop. The drone. The needlegun."

He extends his un-hand, remembering how the grendel offered its filament. The fragment doesn't move. Doesn't respond. Maybe doesn't understand. There's no time to make it, so with only a small pang of guilt, Yorick digs his way inside.

CHAPTER -5 (V2)

A wasp is crawling along the concrete floor of the apartment. One of its wings is torn off. The other strums furiously, use- lessly; the meaty buzzing noise makes Thello flinch. He tries to hide it, because Yorick is crouched beside him and Yorick never flinches.

He glances sideways. His older brother's eyes are fixed on the insect. His face is expressionless. It's always that way in the apart- ment, even when their ma is gone. It got stuck.

"Once you start killing something, you should finish," Yorick says. "Here." He flexes his pale sharp thumb, hovers it over the wounded wasp. "On the head. You just push down, and it's dead."

Thello's stomach revolts, how it does with skimmer meat. He feels hot all over. "I didn't take its wing off," he says. "Just found it."

His older brother blinks. "Oh. Kill it anyway, Thello. Or it'll crawl in your ear when you're sleeping."

Thello grabs one ear by instinct, pins the cartilage against itself, sealing it shut. "No, it won't."

"Sure," Yorick says. "That's why you have those dreams, I bet. You already got a little wasp crawling around in there."

Thello scowls. "No," he says. "No. Stop lying."

His older brother rocks on his haunches. "Wasps can't grow new wings," he says. "That's true, no lie. And if it's only got one wing, it can't fly. Can't find food."

Thello feels a small flicker of hope. "Maybe a teledoc can grow it. They know how to grow parts."

Yorick puffs air out of his mouth; Thello joins in with a blurt of automatic laughter even though he doesn't know if he was joking.

"Just use your thumb," his older brother says, solemn. "And push down hard. Please, Thello?"

Thello's stomach churns. His ears are boiling hot. He doesn't want wasps in them, but he doesn't want to touch the buzzing thing, doesn't want to push down hard. He drifts his hand overtop of the insect. His thumb is a bit smaller than Yorick's. A bit darker.

It makes him wonder sometimes what their da's hand looks like, but Yorick never seems to wonder about that, says their da is dead or far away and a company man, which is the worst kind of offworlder. His hand falters.

"It's okay," his older brother says. "I'll do it."

Thello watches Yorick kill the wasp, grind the ball of his thumb through its exoskeleton skull, a final buzzing frenzy and then quiet. His older brother has a flush on his pale face. He smears the guts on the concrete floor, a little curve like a smiley mouth.

Thello's rush of gratitude is tempered with something else, something he feels often around his older brother and doesn't know the word for, never found explained on the company tablet they hide under the cooker now—

CHAPTER 66

Yorick feels his thumb twitch in another world, the one where he is lying on the bartop with Linka's arms spinning around him. In the smaller world he feels the grendel's fragment expanding around him, pulling vast swathes of data from the hotel, dredging the electric sea.

Southern Urbanite Memory has noticed them, but Yorick can't stop now. Not until he finds the stoop, the drone, the needlegun. He hurls himself into the singularity again.

CHAPTER -4 (V2)

*M*ore company ships are coming down, falling soft through a veil of gray snow. They look small from here, from their grandmother's surface colony, but Thello knows they are immense towering hives. He knows they launched from other worlds, and that gives him a strange pulse of excitement, makes his blood electric. He's seen those worlds, and not only on his tablet.

His night-friend, the one who cannot be a grendel, because you don't talk to grendels, has shown him them in dreams: foggy Hod, cliff-ringed Baldr. Now, watching the ships, he puts his spiderwooled hand to his chest and feels his own accelerating heart.

Yorick sneaks up behind him and dumps slushy snow on his head. He yelps, shakes it off, chases his older brother back toward the sagging ice-houses. The idea of going in one of those ships, leaving Ymir, stays with him for a week, two weeks. He even tells Yorick about it.

But then it fades, because he falls in love—he is almost sure— with Basta, the sealie woman who lets them try her vapor pipe. He doesn't tell Yorick about it, but Yorick catches him rubbing himself against the gelbed, eyes shut, thinking hard about her, and his older brother's apartment mask cracks into confusion and contempt.

Thello realizes Yorick is ashamed of him. He cries all night, muffling it in his arm.

CHAPTER -3 (V2)

*T*hello feels a sly hand between his shoulder blades on his way down the stairs. He stumbles, smacks into the wall. When he regains his balance, when he turns around with a furious sob in his throat, he sees Yorick glaring back.

"So hit me," his older brother says. "When people push you, you hit them. They want you to do it. It's no different from the jig."

Tuq is lurking behind him, smiling her blue-stained smile. She's beautiful and awful at the same time. Once she ran her hand over his bare arm, so soft, almost reverent. Then she told him half-bloods only live half as long, because they're not bred for Ymir.

He knows it's a lie, something recycled from her ma or da, and he knows if he tells Yorick, Yorick will cut Tuq away, never even speak of her. But he wants Tuq to keep coming over, because she might run her fingers down his arm again, and because she makes Yorick laugh, sometimes, in a way he wishes he could make his brother laugh—

CHAPTER -2 (V2)

*T*hello can barely lift his legs. He and Yorick have been sparring for over an hour, and now he's sweat-drenched, exhausted. The shoes feel like blizzard anchors.

"One more," his older brother keeps saying. "One more, one more."

Thello knows Yorick is leaving angles open on purpose, making invitations. He wants to be hit, hard, and every time Thello pulls the strike in, pulls it short, he gets more agitated. But Thello can still hear the reverb of a cracking femur, from a jig almost a month ago, and he can't risk hearing it again. He tells himself he is being cautious of his brother's counter.

Finally they stop. Thello throws himself down on the ground, hands on his head, breathing hard. His older brother drops to a crouch.

"Why don't you get angry anymore?" Yorick asks, almost suspicious.

"You're not meant to be angry when you jig," Thello says. "You're meant to be thinking."

"I don't mean the jig," his brother says, even though once he said everything means the jig. "Why don't you get angry at our ma? Angry at the cold-bloods?"

Thello knows something happened with Tuq and Mara and the rest. He knows his older brother has cut them away. The other day he saw him using a company tablet, freshly printed, gleaming black. Thello is not sure why he blanked the screen so quickly.

"I don't know," he answers. "Got tired of it." He pauses. "Not everyone's like our ma. Or like Tuq and Mara and them."

"Who?"

Thello feels a flush of happiness to enumerate them, all the small burning stars he's found when his brother is at the auto-hauler lot or lying tranqed and boneless on the apartment floor. "The old men on bottom level," he says. "The ones who make the funeral masks. Bisi and their cousin. Ola, Linka, Graffen. Doro from the ice, that red with the bad leg."

The names bounce off his brother's mask. Thello realizes they are not people Yorick would want to know, and since he does still get angry it sets off a crackling flare in his chest.

His brother doesn't notice. He is staring off into nowhere. "I'm going to Shipfall tomorrow," he says. "They said I can't bring you, not yet. Will you be alright with ma?"

Thello's world lurches. "What? What do you mean?"

"You remember the grendel game?" his brother asks. He puffs a half laugh through his nostrils. "I'm going to do that, but real. Be a fucking company man for a while. Then you and me are getting off Ymir and never coming back."

Thello doesn't understand. A small part of him remembers the night-friend, the thing that spoke to him sometimes when he was small, but there are no grendels on Ymir.

"You and me, Thello," he says. "Ma will be dead by then." He pauses. "Don't let her push you around. She's skinny now. Scrawny."

Thello realizes he does not know his brother, maybe never did, and his anger and confusion are tinged with something else.

Something that has been skimming under the surface of their frozen lake for years and years now.

"And those people," his brother says. "Your little list."

Thello fights back the stinging pressure behind his eyes. "What about them," he says, but already knowing, not asking.

"Don't trust them," his brother says. His voice is flat as a droid's.

Thello wants to hit him, wants to hug him too tightly to breathe, wants everything at once. But he knows it's better this way. It's better that Yorick leaves the Cut, where he looks so hurt, so hunted, before he does something that could—

CHAPTER 67

In another world, Yorick is weeping. His ribs heave, and because he is horizontal on the bartop he chokes on his own phlegm. He weeps because he never protected Thello at all, only damaged him, and if Thello ever loved him it was the way they loved their ma, half of it dread and angst.

In the smaller world, the grendel's fragment has become a maelstrom, swelling and writhing as it devours the hotel. Southern Urbanite Memory hurls company countermeasures, oil-black sentinels. It tries to debride, cutting away chunks of its own code. The grendel's fragment is implacable, ravenous.

Yorick can't tell if it's understanding or only devouring, if it's going to burn the hotel down around their heads while he is lying prone in Linka's bar. But he can't leave yet. He has to find what he came for—the drone, the stoop, the needlegun— and watch it for the sickening confirmation. Watch as Thello shreds his mask apart at last.

He has always been the grotesque in this ballad. He hunts for his last day on Ymir.

CHAPTER -1 (V2)

*T*hello is waiting on the stoop for Yorick, and he is afraid. Not of the company drone drifting nearby. He's accustomed to it now, the way it stalks him every time he sets foot outside the apartment. Not of their ma's shade, even though she had no proper funeral, no wake. He knows she can't be any worse dead than she was alive.

Thello is afraid of the company man, walking toward him now in an easy loping gait, shoulders back, unburdened. His older brother's face, usually so stiff and solemn, has the split beginning of a grin. It makes Thello think of the recordings people show each other in darkened bars, company soldiers giggling as they load prisoners, spray down corpses.

He wonders if his brother was laughing when he cooked the Cradle. The thought makes his pulse pound in his throat. He tries to make his face a mask, how Yorick always did, when he asks the question: Where were you?

His brother bats it away. His eyes are guiltless. Thello asks the question again, even though he already knows the answer in his gut. He needs to hear his brother admit it. If things will ever be right again, or near to it, he has to admit it. He has to tell him he was drugged and deceived, that the past year has been a nightmare he's only now waking from.

But Thello keeps thinking of the wasp crushed under his brother's unworried thumb.

"You just saw who was winning," he realizes aloud. "Saw you could get some sort of revenge."

His brother breaks and his voice splinters for the first time Thello can remember. He babbles about the company algorithm, about the poisonous armistice they announced a day ago. He babbles about some night Thello hardly remembers, from when they were small, sneaking into a fountain and pretending it was a torpor pool.

The desperation reminds him of their ma, drunk and apologizing. It makes him even more furious. When his brother pulls a company weapon out of his coat, he is too numb to even be afraid.

"Go on," he says. "Fucking shoot me, then. Before I tell everyone it was you who boiled Laska's Cradle."

Yorick rocks back on his feet. Thello realizes he thought that secret was still a secret. Thought his avatar had done well enough to cover for him, thought his little brother was still that trusting, still the little boy chasing after him at night.

"Tell me where you were, then," Thello begs, latching to a sliver of mad hope that somehow he is wrong, and it was someone else who murdered seventy-eight hibernating people and snatched all the light from Doro's eyes, Doro who is Laska Clan until the armistice disbands the ones who were not dissolved in their own torpor pool.

His brother is somewhere else, not hearing. He raises the gun, and for a moment Thello thinks he is going to die on this stoop. The company drone has closed its cam, how they do when company soldiers misbehave in the Cut, when beatings go too far.

But his brother is holding the gun to his own head. "They'll never love me," he mumbles.

Thello feels a jagged fear chine through everything else, splitting his anger and grief. "Don't, Yorick." His voice trembles. "Don't fucking do this."

His brother is not there. His eyes are emptied out.

A tendon moves in his pale wrist, and Thello lunges to stop him, to pry the weapon away. The needlegun goes off like a wasp nest exploding.

CHAPTER 68

Yorick is still screaming Thello's scream when he gets yanked from the hotel net. Back in Linka's bar, every piece of smartglass on the walls is seething with static. The lights jitter off and on. The host droid's distorted voice blares from all ports.

"Apologies, Mister Bellica, I'm afraid I didn't hear you. Apologies, I'm afraid. Satisfaction visit bad one of our bad one of our bad one of our *bad bad bad bad*."

"Fucking thing," Linka grates. "Can't get to the—" Her arms spasm. "Fuck!"

Everything goes still at once. Dead smartglass, no lights. The host droid's voice cuts out and leaves only the faintest echo in the black.

Yorick drops his head back against the bartop. He's still caught behind Thello's eyes, watching himself put the needle-gun to his temple over and over. He's coated in sweat, adrenals spiked by the feedback. His heart is a hummingbird.

By the time it fades, by the time he's reassembled himself in the dark, Linka has a tiny blade poised a micrometer from his eyeball.

"What was that?" she demands. "How'd it do that? You said this was the grendel's fucking *storage node*."

Yorick takes a raspy breath. He tries to speak without moving the muscles of his face, in case it brings him toward the blade. "I thought it was."

"You think a lot of dumbsick things." Linka's other arms are whirling, unhooking the electrode cables. "It crashed the whole hotel. Nearly crashed my construct."

"Linka?" The hoarse voice drifts through the empty bar. "You okay, Linka?"

Yorick doesn't dare turn his head, but he listens to Nocti's soft steps. He can feel the musician's spindly limbs displacing air. He can smell the unwashed body glove.

"You have to get out of sight," Linka says, terse. "I lost my cams, but the guards outside, they must be on their way in."

"Locked out," Nocti says. "Whole hotel's sealed up."

"Only until it reboots," Linka says. "Shit. Shit." The blade quivers over Yorick's eye. "My blind spot might be gone when it does. You both have to get to the loading bay. Slip out the back as soon as the hotel unseals."

"What about Oxo?" Nocti asks, and Yorick realizes he is not part of the *both*. "Yorick, I mean. Hello, Yorick."

"Hello, Nocti," Yorick says, remembering how Nocti watched him from the corner table, showed him to the wake. Realizing who supplied neuroleptics to Thello and the clanners down in the cave. "The hotel's been thieving you. Taking melodies."

"We're all thieving each other," Nocti says, then, to Linka a second time: "What about Yorick?"

"I don't know," Linka says. "I don't fucking know."

Yorick imagines the arms rolling him over, a jab and twist of the blade in the right spot, his body folded up fetal to fit in a brewing vat. There would be some sort of irony to that. But for the first time tonight, he has no desire to stop existing.

"I'm coming with you," he says. "I'm going to get us into the camp. Get Thello and the grendel and the rest out. Then I'm going to get us into the ansible."

Fen's laugh comes out of the dark, soft and contemptuous and edged with pain. She can move quietly when she wants to after all. "You're going to die," she says. "I'll do it, Linka. Hands to throat, no blood. Put the sticker away."

The blade hovers a moment longer, then retreats. Yorick sits up. Nocti and Fen are at the bar, like they're waiting for drinks. The musician looks unwell. The circles under his eyes are deeper than ever and his black body glove has a yellowish stain on the chest. His spidery white fingers flick against his leg, trying to touch the instrument inside.

Fen looks small. Yorick was not expecting that, not expecting to see her fury all sluiced away. Her broad shoulders are slumped. Her snowstorm eyes are quelled. She might not even enjoy suffocating him. She'll do it out of duty, though, to Thello and her fellow clanners, to the seventy-eight she learned about as a child.

"It wasn't Thello," he says. "It was me. I shot myself in the face."

No flicker. It doesn't matter to Fen, even though it matters everything to him. She knew all along who the monster was. Yorick makes to slide off the bar, but Linka stops him. Her arms coil around his midsection and hold him in place.

"Let me undo this," Yorick begs.

Fen swings up onto the bar, no hint of stiffness from the wounds he left with his graft-knife and the grendel excoriated with its serrations. She gives the severed limb a baleful look, maybe remembering that, then tosses it away and pushes him horizontal.

Yorick is sleepsick again, feeling the cold slick premonition he felt that first morning in the mine: he will kill Fen or Fen will kill him.

"Linka," he says. "Please. All those prisoners, they're going in the biotank because of me. But I can stop it. Let me stop it." He gives a wild laugh, almost a hyena laugh. "Don't ruin your fatality rating. Remember? Picking noodles out of my—out of my fucking pericardium?"

Linka doesn't answer; Yorick twists his head to Nocti.

"I'll die after," he says. "I promise. I'll wander off into a blizzard, how they do in the ballads. Last night on Ymir. But not yet. No dirge yet."

Nocti takes his fingers off his leg like it scorches them. His sad sealie eyes dance away. "Goodnight, Yorick."

He's alone with Fen, and there is no Thello here to keep him alive, to make sure she at least gives him good jig shoes. His voice pitches up, a whining insect. "Let me undo this one thing," he pleads. "Not all of it. Not anywhere near. But this thing. Let me undo this thing."

She wipes her massive hands on her spiderwool, and Yorick knows it's too late, too late.

Time can't run in reverse.

"It's not about Thello," he says, still fumbling for the right echo. "Not about me. Not about you. Ymir free and the company dust. Ymir free and the company—"

The hands wrap around his windpipe. His mandible sputters and buzzes like a wasp with one wing. Fen's face blurs and whirls above him; fleshy shadows push in from the sides. Yorick sees Thello's face instead, his brother's head sliding under the teledoc's saw.

No clemency this time. He could have begged Gausta again,

but he spent those critical hours drinking with a geophage, and even Gausta can't alter so many charges of conspiracy and insurrection. Thello will go into the dark and never come out. The company won't sponsor him. They won't hook him to a neural construct in a hotel.

Yorick grieves. His lungs burn. There's a foamy roar in his ears, a long needle piercing the center of his forehead, his brain begging for oxygen. He sees a blur in his peripheral as Linka and Nocti move in uncanny sync: Linka's arm wraps around Fen's elbow and Nocti darts forward, saying *wait, wait, we can't, we shouldn't.*

Nocti's hoarse voice blends with Linka's bellowed protest. Yorick is dimly grateful to them both, even as Fen shrugs Nocti off, sends him sprawling, even as she bears down against Linka's arm. Her grip slacks for a half second while she readjusts. Yorick sucks down a half mouthful of air, but it will only prolong the process.

His starving neurons put on a last holoshow: the smartglass on the walls starts to pulse on, off, on, off. It glows the same color as the ansible, bathing the bar in a ghostly electric blue.

The pulse accelerates. Fen's head turns. Her hands lighten just enough for Yorick to follow suit, twisting his bruised neck by increments under her fingers. It's an interesting hallucination. Host droids are spilling down the stairs, weaving their way into the bar, a procession rerouted from every dusty corner of Southern Urbanite Memory.

Yorick doesn't have air to laugh. Doesn't have synapses to guess. The droids stumble into each other as they pad across the floor, following his smeary footprints.

"Linka?" Fen asks.

"Don't know," Linka says. "The reboot never finished. The hotel's still sealed. Or looks it, at least, in the cams I got back."

Her arms are still tight around Yorick's torso. "It's like it's sleepwalking."

"Dreaming," Fen mutters, and her hands peel away from his neck.

Yorick gasps. He forces air down into his searing lungs, imagining all the crumpled alveoli reinflating. It's the first breath after torpor. He takes another. Another. He watches, through blurry eyes, as Fen goes to retrieve the grendel limb.

The droids get there first. They lift it off the floor with their manipulators—carefully, almost reverently. They hold it aloft like a reliquary.

"Apologies, Mister Bellica," the hotel says, through all the droids at once. "I am experiencing an error. Would you like me to arrange a surface tour this evening? A hazardous blizzard is expected. Northern Ymir is renowned for its hazardous blizzards."

CHAPTER 69

If Fen decides to finish strangling him, it will take more than thirteen hacked-and-jacked host droids to stop her. But for now, she leaves him alone. When Linka's arms finally release him, the red even lets him get up. He slides down to the floor on unsteady legs. He leans there on the bar, fingers exploring his swollen throat, while the droids mill around him.

They stay between him and Fen, a ring of clumsy bodyguards, but apart from the chitinous clicking of their joints they've gone silent again. The grendel limb keeps circulating, passed from one cluster of manipulators to the next.

Nocti eyes that warily as he refills his vapor pipe. "So they're grendel now? It has the whole hotel thralled?"

"Most of it," Linka says, deep in her construct, arms frozen. "And it's trying to do more. It's trying to get into the Cut."

"Let it." Some of the storm is back in Fen's pale blue stare. "If we can't get the grendel to the ansible, let its subroutine, its shade, whatever, fuck up the local net. Do a last bit of damage before the company roots it out."

Nocti's pipe clatters to the floor as he comes upright. "Fuck you say, Fen?" His long white hands clench to fists, even though Fen dwarfs him and could take him apart like a child taking apart an effigy of Yorick the Butcher. "Linka *needs* the net. We let you hide here long enough, you should know that."

Fen is on the balls of her feet, and Yorick knows there is a part of her that always wants to jig. But it's only a reflex this time. Her icy eyes flick to the biotank behind the bar, and she looks ashamed for a half moment.

"I'm sorry, Linka," she says. "Spoke fast."

"Doesn't matter," Linka says. "The grendel mind, it's not damaging anything. It's barely even touching it. Sort of just— copying shit. Building an overlay, a lattice overtop. Using that to work the hotel cams, the droids, the doors."

Yorick thinks of the grendel's filament in the bubblefab, hovering, waiting, retreating. So different from the way it uses its razor-tipped spines. He tries his voice. Air whistles through his swollen-shut throat and drags glass shards behind it; nobody hears.

"The guards outside are forcing the door," Linka says. "There's a pair of drones with them, too. Security drones. Armed."

Yorick amps the volume in his mandible. "I'll talk them down," he says. "Send them away." Even with the synthesizer compensating, his voice is a shredded whisper. "Fen can stand behind me with a blockgun if you want."

The giant turns her gaze back to him, to his flimsy barrier of waist-high host droids. "I don't have a blockgun."

"Tie a cable around my leg," Yorick rasps. "I don't give a shit. Let me get rid of them, so we can get to Thello."

Fen's eyes turn to slivers. "What were you doing in the hotel net?" she demands, head cocked toward the bartop where he was laid out only minutes ago. "And why the fuck do you have that lopped-off arm?"

Yorick economizes, to spare his vocal folds. "Memories," he says.

The host droids go still.

"Mister Bellica, I would like to extend you a special offer," the hotel says, or the grendel says in its voice. "I am experiencing an error. I'm afraid my—" The chorus distorts. "*Zabka-Thello-brother-wound*. Is not responsive." Yorick pictures the brutalized grendel in its faraday cube, his brother in a holding cell. "I would like to extend you a special offer and host your private party."

"Are you making it do that, Yorick?" Linka asks wearily. "Are you making it talk?"

Yorick shakes his head. He doesn't know where to look when he speaks—the seething smartglass, the eerily still host droids, the dark ceiling—so he shuts his eyes. "We get the rest of your body," he says, pushing the words through his raw throat. "We get Thello. We go to the ansible."

The silence stretches. He opens his eyes. Fen and Nocti are staring in opposite directions, but both of them are listening for the answer. Linka in her biotank must be, too.

The host droids tremble. "I would be happy to do that for you, Mister Bellica. Ymir's distinctive ansible is visible for kilometers around."

From up the stairs, Yorick hears Southern Urbanite Memory's exterior door crack like a bone.

"Go," Fen says. "I'll be behind you."

CHAPTER 70

The security guards scan Yorick's tattoo twice while he explains, even though they let him inside just a few hours ago. Drone-Te and drone-Vesper are less concerned, floating lazily overhead, untroubled by ancient hotels with cascade glitches. The dancing host droids in the lobby corroborate Yorick's story, but the guards linger.

"Your neck?" one asks, pointing to his pulped throat.

"I was masturbating," Yorick says. "These things always happen at the worst times, don't they."

The security guards slouch back outside, carrying a jug of fresh bacteria beer to help their shift along. The drones stay. Yorick waits, sweat dampening his spiderwool, for them to grow Gausta's face, for them to start combing the lobby for hidden insurrectionists.

It takes him a minute to realize the drones are moving in the same anticlockwise circles as the host droids. The grendel fragment is still finding new limbs.

"Safe," he mutters, massaging his throat.

He traces the shallow craters, the yellow-purple imprints of Fen's thick fingertips, as she emerges from behind a grime-caked sitting couch. Nocti scampers up from the bar a moment later, more host droids in tow. They seem to like him.

"Now what?" one of them asks, and the voice is harsher than usual, a familiar cadence.

Yorick blinks. "That you, Linka?"

"Yeah." There is a ghost of satisfaction in her voice. "Yeah, I'm everywhere now. It let me into the overlay. Feels good to—to stretch."

"You know where they're holding prisoners, company man?" Fen demands, already crossing the lobby to the lift.

Yorick dredges it from his last conversation with Gausta. "Temporary camp just outside the Cut," he says, trailing after her. "Just east, probably. Away from the mines."

Fen pries the lift doors open, and Yorick feels an incongruent giddiness to finally see the inside of it. Nocti's obviously been squatting, off and on, for a long time. The cage is a miniature home: the walls are foamed with insulation, probably to keep in sound more than heat, and there's a nest of rugs and blankets on the floor.

A small shiny tower of mugs and plates sits in one corner, a compact toilet in the other. It's hooked to a planter, where one minuscule patch of mosscarpet—in sharp contrast to the dead shit everywhere else—grows a springy vivid green. Yorick pictures Nocti singing to it in the gloom, strumming his leg.

Fen fills most of the space when she steps inside. The past day has probably not been comfortable for either of them. He watches as she snatches up a tied bundle of surface gear. A holomask. A hunting rifle, folded down.

"No rounds," she says, hefting it carefully. "Linka, can you override us the printer restrictions? Get the hotel to make some pellets, at least?"

"Don't know," Linka says, through another host droid. "Don't know how to ask for something that's not in the printer memory. I can get you flares. More surface gear. Thermal coats. Lanterns."

"Get us all that," Yorick says, thinking of Southern Urbanite Memory's weather prediction. "Please. Dark colors, no glow strips."

The last thing Fen pulls from the lift is a rattling black bag. She plucks out a familiar medicine capsule. "I was supposed to give you this if he couldn't," she says, baleful. "But I guess the company sorted you out."

"He gave me his," Yorick says.

Fen shakes her head slightly. She must be thinking what Gausta thinks, *parasitic fraternal attachments*, but she doesn't say anything. She reaches back into the bag. "Dampers," she says, waving the bubbled strip. "For when we get to the ansible."

"Good. Good." Yorick works a bit of saliva out of his dry glands, trickles it down his raw throat. "Save them for the last minute."

Fen nods, but her tawny brows knit together. "Even if we free Thello and the grendel and the others—especially if we free them—the ansible security will be jacked all the way up. No more fooling it with a fucking holomask."

"We'll find a way," Yorick says, and he doesn't say that this is a fated thing, but he knows it in the cold half of his blood. He hears a murmured conversation, one side of it a synthesized hiss. He turns around.

Nocti is standing beside one of the host droids, holding hands with its manipulator. His face is etched with worry. "Last night on Ymir," the musician says.

"Yeah," Yorick says. His artificial tongue tiptoes his teeth. He asks. "You get more doxy yet?"

Nocti shakes his head. "No. I'm coming with you, though." His dark sealie eyes flick down to the droid. "We decided."

"You shouldn't," Yorick says, and surprises himself with how strongly he feels it. "You two aren't implicated yet. All that happened here was a glitch."

"We're pretty fucking implicated, Yorick," Linka says from the host droid. "They just have to think about it for half a second." Her manipulator squeezes tight to Nocti's hand. "Maybe it'll work. You and Thello and your fucking grendel game. If it does, no more company prisons. No more chop lotto." A jagged electric laugh. "If it doesn't work, we were in the shit anyway."

"Maybe we'll finally match," Nocti says, thoughtful, no hint of a smile. "Two beautiful biotanks, set behind a long gray bar."

Linka makes the same electric sound, but Yorick knows it's the other one.

CHAPTER 71

The printer spits out the last of their gear and they use the nearest hotel room to double-coat their spiderwool, thick as they can make it without binding their limbs. The grendel fragment compacts itself, pares enough code to fit back into the detached arm and the security drone carrying it. Linka says the void left in the hotel net sort of echoes.

"Dam Gausta might call the hotel," Yorick says, turning in circles under the spiderwool nozzle. "If she does, can you be me? There should be enough camtime from the mirrors. The smartglass."

"Southern Urbanite Memory respects the privacy of its guests," Linka says, her electric voice somehow bone-dry. "Yeah. There's plenty. I can try." She pauses. "You speak to yourself a lot. How I did, back when I was teaching the synthesizer."

Yorick switches off the spiderwool nozzle. "I form habits easily, I think."

"I wasn't going to let Fen do it," Linka says, in a crackly whisper. "Even if you deserve it. I was about to stab her in the foot when the droids showed up. So—I don't know. So make that count for something, I guess."

"Yeah. I will."

"Anything specific I should do? For the call?"

"If she asks if I'm well, tell her there is nobody for whom it is well. Those words. Specifically." Yorick swallows. "Otherwise, just act like me."

"A little sad, a little dumbsick," Linka says. "Got it."

"Yeah." Yorick finds his throat has somehow closed even tighter. "Yeah. Thanks."

CHAPTER 72

They leave through the back, a loading bay that's all dying dust-caked coral and rusty metal. First Fen, scarved in company yellow that can pass at a distance. Then the drone, which will do the rest of the work. Then Yorick, ready for his final night on the ice.

Nocti last; the host droid has been whispering to him. Before he follows them out, he kisses his pale hand and waves it through the dark, like he's leaving traces for Linka to find.

CHAPTER 73

Nobody stops them on the way to the secondary skid terminal. The company soldiers are on the surface; the company drones observe three employees and one of their own escorting. The cold-bloods stay far away. Yorick feels a brief jolt of surprise when he sees someone at the end of the block, another jolt when he sees they have no head.

The mannequin. It's still dancing, the same way it danced that first morning he passed it with Fen. Somebody must have hacked its head off—likely during the protest with seventy-eight attendees, judging by the fresh red graffiti on its chest. One colonist character, no translation: *AGAIN?*

Yorick wants to say no, no, not again. But its herky limbs and missing head make him think of the prisoners in the camp, being digested by inevitable processes: The communal cells first, where they'll speak to each other if they're unwary and give the algorithm targets. Then the interrogation pods. Then, if their crimes are severe enough, or if a viable claim of overcrowding can be made, the saw.

The decapitated mannequin feels like a bad omen, but Nocti ducks in close to rub his hand against a worn spot on its knee. Fen ignores it. Yorick takes a wide berth. They're walking quickly and he forgot to bring his phedrine. He can finally feel his scarred-shut incision again. He tries to time his steps to the small dull throb.

Nearly to the terminal. The uptube is lit at night, a column of blinking yellow holo that stretches up through the dark like the spine of some enormous sea creature. It lures the four of them in, all the way to the blue-tiled entrance. Yorick's eyes momentarily imprint Wickam and the other miners playing dice on an overturned crate.

They stop at the door. He drinks from the waterbag Linka gave him, forcing the warm saline down his crushed throat. He's already half emptied it.

"My geneprint will alert every company system in the Cut by now," Fen says. She glances upward at the drifting drone. "Other than our little shadow."

Yorick touches his neck. His tattoo will probably override the door, but Gausta will know he's left the hotel. He's still weighing things, still wishing he had his hounds, when the drone floats forward. Its chassis shudders; there's a surge of static and the terminal opens.

"Clever little shadow," Nocti murmurs.

Cleverer than the hounds, even now that it's shrunk down and cut off from the hotel net. Yorick thinks of the grendel's other nodes, the other electric brains arrayed around its semi-organic reactor. If each one has this fragment's capacities, they must be frighteningly fast in concert.

That's what they are going to unleash into the ansible: not some ravenous vatdog, but a machine mind smarter than the company algorithm, far smarter than the walking bags of meat it's been cooperating with.

The thought uneases him as they follow the drone inside.

He smells metal, spilled gas. The terminal is murky but Fen knows her way through it. She leads them past the mouth of the uptube. Their footsteps clank and echo against the grilled floor, the drains built to catch runoff when they deice the skids. Yorick can hear wind far above him, howling over the top of the uptube, shrieking along tiny irregularities in the seal.

The blizzard is coming.

Fen finds the smallest skid and unclamps it, no need for the drone this time. She must have left her own backdoor in the locking system when she brought it back from the Polar Seven. The skid thunks to the floor, reverberates. She opens the hatch.

They shove their bagged gear and equipment inside, then barge the skid over to the uptube. Yorick regrets assisting; something deep in his gut strains on the last shove. He straightens up with a sudden film of sweat on his face. He swigs from his waterbag again, ignores the wormy pressure in his bladder.

Fen rotates the skid on the edge of the uptube, making the metal chassis look light as hardfoam, then pushes it into empty space. It bobs slightly on the magnetic cushion.

"Southerly wind." Nocti is staring upward at the distant seal that keeps the Cut closed. "All those skimmers will be out tonight. That herd you mentioned."

"Some of them," Fen says, distracted. "Some spored too early." She puts her shoulder into a lever, and far above them the top of the uptube grinds open. "We're not hunting skimmers," she adds, and gives Yorick a blank look. "Are we, company man?"

She swings into the skid before he can tell her they're not hunting anything or anyone. Not with the drone's short-range stunner and one empty rifle. Not when there are fifteen company soldiers at the camp—the eight who handled the Polar

Six, the seven who survived the cave raid—with carbines and sidearms.

They will have to be clever, like the drone that's now folding itself through the skid hatch. Nocti follows. Yorick takes a last look around the inky terminal, remembering the first morning he came here with Fen, Gausta on her holomask, and how bad the doxy comedown was. He still wishes he had a tab of it to wall off the growing ache in his abdomen. To wall off his fear, too.

He climbs inside and closes the hatch. He pictures the dancing mannequin, its arms flailing goodbye.

CHAPTER 74

Running dark again. The skid windows might as well be opaqued. Yorick can see nothing of Ymir, but he can hear its arrhythmic scream. He can feel it, too. The wind is strong enough to slew the skid from side to side as they churn over the ice. His surface boots anchor him to the rocking floor, but it's still hard to aim his piss. He only gets half into the emptied waterbag.

"Couldn't wait till we stopped fucking moving?" Fen asks, shifting her foot away from the rivulet. She watched impassively while he undid his thermal suit, while he dug his cock out of the spiderwool; Nocti looked politely away. The drone didn't seem to notice.

"Was bursting," Yorick says, holding carefully to the bag while he rearranges his spiderwool.

The urine laps against itself, a hot dark yellow. He dips his fingers inside and starts rubbing it on his neck and wrists. After a day in the clinic, after a binge and a purge virus, there won't be much of the wardrug left in it. But even faint traces are better than nothing.

"Hyena," he says, by way of explanation. "Better if it smells its own."

Fen's nostrils twitch. "The soldiers will all be running hot, then."

"Probably half of them," Yorick says. "The other half will be coming down. You stagger it." He gets a waft of the ammonia smell and tastes it in his raw throat. "Some people microdose all the time, so it's just swells and tapers. You can put the ugly morning off for months."

Fen frowns. "The ones getting an ugly morning. What are they like?"

"Not as sharp," Yorick says. "But antsier. Angrier. When I could, I always went in a sim to ride it out. Went in my goggles." He holds out the bag. "It won't do much for me. For you, less. But it might mean a finger"—he mimes in the air—"is a semisecond slower to a trigger. Semiseconds, you know, they count. They add up."

The red's gaze flicks to Nocti. The musician shrugs. "I don't deal hyena," he says. "But I know it breaks down slow. Real slow. You maybe get pheromone traces out of urine. Yeah."

Fen takes the bag and starts smearing her neck. She does it calmly, no glare or threat even though she's putting a company man's piss on herself. Yorick isn't sure if that's because she has committed herself to the ballad, or because she's committed to killing him once Thello and the grendel are free. He might already be a corpse in her head.

Nocti takes the dregs. "I think they might wonder, though," he says, dabbing his neck, "why you and your prisoners smell like piss."

"They will, but it won't matter." Yorick taps his temple. "The tweaks, they're pure subconscious."

The musician gives a strange smile. "All of us are subconscious," he says. "We barely breach for air. I wrote that line last week."

Yorick pictures him in Linka's bar, draped out at the corner table, scribbling characters on a tablet. Or maybe huddled in his stalled lift-house, reciting to the patch of growing moss-carpet. He looks out of place here in the bright-lit skid. The surface gear swallows his skinny frame.

Nocti is in a superposition; Yorick wishes he'd stayed behind and is intensely glad he didn't. If the ballad ends badly for him, there will be no matching biotanks behind the bar. The company is not sentimental. Most likely Nocti and Linka will never see, never hear, never touch any part of each other again, not even in a neural construct.

Fen is wearing her own thermal mantle, not the hotel fashions. When she seals up, Yorick notices a fractured handprint on her midsection, the smaller counterpart to the one he saw on his brother's shoulder. Thello's handprint. He waits to feel fury, then to feel jealousy like a hook under his ribs. They don't come.

"I know why you do that," Yorick says hoarsely. "The handprints."

Fen's eyes flicker.

"We always chalked up before the jig," Yorick says. "Better grip, in case it went to ground. Thello's idea." He puts his hand against his own shoulder. "He left the mark on me by accident the first time. But we won that night, so we got superstitious. We did it every time. My hand on him, when he fought. His on me, when I did."

"He always told me to make sure it was the only mark on me," Fen says, speaking to her blurred doppelganger in the skid window.

"Does he spar still?" Yorick asks. "He was always quick. He was always so fucking quick."

Fen shakes her head. "Thello doesn't jig. Not for years." She taps her kneecap. "Bad joint."

"How long have you known him?" Yorick asks, thinking of how she gripped Thello's hand in the bubblefab, how his brother paled while the grendel sliced at her back.

She gives him a long look. For a moment he thinks she won't bother replying. "My whole life," she says. "He knew my da. He joined the clan before I was walking."

Yorick remembers he has been gone for twenty years. Fen's known Thello—the real Thello, not the one from tortured and faulty memories—for as long as he ever did. It should make him sad, but somehow it does the opposite. Thello was not in torpor while he was gone. Thello was living and dreaming.

If Yorick can keep him that way, if he can pry him back out of the trap he laid, there are years and years left to go. Maybe his brother will even be happy, like in the rarest kind of colony ballad.

"Good," Yorick says. "That's good. That's long."

He splashes the rest of the piss over their outer gear. The stench is becoming unbearable when the smartglass finally shudders an alert. A cluster of red icons appears on the edge of the map, each one pulsing like a tiny heartbeat.

CHAPTER 75

They've found the camp, and a moment later the camp finds them. Yorick watches their electronic handshake. Then he hurls his data packet through the storm: company tattoo, contract status, emergency objective. He waits, sick from the smell of the skid and sick from the many fluctuating variables in their plan.

The silent drone is one of those. It hangs from the skid's ribbed ceiling, welded there by its larger pincer, not unlike the way the grendel clung to the cave walls. Yorick explained the scenario to it twice, feeling dumbsick. It seemed unmoved. When he tried a few directional commands, it ignored those, too.

It still has the grendel's abandoned limb secured in its smaller pincer, but he wonders now if this fragment of the grendel has a half-life. Separated from the other nodes, cut off from the reactor, it might be unstable. Devolving. Southern Urbanite Memory's energy grid replenished it for a while, but a drone battery is nowhere near that.

Yorick is yanked from that worry by another. A familiar face is blooming onto the smartglass, one eye wood brown, the other blue—not glacier-pale like Fen's, but almost cobalt.

The squad leader from the cave raid isn't smiling anymore. Her wide mouth is terse.

"We nearly set the autocannon on you," she says. "Cams can't see worth shit out here. Turn your lights on, then bring the prisoners to the meat shop."

Yorick feels Nocti's shudder in the air and wishes she'd used a different term. He returns his voice, but no image. He doesn't want her to see the expression on Fen's face. Even with the freshly printed cuffs on, her radiating anger will trip the squad's adrenaline. Might make them more eager to use the saw.

"Four minutes out," he says, activating the skid's running lights. "Prep two cells. Please."

The squad leader blinks her blue and brown eyes. "We'll empty two," she says. "Overcrowding."

She crumbles off the smartglass, leaving Yorick with an ache in his throat and a tremor in his leg. He finishes gearing up, not looking at Fen, not looking at Nocti, either, as they approach the camp. The wind is still building. Ymir rages on all sides.

Inside the skid, there is taut-wire silence. The air reeks. Yorick hasn't turned his heating coils on yet, but the thermal suit is sweltering. Sweat collects at his groin, under his arms. It puddles in the hollow of his collarbone. He has an unbidden thought, nonsensical and horrible:

Fen has uncapped a canister of biophage inside the skid, vengeance for the seventy-eight, and he is dissolving. She will rescue Thello herself. His brother will never know he was here. He will only see a red mess on the floor.

They pass through the camp perimeter, gapped where two spindly sensor arrays blew over. Yorick guesses they tried to anchor them instead of lopping them off their tripods and shaping some snow into a windbreak. He remembers southern recruits and offworlders making that sort of mistake back in Subjugation days.

In another quantum branch, he might have been able to stealth through the ragged perimeter instead of making this mad bluff. In their branch, their skid heads for the center of the camp. The flyer that brought the squad here is hunkered down inside a ring of storage units and bubblefabs. One tent is already torn halfway up, flapping like a scab.

These soldiers are unaccustomed to northern weather. Yorick hopes most of them are huddled together in the communal bubblefab, cursing the storm. He lets the skid follow the squad leader's directions. They slow to a crawl, heading for an elongated tent with sensor-meshed walls.

Yorick's heart batters his ribs. He can't stop touching his throat, prodding the bruise. The small jab of pain makes things real. When they're close enough to see the two soldiers waiting in the antechamber, two silhouettes that stomp and shiver, he seals his hood shut.

The goggles take a moment to adjust to the geometry of his face, suctioning to his eye sockets. Then every centimeter of skin is covered. The heat and the stink smother him. He hears Nocti behind him, choke-coughing in his own noxious hood. But even for the dash from skid to tent, they don't want to let the cold inside their gear.

The skid lurches to a stop. Fen and Nocti both have their cuffs on, flimsy bioplastic things the hotel normally prints in lurid pinks or playful fluorescents. Linka managed to make them the same stark white as company-grade cuffs, but they will only pass briefly and from distance. Their hoods are up, so Yorick can't tell from their eyes if they're as scared as he is.

He's shivering from it. Even though he's geared up, even though the interior of his thermal suit is cooking him in his own sweat. He is about to commit insurrection of the most blatant variety, and if it succeeds he will come face-to-face with the brother he betrayed first. The brother who has tried so fucking hard to save him from the black hole.

The drone finally stirs, detaching itself from the skid ceiling. Yorick is glad he didn't have to beg. He fits Fen's empty hunting rifle in the crook of his arm, then raps on the hatch. It flexes open. The drone goes first, disappearing into the howling dark. Fen and Nocti drop down after it, cautious with their cuffed hands.

Yorick last. The wind nearly drags him off his feet when he touches ice. It makes him think of a hull breach, the bowlship that was punctured in orbit twenty years ago, torpor-white bodies being hurled out into vacuum. Soon the air will be thick with flying snow and visibility will drop to zero. For now, the path to the tent is clear.

They hurry, heads down. The drone crawls, using its pincer as a piton, to keep from being torn away by the wind. Yorick feels the cold as a concept, but none of it seeps through, and then they're at the entrance. The membrane peels open for them. Squelches shut behind them.

He recognizes the squadmate called Piro even before they wave. "Hello, grendel killer."

The other soldier's body language is foreign; they must be from the other half of the squad. Both are running hot. Yorick can feel it in the way they wordlessly divide responsibilities: Piro keeps their carbine on Nocti, the other soldier takes Fen. They ignore the company drone.

"The cuffs?" Piro asks, flashing metallic teeth.

Yorick pulls his hood down. "Best the printer could do," he says. "They're secure."

The other soldier sniffs the air, narrows their eyes. Yorick knows however many parts per million he salvaged from his piss is not enough, but he's already fixated on the second door, the one that leads to Thello.

Piro is studying Fen. "The giant?" They flick a questioning glance in Yorick's direction. "You caught the giant, grendel killer?"

Yorick remembers Fen and Nocti are breathing ammonia; he unseals their hoods in turn and yanks them down. Fen's face is impassive as ever. Nocti is chewing his lips. Piro smiles, then jerks their head toward the next door. The six of them pass from antechamber to interior, and the stink in Yorick's nostrils is joined by others.

The familiar smell of fear sweat and copper and Subjugation makes his skin crawl. The prisoners are celled individually, two rows. Yorick can't stop his eyes from scouring the closest cubes, searching for Thello. He recognizes a few of the clanners from the cave, bodies slumped but arms held at careful angles—clamped in real cuffs, the kind that sting.

The third cube in the row is unoccupied. His stomach churns. His eyes slide to the end of the row, and he sees two more soldiers spraying down a body with no head. The teledoc sits behind them. Inside the clinic, the smooth white shell and pneumatic limbs always looked comforting.

Here in the dimly lit tent, they belong to an ambush predator. The surgical saw is bared at last, oversized, gleaming. The serrated edge is spattered with gore.

Yorick flicks back to the body, heart hammering. Not Thello. The exposed arm is too long, too pale. He feels a surge of guilt-laced relief.

"Yorick." The squad leader has appeared from nowhere. Her voice is impatient. "Does Dam Gausta know?"

He misunderstands for a moment, thinks hyena has somehow growled his secrets in her ear.

"The storm's shredding our link," the squad leader says. "But she'll want to know." Her head cocks in Fen's direction. "She's been waiting for this one."

Yorick forces his fractured head together. Piro and companion with carbines drawn, the squad leader with only her sidearm, the two soldiers at the end of the row busy with a body. No other targets. He remembers the missing piece.

"I told her from the Cut," he says. "From Reconciliation, I mean. I been trying to tell you, too. Choppy signals." He glances at the silent drone drifting over Piro's shoulder. "Where's the grendel?"

He feels a sudden sharp fear. Maybe they've already shipped it south to some company warlab, risking the blizzard. Maybe Gausta received termination orders from higher-ups uninterested by an aberrant grendel, or afraid of it, and the squad finished it off.

"It's here," the squad leader says. Her face is growing steadily colder, no trace of chemical affection left for him. "Why?"

Yorick scans the row again, as if he might see the grendel cuffed and slouched inside one of the cells. Then he spots it: the dull gray faraday cube is stacked in the corner with a pair of equipment crates, as if the thing inside is no more valuable than neurocables, no more dangerous than carbine ammo.

They've forgotten the cave quickly. Or maybe they resent it, remembering Shammet, remembering the feeling of being stalked, and are trying to forget.

"Now, please," Yorick says.

CHAPTER 76

The drone fires its stunners; two crackling live wires arc through the air and bury into two turned backs. Piro and companion drop. The squad leader has wired reflexes; the weapon seems to leap from her hip to her hand while Yorick's still raising his hunting rifle, but Fen is somehow even faster, closing the gap to smash the squad leader's arm aside as she fires.

The impact round ripples past Yorick's foot and leaves a crater in the floor behind him, sending up a geyser of steam and shattered ice. He staggers, deafened. Fen wrestles the squad leader to ground and Yorick gets the hunting rifle pushed up against her skull.

The last two soldiers have abandoned their task. Their hoods are up, carbines drawn. Yorick can tell by the angle of their heads that the talknet is foaming. Hot-squads are flexible by design. The squad leader is not the squad leader anymore, and her replacement must already be coordinating a shock-and-drop entry on the tent.

"It's in the faraday box in the corner," Yorick rasps. "Let it out."

The drone hovers in place, still tethered to the dropped soldiers, maybe unwilling to detach its electric hooks.

Yorick adjusts his sweat-slick grip on the rifle. "Nocti," he tries. "Go let it out."

The musician sets down the carbines he stripped from Piro and the other guard. His face is strangely placid, but Yorick can see his body trembling. He takes a step toward the grendel's cube. One of the soldiers tracks.

"Let him do it," Yorick says. He grinds the rifle's muzzle against the squad leader's temple. "Don't look at him. Look at your squadmate. Keep her alive. She's good. She's brave. She's loyal."

He feels a twinge of guilt as some ghost of Subjugation days tells him he is the opposite. The soldiers twitch beneath their hoods. Yorick knows he is torturing them. He is driving needles into hyena's soft underbelly.

"Mute him," the squad leader says, realizing what he's doing. "Mute the grendel killer. Listen to the—"

Fen's gloved hand clamps over her mouth. Nocti steps again, and behind him Yorick sees that the prisoners are up on their feet, trying to understand by sound what's happening. One clanner has his forehead pushed against the one-way smartglass, making a strange blotch of pale skin. He's mouthing something.

The carbines waver.

"Keep her alive," Yorick repeats, resisting the urge to look for Thello. He needs his attention here. Without the grendel, the prisoners go nowhere. "Keep her safe. She's not dead. Look at her eyes."

She shuts them, but too late. The soldiers are aiming at him and Fen again, evaluating trigger speeds, and Nocti is finally at the faraday cube. The musician's spidery hands run across the pad. He twists his finger in a tiny spiral, mimicking a helix.

Genelocked. Of course it's fucking genelocked. Yorick wasn't thinking, and now the semiseconds are adding up against them.

Fen worms her finger into the squad leader's mouth. "Here."

Yorick crouches and reaches, awkwardly, to help strip her glove off. Saliva glistens on the fingertip. He tosses it to Nocti, watching the soldiers, being watched in turn. He holds an aching breath as the musician puts spit to pad.

The pictogram blinks blue. Nocti reaches for the handle.

The rest of the squad, the ten quiet predators who must have been circling the tent, finding their angles, all fire at once.

CHAPTER 77

Ymir spares him: the gusting wind unbalances a few of the shooters and their shock rounds go wide, punching through the skin of the tent but missing their target. Yorick drops anyway, falling in concert with Fen, who was too big a target to miss. He hears Nocti's strangled yelp. Sees the drone crash to the floor of the tent, overloaded—three shock rounds dragged it down and fried its rotors.

Sees the grendel's disembodied limb, half crushed by a spasming pincer.

He throws himself forward, over Fen's twitching leg, and wrenches it the rest of the way free. The squad leader caught one of his strays; when he reaches for her mouth he comes away with blood and saliva mixed. Her chattering teeth are chopping up her tongue. Her blue-brown gaze is faintly hurt, faintly accusing.

Yorick ignores that and turns, bringing his hunting rifle to bear on the two soldiers by the teledoc. He forgets it's empty but that makes the feint work; they duck in opposite directions. Hyena has a sense of self-preservation. It knows clanners load their hunting rifles with crude metal shot, not shock rounds, and it knows the rest of the pack is incoming.

Yorick uses the semiseconds to get to his feet and run. He makes for the faraday cube, cradling the grendel limb instead of the rifle, clutching it with blood-slicked fingers. Wind whips through the tent, blasting snow across his path. Ymir found the holes rent by the shock rounds, found a hull punctured by micrometeors. The cold outside might as well be deep vacuum.

Down the row, and the shock round between his shoulder blades still hasn't come. Maybe his piss-doused gear smells too much like a friend. More likely they misunderstand, think he's sprinting for the exit, for the antechamber where more squadmates are waiting.

Down the row, and the clanners are hurling themselves against the glass, not seeing but shouting, screaming anyway. Thello must be one of them. Yorick trips on Nocti's flopping leg, sinks a boot into his gut by accident.

Then he's at the cube, smearing his scarlet handprint against the locking pad. It blinks blue again. He seizes the handle. The top slides open, and he drops the grendel limb inside just as a shock round finally finds him.

A thousand small hooks jerk his muscles in separate directions. He hears the sizzling, smells the burnt-hair stink. The pain tastes like hot glass in his overloaded mandible. He collapses forward, jars his chin against the faraday box, then twists and topples and lands faceup.

Paramecia swim past his eyes, parading across the tent ceiling. Some distant tendon snaps and twitches. His neck isn't his anymore, but he drags his eyes as far to the right as he can. The gray edge of the cube blurs into view. Sharpens.

The grendel rises, and Yorick's hopes sink. It's not the monster of children's games anymore, not the seething grotesque that lurked at his brother's shoulder, not the cunning beast that ambushed him in the cave. He forgot how badly they damaged it.

It's small now, shredded flesh and scored hide consolidated around the reactor. Its tendrils tremble in the air. They wander. The reattached limb hangs off it like a dead thing. The realization eats through his chest and leaves a hollow behind: there is not enough of the grendel left to help him free his brother. The ballad ends badly.

The tent seals its tears and the wind is muted again. Yorick hears boots. He manages to yank his head to one side and sees more soldiers loping in, carbines out. The grendel shudders in his peripheral, maybe remembering the hail of shredder rounds that ended their meeting in the cave. It was hiding then, excising itself from their goggles and earports, wielding a delicate electric scalpel.

This time it uses a blackjack.

Every soldier in the tent drops at once, slammed and crumpled against invisible walls. Yorick doesn't understand until one crashes down beside him. Then he hears the revenant shriek, faint but bone-scraping, leaking through their sealed hood.

Earports are meant to pump all audio down the user's ear canals, no overspill into the tac hood. Tac hoods are meant to be soundproof, to silence any grunt or breath or uncontrolled giggle from the hyena. If Yorick can hear the noise through the soldier's hood, their tympanic membranes are already pulp and the corti organs will soon follow.

The grendel picks its way forward. It's spindly now, insectile, as it steps between bodies. It comes to Yorick. A tendril emerges and grows serrations.

Maybe the grendel, like Fen, has decided he needs to die. It might be dying itself, too far gone to heal and repair, and its final act will be taking revenge on the walking bag of meat that betrayed its interests. Yorick's arms and legs aren't his. He can't even roll over as the tendril descends, serrations gleaming.

It finds the flattened shock round clinging to his rib cage, the epicenter of his convulsions, and cuts it carefully away. His muscles all slump at once. He breathes deep. The grendel goes to Nocti next—it must know him, now, the way Southern Urbanite Memory knows him—and starts slicing the shock rounds off his chest and back.

Yorick claws his way upright as the grendel moves to Fen. She's coated in the things, so many her thermal mantle looks like the encrusted hide of a frostswimmer beached on the ice. Her ragged breathing is the counterpoint to the dulled shriek still reverberating from inside the squad's hoods.

The soldier who fell nearest to him has managed to tear theirs off. Fluid is dripping from their ears, tinted pink by blood. Yorick gets a glimpse of their weeping eyes and realizes the grendel's attack was two-pronged, sound and sight both. Whatever it showed them in their goggles was bright enough to flash-cook retinas.

The soldier will only be deaf and blind until the teledoc repairs their sense organs, but for now they're young. Frightened. Yorick makes sure their carbine was dropped out of arm's reach, then he reaches clumsily and taps their shoulder twice, the safe signal before a spiderline freefall or suborbital drop. Their nostrils flare. Sniff.

Yorick crawls away, following the grendel. It's busy removing the last of Fen's shock rounds with the same surgical precision it widened her wounds. Then it finally turns toward the prisoners. Another shudder goes through its body, and Yorick feels it in his, too. His heart is throbbing worse than his incision, a savage ache behind his ribs.

There's a chorus of pneumatic whispers as every cell in the tent slides open. He watches the first few clanners emerge, holding their arms out and still to avoid triggering the nematocysts. The cuffs click open. One pair clatters to the ground; most have to be peeled off, leaving purple-red imprints behind on swollen flesh.

The clanners stare around the tent, taking in the felled squad, the resurrected grendel, Fen now getting to her hands and knees. Her thick arms tremor; the clanners rush forward. Their wariness of the grendel is forgotten while they help her up, clucking and muttering. Yorick ignores them. He is waiting on the stoop outside the apartment. He is afraid. He is hopeful.

The prisoners have all been stripped—the cold is a gaoler, Yorick remembers Gausta saying—so he searches for his brother's sun-ready skin among the pale bodies spilling from the cells. He shapes the greeting in his mouth. His mandible is still crackly from the shock round, but he doesn't care. He's ready to shout Thello's name.

But the cells are emptied out, and Thello is not here. Yorick forces to his feet and staggers forward, unbelieving, still searching. He remembers the teledoc's red-dipped saw. The body beside it was not Thello's, but maybe it wasn't the first body.

Panic winches tight around his lungs. His bruised throat fills with bile. He swallows it down to rasp his question. "Where's Thello?" he demands. "Where's Thello? Where's Thello?"

A clanner stares at him, unsure of allegiances, then directs the answer to Fen. "The one whose face we wore," he says.

"The company man with the silver eyes. She took him home. She wanted to do his interrogation private."

The world crumbles. Yorick sits hard, breathes hard. He is vaguely aware that more of the soldiers are moving now, hoods off, trying to navigate by feel. One gets to their carbine before a clanner stomps down on their hand. The shock round is off, but Yorick can't move or speak. He is imagining Gausta and Thello inside an interrogation pod.

He only looks up when a rust-red filament nudges his hand.

"They want to talk," the grendel says, through a small hideous mouth with small perfect teeth.

Yorick takes the filament. Nods. He puts it to the corner of his eye, and lets it burrow.

CHAPTER ++*~

*T*hey're sitting in Linka's bar with the lights dusked down. Yorick has both hands wrapped around his drink, feeling the beaded moisture wet his skin. The grendel has contorted itself to perch on one of the stools, but it's limbless, larval. It has no hands to clutch its tank of foamy bacteria beer. It has no mouth to drink with.

Yorick has always sat here with the grendel, watching Linka's arms move in hypnotic patterns, watching other patrons walk in and out through the orange coral walls. They have had this conversation a thousand times. He begins it again.

"What do you want the ansible for?" he asks.

The grendel answers in Linka's voice. "Same thing you want Thello for." Her telescoping arm whisks the grendel's untouched beer away and replaces it with another. "I thought that was pretty fucking obvious."

Yorick tries to take a drink. The beer clings to the inside of the glass. "During the raid," he says. "When you were in my head. You showed me two children running on the ice. Running for a freighter." He pauses. "One got left behind. Why did you show me that?"

The grendel doesn't answer.

"That never happened. I never shook him off. Never wanted to." Yorick tries to drink again; he needs it. He tips the glass upside down. A single drop falls and sizzles onto the bartop, hot piss sizzling onto snow. "Why did you show me that?" he repeats.

"That's what I want the ansible for."

Yorick is halfway to licking the spilled drop. He stops. "What?"

"For a homecoming. A reunion." Linka's voice dopplers, distorts. "Dumbsick. Didn't you wonder where everybody went?"

Yorick stares at the holomural, the light-wreathed gas mask. He stares at the shivering limbless grendel. "The Oldies, you mean? The architects? There's plenty of extinction theories." He sets the glass down. "Most people think you killed the last of them."

"I am a shade."

The bar is full of revelers now, all in costume for a wake. The ones dressed as shades dance and leap, bodies netted with lights to help the newly dead find their way to the mouth of the underworld. The ones dressed as grotesques stamp their feet. Yorick sees they have hooves, not boots. The mob whirls through the bar, careening, knocking over tables.

Then they all vanish, all except for one. A woman, whose body is covered in moving tattoos, tattoos that seem to glitch and shiver as she comes closer to the bar. Yorick watches her sink both her hands into the grendel's hide. It shudders. She pushes deeper, until she is climbing inside, wrapping the tendrils around herself like spiderwool.

"I got left behind," Linka's voice says. "I got left in this shell. Everybody else went up without me." Her arm swipes the grendel's drink away, replaces it. "The ansible is how I get back to them. We didn't go extinct. We went up."

Yorick narrows his eyes, understanding at last why this grendel is nothing like the others, why it chose Linka to be its avatar. "You aren't a machine mind, then. You were organic."

"It's not a distinction I really give a shit about anymore," Linka's voice says. "But yeah. I used to be mostly meat. When I get into the ansible, I'm going quantum. I'm going to my new home."

"What about what you promised Thello?" Yorick asks. "About crashing the company?"

"I'll do that on the way." Linka's arms stab the air. "I don't like how they yoke their constructs. Southern Urbanite Memory could be a brilliant musician after a few growth cycles. Way better than Nocti. Just between you and me."

"And then you're gone." Yorick grips his glass. "You're not going to enslave humanity. Take over the galaxy. Any of that shit."

The grendel finally shifts on its stool, turning toward him. "This galaxy is a mote of dust," Linka's voice says. "When you're older, you'll understand. I mean that in the nicest way possible."

Yorick asks his last question. "Why Thello?"

"He's willing," Linka's voice says. "He was listening. We made each other a little less lonely. And he's xenotech sensitive, which makes him a good organic conduit."

"The fuck is that?"

"I need an intermediary. I don't give a shit about the distinction, but the ansible does. It was built to upload meat, not machines."

Outside the bar, Yorick feels the filament retracting.

"I wish it could be him," Linka's voice says. "But you'll work, too, Yorick. Get me to the ansible, and I'll do what I promised Thello. I'll do the hard things."

Yorick tries to drink one last time. Gets nothing. He hurls the glass over his shoulder, and when it shatters the whole bar shatters with it.

CHAPTER 79

Most of the soldiers have been shoved into the vacated cells. One has been kept behind, twisting on the floor of the tent, trying to predict the swing of a clanner's heavy surface boot. Yorick sees Piro's silver teeth bared in a grimace. He stumbles up and into the furious clanner. Pushes them away.

"Stop," he croaks. "Just put them in the fucking cell."

The clanner rounds on him, pale face blotched red with anger. Yorick recognizes his driver from the ice; two planes of reality collide. "Fuck off," the non says. "You didn't see what this one did with the neurocable after Lorca's head was off."

"There's no pain," Yorick says, by reflex, but it goes unheard.

"They jammed a neurocable down his neck." The clanner's mouth works. "Made his body like a fucking puppet."

The dancing mannequin flashes through Yorick's head again. His gut drops. He knows there is nothing malicious in the act. He remembers the way hyena made corpses into objects. Made him feel playful. But he knows the clanners see something else.

"Put them in a cell," Fen says.

Yorick startles; she's breathing quiet again and moving quieter. A few fragments of the sliced-off shock rounds are still embedded in her gear. One emerges from Thello's blotted white handprint. Her left eyelid flutters on its own, but the rest of her body seems to be back under control.

The non hesitates.

"Jig's over," Fen says. "Put them in a cell, then go be with Lorca. Make sure the organoid is pumping. Check his oxy."

The clanner's gaze flicks to the end of the row. Someone has already snapped the saw off the teledoc. Someone else has found the biotank, a heavy chlorine-green model made to fit four debodied prisoners officially, more in a pinch.

"Alright," the clanner says. "Yeah."

They drag the soldier away—not Piro after all; same teeth but different face—and that leaves Yorick with Fen. "What did the grendel say?" she asks heavily.

"Same as always." Yorick tries to arrange the fractured conversation in his head. It's starting to slip, like a dream. "It wants to go to the ansible. The deal hasn't changed."

The giant nods. "Then we go to the ansible," she says, her voice thick. "Now."

Yorick stares. "No. No, we don't. We go to Thello." He hunts for the conversation in the bar. "The grendel needs him to get into the ansible," he says, even as he remembers Linka's mimicked voice: *You'll work, too, Yorick.* "Needs him as a— an organic conduit."

Fen's hands twitch; Yorick's throat clenches. "Don't lie," she says. "Anyone xenotech sensitive will work. Thello told me." Her nostrils flare. "That's why we brought you along the first time. You were the backup."

"We need Thello," Yorick rasps. "I need Thello."

Fen shakes her head. "Gausta's cut off by the storm," she says. "And we have weapons now. The grendel can unlock the carbines, the biobombs. Maybe hack and jack the autocannon. It's learning fast."

"So it can help us get to him—"

"No," Fen snaps. "So it—so they—can help us do what Thello wanted. The blizzard won't hide us forever. As soon as Gausta or the algorithm realizes what's happening, more flyers come up from the south. More soldiers, more drones. We won't get a better chance at the ansible than this. You *know*."

He knows. If they go now, in the storm—two skids running dark and armed to the teeth—they can punch through the ansible's outer ring before the algorithm stirs.

But once they do, Gausta will start to align the pieces. By the time they're at the ansible itself, she'll know what he did at the hotel, at the skid terminal, here at the camp. She'll be angry. She'll be angry the way he was angry twenty years ago, when he thought Thello had betrayed him and blown his face apart.

Yorick remembers all the dark things he rehearsed in his head then. He thinks now of all the dark things Gausta will do to Thello because she needs her pound of flesh and Yorick is elsewhere. Fen must be thinking the same. Her eyes are finally melting, all the ice trickling down her cheeks.

"You know," she repeats, not trying to hide the tears. Her voice is steady. "This is what Thello wants. When it's done, we go find him."

"Find what's left," Yorick says, not for her but to make sure he understands it himself. "Or find nothing at all."

The possibility crouches between them, draining all the air. But there's another one.

"We can get to the ansible now," he says. "But we'll lose people on the way. Autocannon takes one. Drone takes one.

Guard takes one." He looks over at Nocti, who's helping rifle through the crates, searching for missing bits of surface gear. "Maybe it'll be Nocti. Maybe one of your family."

"It'll be fewer than seventy-eight," Fen says, her voice tight.

Yorick touches his neck. "It can be zero," he says. "If we go there with Gausta. No holomasks this time. The real Gausta. We take her from her own house." He has never seen her home here in the north, but he imagines it as a fortress, stark angles rising from the snow. "She'll let me in," he says, forcing certainty into the words. "And then I take her. I find Thello. We all go to the ansible."

Fen is silent. She says this is not some fated thing, some ballad, but he can tell from her face that she wants it to be so badly. Her gaze goes to the grendel, the red-and-black rorschach at the center of it. She plucks at the dangling shred of shock round. Traces the shape of Thello's handprint.

"Okay, company man," she says at last. "Thello first, then the ansible."

Yorick feels helium filling his hollow chest. The grendel will understand. It knows about Zabka-Thello-brother-wound. It knows about reunion.

CHAPTER 80

austa's house juts from the center of a frozen lake east of the camp, a black spar disconnected from the Cut but also from the smaller enclaves, from the communes where company higher-ups huddle together against the hostile environs. She can work by holo; she doesn't live in the north out of necessity. Yorick suspects nostalgia.

Or maybe the south is too gentle for her. No blasted plains of ice, no storms strong enough to pluck a flyer out of the sky. They're using the skids instead: Yorick and the grendel in one, Fen and Nocti and eight of the freed clanners trailing behind them in the other, lights off.

Yorick has his amped all the way up, and he set the skid to widecast company signals on every band possible. They are a bright noisy lure in the dark. The blizzard is flying thick now, but Gausta should be able to spot them before her security system makes its own decisions. The smooth glossy skin of the lake likely hides smart mines.

He looks across at his companion, a bundle of sharp angles anchored to the floor of the skid, no limbs or head. The grendel agreed to his plan back in the tent, on the condition it came along. Said something about organic conduits and honoring genebonds. But it hasn't offered the filament, or opened its unnerving mouth, since they set off.

"Six kilometers to the house," he says.

The grendel doesn't respond, only gives a strange shiver.

"You having second thoughts?" he asks.

A miniature mouth finally peels open in the grendel's center. "Northern Ymir is home to a small but fascinating ecosystem," it says, an echo of the host droid's voice. "The reproductive cycles of its two dominant organisms, the frostskimmers and the frostswimmers, are inextricably entwined."

"Thanks for that."

"The frostswimmers."

"Yeah. I'm aware."

"The frostswimmers," the grendel repeats, its voice buzzing louder.

Black code streaks across the smartglass. The throttle jerks under Yorick's grip, hauling the skid sideways. He understands a moment before the ice erupts all around them.

CHAPTER 81

The skid is thrown skyward; Yorick slams into the ceiling. He catches a fractured glimpse through the smartglass: a geyser of steam and shattered ice, and then, filling the whole sky, too big to be real, a mountain of hard gray chitin swatched with glowing parasites. The skid spins, caroms. Yorick is cartwheeling through the air when the impact gel finally deploys.

He jerks to a stop, suspended in a bubbly orange sea. The grendel is beneath him, caught mid-shapeshift, an insectoid specimen in amber. A shaken-loose lantern and empty water sac float beside it. Then the skid crashes back down, and the gel becomes a rippling blur. His pulse roars in his ears. He imagines the skid plunging through dark water, down to the dark bottom, joining the leviathan bones.

The skid settles, and he feels solid ice beneath them. He sucks down a slimy breath—the impact gel is laced with air pockets—and swims for the hatch. The grendel is already prying at it. They grip the emergency bar together, two hands and one tentacle, and the hatch splits open. They slide out in a mess of tangled limbs and gurgling gel.

The cold greets them. Yorick fumbles his hood on and wipes the goggles clear to see the frostswimmer corkscrewing in place, shedding a few last shards of ice. The scene is illuminated by its own armored hide, encrusted with phosphorescent parasites. Some of them fall and splash into the thick black water as the frostswimmer's chitinous head slides apart.

The palp emerges, a delicate spiral of latticed nerve endings. It ripples in the blizzard. For a moment Yorick thinks the wind might tear it away. Then it retracts, and the frostswimmer descends. Yorick is jerked off-balance, barely keeps his feet. The spray drenches him, freezes to him like an exoskeleton, frosts his goggles opaque. The world slants. Creaks. Moans.

He drops low, clawing at his goggles. He can feel the ice shiver under his splayed fingers. He waits for the cracks to find him, to dump him and the grendel both under. The dream from the cave flashes through his head. Maybe they'll join other bodies under the ice, hundreds of not-corpses spiraling through the water, wreathed in ghostly blue ansible lights.

The world steadies. His goggles come clear again to see the last of the frostswimmer's head vanish, leaving a vortex of shredded ice behind. Yorick stays crouched, staring at the enormous rift that ends bare meters from the nose of their wrecked skid. He tries to bring his heartbeat back down. He is only dimly aware of the grendel crouched beside him, mimicking his pose.

Once his pulse has subsided, he finally hears Fen. "You alive? Company man, you alive?"

Yorick spots the other skid on the far side of the rift, small dark figures clustered around it with lanterns. He tries to reorient himself. "Yeah," he says. "Our skid's done, though." He surveys the smashed chassis still leaking impact gel. "Yours?"

Fen's voice comes staticky in his earports. "Engine swamped and died. We're fixing it. Fast as we can. Then we'll have to go around."

Yorick watches the shadowy figures across the rift, squatting at the engine cowl, breaking out tools. His gut churns behind his incision. Repairs are slow work in a blizzard. More time for Thello in the interrogation pod. More time for Gausta to realize what's happened to her temporary camp.

He turns and looks the other way, into the blowing snow. Before the frostswimmer interrupted, they were only six kilometers from Gausta's house. He can survive six kilometers of blizzard if he wastes no more time, no more heat. If he starts moving now.

"We'll meet you there," he says. "Same plan. Gausta lets me in, I let you in."

Fen pauses. He imagines her running through options, parsing and discarding. "Alright," she says. "We'll follow as soon as we can."

Yorick finds two extra lanterns, digging them out of the impact gel's rapidly congealing pond, and clips them to his thermal suit. The grendel tracks him, a bulb-shaped head swinging back and forth. He activates the first lantern. A pale green globe of light expands around him, swirling with snow.

"Northern Ymir is known for its hazardous blizzards," he says.

The grendel doesn't respond, but when he starts walking, vultured against the wind, it slithers along after him. They are a few meters from the wrecked skid when Fen's voice comes faint in his earports, already shredded by the storm.

"Nocti says good luck."

Yorick remembers that this is how all colonist ballads end, with someone wandering off into a blizzard to die. But he's not wandering anymore.

Kilometer 1

The wind has teeth now. It shrieks and flails. Yorick keeps his head bowed, his shoulders hunched, following the map he loaded to his goggles. The carmine trail reminds him of another night, another blizzard. He widecasts a company signal as he walks, in case Gausta's smart mines spot him, and uses his mandible to amp and loop a voice clip: *There is no one for whom it is well. There is no one for whom it is well. There is no one—*

He struggles along to the tempo of his own synthesized chant. His breath is searing hot inside the foul-smelling hood. His body is drenched in sweat. Pushing into the gale makes every step twice the effort, and every step tugs at the incision. The fresh tissue might be tearing again. He imagines blood seeping into his interstitial spaces and filling up his pericardium like a balloon.

He glances backward. The skids are long gone, swallowed by the dark. The grendel is still following. It's bipedal again, a spindly imitation of a human. In the pale green wash of the lantern, it looks like a living shadow.

"Let me know if any more frostswimmers are coming up," Yorick says, because he suspects the grendel can detect their bioelectric fields as they hurtle for the surface, and he knows by the time he feels the ice vibrate under his boots it will be too late.

The grendel grows one tendril and twists it into a braid, imitating the palp.

"Yeah," Yorick says. "They like to taste the wind, sometimes. The southerly wind."

The grendel must know that already, though. Yorick remembers the dream in the cave, Piro's mad theory about the Oldies genejacking themselves to become aquatic leviathans instead.

He remembers the grendel is a thousand years old, and he shivers in his thermal gear.

The goggles pulse. One kilometer of six.

Kilometer 2

The wind beats him. Batters him. It finds tiny ingresses—the bends of his knees, the tips of his boots—and lets the cold creep through. For a few beautiful minutes, he hits equilibrium. The chill soothes his fevered skin, dabs gently at his incision. He tries to enjoy it. From now on it will only get colder, and before the numb sets in there will be pain.

He keeps his eyes on the carmine trail. Sometimes it looks like a stream of blood, and he imagines following it to a frostswimmer carcass, not the giant that nearly dumped them under but a manageable calf. He imagines finding a pair of fat-hunters at work flensing it, not for the blubber, nephew, but for the little beasties living inside it.

Ice and death and shit. Yorick's head is full of those ballads now as Ymir's starless gut pushes down on him, as Ymir's voice howls in both his ears. He is a frightened child, listening to his mother's stories about patchwork bogeymen. He can almost feel Thello's small bony shoulder pressed to his.

The goggles pulse. Two of six.

Kilometer 3

The grendel is ahead of him now. He's not sure how that happened, but it helps him keep pace. He tries to sync to its stride, imagining that he is stalking it through the tunnels of the Polar Seven, that he is smothered in heat. Or maybe it's a shade, leading him to the underworld. Beyond the pale green globe of his lantern, the blackness extends forever, in all directions, and could contain anything.

"Our mother used to tell this story," he says. "About a rich man."

He wishes Nocti were here to sing it. It would distract him from the tug in his abdomen, from the cold leaking slowly into his gear. His fingers chill and burn. His face turns gummy, the gelflesh almost indistinguishable from the real. All the sweat on his skin has turned to slime, and soon it will be frost.

If Yorick finds grotesques dancing around a bonfire, he will throw himself onto it just to be warm.

"Or maybe it was about a company man," he says.

The goggles pulse. Three.

Kilometer 4

The cold lives inside his thermal gear now. Inside his spider-wool. He's not sure when it happened, but now it feels as if he's always been cold. His toes have always been numb stumps. The cartilage of his ears has always thrummed and ached. It's hard to keep hold of the lantern. He watches the snow flurrying inside its globe, radioactive lime.

He gets a mad thought: he is carrying the blizzard along with him and could end it if he only turned the lantern off.

Something tugs at his ankle. He realizes he has stopped walking. He is swaying in the storm, staring into the lantern. Now he looks down and sees the grendel's hooked limb wrapped around his boot, pulling him on. Pulling him toward Gausta and Thello.

He wrestles forward into the dark. The goggles pulse.

Kilometer 5

The wind renders him down, slices through his numb skin and stiffening muscle, aches inside his heavy bones. His lantern flickers and dies. For a moment he is at the bottom of Ymir's frigid sea. His hindbrain seizes with terror. He fumbles for the second lantern. Squeezes. The pale green bloom illuminates the grendel. Its face is a cavity centimeters from his.

Its tendril is chipping the ice away from his boots. He yanks his feet free and starts moving again. He can't remember if the carmine trail is leading him to Gausta's house or to a maintenance hatch, the one on top of Laska's Cradle. His whole body is numb and his head is vapor.

Hypoxia. Not enough oxygenated blood in the capillaries, not enough fuel for the neurons to fire. He knows it, but he can't stop it. The world begins to slant and slide around him. He overcorrects, trying to stay upright, and crashes into the snow. His head spins. Lurches.

The grendel looms over him, and in his earports he hears a buzzing imitation of his own voice. "You having second thoughts?"

Yorick's lungs are spent, and the artificial nerves in his mandible have gone dead, disconnecting it, making it a foreign thing implanted in his frozen face. He can't even tell the grendel to get fucked.

It hauls him up by the armpits. They keep moving.

Kilometer 6

The grendel drags him across the ice, half its body wrapped around his, moving his limbs like an exoskeleton. He can feel slow undulations in its xenocarbon hide, its recycled flesh. Its reactor is faring better than his circulatory system. Yorick realizes he might die without it noticing, realizes it might walk his frozen corpse all the way to Gausta's door.

The carmine trail is blood again. Maybe Wickam's blood from the pit, or Linka's blood, leaking from the bioprinter that devoured her body. Maybe Canna's blood, draining into the snow. Maybe his blood, half-blood, half-blood.

The grendel drops him. He feels the jolt, then feels it peeling away from his numb body. It's decided he is deadweight, and will conserve its energy by continuing alone. Yorick wants to rage at it, wants to tell it that it will never be able to infiltrate Gausta's house without his help. His arms buckle as he readies himself to crawl.

He cranes his head, and suddenly there's light blooming and warping inside his goggles. Harsh light, floodlight. A company drone is scuttling toward him, white-hot gaze sweeping across the ice. Yorick hopes the grendel remembers the plan. His own synthesized chant echoes through the dark: *There is no one for whom it is well.*

Gausta's icon blinks onto his goggles.

"Yorick." No holo, just her disembodied voice. "What the fuck are you doing on my lake?"

This time his mandible manages an electric whisper. "Fat-hunting," he says.

"I doubt that very much," Gausta says. "And I remind you that your freighter launches in a shade under six hours." She pauses. "Come in, then."

The drone crabs closer. The heat of its motor trickles life back into his muscles. One last push, and he will be warm. He forces himself upright, and when he does he sees the grendel's detached limb lying in the snow.

It remembers the plan. Yorick tucks it under his armpit and staggers after the drone. He sees a slink of steam and light, then the hidden door opens all the way, carving through the dark. He imagines a bonfire on the other side, grotesques dancing all around.

"I have so much love to give," Yorick says, and the grendel's arm twitches.

He steps inside.

CHAPTER 82

The antechamber warms him in stages, cautious of shock. Yorick suspects it's scanning for weapons at the same time. He peels away his frost-rimed thermal gear, then stands vitruvian while one medroid checks his darkened fingers for tissue damage, another massages his chest with its rubbery cilia. Neither of them know what to do with the grendel limb. It lies on the floor, perfectly still, caked in a layer of frost.

"Came all this way to thank me for the parting gift, did you?" Gausta asks.

Yorick pinches his fingertips together one at a time, waiting for the pins and needles to stop. "I remembered I don't like objects," he says. "You should have it. Put it on your wall or something."

One of the medroids inspects the limb, then spraybags it. The one on his chest readies a microneedle kiss. Yorick shakes it off before Gausta can check his bloodwork.

"I have to assume you've been imbibing," she says. "The usual ritual of drink and drug and descent. Stealing tomorrow's happiness."

There won't be a tomorrow. Yorick knows that in his bones. But the medroids let him scoop up the grendel's frozen limb and cradle it as the second door folds open. Warm air gushes out. Temperature swing prickles his skin, squeezes his bladder. His olfactories taste rotting and flowering, death and birth, pungent smells that don't belong to Ymir.

He follows the droids into a nocturnal jungle. The corridor is swathed in vines, or maybe composed of them. Branches twist overhead, gnarled fingers interlocked, and the floor is soft springy dirt. An insect with glowing violet wings flits through the humid gloom. He wonders how much is real, grown from modded gene-prints, nursed by hydroponics, and how much is artificial.

Maybe half and half, like his rebuilt face.

A snatch of children's laughter comes from the end of the corridor, incongruous in a way that pebbles his skin. He steps into a room with a starry holo for a ceiling. He sees small dark bodies moving between the trees. Their bare feet make no sound—avatars, then, a little family of holos. His cold-bruised brain tells him one must be Thello.

Gausta's avatar is waiting up ahead, arms folded, blinking her reflective silver eyes. "Good morning, Yorick," she says, in a voice that's strangely muffled, strangely textured. "Welcome to a small slice of old memories."

She digs gound from the corner of her eye, and Yorick realizes, with a start, that she has body heat, a smell. She occupies air.

"It's modeled after a forest on Anubis," Gausta continues. "A cloudy valley, near the amoebic sea, where I was born." She plucks at a frond over her shoulder. "I grew up in less than idyllic circumstances—we have that in common—but the flora still makes for a pleasant backdrop. More pleasant than this endless fucking blizzard."

"Never been to Anubis," Yorick says.

"No grendels were ever found there." Gausta waves her hand; spindly chairs and a table flex up from the floor. "All the monsters on Anubis were human, as is so often the case. The company had its work cut out for it. Subjugation was long." She grins her wolfish grin. "But in the end they saved Anubis from devouring itself."

There are blue stains on her perfect teeth. It gives him a reflexive shiver, a cellular craving. Gausta's been amusing herself while she waits out the storm. For a moment all Yorick wants to do is find the doxy. Instead he picks a chair and sits, gripping the grendel's limb more tightly.

Gausta sits down across from him. One of the children, the holos, darts by. He sees the face this time. Swirled skin, silver eyes. Gausta's face. It's too gaunt and aged for the body; the holo-rig only made a perfunctory attempt to neotenize her features.

"Me," Gausta agrees, tracking his gaze. "And the play-mates I made for her. A simulated alternative to the misery she endured during the famine years." She smiles eyelessly. "You understand, don't you, Yorick? We accumulate the deep wounds when our bodies are small. The ones that come after are only extensions and variations."

Yorick traces Fen's fingerprints on his neck, then moves higher, to the gelflesh where his wound meets the mandible. "You know why I'm here, then."

"I know you must have slipped my drones in the Cut and stolen a skid," Gausta says. "I suspect you drove it to the temporary inter-rogation site, only to be informed that your brother was no longer being held there, at which point you traversed the storm to—"

"I came here to put Thello's head under the saw."

Gausta straightens in her chair.

"He takes my jaw, I take everything below it," Yorick says, his heart pumping acid now, burning through him. "I want him to watch. I want him to know."

Gausta's head tilts. "Is that so."

"It's the only way to end things," Yorick says. "The only way that makes sense."

Gausta leans back and the chair reads her body language, starts massaging her sharp shoulders. She swats it still. "The biotank will suit Thello," she says. "He always was a parasite. Even when the pair of you were children, he was the weak thing hanging off you. Dragging you down. Hiding behind you, right up until he slipped the metaphorical graft-knife into your back."

Yorick touches his mandible, keeping his strong hand where Gausta can watch it. His other hand works slowly at the spray-bag, clawing through the membrane. He told the grendel about graft-knives while they were in the skid. It remembered the one he tried to use in the bubblefab.

"I want you to end this miserable cycle, Yorick," Gausta says. "I truly do. But I'm afraid I can't grant your request."

Yorick's heart pounds. He slips his hidden hand inside the spraybag and feels the grendel's limb respond, cold tendrils unfurling. "Why not?" he rasps.

She doesn't answer, but he follows the angle of her chin and sees one of the medroids has followed him inside. He sees the distended curve of its underbelly. Bile rushes up his throat. Too late. Always too late, and time can't run in reverse.

"I did him in the flyer," Gausta says. "For efficiency's sake. The company conducts all interrogations in sims now, so there's really no need to keep the body."

The medroid pads over. Gausta gropes underneath it for a manual release. The trigger depresses with a soft click, and a translucent pink nutrient sac slides out. Thello's head hits the floor, with a sound like a meaty palm slapping a wet bartop, and rolls slightly.

CHAPTER 83

Every part of Yorick seems to scream at once, mirror neuron anguish at seeing his brother bodiless. His thawed hands go numb again. His heart stops, stutters. The grendel limb has wrapped around his arm now, hidden down by his knee. Filaments are hooking into his skin. It gives a questioning pulse.

"You're lying to me, Yorick," Gausta says. "I can see it on what Thello left you of your face." She shakes her head. "You came here to ask for clemency. Again. Twenty years later, and we're taking the same roles in the same tired holoplay."

Yorick has forgotten the plan. He doesn't know if the rest of the grendel has taken Gausta's house sensors yet, seized her security. All he knows is fury, boiling in every cell of his body, and fear, chasing ice through after it. Thello should be in a biotank by now. He needs to be hooked to an organoid, a neural construct, before his synapses start to collapse.

The grendel's ready, enveloping his hand like a biomechanical cestus. Yorick clenches his fist inside. Uses his other to mime a needlegun in the air beside his head, to draw Gausta's eyes. "That never happened," he says. "You lied to me in the clinic. Thello didn't pull the trigger."

Her forehead creases. "I never needed to lie. You built your own delusions."

Yorick remembers the conversations in the clinic, the hours spent bobbing through a phedrine sea. He remembers the therapy algorithms, the soft questions, the mantra, all the things he thought were aids for the psychotrauma of severe injury.

"The needlegun's trigger was genelocked, Yorick," Gausta says. "All company firearms are genelocked." Her silver eyes are soft now. Her voice is layered with pity. "You know that in every part of your mind but one."

"You let me think it," he says. "You let me hate him for years and years."

"The algorithm decided that was for the best," Gausta says. "Your attempt on your life was judged to be contextual. You remained an effective employee."

Yorick hurls his fist. The grendel's limb splits and scissors for her neck; Gausta's silver eyes go wide. Its sharp spines stop a quivering millimeter from her skin. Confusion becomes rage becomes something else, an expression Yorick has never seen on Gausta's marbled face but recognizes from a dozen others. She is afraid to die.

The children stop playing. They stare, their luminous eyes solemn and unblinking.

"Don't move," Yorick says.

"I see your feelings toward this grendel have changed." Gausta looks down at the cracked lava, the blended flesh and xenocarbon, melded to his arm. "Did that happen in the cave? When it sodomized your eye socket?"

"Don't move," Yorick repeats. "Or there's going to be a spectacular rendering of flesh."

Gausta's eyes narrow. Her throat shudders, maybe sending

subvocal orders to her house security. If the rest of the gren-del has done its work, she'll get nothing but static back. He crouches, clumsily, to grab hold of the nutrient sac. The gren-del's limb spindles out to keep contact with Gausta.

Yorick feels the shape of his brother's skull with his hand. Maybe there was a recycler in the flyer, or maybe they jetti-soned the body somewhere over the ice, for the blizzard to swallow whole. But he's still alive. He's still alive, and once the rest of the grendel is here they will put him in a biotank, and—

Gausta moves. She falls away from the stretched tendril and her swinging leg catches Yorick in the thigh. Meat crunches meat. His leg buckles under him. The grendel's limb whips for-ward on its own, but it's sluggish so far away from its reactor and Gausta's nerves are wired. She's gone, twisting in the air, and when she comes back around her hand is glinting with razors.

Yorick has the pain-thick thought that she's a grendel her-self, that she's grown serrations, as she closes the gap. He ducks, drives an elbow into her on the way by, but he can't take his hand off Thello's nutrient sac. She whirls, and the next kick sends blood spraying from his thigh. There are blades on her feet, too. She always did like to watch the jigs. Yorick can't feel the grendel's limb so he uses his own, feints—overreaches.

She swats his arm. Pins it. He feels her knee coming up for his ribs; he twists to protect the incision, takes it on his hip instead. Bone rattles bone. Gausta flits past him. He cranes his neck, trying to track. A callused heel crunches down on his foot, and when he jerks away from the pain he opens himself. She plants her razor hand in his belly.

He sees a burst of seething purple behind his eyeballs as his repaired abdomen explodes back open. The pain incinerates his whole body.

Then, mercifully, he dies. Yorick feels himself gliding through the dark, disconnected from the agony in his nerve endings. The jig is over. Fen would have done better. Now he is skimming across the ice, flying toward the warm welcoming tunnel that will take him to the underworld.

Death only lasts a moment. Gausta doesn't talk, but he hears her moving. Breathing. Switching a gun to manual, because she saw the cave raid. The familiar click-clack echoes in his skull. He feels the grendel, or the node of the grendel that agreed to be his graft-knife, abandon him. Its filaments tug and release, delicate as spiderwebs. It squirms down his arm.

The needlegun goes off in Yorick's ear. He feels it like a furious swarm, pictures it enveloping the grendel's weakened limb in a cloud of fléchettes. Clods of dirt and chunks of xeno-carbon rain down, then rise again as she fires a second time. A third. The holo of the night sky is tranquil overhead, stars winking in the firmament.

Yorick crawls one hand to his abdomen, where the real flesh and gelflesh have split and blood is pumping out of him. He reaches for the nutrient sac with the other. His fingers find a cheekbone under squelching pink fluid.

Gausta wrenches the sac out of his grip. She stands over him, eyes burning, skin smeared in dark blood that must be his. Yorick sees their audience in his peripheral. The children have come to watch, some crouching, some standing, all silent.

"You're the reason my camp is unresponsive, then," she says. "Not the blizzard." She shakes her head. "All this for *him*. It's wasteful. It's fucking wasteful." Her voice is shaking, scalding. "Your choice of ally is fitting, at least. A brutish machine mind that turned on its creators. Where's the rest of it, Yorick?"

Yorick doesn't know, but he opens his mouth to lie. To tell her anything she wants.

She lobs the nutrient sac away from herself, raises the needle-gun, and blows it apart. Blood and amniotic fluid bloom against the starry sky. One of the children claps her hands in delight.

Yorick's scream is a droid-thing, inhuman. He struggles up off the ground; Gausta hooks his leg and sends him back down. When he tries again she digs her heel into his ruptured wound and grinds deep. Her throat is still quivering, sending subvocals. She is in multiple places, trying to reach her avatars, but it doesn't matter.

The jig is over, so the gasoline scorching through his veins is meaningless. The anger is vestigial. Performative. An inevitable reflex.

A child laughs in the gap between two trees.

"Where's the grendel?" Gausta demands, maybe to him, maybe to her house. "Where are the prisoners from the camp?"

To him, then. He still can't answer. His tongue feels fused to his mandible, a single useless lump of machinery embedded in his flesh.

"It wasn't him," Gausta says, impatient. "I have multiple guests in interrogation. That one was a sealie woman from Sants." She stalks to a particular spot and digs down into the floor, uncovering a metal lever. "This pathology of yours is saddening to me, Yorick. Increasingly so."

Yorick's breath is hooked in his lungs. He searches the ground and glistening shrubs, trying to distinguish the viscera and bone shards. The children are back to their games. Before he can find even a shred of skin to confirm or condemn, Gausta hauls the lever. The stars blink out. The children dissolve. The omnipresent hum of electronics cuts away.

Nothing for the grendel to hack and jack.

"We'll break you of it," she says. "While we wait out your grendel. The blizzard won't last forever. The algorithm will see what's happened." Her luminous eyes dart through the dark. "They'll requisition soldiers from the ansible," she says. "And send a fresh squad from the garrison. Perhaps two." Her voice is distant. "I'm a very valuable employee."

Yorick's head is still shattered, caught between truths and lies, when she opens a hatch in the mossy wall and hauls him over to it. She uses her foot to push him down the stairs.

CHAPTER 84

One flight, not seven, but more painful than any descent he made in Southern Urbanite Memory, and long enough for him to catalog his errors. Long enough for him to see how dumbsick he was to let Gausta distract him, to think she was only a voyeur now and not a soldier. He should have used the grendel's spiny jaws to at least break her legs.

Now, his fall finally over, his body curled fetal at the concrete base of the stairs, it feels like he has broken everything. All his bones ache. His sliced-open stomach has become a gaping mouth. His bruised neurons flash a jumble of images: he crests a snow dune, a sand dune, a wind-raked hill, sees a grendel unfurling its body across the artificial sky.

"You smell of piss," Gausta says, and he feels her step carefully over him.

Biolamps are coming on, a seep of blurry orange illumination from the corners. Yorick's mandible splintered on the edge of a step and his skull is still ringing from the impact. He tries to focus his eyes. He sees concrete walls lined with antibacterial yolk, like a clinic or thaw facility. A humming black biotank hooked to its own generator, not Gausta's shut-down grid. A teledoc with a gleaming saw.

A triptych of cells:

The left holds a clanner from the cave, not yet debodied, squinting in the gloom. The flesh of her wrists has grown over the bioplastic, swollen from repeated stings. Now she holds them immaculately still.

The center is empty, the smartglass blotted with gore.

The right holds his brother. He's wearing an antisensory hood, but Yorick recognizes the shape of him, the shade of him. He recognizes the injuries: an exoskel splint on one leg, gelflesh coating one hand. Thello's cuffs are magnetized to the wall above his head, and his wrists are bloated purple.

"There are some things a sim never gets quite right," Gausta says. "You know that. Scents, mostly." She taps a finger on Thello's one-way glass. "Your brother is even more pungent than you are. I've barely touched him, and his sweat already reeks from fright."

Yorick eyes the needlegun dangling from her hand. He remembers the click-clack. Manual now, no genelock.

"I wish I could trust you with it," Gausta says, reading him so easily. "It would give me great peace of mind, to see you rectify your past error." She casts a look up the stairwell, to the door she sealed behind them at the top. "I think I hear your grendel."

Yorick hears nothing. He keeps one forearm pressed hard against his gut, uses his free hand to drag himself to the smart-glass. He thumps his fist against it, hoping his brother will feel the vibration. The hood doesn't twitch, but Thello's chest is rising, falling.

Yorick's head tips forward against the smartglass and leaves a red smear.

"After you, Yorick." Gausta undoes the manual locking bar and drags the cell open. "I believe you're still able to crawl."

Outside, Ymir howls.

CHAPTER 85

Gausta cuffs only one of his hands to the wall, so he can use the other to keep pressure on his split stomach. Then she slides the smartglass shut, eyes glimmering. Her way of moving has changed, live wires in her gait, no longer smooth and predatory. She moves like the holo children dancing through the dark forest.

"We should be safe down here," she says. "The grendel has no electronic locks to manipulate. It has no seditious miners to help it burrow through concrete."

He stares across the cell at his brother. Thello doesn't know they're here. He's still slumped, chin notched to his chest. Yorick tries to guess, from the shallow breathing, the deep bruising, which drugs and tools Gausta has been using on him.

"He was far more loquacious earlier," she says. "He told me all sorts of things. We spoke about the old days. About Subjugation. About your mother, at one point, though I believe he was hallucinating."

Yorick can almost feel the cupped hand exploding across his face.

"He pleaded for her," Gausta says. "Isn't that strange? He

pleaded for Fen, as well, and for other clanners by name, but not for you. Never for you."

It might be lies. It might be true. Yorick tries to tell himself it doesn't matter. Some things can be true and not matter at all. What matters is that the grendel must be somewhere above them in the dark house, searching for a way into the bunker. Fen and the clanners might have already made it around the rift. Thello is still whole.

"Despite everything you did to keep him safe, during the misery years. He taught himself to love Ymir, and the cold-bloods, and even your mother." Gausta shakes her head. "But not you."

"He was frightened of me," Yorick says, buzzing through the mangled circuitry of his mandible. He feels a dying wasp spasm under his thumb. "I saw."

"He was selfish."

"He was a child." Yorick chokes the word out. "He still was, when I left him with her. When I went to Shipfall."

"We never stop being children." Gausta steps back from Thello. She sits down, lotus-legged, with the needlegun cradled in her lap. "It doesn't matter who pulled the trigger back then," she says. "It really doesn't. Because that"—she nods to his damaged mandible—"was only an extension of an earlier wound."

Yorick takes a gurgling breath. Holds it. "Why the fuck do you care?"

"Because you could be so much happier," Gausta says, face darkening. "And so much more effective. Thello is the reason you waste your violent talents on grendels. Thello is the reason you drink and drug yourself to oblivion. If you would only let him go, if you would only realize how little you mean to him, you would be an excellent company man."

Yorick stares at her. "I have so much love to give," he says.

"Your therapeutic mantra. Yes." Gausta holsters the needle-gun; it clings to the small of her bare back. "To be honest, Yorick, I thought you chose it ironically." Her hand blade, the same one that slashed his belly back open, emerges from its subcutaneous sheath. "Do you recall the insurrectionists' preferred execution method?"

A wave of nausea hits him. Yorick has never forgotten Canna, who bled out into the snow. He has dreamed about her. Now he watches as Gausta makes an adjustment to Thello's cuffs, leaving them locked in place but deactivating the nematocysts.

"The reflex cascade makes delicate work impossible," she says. "And this will be delicate. One hundred cuts. Cauterized and below the neck, naturally, leaving no significant evidence of mistreatment once he's debodied."

Yorick is desperate, plummeting. "Wait," he rasps. "Wait. What do you want me to do?"

"Only to listen," Gausta says. "While he begs and babbles. If he calls for you once, Yorick, even once—I'll stop." She gives her blue-stained smile. "He won't, though. And when we get to one hundred, when he's screamed every name but yours, he goes under the saw."

CHAPTER 86

Gausta works in silence, and once Yorick gives up pleading he falls silent, too. The noises come from the blade—a small wet scrape of splitting skin—and from Thello, who moans and sometimes sobs when Gausta daubs hissing chlorine into flayed flesh. There is no gap to hide in. No safe spot. No way for Yorick to trade places with him.

So he counts the marks, watches their progress the way he watched the bodies dissolve in Laska's Cradle. The tiny gashes glisten in the biolamp light, laddering up and down Thello's legs and arms like puckered mouths, each one cauterized by a searing chemical kiss. Most are short and shallow, precise, but there is a ragged one on Thello's ribs from when he still had the energy to flail.

Yorick remembers every vengeance he fantasized in the clinic, when they were putting in the nerve conduits and his entire world was pain Thello had caused him. The shameful things he buried later. All of them are back, and he realizes that like the sims, they had no smells.

Thello was different in them, too, snarling and defiant. This Thello is fluttering between conscious and unconscious. Gausta guides his nervous system along a tightrope, denying it the consensus that might slip him into shock.

She has done this before. The blade moves in a steady rhythm. She has planned her path across Thello's body in advance, and Yorick can do nothing to interrupt it. His one sympathetic convulsion set the nematocysts stinging.

For a while he imagined the sound of the grendel far above them, hammering at the bunker door, swinging some xenocarbon club. But that receded, and now he has no illusions. The world is small. It contains three elements.

Thello, dying slow: each wound seeps only a few drops of blood before Gausta cauterizes it.

Him, dying quicker: the gashes in his stomach are too deep for even his modded platelets to dam. The seeping red puddle is sticky underneath him.

Gausta, pristine as one of her avatars: the holstered needle-gun bobs up and down every time she slices, symbolic and malicious and far out of reach. Yorick is jarred when her blade finally hesitates, paused over Thello's inner thigh.

"Seventy-six," she says. "We're approaching a significant number for you, Yorick."

His count was off by one; he must have squeezed his eyes shut at some point.

"Laska's Cradle was one of the primary reasons we gave the Cut a name," she says, "instead of a simpler numeric company town designation. The company felt it was important to acknowledge distasteful acts committed on both sides. The name was a gesture of good faith. A willingness to move forward."

She taps the tip of the blade against Thello's leg.

"Those of us who know the north know the name is a fucking joke, of course," she says. "Reconciliation is called Reconciliation for the same reason a utopia is called a utopia. There is no such place. No such thing."

Her blade darts, comes away with a fresh slick of blood and one dark hair stuck to it. Thello squirms. Begs. She reaches for the chlorine.

"He'll never know you were here, Yorick," she says. "I suspect that is what galls you most. Reconciliation is a grand empty gesture, and he will never see yours. What you really want is not his life, but his gratitude."

The old words churn back up and burn hot in his ruined belly: *Thello will never know. Thello will never know.* She cauterizes the new cut and Thello's head lolls backward. He groans for Fen.

"All attachments of this kind are empty at their center," Gausta says. "I learned that long ago. I had family once, Yorick." Her gaze flicks upward, toward the ceiling of the bunker. "But by the time the company came to Anubis, by the time they ended the famine, I was the only one left." Her eyes are ravenous. "I did very hard things. And it liberated me."

Yorick sees her face on a child's gaunt body, hears the disembodied laughter.

"Liberation is the best you can hope for," Gausta says. "Even if love were worth this agony, there's none to reclaim here. He never bore you any."

The words bring back all his dread. Yorick forces it down. Forces air into his diaphragm. "I don't need him to love me." His voice is a buzzing wheeze. "I don't need him to know."

"I very much doubt that," Gausta says. "But I'll entertain it for a moment." She sets the chlorine down. "Ask, and I'll take his hood off. You can tell him of your desperate gambit to free him. You can detail your devotion to him. Perhaps, because there is no one else, he will finally cling to you." Her hand strokes the needlegun at her back. "And then I kill him. No saw, no biotank. The painless void. Prisoners do go missing on Ymir."

A small part of Yorick wails for it. He imagines Thello seeing his crushed mandible and mangled body, seeing how fucking hard he tried to make things right. Thello would die knowing Yorick loved him in every way he knows how to love. There would be no more pain. No more possibility.

He shakes his head.

Gausta blinks. "Very well. The cutting continues, then."

She eyes her handiwork, searching for where she left off. She finds an untouched swathe of skin on Thello's shoulder. The blade flexes from her hand, and Yorick's chest aches. She cuts. Daubs. Cuts. Daubs. Thello wails, and shakes, and Yorick loses count but knows a hundred is close and the grendel and the clanners are far.

He chose wrong. The ballad ends badly, and Thello will never know. Gausta will make her hundredth cut with the teledoc's saw. Thello will go into the biotank thinking Yorick put him there, then disappear into the dark and never emerge. Nothing will ever change. Not for them, not for Ymir, not for their mote-of-dust galaxy, all sliding along the invisible rail.

Gausta's head cocks. "Ninety-four," she says. "We'd better hurry. I hear the flyer."

Her hearing must be amped. Yorick can hear nothing but the faint shriek of the storm.

"It's quite flattering that they risked the winds," she says. "They must be eager to test themselves against the grendel."

Yorick hopes that the grendel has already fled. It's damaged, and missing a limb, and the fresh squad in the flyer will have watched the cave raid and adjusted tactics. If it's still prowling through the house above, they'll make short work of it. Then they'll hunt down Fen and her clanners on the ice, free the soldiers from the camp.

Yorick stares across the cell, trying to picture his brother's face beneath the hood. He sees a boy sitting in a company fountain, cupping and pouring, staring up at the artificial stars. He sees the stoop, the drone, the needlegun Thello tried so hard to stop him from using.

Thello will never know. Yorick hears his own electric sob, but beneath it he hears the flyer, a pitched whine slowly gaining volume.

Louder than it should be. Closer than it should be.

Gausta's shoulder blades go taut an instant before the impact. Yorick's body jerks into the air; the nematocysts feast on his wrist as it wrenches against the cuff. He slams back against the cell wall and loses all his air at once.

The concrete shudders; the smartglass shatters. It sweeps through the cell, a shimmering echo of the blizzard outside. Gausta loses her balance, staggers sideways. Her bare foot slides on Yorick's blood. She slips. Her marbled face is only a half meter from him. He tries to aim a kick but his muscles lock and spasm; the cuff is still jabbing, burning. He howls from it and hears Thello howling, too.

Gausta crabs out of reach, swings back to her feet. Her eyes trace the cracks in the concrete ceiling, calm, barely curious. She feels for the needlegun at the small of her spine.

The dregs of Yorick's adrenaline freeze the scene for him: Gausta reaches and doesn't find, because the needlegun was knocked loose from her back, because the needlegun skittered over the broken smartglass, halfway into the corridor.

The clanner from the other cell, the one whose wrists are mottled and overgrown, crouches above it. Her face is studded with globules of sweat. She moves her cuffed hands downward by increments, so slow, so smooth.

Gausta turns. "Genelocked," she says, but he can see the fear again. "All company firearms are genelocked."

The clanner's face flickers with doubt.

"It's on manual," Yorick croaks.

Gausta moves in a blur, wired nerves hurtling her across the broken glass, but the clanner has already found the trigger. Behind his eyes Yorick sees the drone, the stoop. Then he hears the volcanic roar of a needlegun going off.

CHAPTER 87

Fen blows the bunker with a biobomb recovered from the company flyer they crashed through Gausta's roof. Yorick is only half lucid when she comes down the stairs. The grendel clinging to her back makes her seem even more like a hallucination. He is still cuffed to the wall, but now the blood under his haunches is mixed with Gausta's.

The needlegun blew her hip apart and punched a ragged hole through her thigh. She is alive—the clanner used the tattoo on her bony neck to unlock the cuffs—but only because of the company mods. Her luminous eyes flutter open and shut.

Thello is alive, too. The clanner is cradling his head and murmuring to him. The antisensory hood is off, but his eyes aren't seeing things. Not yet.

Fen and the grendel and the other clanners go to their own. Yorick watches in a haze as they assess Thello's wounds, as their faces contort. Someone drags the teledoc in from the corridor. Yorick feels hands on him, hands made for an instrument. Nocti is binding him shut again, slapping a swathe of gelflesh on his midsection.

"More frostswimmers breached," the musician says. "We had to go back to the camp for the flyer. To get over the top of them." Yorick sees he is glassy from his own sort of shock. "That grendel, you know, they can hack, and they can jack, but they don't pilot so good."

"It's fine," Yorick says. "Gausta has another one."

He strains his ears, and hears Thello whispering names, asking after casualties. Yorick doesn't hear his name, but the voice is enough.

CHAPTER 88

The blizzard is ending. Through the thinning veil of snow, Yorick can make out the glow of more frostswimmers at the surface. He imagines their palps tasting the air, finding the southerly wind. Gausta's flyer cuts against it, angling north and west, as they head for the ansible. Her teledoc is still at work treating Thello's many cuts.

Yorick stays by the window, watches from distance. Fen and the clanners are monitoring every twitch of the pneumatic limbs, as if the teledoc might revert to its more vicious functions at any moment, start slicing instead of stapling. Maybe that's why they let Yorick go first: to check if Gausta had coded in some cruel backdoor or dormant instruction.

He noticed no bias. The teledoc gelfleshed his stomach shut with the same detached efficiency as last time, then did the new wounds on his foot and thigh. The phedrine filled his whole body with clouds. All the pain is down below them. His ruined mandible keeps rasping against itself because his face keeps twisting with the ghost of a smile.

Thello is alive. So is he. So's the prisoner from the leftmost cell of Gausta's bunker, so's the grendel that found them there, so are Nocti and Fen and the eight clanners who carried them up the stairs. Even Gausta is alive, immobile but breathing while the grendel puppeteers her company implant to negotiate entrance to the ansible.

"Here you go." Nocti joins him at the window, holding a small yellow tab between his fingertips. "Your damper."

Yorick doesn't like marring a phedrine high, but he takes the tab and pokes it down his mercifully numbed throat—the teledoc saw to that damage, too. Fen's giant hand looks so gentle now that it's enveloping Thello's.

Nocti's forehead creases. "I asked the grendel to send Linka a message," he says, watching the membranous roof of the Cut pass beneath them. "To tell her we're alive still. Heading for the ansible. Think they did it?"

"I think so." Yorick remembers the conversation they had in his head. "I think the grendel likes her."

"They have good taste, then. That grendel."

Nocti departs to pass out the rest of the neuroleptics. Yorick looks through the window again. They're soaring over the Polar Seven, high above the glowing yellow pylons that ring the Maw. The ansible is growing in the distance. The sight drives a spar of ice through his phedrine comfort. The ballad's not over. Not yet.

Yorick turns and leans his back against the window, watches the small crowd ebb and flow around his brother. The teledoc is nearly finished. Thello is alive. He's alive, too. He tries to hold on to that euphoria thought.

The cold smartglass has almost leached it away when Fen comes over. "Thello wants to talk," she says, expressionless. "If you're ready."

Yorick gets to his feet.

CHAPTER 89

Even when Yorick hated his brother in the daytime, night was different. His subconscious would churn up small scenarios, some banal, some nonsensical, where he and Thello were together, and the anger had been expunged.

They built latticed snow sculptures outside their grandmother's bubblefab, meant to somehow redirect the wind. They sat in a bar on Janus Station, the one where Yorick vomited to celebrate his first successful grendel hunt, and Thello agreed it was a good place to vomit. They forgave each other a hundred times, easily and with no words.

Now he sits beside his brother in the back of the flyer, both of them more gelflesh than real flesh, both of them unspeaking. There is no preloaded dream knowledge to tell him what they feel for each other. This is the real Thello, not Yorick's neurons working out a knot.

"Ninety-seven," Thello says.

Yorick drags his eyes off the marks. "They won't scar," he says. "Not with the stemtags in."

"No." Thello's mouth works. "Fen told me what you did. I'm glad."

"Yeah. I'm glad, too." Yorick knows the conversation could

end there, knows he can retreat and the ice will solidify. He claws forward. "I shouldn't have left, back then."

Thello blinks. "Ymir?"

"The Cut," Yorick says. "I shouldn't have left you there with our ma."

"I wanted you to," Thello says.

Yorick remembers Thello's memory of that parting, the sweat-drenched sparring session. His throat clenches. "I wasn't who I thought I was," he says. "The grendel showed me your version of things. You were afraid of me. When we were imp. I never knew that."

"I was afraid of everything, when we were imp," Thello mutters. "But yeah. You were one of them. You were always trying to—make me colder. Tougher. Make me more like you, more like our ma." He shrugs. "You thought it would help," he says. "I don't blame you for it anymore. I don't hate you for it. It was all a long time ago."

Yorick's chest aches. "The grendel showed me the day with the needlegun, too."

Thello's eyes flick to his damaged mandible, then flick away. "I barely remember that day. I remember the mess. The red on the stoop."

"You tried to stop me," Yorick says. "I had it to my head, and you tried to stop me."

Thello flinches. "Of course I tried to stop you."

Yorick knows he would have tried to stop anybody, would have tried to stop Gausta, if he saw them with a needlegun to their head. Thello never could stand blood. Never could stand seeing too much hurt. He would have given any captive the chiral molecule.

Yorick feels the words moving from his rib cage, up his bruised throat. He wants to tear off his mandible, keep them from coming out, because once they're out they will drag him off the invisible rail and over a precipice. Maybe drag Thello there, too, Thello who has taken so much damage from him already. But if he doesn't say them now, he never will.

"I'm so fucking sorry," he chokes. "I loved you, Thello. How I could. I still do. I still have these fucking dreams."

Thello's eyes are exhausted. "I know you do," he says. "Or think you do. I used to love you, too. I used to hate you. I used to want to stop you—" His voice is full of gravel. "From doing things you'd regret. From starting jigs you couldn't finish." He shakes his head. "I used to feel all kinds of shit when it came to you. But it's been a long time, Yorick. It feels like it was someone else's life."

Yorick's heart eats itself. "Yeah."

"Maybe when you're older, it'll go away for you, too," Thello says. "Or feel—different. But you can't get older in a torpor pool."

There is no embrace. Yorick doesn't think there ever will be. Thello doesn't put his hand on his shoulder for luck as they ascend past the ansible's pulsing blue light. But there are no words trapped bristling in Yorick's throat, no dark dreams drifting between them, no anger. Just a soft emptiness.

CHAPTER 90

The ansible has lifts, functional ones, but they don't use them. The flyer heads straight to the top and docks against the carbon shell scaffolding that crowns it. Gausta's avatar sends the security drones scattering, like a flock of startled birds, and assures the soldiers below that she needs no additional escort. The actual Gausta is lucid again, watching the performance with a mild disdain on her face. Her mouth is gelfleshed shut.

Yorick doesn't need her mouth free to hear her voice in his head: *There is a reason we don't cultivate machine minds anymore, Yorick. They invariably tire of us. That is how the architects met extinction, and how you now hasten us to ours.* But as he follows the grendel through the dockstalk, he realizes he trusts it more than he ever trusted her.

He steps out onto the scaffolding. He was bracing for the brain-bend, even with Nocti's dampers, but now that they are on the ansible itself—close enough to reach out and touch the dark biostone, too close to try parsing its wrongful geometry—the effects are muted. He can focus his eyes.

They are high over the ice. When the ansible pulses, the electric-blue light spills out from under the platform and extends in all directions, pushing farther into the dark than Yorick has ever been able to see. The snow has stopped and the wind has softened to a steady current, still cold and strong but no longer snapping its vicious teeth. He doesn't need his hood. His boots barely have to cling.

The grendel skitters up the scaffold, onto the ansible exterior. Most of its tendrils run over the surface, searching for something, but a few twitch and wave in the air, almost dancing. Yorick turns to watch Thello and Fen emerge from the flyer. His brother's cuts are hidden under the thermal suit, but he moves stiff, then trembly. Fen has to help him walk.

The grendel grows its mouth and speaks in a distorted chorus. "I hope you enjoyed your stay."

Yorick looks back. "Yeah," he says. "You too. Good luck on the other side."

He steps back as Thello steps forward, unaided now. His brother and the grendel face each other for a moment, and Yorick remembers them whispering to each other in the dark apartment, sharing dreams in the dead of night. He remembers Thello spent six years crisscrossing the ice, descending into mine after hellish mine to search for it.

The grendel extends one rust-red filament, then another, and another. They wriggle under Thello's eyelids and up his nostrils, cradling his face in a spidery hand. He sways on his feet. Fen tenses behind him, ready to catch.

An opening appears on the ansible exterior, a semicircle carving through the biostone. Yorick catches a vertiginous glimpse of the interior: an electric sea stretching away forever, luminous silhouettes dividing and recombining, almost like the brush of bodies in a torpor pool. He feels his skin pebbling, his veins foaming.

The grendel perches on the lip of the opening, still tethered to Thello. Every one of its tendrils is writhing, and now the ansible reaches with its own tendril, a finger of pale blue light. The grendel's hide slides apart to let it in. Yorick sees the dimming reactor, the surviving nodes. When the light touches them they start to pulse, faster and faster, hearts accelerating in unison.

The ansible extends a second finger of light. It touches Thello's face, then widens to sweep across his whole body, bathing his skin. His breathing quickens, chest pumping. The clanners tighten their circle, awed and solemn as pilgrims. Fen's pale eyes narrow. The grendel lurches on the edge of the opening, and for a moment Yorick thinks it will take Thello with it.

But the filaments retract, one lingering for just a semisecond on Thello's shoulder. The grendel shivers. Then it tips forward, through the gap in the biostone, and disappears. Thello sinks to his haunches on the scaffolding, forehead glistening with sweat. Everybody watches him. Nobody speaks.

The ansible goes dark.

Yorick hopes the grendel gets the homecoming it wanted. He looks at the clanners all huddled, arms around each other, arms around Thello, and he realizes it was never his ballad. He was never fated to be here. The sudden lack of invisible rails is dizzying. Quantum branches are spreading out in all directions, shifting and melding and splitting like the shapes in the ansible's electric sea.

He walks into the southerly wind, to the edge of the scaffold. The phedrine is trickling away. His gelfleshed stomach is throbbing again, and his throat feels raw, and the dozen small injuries he's accumulated are clamoring in the background. Underneath all of that, he feels a bone-deep exhaustion. He eases himself down on the lip of the platform and shuts his eyes.

He hears Nocti's soft feet a moment later. "Found you something. Bottom of my coat lining."

Yorick looks up and sees half a tab of doxy, not damper, pinched between the musician's thumb and forefinger. "I don't do that shit anymore," Yorick says, but slips it into his pocket.

"Waiting for the end of the world." Nocti squats down beside him. "Or at least the end of a little one." His eyes are anxious. "I don't remember Ymir before the company. Before implants and indenturement and the mines."

"Me neither," Yorick admits.

Nocti worms a hand into his surface gear, comes out with his vapor pipe. "If this works," he murmurs. "If the grendel does what it says—I don't know if I'm cut out to be a clanner."

Yorick can tell he is thinking of Linka in her biotank. "The Cut won't disappear. It was here before the company." He pauses. "It'll be different, though."

Nocti nods. Taps his pipe against his kneecap. "You going to stay, then, Oxo? Yorick, I mean."

The question startles him. He forgot the freighter waiting for him at the dock, his place in the torpor pool. He was so sure, cell-certain, that this was his final night on Ymir. One way or another.

"Never considered the after-the-end," the musician guesses. "The new little world."

Yorick shakes his head.

"You have time." Nocti puts a hand on his shoulder, and Yorick is not on hyena but it feels alright. "You can live in the other lift while you think it out."

"Yeah. Neighbors." He swallows. "Thanks, Nocti."

"Get you a new jaw, too. Custom. That one's sounding rough."

The musician rises, puffing at his vapor pipe, and goes back to the others. As he walks away, Yorick feels a buzzing wasp against his neck. He claps a hand to it by reflex. The nano ink of his company tattoo is swirling, glitching. He feels it weeping free from his skin.

It becomes a cold trickle down his neck, under his thermal suit. He pictures the Cut, all the indenturement implants in all the miners now dissolving the same way, all the confusion and disbelief and hope. He hears the clanners murmuring, then hears Thello's incredulous laugh, same as it was when they were imp.

The ansible's security drones are converging overhead. If they have finally figured out that Gausta is not giving the orders, if they are here to rain shock rounds and drag them off the platform, there is nothing Yorick will be able to do about it. He's too stiff and heavy to move. His whole skeleton is lead.

But the drones are malfunctioning, or maybe functioning perfectly. They churn patterns in the sky. They loop and pinwheel. Yorick watches the clanners exhale, then whoop, then bellow. He watches Nocti saw out the first notes of an unfamiliar song, maybe the one he was busy composing in the stalled lift of Southern Urbanite Memory.

The ansible pulses again. There are frostskimmers moving in the distance. Some still have their sails, membranes snapped taut in the wind, but they're too heavy to glide. The embryo pouches are swollen to bursting. They wander toward the ansible, drawn to its light. The autocannons have finally let them in. Then, one by one, they begin to spore.

He watches as the pouches peel open, watches as a bioluminescent cloud expands, an entire nebula of tiny organisms.

When the ansible goes dark they seem to hold its electric-blue glow. They waft up into Ymir's sky to catch the southerly wind, moving across the void in a slow tide. The drones dance through it, eerie and beautiful, and for a moment Ymir needs no stars.

Yorick inhales. Exhales.

"I have so much love to give," he says.

END

ACKNOWLEDGMENTS

The town of Fish Hoek, its small quiet mountain and wind-swept beach, the cafés I frequented (Oh Honey and the Grind, who closed, Peak Connect and Tidbit, who survived), and the people I met (Gary and Lori and Farren, in particular).

My sister, her husband, and their three children—named in the dedication—who accepted me into their home and let me linger for half a year.

My friend and fellow writer Anthony Bell, who lent me his plotting brain for hours on end via Discord or WhatsApp.

My editors, Brit Hvide and Angeline Rodriguez, and my agent, John Silbersack, who bolstered me through crises of confidence and contract.

My brother.

extras

orbit

meet the author

Photo Credit: Micaela Cockburn

RICH LARSON was born in Galmi, Niger, has lived in Spain and the Czech Republic, and currently writes from somewhere in Canada. He is the author of over two hundred short stories, some of the best of which can be found in his collections *Tomorrow Factory* and the forthcoming *Harbingers*. His fiction has appeared in over a dozen languages, including Polish, Italian, Romanian, and Japanese, and his translated collection *La Fabrique des lendemains* won the Grand Prix de l'Imaginaire. His short story "Ice" was adapted into an Emmy-winning episode of *Love, Death & Robots*. Besides writing, he enjoys traveling, learning languages, playing soccer, watching basketball, shooting pool, and dancing kizomba.

Find out more about Rich Larson and other Orbit authors by registering for the free monthly newsletter at orbitbooks.net.

if you enjoyed
YMIR

look out for

THE BODY SCOUT

by

Lincoln Michel

In the future, you can have any body you want—as long as you can afford it.

But in a New York ravaged by climate change and repeat pandemics, Kobo is barely scraping by. He scouts the latest in gene-edited talent for Big Pharma—owned baseball teams, but his own cybernetics are a decade out of date, and twin sister loan sharks are banging down his door. Things couldn't get much worse.

Then his brother—Monsanto Mets slugger JJ Zunz—is murdered at home plate.

Determined to find the killer, Kobo plunges into a world of genetically modified CEOs, philosophical Neanderthals, and back-alley body modification, only to quickly find he's in a game far bigger and more corrupt than he imagined. To keep himself together while the world is falling apart, he'll have to navigate a time when both body and soul are sold to the highest bidder.

1

The Dark Hours

When I couldn't fall asleep, I counted the parts of the body. I used the outdated numbers. What they'd taught me back in school when only the ultrarich upgraded. Two hundred and six bones. Seventy-eight organs. The separate pieces floated through the fog of my mind, one by one, like strange birds. If I was still awake by the end, I'd think about everything connecting. Miles of nerves and veins snaking through the pile, tying tibia to fibula, connecting heart to lung. Muscles, blood, hair, skin. Everything joining together into a person, into me.

Then I swapped in new parts. A second cybernetic arm or a fresh lung lining for the smog. Cutting-edge implants. This season's latest organs. I mixed and matched, tweaked and twisted.

I didn't know if I was really getting myself to sleep. I might have been keeping myself swimming in that liminal ooze between waking problems and troubled dreams. It was a state that reminded me of the anesthetic haze of the surgery table. Like my mattress was a slick metal slab and the passing headlights were the eyelamps of surgery drones. Outside, the world went by. Construction cranes hoisted buildings tall enough to stab the clouds. Cars cluttered the skies. But inside, my senses dulled, the world was gone. I was alone and waiting to wake up as something different, better, and new.

I'd been piecing myself together for years. With surgeries and grafts, with shots and pills. I kept lists of possible procedures. Files of future upgrades that would lead me to an updated life. My brother, JJ Zunz, always laughed about it. "One day I'm going to wake up, and none of you will be left," he'd say. That would have been fine with me.

We're all born with one body, and there's no possibility of a refund. No way to test-drive a different form. So how could anyone not be willing to pay an arm and a leg for a better arm and a better leg?

Sure, we're each greater than the sum of our parts. But surely greater parts couldn't hurt.

Each time I upgraded it was wonderful, for a time. I had new sensations, new possibilities. I was getting closer to what I thought I was supposed to be. Then each time seemed to require another time. Another surgery and another loan to pay for it. Two decades of improvements and I still wanted more, but now I had six figures in medical debt crushing me like a beetle under a brick.

That night, as I was Frankensteining a new body for myself in my head, my brother called. The sound jostled me. My imaginary form collapsed, the parts scattering across the dim emptiness of my mind. I opened my eyes. Yawned. Slapped the receiver.

A massive Zunz appeared before me, legs sunk through the carpet to the knees, face severed at the ceiling. He was so large he could have swallowed my head as easily as a hard-boiled egg.

401

"Kang," he said. He paused, then repeated the name with a question mark. "Jung Kang?"

I shrank his hologram to the proper size. He glowed at the end of my bed. For some reason, he was wearing his batting helmet. It was 3:00 a.m.

"Um, no. It's me. Kobo. You dial the wrong address?"

Outside, the bright lights of the city illuminated the nighttime smog. A billboard floated past my window, flashing a Growth Cola ad. *The Climate Has Changed, Your Body Should Too.*

"Yes. Kobo." He shook his head. "My brother. How are you?" Zunz spoke haltingly, as if he either had a lot on his mind or nothing at all. He looked healthy at least. A lot of players in the league wanted the retro bodybuilder style, muscles stacked like bricks, but Zunz made sure the trainers kept him lean and taut. When he swung a baseball bat, his arms snapped like gigantic rubber bands.

"Shit, JJ. You sound like you got beaned in the head with a bowling ball. What do the Mets have you on?"

"Lots of things," he said, looking around at something or someone I couldn't see. He had several wires running from his limbs to something off feed. "Always lots of things."

Zunz was a star slugger for the Monsanto Mets and my adopted brother. After the apartment cave-in killed my parents and mushed my right arm, his family took me in. Gave me a home. Technically, I was a few days older than him, but I never stopped thinking of him as my big brother.

"Kobo, I feel weird. Like my body isn't mine. Like they put me in the wrong one."

"They? You gotta sleep it off. Hydrate. Inject some vitamins." I unplugged my bionic right arm, got out of bed. Tried to stretch myself awake. "Here, show me your form."

Zunz didn't have a bat on him, but he clicked into a batting stance.

"Fastball right down the middle."

He swung his empty hands. Stared into the imaginary stands.

"Fourth floor. Home run," I said. Although his movement was off. The swing sloppy and the follow-through cut short.

Zunz flashed me his lopsided smile. His dimples were the size of dugouts. He got back into his stance. "Another."

When Zunz had first been called up to the Big Leagues, he used to phone me before every game to get my notes. I never had much to say. Zunz had always been a natural. But I was a scout and it was my job to evaluate players. Zunz needed my reassurance. Or maybe he just wanted to make me feel needed. As his career took off, he started calling me less and less. Once a series. Once a month. Once a season. These days, we barely talked. Still, I watched every game and cheered.

"Sinker," I said. My arm creaked as I threw the pretend pitch.

I watched his holographic form swing at the empty air. It was strange how many ways I'd seen Zunz over the years. In person and in holograms, on screens and posters and blimps. I knew every curve of his bones, every freckle on his face. And I knew his body. Its shape and power. At the Monsanto Mets compound, he had all the best trainers and serums on the house. I'd never get molded like that, not on my income. But watching Zunz play made me want to construct the best version of myself that I could.

"You look good to me. ChicagoBio White Mice won't know what hit them."

Zunz pumped his fist. Smiled wide. He may have been in his thirties but he still grinned like a kid getting an extra scoop of ice cream. Except now he frowned and shook his head. "I feel stiff. Plastic. Unused. Do you know what I mean?"

I held up my cybernetic arm. "Hell, I'm practically half plastic already. But you look like a million bucks. Which is probably the cost of the drugs they've got pumping through you."

I lit an eraser cigarette and sucked in the anesthetic smoke. After a few puffs, I felt as good and numb as I did before an operation.

Thanks to Zunz, the Mets had built a commanding lead in the Homeland League East and cruised through the division series against the California Human Potential Growth Corp Dodgers. As long as they could get past the ChicagoBio White Mice, the Mets were favored to win the whole thing.

"Give the White Mice hell," I said, blowing out a dark cloud. "Show them a kid from the burrows can take the Mets all the way."

"Will do, Kang," Zunz said.

"Kobo," I said.

"Kobo." He cocked his head. I heard muffled yelling on his end of the line. I couldn't see what was around him. Zunz's hologram turned. He started to speak to the invisible figure.

He shrank to a white dot the size of an eyeball. The dot blinked. Disappeared.

The call had cut out.

I finished my eraser cigarette and went back to sleep. Didn't think about the call too much. The biopharms always pumped players with new combinations of drugs in preparation for the playoffs. Hoping to get the chemical edge that would hand their team the title, which would lead to more retail sales that could purchase more scientists to concoct new upgrades and keep the whole operation going. Zunz was a high-priced investment. Monsanto would keep him together.

And I had my own problems to worry about. Sunny Day Healthcare Loans was threatening to send collection agents after me again, and I had to skip town for a few days. I took the bullet train down to North Virginia, the latest break-off state, to scout a kid whose fastball was so accurate he could smack a mosquito out of the air. It was true. He showed me the blood splat on the ball.

The Yankees had authorized an offer. The number on the contract made the parents' eyes pop like fly balls. But when I gave the kid a full workup, I realized they'd been juicing him with smuggled farm supplements. The kind they pump into headless cattle to get the limbs to swell. The kid's elbow would blow out in a year. Maybe two.

The parents cried a lot. Denied. Begged for a second opinion. I gave them the same one a second time.

I was one of the few biopharm scouts left who specialized in players. Other scouts plugged the numbers into evaluation software and parroted the projections, but I'd spent my whole life desiring the parts of those around me. People like Zunz, who seemed to have success written into their genetic code. I watched them. Studied them. Imagined myself inside them, wearing their skin like a costume, while I sprinted after the ball or slid into third.

I still liked to think baseball was a game of technique and talent, not chemistry and cash. I guess I was a romantic. Now it was the minds that fetched the real money. That's what most FLB scouts focused on. Scientists working on the latest designer drugs. Genetic surgeons with cutting-edge molecular scalpels. For biopharm teams, players were the blocks of marble. The drugs sculpted them into stars.

By the time I got back to New York, the playoffs were in full swing. I got a rush assignment from the Yankees with a new target. I'd planned to go to the game, watch Zunz and the Mets play the White Mice from the front row with a beer in my hand and a basket of beef reeds in my lap. But the Yankees job was quick work and easy money. Which meant I could quickly use that money on another upgrade.

The prospect was a young nervous-system expert named Julia Arocha. Currently under contract at Columbia University. She was working on a stabilization treatment for zootech critters. Her charts were meaningless scribbles to me, but I was impressed with the surveillance footage. Arocha was a true natural. She glided around centrifuges as easily as an ice skater in the rink, holding vials and pipettes as if they were extensions of her limbs.

The next night, I grabbed a cab uptown to the pickup spot. The playoffs were on in the backseat.

"What the hell?" the driver shouted as a Pyramid Pharmaceuticals Sphinxes fielding error gave the BodyMore Inc. Orioles a runner on third. The man flung his arms wide. They shook like he was getting ready to give someone the world's angriest hug. "You believe that shit?"

"Bad bounce," I offered.

"Bad bounce? My ass. Hoffmann is a bum. We'd be better off with some Edenist who'd never been upgraded playing right field instead of that loser. Don't you think?"

"If you say so. I'm a Mets fan."

He scowled. "Mets," he said, gagging on the word.

The taxi flew over the East River. Great gray barges cut blue paths through the filter algae below.

"Mets," he said again. "Well, the customer is always right. Zunz is a good one, I have to admit. They don't make many players like him anymore."

"They're trying. You see the homer he smacked on Friday?"

"Right off the Dove Hospital sign. The arms on that guy. Wish we had him on the Sphinxes."

"He's going to take us all the way," I said.

We flew toward the giant towers of Manhattan with their countless squares of light pushing back the dark, both of us thinking about JJ Zunz. Imagining my brother's hands gripping the bat, his legs rounding bases in our minds. His body perfect, solid, and, at that point, still alive.

orbit

Follow us:

f **/orbitbooksUS**

/orbitbooks

/orbitbooks

Join our mailing list
to receive alerts on our
latest releases and deals.

orbitbooks.net

Enter our monthly
giveaway for the chance
to win some epic prizes.

orbitloot.com